THE DRAGON RETURNS

BOOK 4

THE FALLEN KNIGHT

PETER WACHT

The Dragon Returns
By Peter Wacht

Book 4 of The Fallen Knight Series

This book is a work of fiction. Names, characters, places, and incidents are the product of the author's imagination or are used fictitiously. Any resemblance to actual events, locales, or persons, living or dead, is coincidental.

Copyright 2025 © by Peter Wacht

Cover design by Ebooklaunch.com

Published in the United States by Kestrel Media Group LLC.

ISBN: 978-1-950236-70-1

eBook ISBN: 978-1-950236-69-5

Library of Congress Control Number: 2025909377

 Formatted with Vellum

ALSO BY PETER WACHT

THE FALLEN KNIGHT SERIES

The Death of the Dragon (short story)*

The Dragon Awakens

Duel With a Dragon

Beware the Dragon

The Dragon Returns

THE REALMS OF THE TALENT AND THE CURSE

LEGEND OF THE DRAGON LORD

A Painful Truth (short story)*

Stealing the Light

Sacrificing the Queen

Roar of the Broken Bear

Rise of the Dragon Lord (Forthcoming 2026)

THE TALES OF CALEDONIA

(Complete 7-Book Series)

Blood on the White Sand (short story)*

The Diamond Thief (short story)*

The Protector

The Protector's Quest

The Protector's Vengeance

The Protector's Sacrifice

The Protector's Reckoning

The Protector's Resolve

The Protector's Victory

THE TALES OF THE TERRITORIES

Stalking the Blood Ruby (short story)*

A Fate Worse Than Death (short story)*

Death on the Burnt Ocean

Monsters in the Mist

The Dance of the Daggers

Bloody Hunt for Freedom

A Spark of Rebellion

Shadows Made Real

Shadow's Reach

Storm in the Darkness

THE SYLVAN CHRONICLES

(Complete 9-Book Series)

The Legend of the Kestrel

The Call of the Sylvana

The Raptor of the Highlands

The Makings of a Warrior

The Lord of the Highlands

The Lost Kestrel Found

The Claiming of the Highlands

The Fight Against the Dark

The Defender of the Light

THE RISE OF THE SYLVAN WARRIORS

Through the Knife's Edge (short story)*

YOUR FREE STORY IS WAITING...

This eBook is a prelude to the events in *The Fallen Knight Series* and is free to readers who receive my newsletter.

Join Peter's newsletter and get your FREE short story.
PeterWachtBooks.com

1

KILL ORDER

Arthur Pendragon stood hands on hips atop the long flat rock that extended out from the crag. Sword hilt sticking up over his left shoulder, he wore his black leather armor, which because of its matte finish sucked in the bright sunlight. All the better to ensure that the dozens of Teg down below could see him easily.

He gazed upon the various practice combats with a gravitas and imperiousness that he had perfected while ruling as the King of the Teg for more than a thousand years, and a thousand and more years to come if he had his way.

Arthur understood the importance of perspective. How an individual's standpoint played a key, often outsized, role when deciding on what was and was not the truth.

Thus, the care he took to ensure that those serving him always saw him as he wanted them to see him. Thereby shaping and managing their bias in a way that suited him best.

In essence, thinking of it crassly, he sought to project and protect his brand. And the best way to do that was to manage every last detail that could affect another Teg's perspective of him. That all began with the image that he presented.

One of the benevolent lord more focused on the interests of the Teg rather than his own.

He understood that. He had mastered it, actually. But to him it was so much more than just that.

For him, protecting his brand served another purpose as well. A more critical purpose.

Because in his mind, putting forward and protecting his brand – not only the image he presented, but also the associated message, the decisions that he made, the actions he took, and the many more concepts and details working together as a part of the larger narrative he presented – was the same as protecting the Teg.

And that above all else was his primary objective.

His sole objective, in fact.

Everything he decided, everything he did, everything he said, was geared toward achieving that objective.

Because he was not only of the Tylwyth Teg as well as the celebrated and necessary leader of the Teg, but he *was* the Teg.

An indisputable although not always understood fact.

Therefore, Arthur spent a great deal of time educating his people in the story that he had crafted so long ago and had built upon over the centuries. And, in large part why with all the other matters he needed to deal with, he made sure that he always attended the last few days of training here on his estate in northwestern Westchester County in New York, not too far away from Cortland.

He smiled with a confidence that few among the Teg could match, grunting softly in satisfaction, even offering a brief nod or two when one of the prospective Knights took a break from their training and glanced up at him.

His being there helped his soon-to-be Knights of the Round better understand who they served and why. His presence not only functioned as the mortar used to build the esprit de corps required among those selected to join his elite fighting force, but just as if not more important it strengthened the ties his Knights had to him.

The Knights of the Round fought for the Teg. That was an undeniable truth. But his Knights were loyal to him. The King Teg.

And what was good and right for the King Teg also was good and right for all the Teg.

Arthur knew from long experience that taking the time to be there demonstrated to these Knights in training his belief in them. When he spoke to them after today's session, he would impress upon them why serving faithfully as a Knight of the Round was critical to the survival and success of the Tylwyth Teg.

He would emphasize the essential role they would play, serving as the primary bulwark against the dangers that threatened the Teg.

And there were a great many dangers indeed.

The bulk of those dangers from beyond the Teg, biting at the edges. Always seeking a weakness. Always searching for any opportunity to unseat Arthur as the King of the Teg and thereby put the magical world he created and controlled in turmoil.

A few of the dangers he kept a wary eye out for were more sinister.

Dangers from within.

Because of that alarmingly weak link, he needed these prospective Knights to understand what he expected of them.

He needed them to believe in what they were doing.

He needed them to believe in him.

That was crucial, because some of these Knights would die in his service, and he needed them to do so willingly and with a fervor driven by their absolute belief in their comrades and in the King Teg.

He needed them to believe that making the ultimate sacrifice was not a terrible burden or loss. Rather, it was a gift to him and all of the Teg.

Learning that, becoming a part of the culture of the Knights of the Round, began months before, and would continue until that belief was fully ingrained within each and every one of the Knights who swore their allegiance to the King Teg today.

And, from what Arthur had observed for the last few hours, it seemed that this latest class of Knights was well on its way.

Arthur was quite pleased by what he saw. The skill that these prospective Knights exhibited impressed him and filled him with a hope that they could address the future challenges that bore down upon him.

Although he wasn't really surprised by their competence. It was to be expected considering who was responsible for their training.

To that end, a massive field had been cut from the long grass on this section of his estate. It was finely mowed and land-scaped to the point where a Premier League football match could be played on the surface.

And on that pitch fifteen combats were taking place.

Short swords only.

The preferred weapons of the Knights of the Round.

Arthur studied all that played out before him impassively even as his keen eye identified those individuals who he thought might have the chance to fly up the ranks quickly. *Might* being the key word.

Because martial skill was only one determining factor for advancement within the fighting force charged with protecting the Teg while also maintaining discipline and order among the Teg. A difficult task because of the Teg's noted unruliness and obstinacy.

There were other variables. In particular, an undying loyalty and willingness to carry out his orders ... no matter what those orders might be and no matter what they might cost.

"You've done well with these recruits, Gaheris."

"Thank you," the Knight of the Round replied as he reached the top of the steps carved into the back of the rock and came to stand next to his king. He was an older man of indiscriminate age, dressed just like Arthur, although his black leather armor had seen a great deal more use. Worn away along the edges. Scratches and rips visible. It also didn't consume the light the way the King Teg's did.

"Nothing else to say, Gaheris?"

Gaheris shook his head. "No, just tired. This class has been more challenging than the last few."

"Why do you say that?" Arthur didn't pull his gaze away from the practice combats taking place below, even though he found his friend's comment slightly concerning. "They all seem to be doing quite well. In fact, several have captured my interest."

"Though I do worry about a few, not so much the quality. Rather, the fact that among the Teg, the desire to join the Knights of the Round isn't as strong as it used it be. We're not pulling the numbers we used to."

That revelation captured Arthur's attention. He fixed his penetrating stare on the man he had known since not long after he pulled Excalibur from the Stone. "What do you mean? Usually we have to beat away the applicants."

"Not in the last few years, Arthur," Gaheris replied calmly. He ignored the tic under Arthur's right eye, well aware that it meant his liege was getting irritated. Gaheris had never failed to tell Arthur what he thought, even when Arthur didn't want to hear what he had to say, and he wouldn't stop doing that now despite his king's more frequent and mercurial moods and the possible consequences of pissing him off. "To ensure that we get a full class, because we know that we will lose a certain percentage during the training, whether because of injury, illness, or death, we've had to lower our standards. It's been the only way to fill the ranks."

"How long has this been going on?" Arthur demanded. "Moreover, why is this the first that I've heard of it?"

"To your last question, I've told you several times before, usually right here the last five years or so. You didn't demonstrate much interest in hearing what I had to say, each time telling me that I was crying wolf and that there was no need to consider the solutions I offered you for addressing the problem."

Gaheris gave his response in an even tone. He couldn't let his own irritation show. It would do little good and only aggravate Arthur all the more, ensuring that this conversation devolved into another argument, which was becoming more and more common between them in recent months. Then Arthur could stalk off and stew as was his want when he received news that he didn't like.

That last, Gaheris believed, based on past practice, a distinct possibility because of what he was going to say next. "As to your first question, it began not long after the Dragon died."

"The Dragon," Arthur repeated in a lethally quiet voice. "How is he connected to this?"

More than just a sore point for Arthur. Gaheris understood why, although he didn't agree with his liege's perception of what had occurred between him and his son. "Yes, my King. The number of recruits dropped substantially the year after Draig's death and has dropped year over year since then. Now, we have half as many applicants as we did ten years ago."

Arthur nodded, taking in that information as his peremptory expression twisted into a scowl. Now wasn't the time to give free rein to his anger. Not with so many eyes watching. "Any thoughts as to why?"

"You sure you want my opinion on this Arthur? The last few times I've given it, you had no interest whatsoever."

The tic beneath Arthur's right eye started to pulse faster. "You're afraid to offer your opinion, Gaheris?" Arthur said with a forced calm, ignoring his second in command's veiled challenge. "This would be a first for you as I've never seen you cowed by anything or anyone."

"Not afraid, Arthur," the Knight replied calmly. "I just don't want to waste my breath if you don't want to hear what I have to say."

"I always want to hear what you have to say, Gaheris. Even though lately I haven't liked what you've had to say."

Gaheris wasn't taken in by Arthur's deceptively welcoming tone. Instead, he focused on the fire burning in the back of his liege's eyes.

Still, Arthur was correct. Gaheris had never shied away from giving Arthur the truth, or at least the truth as he saw it. And despite his reservations, he wasn't about to start now.

"Draig was known as the Dragon for many reasons. Among the Teg, in particular for what he did for you."

"That was common knowledge. How he served as my hard man."

"Exactly so," Gaheris confirmed with a nod. "He was the one you sent to deal with the more difficult cases among the Teg. Your enforcer."

"Tell me something I don't know, Gaheris."

"Draig's reputation among the Teg was well deserved and well earned."

"Again, tell me something that I don't know, Gaheris," Arthur growled, beginning to lose patience with one of his oldest friends and supporters.

"Draig accomplished missions that no one else among your Knights could." Gaheris held up his hands to forestall the protest on the tip of Arthur's tongue. His liege's annoyance becoming more obvious. "Because of that, the Teg feared him, and for good reason. Many of the Teg hated him, in fact, and for good reason as well. But what you may not have realized, what I didn't realize until he was gone, was that many of the Teg respected him as well."

"Respected him?" Arthur snorted, not quite believing what he was hearing. "How could they respect him after all that he did? How could they respect him if they feared him as well? His reputation wasn't just tarnished. It was drenched in blood."

"From what I've learned, it was a grudging respect to begin with," Gaheris admitted. "Again, Draig built up quite a reputation because of his exploits, and a much deserved one at that. Although some of the Teg didn't like why he did what he did, they were impressed by some if not all of what he did. And he demonstrated a personal integrity that struck a chord among the Teg, even those who wanted to kill him."

"Why would a grudging respect affect our recruitment?" Arthur almost shouted, though he stopped himself just in time. He didn't want the men below him to hear. "You said they hated him as well. It doesn't make sense."

"That grudging respect shifted to admiration for some of the Teg not long after your encounter with him at Belvedere Castle."

"Why would that be the case?" Arthur growled, barely able to contain his aggravation. "He was a traitor. And I won that combat. He died. Or at least we thought he died until he decided to crawl out from under the rock he had been hiding."

"Yes, my King. That's what the Teg believed. That he died by your hand." Gaheris shrugged, unable to offer much more. "For whatever reason, that strengthened their admiration for him."

"I don't understand. How is that possible?" Arthur demanded. "That doesn't make any sense." The tic below his right eye was pulsing with even greater urgency, his irritation quickly building into a rage. A much-too-common occurrence for him these days. "I beat him that day. I showed the Teg who the better fighter was. Who the better man was." By the end of his diatribe, Arthur was hissing out his words. "I showed the Teg what their King really was made of."

"For some, you killing your own son had the opposite effect from the one you intended. These Teg viewed Draig's death as a form of resistance."

"Resistance?" Gaheris' comment forced Arthur to think more than he cared to. "To me, you mean? That's preposterous. Why would any of the Teg feel the desire to resist me? All I do, I do for them. Always. That's the way it's been. That's the way it always will be."

Gaheris didn't disagree with Arthur. Of course, he didn't agree with him either. He allowed the matter to hang there. Not wanting to waste his time or his breath, he moved on to what he believed was a more salient topic. "After that combat and word of the Dragon's death spread some rumors spread with it."

"Rumors? What rumors were those?"

"It seems that more and more stories about Draig were being shared among the Teg."

"Why would that have any impact? All of the Teg were quite aware of what my son did for me. They viewed him as a killer. No more than that. A boogeyman for any who failed to adhere to my rulings as the King Teg."

"Yes, my King. But these stories weren't coming from us. They were coming from the Teg ..."

"My son aided without my knowledge or approval. A gross abuse of my trust." The fire within Arthur sparked out in an instant as the truth struck him a hard blow right in the gut. He should have assumed this would happen, but he hadn't, his focus taken up by what he believed were more important matters than the death of his son.

"Yes, that's correct, Arthur. It seems that your public relations machine either missed them or didn't give these claims enough credence to be worthy of consideration or action. That mistake has cost you." Gaheris knew that Arthur would fixate on his last comment not understanding that it was actually directed toward the King Teg deciding to eliminate his son rather than the aftermath of Draig's death.

"Don't challenge me, Gaheris." Arthur knew that he had no right to blame Gaheris for this. Still, he needed to blame someone, and Gaheris was closest. He would deal with his PR hacks and their failure later.

"If I challenge you, you'll know, Arthur, just as always." Gaheris followed Arthur. He obeyed him as his rightful king. But he didn't serve him blindly as some of the other Teg did. And he would not hesitate to take his ruler to task if he believed that doing so was necessary. Or at least he hoped that he would not hesitate. He had come close a few times during the last few years, debating whether challenging the man who pulled the sword from the stone was worth the repercussions. Each time that happened Gaheris thought that perhaps it was time to move on from his millennium-old position. Yet still he was here at the King Teg's side. "I am telling you the truth. If you don't want to hear it, I'll leave you here to simmer so I can get back to my real work." He nodded toward the men learning to fight with short swords infused with the Grym.

Not all of the Knights in training had the skill to call upon the Power of the Ancients to the degree that might be required to address some of the challenges they inevitably would face when they began to serve the King Teg. The magic that was a part of their blades would help to remedy that weakness, offering them additional power as well as the ability to defend against attacks by those who might be stronger than they were in the natural magic that strengthened and protected the Tylwyth Teg.

Before Gaheris could head back toward the stairs, Arthur

nodded, reaching out and grasping Gaheris' forearm in a strong grip, holding him in place. "Tell me."

Gaheris did not respond right away. The fury that had become a much larger part of Arthur's personality these last few years as his challenges as ruler of the Teg mounted was there just below the surface, ready to be released.

Normally, Gaheris would seek to calm his friend. Another of Arthur's more frequent emotional explosions would do little for either of them and only serve to harm the image that he was trying to present to this latest class of Knights.

But right then, Gaheris didn't care. He cared about the fighters who swore to protect the Teg from all threats.

Many of the problems affecting his beloved Knights of the Round could have been avoided years ago. Yet Arthur hadn't wanted to hear about them then or the many other times Gaheris had raised them. As a result, Arthur had done nothing to prevent those problems from growing and multiplying.

More fixated on himself and his own issues, Arthur had forgotten that there was more to his rule than just him playing a role. As the King Teg, he needed to make hard decisions. More important, he needed to make the right decisions.

And he hadn't been. A fact that Draig had determined and acted upon well before anyone else within Arthur's inner circle recognized the danger that threatened to weaken the Teg, perhaps irrevocably.

"The stories that spread upon his death spoke of Draig's kindness and mercy. How, during the last few years of his time serving you, instead of killing the Teg you identified for elimination, he helped them instead. He aided them during their escape and then assisted them by finding a place for them to live without fear of being discovered."

"Kraken Cove," Arthur murmured just above a whisper. His son had turned that small town on the northern coast of Maine into a refuge for the Teg Arthur had charged him with killing.

From all reports, it was a thriving community. In large part because it had stayed well beneath Arthur's radar until the Witch who had been working for him showed her true colors and forced the Dragon to reveal that he wasn't dead.

"I doubt that Draig had anything to do with it, Arthur. You better than most understand how stories spread. How they take on a life of their own."

"That I do," Arthur admitted. Thanks to Merlin, he had mastered the skill of ensuring that the story he wanted to become the lore of the Teg did so. "Kraken Cove needs to be dealt with, Gaheris."

Gaheris' face scrunched up with displeasure. "I would advise against that, Arthur."

The King Teg snorted again. This time not in humor. Rather in disgust. "Are you afraid of what might be required if I give you the order to deal with those Teg who so blatantly challenge me? Do you not have the courage to deal with the Dragon who should have stayed dead?"

Gaheris took quite a long time before replying, needing a few minutes to tamp down his own anger. He did not like having his bravery and integrity challenged. "You know me better than anyone, Arthur. I will follow any lawful command you give me." The Knight was taking a risk. He knew that. But he couldn't help himself as he could only take so much.

Arthur turned to face Gaheris, squaring up to him, almost as if they were in one of the practice rings cut out from the long grass below. He hadn't missed the key qualification that Gaheris had included in his response. He couldn't have.

"No matter what some small segment of the Teg might believe, what my son did, Gaheris, what he refused to do, were the acts of a traitor."

"As defined by you, Arthur," Gaheris clarified.

"As defined by me," Arthur confirmed with a slow nod. "As is my right as the King of the Teg."

"That may be, Arthur, but that's the hiccup. That's what some of the Teg are picking at."

Arthur either didn't care or he chose to ignore Gaheris' insinuation. "I am the law, Gaheris. It's important that you remember that. It's important that all the Teg remember that. Our future depends upon that belief. Our future depends on *me*."

Gaheris had several immediate and pointed comments to offer Arthur that challenged his self-serving perspective. He held them all back.

He didn't have any desire to get into an argument on this issue with the man who had been his friend for so long. There was little point. Arthur wouldn't listen to him just as he hadn't been listening to him for quite some time now.

There was a growing resistance to Arthur's rule for a variety of reasons. Some stood out more than others.

Telling Arthur that he had been using the law and other facets of Teg society to function more as a dictator rather than as a fair and just leader, as he had begun those many long centuries before, would fall on deaf ears.

No, that wasn't quite right, Gaheris corrected. Arthur would hear all that. Every word.

Then he would take action against Gaheris. Swiftly and without remorse. No matter their friendship. No matter the history between them.

So best that he keep his opinion on that matter to himself for now. Still, he felt a responsibility at least to try to get Arthur to think about some of the ramifications of what he was saying and what he had been doing since Draig had left his service.

"Arthur, if I may ..."

"You may do nothing other than what I order you to do, Gaheris," Arthur cut in, having lost patience with his friend and the dialogue. "And what I order you to do is to reinstate the kill order on Draig. As soon as we are done here, you will spread the word within the Knights of the Round and our allies among the Teg. Draig is to be killed on sight. Is that clear?"

Gaheris' face turned white at his liege's command. Though not from fear. Rather from a cold rage, believing that based on the circumstances what Arthur had just ordered was the absolute worst decision he could have made. "Arthur, please, just allow me to ..."

"We are done here, Gaheris. Do your duty. That is all I require of you. That is all that I have ever required of you. Do your duty or I will find another Teg who will."

Arthur stared coldly at Gaheris, watching as a flurry of emotions passed across his friend's face. He was curious to see on which emotion Gaheris would come to rest. Even more so, what that would mean for how this conversation between them ended.

Gaheris wasn't hotheaded, but he could be pushed only so far. With that in mind, Arthur flexed his fingers, prepared to reach for the sword on his back if it came to a duel.

It didn't. A few seconds later, Gaheris' eyes narrowed and revealed an emotion that Arthur couldn't interpret, and that worried him. Then Arthur's second in command nodded. "By your leave?"

Arthur locked eyes with his friend. He waited almost a minute before nodding his approval, wanting to make sure as to Gaheris' intentions. Also wanting to ensure that Gaheris remembered his place.

When Gaheris reached the top of the steps, Arthur's voice held him in place. "Remember, Gaheris, if you can't do as I require, if you can't do your duty, I can easily find someone who will."

Gaheris didn't reply right away, standing there, back to Arthur, clearly struggling. Thinking about what Arthur had said. Moreover, what his friend of so many centuries had revealed about himself in just the last few minutes of their brief conversation.

When Arthur spoke of duty these days, Gaheris felt slightly sick to his stomach. Because more often than not, what Arthur required of him under the guise of duty felt wrong and threatened the code by which he lived.

Gaheris had adopted the chivalric underpinnings of Camelot, striving all his life to uphold them. Even as he watched the one who had instituted those strictures drift farther away from them.

All that distinct from the fact that Draig was a friend. Almost a son to him, in fact.

Gaheris had trained the lad when he first started in the Knights of the Round. Draig had been his best pupil, becoming the very best of the Knights. Until his father had pushed Draig down a road that no one, in particular his son, should have been made to follow.

Gaheris remembered when he had asked Arthur about what he was doing to his own son. The King Teg had offered several reasons as to why he had selected Draig, then told him to mind his own business.

He should have fought Arthur's decision back then with greater vigor. It might have saved Draig a great deal of pain. And just as Gaheris feared, Arthur setting Draig onto that path had only come back to bite the father in the ass.

Just as it should have.

Yet there was a deeper, more intrinsic problem for which Gaheris could not identify a solution.

Because of the mistakes Arthur had made with Draig, and because of what Draig had done in response, the King Teg believed that he appeared weak.

And if there was one thing to know about Arthur Pendragon and one thing only, it was that he could never, ever appear weak.

A sad truth from which Arthur couldn't escape. Nor could the Teg.

The only question now was whether Arthur's fear of appearing weak would come back to bite all of the Teg in the ass.

Shaking his head sadly, without another word Gaheris continued on his way, barely acknowledging the man who had snuck up the steps and been standing there listening to the conversation between the two warriors.

Rather than approaching Arthur, who had returned his attention back to the training, and knowing that he would be less than receptive to anything that Merlin might have to say, he hustled down the steps and caught up to Gaheris at the bottom of the crag.

"Does Draig still trust you?"

Gaheris thought about Merlin's question, remembering the last time he had spoken with Draig. Just a few short days in the past that seemed like a lifetime after talking with Arthur. He nodded. "He does. For now. After reinstatement of this kill order ..."

Merlin frowned, his worry increasing tenfold from one breath to the next. Draig didn't reenter the Teg world just because of the Witch.

He risked the life he had created for himself and those of the Teg he felt responsible for because of something bigger than himself.

Just like Draig.

Doing what he believed was right.

Not because it was right for him, but because it was right for the Teg.

An admirable trait, but also one that could very easily get him killed, even without his father's order for his execution.

2

THE WRONG CATCH

"Do you think we'll have any luck today?"

Seamus stood on the helm of the *Kraken*, rough hands sure on the wheel of the charter craft. "She's close. I can feel her in my bones."

Draig chuckled. His friend's comment made him think of the scene from *Jaws* when Roy Scheider first went out with Robert Shaw to look for the shark terrorizing Amity Island. "How can you be so certain?"

"I know her."

"We're going to need to talk about your choices for female companionship," Draig murmured with a hint of faint disapproval. "The daughter of Typhon? Really? Out of all the women ..."

"The heart wants what the heart wants." Seamus gave Draig a knowing look. "Be careful, now. We could have the same conversation about you and your choices, my friend."

By the gleam in Seamus' eye, clearly he was quite pleased with himself for turning the focus of the conversation onto Draig so quickly.

"Fair enough." Draig sighed as he scanned the surface of

the Atlantic Ocean. They were several miles from the coast and a league or so from Kraken Cove. "If you can feel her in your bones, do you know where she is specifically? It's a big ocean."

Seamus shook his head. "No, it's not like sonar. Besides, being atop the water rather than below makes finding her a bit more difficult." He gave Draig a wily grin. "Have no fear, though. Once I go below, Jinx won't be able to resist me."

Draig nodded, giving his friend a lift of his eyebrows and holding back the host of less-than-helpful comments and questions that popped into his mind. "Quite confident, aren't you?"

Seamus nodded then grinned. "Once a woman gets a taste of the Kraken, they only want more."

Draig had no response to that. At least not a useful one. And he didn't want to encourage his friend. Still, he felt like he should say something. "You do realize that you can't make a comment like that in mixed company, right?"

Seamus nodded quickly, some of the air leaving his sail. "Of course. That's why I save them for you. I'm well aware of what Peggy Rose or Cerridwen would do if I said something like that in front of them."

"I'm glad you still have a little common sense." Nevertheless, Draig was finding it exceedingly difficult getting past Seamus' romantic taste. "But Jinx? Seriously?"

"Would you just let it go?" Seamus grumbled. He shrugged. "I was going through a bad patch. She was as well. It made sense at the time. Looking back, I realize that I may have been thinking with the wrong head."

"Thanks for sharing," Draig replied with a distinct lack of enthusiasm, "although you shared a bit too much."

"It's your own fault. You should have stopped while you could."

"You got me there," Draig admitted, accepting a small portion of the blame.

Seamus perked up then, eyes narrowing. He started to

study the waves, spinning slowly though always keeping one hand on the wheel. Draig followed where his friend was looking, not seeing anything other than three- and four-foot swells.

"What's the matter?"

Seamus pursed his lips, although it was hard to see because of his thick beard, the long and scraggly whiskers covering most of his mouth. "Doesn't feel right."

"What doesn't feel right?"

"The ocean."

Draig nodded as he searched around them, not seeing anything that gave him any cause for concern. Still, he trusted in Seamus' senses. Instincts as well. When they were on the water at least. "Could you be more specific?"

"I was kind of hoping that a great white would be our biggest concern."

"How so?"

"We're not alone."

Draig closed his eyes and pinched the bridge of his nose between his thumb and his forefinger, needing to take a breath so that he didn't lose his temper. Whether intentional or not, Seamus had a way not only of drawing matters out longer than was required, but also adding some unwanted drama, and Draig only had so much patience.

"Again, specifics?"

"I can sense Jinx drawing closer, just not exactly where she is." Seamus frowned, brow coming together. "If I'm right, I think she brought one of her pets with her."

"Wonderful," Draig muttered. "Any idea which one it might be?"

Seamus shook his head. "There's only one way to find out, although I think what we discover will likely be a lot larger than a great white."

"No idea what to look for?"

"None whatsoever," Seamus confirmed. "She's using the Grym to mask herself and whatever she has with her."

"Yet you're sure that Jinx is close?"

"More than sure."

"How can you tell?" Draig challenged.

"My balls are itching." Seamus offered his statement with complete seriousness, not a hint of a smile cracking his chapped lips.

"I'm sorry I asked."

"You'll be even more sorry if this fog gets worse."

The wispy grey that had dogged them not long after Seamus motored his cabin cruiser out of the Kraken Cove marina was getting thicker by the minute. "Jinx's doing?"

"She doesn't have the power required," Seamus replied. "Probably Neptune."

"Why Neptune?" Draig didn't understand why the God of the Sea would have any interest in why they were on the water now.

"I was playing cards with him the other week."

Draig nodded knowingly, beginning to understand. "You lost your temper again."

Seamus shrugged. "It was justified," he offered in his defense. "He was being a pain in the ass, and he kept accusing me of cheating."

"Were you?"

"Of course not," Seamus replied, perhaps a bit too hastily. "Maybe being a jackass, but that doesn't matter now. What matters is that he promised to leave me fogbound if I didn't leave him be."

"You were on him for his name again, weren't you?" Draig couldn't stop himself from smiling. There were certain things in the world that bothered Seamus that he just couldn't seem to let go. No matter how trivial.

"How could I not be?" Seamus growled, unable to contain

his irritation. "He kept talking about himself in the third person. And if that wasn't aggravating enough, he kept switching between his names. Poseidon this and Neptune that. Then Neptune this and Poseidon that. He was driving me crazy."

"I can understand why that was the case," Draig responded in a tone that a therapist might use with a neurotic patient with the goal of not riling up his friend any more than he already was.

"Damn right you can." Seamus smacked one large palm on the wheel to emphasize his agreement. "If you speak about yourself in the third person, then you're a jackass. Plain and simple. Even worse, pick a name and stick with it for feck's sake! Who needs two names anyway?"

"A good point," Draig replied just as calmly as before. He decided not to explain why the God of the Sea had distinct Roman and Greek names. They didn't have the time and he didn't have the desire to dive down that rabbit hole.

"I knew you'd agree." Taking a breath to calm himself, Seamus slowed the throttle.

"Have we found our Moby Dick?"

Seamus nodded. "There's only one way to be sure. You want to take the wheel?"

Seamus stepped out of the way so that Draig could take charge of the helm. Draig kept the engine at a soft purr, then set the *Kraken* on a course to complete a slow circle. He hated the idea of being dead in the water with what might be beneath them.

Seamus nodded in approval. Then he looked over the side. Nothing but a murky grey. That didn't bother him in the least, however.

Once he was beneath the waves, he would be home. He would see and hear everything around him as if it were clear as day.

"Too bad we don't have a camera crew around for this," Seamus grumbled.

"You think that would help to boost the business this summer?"

"Without a doubt."

To ensure that Seamus made good money with his sightseeing charters during the warmer months, he liked to create some free press by teasing a scientific expedition whenever they were working on the east coast between Boston and Nova Scotia. He gave them just a glimpse, and a poor one at that, but still enough to make them think they had seen something in the water that shouldn't have been there.

The Loch Ness monster of the East Coast as Seamus liked to promote his escapades. A few articles later in the press and he had a steady flow of customers until well after Labor Day.

"You know, I think I might have a Polaroid camera down in the cabin. Maybe you could ..." Seamus made the motion of snapping some photos.

"The daughter of Typhon is in the water below us with one of her pets and you want me to take your photo?"

Seamus didn't reply right away, Draig's expression hinting that he was questioning his judgment. "Not a good idea?"

Draig didn't bother to reply, shaking his head instead.

"Not a good idea," Seamus confirmed with a nod. Without another word, he dove over the side, barely making a splash when he slipped into the water.

Draig kept the *Kraken* moving in a slow circle once his friend disappeared. Waiting. Watching.

There was nothing but rolling waves for as far as he could see. And he was finding it harder to see. The fog was coming in faster than before, making visibility even poorer as the billowing grey covered the ocean like a pale and silent shroud.

Draig knew that Seamus could handle himself. He was more comfortable below the water than above it.

Nevertheless, that didn't prevent him from worrying about his friend.

Draig reached for the Grym, extending his senses below the surface of the briny ocean.

Where had Seamus gone?

He realized his mistake in an instant.

His search was too broad. Instead of looking in every direction, he needed to focus on one.

He needed to go deeper.

Nothing a quarter mile below.

Nor at half a mile.

A mile?

No. Still nothing.

He extended his senses even farther into the deep.

Finally, he located his friend.

Draig turned the cruiser to the northeast.

He had gone no more than a few hundred yards when he saw the first signs of Seamus making for the surface. The waves in this part of the ocean weren't obeying the currents. They were listening to what was going on in the water below.

Then the rolling waves stopped moving entirely, the strange stillness that resulted seeming unnatural to Draig. That same placid pool dropped several feet in just a breath, as if that particular section of the ocean was being pulled down into a drain. To confirm Draig's speculation, the ocean began to swirl in a clockwise direction, churning in its very center in a way that more resembled the beginnings of a boil.

That boil became even more violent just seconds later. The water seethed, transforming into a frothy white.

With good cause.

Just a heartbeat later, the Kraken in one of his many forms erupted from the sea.

While searching for Jinx and her pet, Seamus had chosen to retain a version of his human shape as he had done when he dueled Morgase on Long Island, although he had grown in size. So much so that if the George Washington Bridge towered above him, he was in danger of hitting his head.

His lower half, a massive tail that resembled that of a shark, pushed most of his colossal mass out of the water. Spiky red shells like those on a lobster protected his chest, shoulders, arms, and legs, serving as a flexible armor that was stronger than titanium.

His face hadn't changed. He appeared to be the same craggy old man as he always did. The one change was his hair. The rat's nest replaced by a thick green seaweed.

Draig had to give his friend credit. Seamus had found what they were looking for.

Jinx's pet.

The gargantuan sea serpent, its body thicker than the hull of a submarine, was wrapped around him.

Although Seamus had located the creature, he wasn't having the success that he wanted against the monstrous animal.

In large part because he couldn't bring to bear the harpoon made from the bone of a sperm whale that he grasped in his hand.

The serpent's coils flexed and moved with a deadly menace, not only keeping the harpoon against his side, but also tightening around the Kraken, seeking to steal his breath with every constriction.

And it was working.

Slowly.

Insidiously.

Despite fighting hard to free himself, Seamus' face slowly shifted from a bright red to a pale white. The blue that would reveal his inability to breathe couldn't be more than just a few seconds away.

Yet that wasn't the only threat Seamus faced nor the most immediate.

Even as each breath became more and more difficult for him to take, the Kraken couldn't extricate himself from the sea snake's grip with his other hand. That meaty paw, thankfully well away from his body, gripped the serpent's head, Seamus using every ounce of strength that remained to him to prevent the animal's fangs from plunging into his neck.

Draig increased the throttle. He needed to get closer before Seamus lost his battle. And Draig could tell that his friend was losing the battle. Seamus' weakening free hand was losing its grip on the serpent's nostrils.

Of course the rocking and rolling waves didn't help him. Draig couldn't make much headway through the chop. In fact, just staying on the helm of the cabin cruiser was a huge challenge, the boat dropping precipitously into a deep trough before Draig guided the bow atop the crest of the next wave, a never-ending cycle.

Seamus' face beginning to turn the shade of blue that he feared, Draig realized that he couldn't wait no matter how unlikely he was to hit what he aimed for while motoring through a pot of churning and swirling water.

Keeping one hand on the wheel, worried that if he wasn't careful an errant wave would capsize the *Kraken*, Draig called on the Grym and shot a bolt of the Power of the Ancients through the worsening fog.

Dropping into a trough, he smiled when he came back up over the crest of the next wave. He had missed, though not by much.

The white-hot energy sliced across the sea snake's jaw, taking with it a furrow of scales and leaving scorched flesh in its wake. Draig had missed one of its platter-sized eyes by only a few feet.

Not a direct hit though enough to force the snake's head back and give Seamus a momentary reprieve.

Still, Draig feared that his effort might not have been enough. The serpent was still coiled around Seamus, its muscular body crushing the life from his friend. Worse, the snake's fangs were snapping back toward him with an even greater vigor.

About to slide off a thirty-foot crest, Draig realized that he needed to take a less precise approach before he fell into the trough below him.

Using the Grym once again, a shield of gleaming energy formed right in front of Seamus' face.

And just in time.

Unable to stop, the serpent's fang-filled maw already darting forward, with a nasty crunch that Draig heard even with the hundreds of thousands of gallons of water surging around him, one of the snake's fangs snapped off.

When Draig emerged from the trough just a moment later, he watched with a great deal of satisfaction as the serpent pulled back with an angry hiss.

It was just a temporary victory.

Seamus' difficult circumstances had not improved by much. The serpent was preparing to strike again. Clearly unconcerned if another barrier blocked its efforts. Instead intent on its prey, Seamus weakening faster now as he gasped for air.

Draig was about to form another shield and fix it in place. He changed his strategy on the fly when he realized that he had hit a fairly stable patch of water, which really wasn't saying much. Ten-foot waves rather than twenty or thirty, though he did appreciate the boiling ocean now was no more than a simmer.

How long it lasted didn't matter to him.

All he needed was a second.

And he made the most of it.

Without the rocking and rolling, Draig's aim was right on target.

A spear of energy sparked from his free hand and sizzled through the thickening fog. The power sliced across the snake's body, ripping away a large swathe of scales and burning into the flesh beneath.

Then again. And again. And one more after that.

Draig didn't stop until the rough water returned.

Even as the *Kraken* pitched wildly to the side, Draig smiled while turning the wheel to keep the cruiser above the surface rather than giving in to the tremendous power of the ocean and capsizing.

Finally, he enjoyed some success that would aid his friend.

Unable to bear the pain of the many wounds torturing its long body, the sea serpent unwrapped itself from the Kraken.

The last spear that Draig threw streaked through the fog, this one aimed for a spot right between the serpent's eyes. It proved to be a harmless throw, the snake sliding beneath the surface before the lance struck.

With the serpent ducking away, Draig almost hit his friend. The bolt of energy would have sliced across his ribs if Seamus hadn't stood straight abruptly. Bent at the waist once more, Seamus sucked into his starved lungs as much air as he could.

"Watch it," Seamus' growled. His deep voice rumbled across the choppy surface, and he gave Draig a look that suggested his last attack didn't need to be so close.

Draig held back his sharp reply, not wanting to antagonize his friend while he recovered. Although he did need to make the point, at least to himself, that hitting his target while captaining a cabin cruiser in rough water that was only getting rougher while a heavy fog drifted in and two leviathans battled atop the surface was far from an easy task.

He shifted his focus back to the sea serpent. It had disappeared, probably licking its wounds. But Draig suspected the animal was not yet done with them.

Reaching for the Grym, Draig extended his senses beneath the surface once again. He didn't have far to look.

The sea serpent was circling Seamus just below the waves and only a few hundred yards away. Using his tail to keep himself in place while he searched for any sign of his adversary, Seamus was turned in the wrong direction.

"Seamus! At your back!"

The Kraken spun just in time at Draig's warning.

The sea serpent burst out of the ocean only a hundred yards away, its long mass of coils propelling the animal swiftly across the surface.

Seamus had less than a heartbeat to react. Heeding his instinct, he threw the harpoon, hoping for a fatal blow. Or at least a wounding blow. At the moment he wasn't all that particular.

Unfortunately, it wasn't to be.

It was a good throw though not good enough. The serpent glided to the side right before the harpoon struck between its eyes, the sharp bone ripping off a few of the snake's scales along its thick hide but doing no real damage.

After that, Seamus had no chance to think about maintaining the all-too-brief momentum he had earned. He could focus only on defending himself as the snake lunged, fangs aimed right at his face.

The Kraken got his hands up not a second too soon, catching the snake by the head. One hand on its upper jaw, the other on the lower, Seamus was able to keep the animal's fangs away from him.

Although not without a great deal of effort.

The sea serpent hissed with anger as the beast bunched the muscles in its neck, engaging in a battle of strength with the Kraken.

But that wasn't the worst of it.

The serpent's long body was curling around Seamus again, seeking to take hold and place him in the same lethal position he had been in just a moment before. And with both his hands occupied, and knowing what would happen if he released the snake's head, Seamus was in no position to prevent it.

Seamus needed to focus not only on maintaining his hold on the snake's head, but also on keeping himself above the water. With the animal's body coiling around him, the weight of the creature was forcing him beneath the waves.

Draig refused to allow that to occur, knowing what would happen if the serpent once again wrapped its heavy coils around Seamus then took him below.

One hand on the wheel as he struggled to control the cruiser in the rough waves churned up by the battle taking place in front of him, Draig blasted a stream of magic from his free hand.

Rather than trying to strike the straining animal, Draig guided the energy around the serpent's neck, tying the glowing line into a lasso that he fitted just below the head.

That task done, Draig closed his fist, the lasso tightening instantly into a noose that bit into the serpent's neck.

The effect on the animal was immediate, a bloody and charred line appearing where the Grym burned into its flesh.

The serpent reared back, forgetting about Seamus. Seeking only to break free from the painful and potentially lethal snare.

However, Seamus didn't forget about the snake. No longer worried about the beast's fangs, he gripped the snake around the neck with both his monstrous hands right below where the sizzling lasso burned through scale and meat almost to the vertebrae beneath.

All thought of trying to kill the Kraken fled from the snake's mind. All the animal cared about was survival. And the only way to do that was to dive back into the deep. To escape from what had become a losing combat.

But that was no more than a hope, and it faded swiftly.

Seamus' face a bright red to match his armor, muscles flexing, he squeezed with all the strength that his current form granted him, wanting the snake to feel what he felt before Draig got in the way.

The serpent thrashed wildly, desperate to get away, unable to snap at the Kraken, eyes bulging as the awful pressure increased.

Finally having gained the upper hand, Seamus fought with a lethal efficiency.

The serpent's thrashing became less wild and then ended after no more than a few additional twitches, its forked tongue flicking a few more times before lying still outside its mouth, the creature's throat crushed.

Yet even though the combat was over, Seamus wasn't done. He felt the need to make a point. To himself and to his real antagonist.

He didn't release his hold around the snake's thick neck until he crushed the flesh and then the bone with such terrible intensity that the animal's monstrous head dropped into the ocean and slowly sank beneath the surface. Staring for a moment with a great deal of contempt at the serpent's body, Seamus flung it away from him toward the east.

Seamus didn't bother to watch the splash. Instead, covered in blood and guts, he turned with a grim expression to face the woman who had almost caused his death.

Yet when Jinx rose up out of the ocean just a moment later, sitting comfortably on a watery throne, she had eyes only for Draig and demonstrated not an ounce of interest in her former lover.

That earned an angry growl from Seamus. He made no

move toward her, however. He knew that if he did so, she would likely disappear.

And Draig needed to have this conversation with her. That's why they had taken the *Kraken* out into the Atlantic in the first place.

Jinx appeared to be not the least bit surprised by the loss of her pet, even offering Seamus a nod of respect and a few silent claps before fixing her gaze back on Draig, who brought the *Kraken* to an idle just a dozen yards away from her in what had become a shockingly placid ocean.

"I told you that we'd meet again."

"And here we are," Draig replied. "It's been what ... a day? You couldn't wait longer than that?"

Jinx didn't bother to reply, instead studying Draig. He really was quite impressive, frightening as well, even more so than the Kraken, Seamus having glided over to hover behind his friend and offer her an angry glower.

Perhaps it was because of the scale, Jinx mused to herself. Seamus was truly terrifying when he went all Kraken on her. Exhilarating as well.

Although not to the level of when she confronted Axel Draig.

Seamus' power was obvious. Draig's less so, though even more potent. Even more frightening when she considered that he was hiding so much from her.

But that wasn't unexpected after what her father had said about him.

The Dragon.

The King Teg's most famous and most accomplished assassin.

A Teg who many believed could not be killed.

Until he was.

And now a Teg risen from the dead.

The Kraken was imposing. She wouldn't deny that. But he had never died and come back to life.

"You've mistaken my intentions, Dragon. I come here as one seeking an ally. Not to fight, which you would know if your waterlogged friend at your back hadn't antagonized my serpent. I'm only a threat if you don't see the logic in my offer."

"Really," Draig said, clearly not convinced. "I find that hard to believe. You'll have to explain. Because from what I can tell, I'm just a piece to be used. Once you're done with me, you'll sweep me from the game board just as your father usually does."

"What do you know of my father?" She was curious. Her father had been away for quite some time, more myth than reality to many of the Teg.

"More than enough to know what usually happens to those working with him. Concrete boots would be a blessing compared to some of what your father has done to eliminate his enemies ... and many of his so-called and very fleeting allies."

"There's no need to be so melodramatic," Jinx challenged, although she sounded more amused than anything else. And she made no effort to correct Draig's characterization of her father.

"You've got the right of it, Draig," Seamus rumbled, staring daggers at Jinx. "That's what he does best."

"I don't need help explaining what I want from an over-grown mix of man and fish. Keep quiet, Seamus, so that the adults can talk."

Seamus growled again, this time more in warning. He hadn't enjoyed his combat with the sea serpent. Although the thought of wrapping his hands around Jinx's throat certainly appealed to him.

Nevertheless, he kept his place, understanding that surrendering to the desire to attack the woman who insulted him and sat so smugly on her throne crafted of seawater would do neither him nor Draig any good. Better to allow this scene to play out and to be ready for any other pets Jinx may have called from the briny deep.

"As you might have guessed, my father and I seek your assistance."

"To do what?"

Jinx chuckled softly, as if his question didn't deserve a reply. "You know what, Dragon. It's the same thing that you desire."

"Right now all I desire are a hot coffee and a freshly baked cinnamon roll."

Jinx stared at Draig even harder, her green eyes burning brightly. Then she nodded. "Yes, I was told that you often got this way. Not just challenging, but also rebellious, as revealed by your attempts at humor."

"I wasn't joking," Draig replied. "I really would like a hot coffee and a freshly baked cinnamon roll."

"Do not test me, Dragon. You won't like me if you do."

"I don't like you now, Jinx. That's not going to change."

Rather than allowing Draig to continue to provoke her, Jinx stayed quiet. Calming herself. Refusing to permit her building aggravation to become anything more than that. She was there for a reason, and she would do what was required of her no matter how hard the Dragon made it.

"Enough with your poor attempt at humor, Dragon. As I said, my father and I know what you desire ... beyond whatever you hunger for in this moment."

"You're going to have to be more specific." Draig knew what she wanted. But he didn't feel the need to make it easy for her. Rather, he wanted to press her, his making the conversation more difficult for her revealing a few breaks in Jinx's composure that he hoped to use against her when the time was right.

"Removing your father from the throne, of course, and you taking his place."

Draig nodded as if he was actually giving serious consideration to the proposal. "I may not like my father, but that doesn't mean I want to take his place."

Jinx laughed. "Of course you do, Dragon. How could you not?"

"I am not like your father. I do not seek to dominate all those around me."

"You know nothing of my father," Jinx countered. "You believe what your father told you about him? What you learned when you trained to become a Knight of the Round? Perhaps what Merlin shared?"

She shook her head, scoffing at the notion that anything close to the truth could emerge from those sources. "My father seeks order above all else. Order. Not control. Because with order you can govern. You do not have to rule, a lesson your father has forgotten or never learned. You can give those you are responsible for what they need to not only survive, but thrive."

"You sound like a candidate for office, Jinx. And not the good kind. The kind that hides their true intentions in a rhetoric that leads only to a terrible end for those foolish enough to believe it and those too afraid to take it seriously."

Jinx ignored Draig's argument, believing that she had identified what she was looking for. "I can see it in your eyes, Dragon. You seek to rule the Teg. You seek to give them the opportunities they deserve. The opportunities that your father is keeping from them."

"I seek to help the Teg," he countered. "No more than that."

"And what better way to help the Teg, Dragon, than to rule the Teg." Jinx leaned forward on her throne, placing her elbows on her knees, hands clasped in front of her. "A fair point, don't you think? You know what your father is doing now. That's why you left him. You know that he is no longer the king he was when he assumed the Teg throne. If you remove your father, think of all the good that you can accomplish."

"Tempting, but ..."

"You are thinking too much, Dragon. It is an easy decision to make. You got in trouble with your father because you chose to help the Teg against his wishes, and you continue to do that now." Jinx's smile broadened, becoming almost predatory. "My father will help you. He will help you take the throne, and he will help you help the Teg."

"He will, will he? No strings attached?"

"The throne of the Teg is there for the taking ... if you want it, Dragon. My father will help you. I promise you that. And that is all he wants to do." Jinx almost pushed herself out of her throne, believing that the moment of truth had come, her excitement at turning the Dragon to her cause almost palpable. "My father seeks from you only one small gift in return. That's all."

Draig nodded, already knowing what Jinx was going to demand and why. "You want the Witch."

"A small price to pay for the throne of the Teg, wouldn't you say? For the opportunity to do what your father should be doing himself?"

"One Teg for all the Teg," Draig intoned.

"Exactly," Jinx confirmed with a smile. "Give me the Witch. She has not met the terms of her contract with my father. She has not delivered to him what she promised, and she must pay for that failure." She gave him a shrug of her shoulders and a lift of her eyebrows. "Not a bad trade at all, wouldn't you say?"

Draig didn't reply right away. He had to acknowledge that Jinx was more than she appeared to be. He had believed after his first encounter with her on the town green in Kraken Cove that she was no more than a blunt instrument. But clearly she was quite clever, although a bit misguided as well and much too sure of herself if she believed that she could turn him so easily.

"I'm sorry, but that doesn't really appeal to me."

Jinx laughed, a throaty sound. "Really, Dragon, you feel the need to play hard to get? I can guarantee that this is the best deal that I'll place before you. The only one, in fact, that does not end in utter despair for you."

"The threat wrapped in the velvet glove," Draig murmured. He had assumed that she was going to start with this rather than offering the sweets first. "And if I don't agree to your deal?"

"Then my father will give me permission to destroy Kraken Cove and kill every Teg you care about."

"Quite the threat." Draig's voice hardened, his reddish-orange eyes bursting into flames. "I don't respond well to threats, Jinx. If you had done more research before coming here, you would know that."

"It's not a threat, Dragon. It's a promise. My father and I have no need of threats."

"Tempting as your offer sounds, Jinx, we've been through all this. My position has not changed. I'm not interested in taking the Teg throne. I'm not interested in working with your father. And I won't give you the Witch."

Jinx leaned back into her watery throne, her expression souring. "I will not ask again, Dragon, and my father will not make this offer again. Decide now. We are either allies or enemies. Choose wisely."

"I much prefer being your enemy, Jinx," Draig replied in a voice colder than ice, not even needing to think about it. "I won't work with you or him. And you can't have the Witch." He saw little need to inform Jinx that Melissa had left Kraken Cove and that he didn't know where she was. He did, however, want to make sure that she understood the consequences of what she was contemplating. "And just to be clear, if you come at the Teg living in Kraken Cove, you will regret your decision. You've already been spanked once. It would be embarrassing if I and my friends spanked you again."

"Is that a threat?" Jinx hissed, hating how Draig talked down to her. A daughter of Typhon! A daughter of an Ancient! Such insolence!

"No, I don't make threats, Jinx. That's a promise."

Jinx stared daggers at Draig, her anger becoming more obvious with every breath she took.

Draig used her few seconds of stewing to appreciate the value of this encounter. When Melissa had entered his life, bringing her chaos with her and upsetting the balance of events in Kraken Cove, he had little understanding of all that was going on behind the scenes. He had viewed her as the protagonist, not realizing until just recently that she was really the catalyst for what was biting at the edge of the Teg world.

Three of the most powerful Teg had been vying for *The Book of Whispers*. All trying to keep that a secret. All intent on using the power contained within the ancient artifact on one, the other, or both.

Two of the three were no longer players in the game.

They knew it. Draig had explained it to them in a way that they couldn't help but understand.

Although that didn't mean they still couldn't cause problems for him. A fact that he needed to address before he took on the third player.

Because he couldn't have those two free to stab him in the back while he assumed the task he had seen for himself while in the Druid's Circle.

Neither of the fates that awaited him appealed. Yet he wouldn't run from them. He couldn't. Not with so much at stake.

He would seek the fate that ensured the survival and the freedom of the Teg, even though that would require more from him than he really wanted to give.

He really didn't have a choice. Because that was the only fate that he was willing to accept.

Before he did, however, he would do all that he could to ensure that he removed the third player from the board before he died again. This time for good.

Draig couldn't escape what he had seen atop the Druid's Peak. He had known that from the start. And he wouldn't try. Even so, he wanted to give himself the best possible chance of succeeding before he met his end.

"I expected more from you, Dragon. From what I heard of you, you were harder than this when you slaved away at your father's side. You did not allow your emotions to guide you. Only cold reason." She bit out her next few words slowly, seeking a reaction that she could use. "With this decision you appear weak to me, Dragon. Vulnerable. Ripe for the picking."

Draig gave her no more than a nod. "Feel free to have a go at me, Jinx. Then when I see your father, and I promise you I will see your father before he sees me, I can tell him how you totally and utterly failed to complete the assignment he gave you."

"You are a sentimental fool, Dragon." Jinx spat out the words, never having been so insulted. "We are done here. I will wipe your beloved Kraken Cove from the face of the earth. I will take the Witch. Have no doubt of that. And when I stand above you with the blade that kills you, you will think back to this very moment and realize that all could have been much different if not for your obstinacy and stupidity."

Before she uttered the last of her threats, Jinx already was disappearing back into the ocean, her throne sliding below the surface with her on it.

"You want me to go after her?"

Draig didn't reply right away, staring at the waves, going through in his mind once again the conversation he just had with Typhon's daughter. "No, I think we got what we needed. Thank you for your help. Great job."

Seamus stood at the helm once more, having shifted back into his human form, soaked to the bone and not caring a whit. He nodded sheepishly, uncomfortable with gratitude or praise, even from a friend. "You think she'll do what she said?"

Draig stared at the ocean where Jinx sank beneath the waves for just a moment longer before replying to his friend with a shake of his head. "No, she doesn't want to look the fool again. Even with her Vipers, she knows she doesn't have the strength to do what she wants. She's more concerned about embarrassing herself than with doing the work to earn a hard victory."

"My thought as well," Seamus said. He and Draig had wanted to tease a reaction out of Jinx. They just hadn't expected to get one such as this. "You know what this means, right?"

Draig nodded. When he turned toward his friend, his expression was grimmer than the grey of the sea right before a storm. "Typhon is almost ready to step out from the shadows."

"The last time that happened the world burned. Even worse, it was almost destroyed."

"Then I'll need to do what I can to prevent that from happening."

"And just how are you going to do that?"

"Kill a god," he replied in a voice that suggested doing so would be no more than him taking out the garbage.

"You can do that?"

"There's only one way to find out."

3

MORE THAN MUSH

"Back again?" Seamus asked, mostly to himself. He didn't want to get into trouble with the prickly personality waiting for them.

He nodded to Riga as he killed the engine, the *Kraken* gliding into position along the pier that jutted out from the Raptor Bay Lighthouse.

Draig smiled and offered the raven-haired beauty standing on the dock a wave. "We've got several matters that we need to discuss."

"Of course you do, you sly dragon." Seamus patted his friend companionably on the back before Draig jumped down onto the pier, the crusty mariner, engines already punched up, turning the cruiser back toward the deeper water so that he could return to Kraken Cove. "Just don't take too long. We don't have much time."

Draig didn't need to see Seamus' wink to understand exactly to what his friend referred. So he chose to ignore it. He didn't want to give Seamus the satisfaction of knowing that his barb had struck home.

"You've got more on your mind than usual." Riga's severe

expression was replaced by one that was a bit more open. Also more mysterious, which was never a good sign.

She leaned back against one of the posts. Just as always, several overlarge ravens flew in the sky above her. Watchful. Cagey.

Not of him. But rather of Butch, Cassidy, and Sundance.

The three cockerpoos were hidden farther up the shore within the sawgrass and scrub. They were only discernible to Draig who knew where to look for them, or ravens who could see all that was visible in the world around them and all that was not.

"Do you really want to know?" Draig asked.

Riga gave Draig a challenging look. "I am not the woman I was when we first started whatever this is we have between us. I hope you've noticed that."

"I have. And I hope you've noticed that I'm not the man I was when we started ..." He offered her a mysterious smile of his own that mimicked the one she had given him when he hopped down to the pier. "As you described it, whatever this is between us."

Riga nodded, then gave him a dazzling smile that seemed more than just a little out of place on the Irish Goddess of Battle and War. "Now that we've got that settled, let's move on. Tell me."

Draig did, providing Riga with a brief synopsis of what happened outside Kraken Cove during their encounter with Jinx and her pet. Perhaps more important, what he learned during his conversation with Typhon's daughter and his thoughts on what that could mean for the Teg.

"I knew that Seamus could exercise bad judgment from time to time, but the daughter of one of the Ancients? You would think that he would want to stay away from a father imprisoned in Tartarus because of his desire to overthrow Zeus.

I don't know if I should be disappointed in him, impressed, or both."

Draig shrugged. He really didn't understand it either. "The heart wants what the heart wants."

Riga snorted at that. "I doubt Seamus was thinking with his heart."

"Probably not," Draig admitted with a soft chuckle, "but we all have our failings."

"That we do," Riga agreed, "and it seems that because of yours, you keep finding yourself in the same perilous situation."

"Meaning?"

"Doing what you must even when that could cost you more than you want to give."

Draig couldn't deny Riga's claim, so he didn't bother to try. "Yes, that does seem to have become a common theme in my life."

"Become?" Riga reached out, grasping his arm and pulling him closer so that they stood no more than a foot away from the other. Her swirling black eyes caught his fiery orbs. "You have always been this way, Axel. The only real change has been your change in circumstances and allegiance."

Draig opened his mouth to reply. Riga cut him off.

"Don't try to argue. You know it's the truth. The difference now is that you can do what is right. You don't have to do what you must."

"Aren't those one and the same? Doing what is right and doing what I must?"

"A fair question," Riga admitted, "although I would argue that there is an important distinction."

"Which would be?"

"When you served your father, doing what you must wasn't always the right thing to do."

"Good point." That was a fact that Draig couldn't argue and have any hope of winning.

"And that's why you did what you had to do to break free from him," Riga stated, nodding sagely.

"Another good point."

"I'm glad you agree, because it was that change in you that made me think that I could change as well. If you hadn't chosen the more difficult path, questioning what your father required of you, then we …"

"We wouldn't have the opportunity that we have now," Draig finished for her. "I'm well aware of that. Grateful as well." Reaching out, he grasped her hand warmly with his. "An even better point."

"I'm glad you're listening. Because we can no longer think only of ourselves. Our lives are more complicated now."

Draig smiled, shaking his head slightly in amusement. "More words of wisdom."

"You seem to be suggesting that I rarely offer words of wisdom." Riga's eyes blazed a little hotter and a bit more dangerously.

Draig believed that it was an act, and even if it wasn't he had never shied away from teasing her when teasing her was deserved. "I would never do such a thing to the all-powerful and all-knowing Morrigan. I know the danger of challenging her in that way."

Riga smiled then and offered Draig a wink, acknowledging his sarcasm while ignoring his attempt at humor. "Just so we understand one another."

"Riga, I understand no one better than I understand you."

For just a few heartbeats, Riga was speechless. Draig's words suggested a closeness that almost frightened her. She didn't know how to respond because no one had ever said such a thing to her. Before her mind traveled down a road it shouldn't, at least not in that moment, she brought the conversation back to where it needed to be. "Enough with all this mush. Let's get down to what needs doing."

"I need to take on Typhon. He's free from Tartarus or soon will be. It's as simple as that."

"No, it's not that simple. Why you?" Riga didn't disagree with him. Nevertheless, she worried for Draig. He had survived a great many trials in his life. But he had never taken on an Ancient. Few among the Teg ever did. Because those who did rarely survived.

"Because no one else can or will."

"So we're back to you doing what you must," Riga tsked.

"No, in this instance, doing what I must is doing what is right."

"Explain it to me."

"Typhon seeks the Teg throne. If he takes the seat, he controls the Teg. If he deposes my father, he can do whatever he wants to the Teg. No one will be able to stand against him."

"You can't just tell your father about this threat and allow him to deal with it? He has been challenged before."

Draig shook his head in frustration. "My father isn't the man he used to be. He's still focused on my aunt and me. So much so that Typhon isn't even on his radar."

"That myopic perspective of his could cost him dearly. What about Merlin?"

"My father isn't listening to Merlin. He's not listening to anyone. Besides, I get the feeling that Merlin is playing a game of his own since he can't rely on my father to do what is required."

"What is required or what Merlin requires?"

"With Merlin, probably both. You know how he is. He's always playing multiple chess matches at once."

"Cy would like him," Riga suggested.

"He probably would at that," Draig nodded. "That schemer enjoys cutting down anyone he deems too big for his britches."

"What kind of game do you believe Merlin is playing?" Riga asked, returning to the heart of the matter. "And why now with the threat of an Ancient right on our doorstep?"

"I don't know what kind of game for sure, but I can guess, and I can understand why."

"Don't make me ask," Riga warned.

"He's looking for other possible solutions because he believes Arthur isn't it."

Riga didn't say anything for a long while, contemplating what Draig just said and understanding what it truly meant. The weight and consequences of a decision like that were immense for all the Teg.

Arthur Pendragon ruled the Teg. He had for more than a thousand years.

But cracks were appearing in his rule. Large ones. Fractures not too far off.

Thanks in part to the constant pressure placed upon him by Morgase and Mordred. Even more so because of the mistakes that Arthur was making all on his own.

All committed in the name of serving the Teg when in truth it was Arthur seeking to serve himself.

One mistake in particular stood out.

Trying to kill his son and failing to do so.

"You're really the only option then," Riga murmured, not liking what she said but having no choice other than to admit the truth.

"It seems that way. Scary thought, don't you think?"

Riga gave Draig a warm squeeze. "Not really, no. Perhaps for Typhon."

"I appreciate the vote of confidence."

"Maybe you should speak with Merlin."

Draig offered Riga a quizzical expression. "Why would I do that?"

"You know what one of his solutions likely is," Riga said,

her tone suggesting that it was an obvious choice. "Perhaps you should speak to him about it. The Knights of the Round at your back might prove useful."

"They probably would be," Draig admitted. "The right Knights at least."

Although he knew that gaining their loyalty would come at a cost that he didn't want to pay. To gain the support of the Knights, he would need to remove his father from the throne, just as Jinx and Typhon wanted him to do. He wasn't ready to do that. He doubted that he ever would be.

Not because he believed in the quality of his father's decisions as the King Teg. Rather because he had no desire to assume the responsibilities incumbent upon such an exalted position.

"Then why not ..." She stopped herself when she saw how his expression darkened. "What you learned in the Circle atop the Druid's Peak." Riga nodded, her understanding plain. "You fear that you would become what your father was trying to make you. Perhaps even someone worse."

"Exactly that," Draig confirmed. "Probably worse based on what I saw. I'd like to avoid that if I can. I'm sure the Teg would like to as well."

"Your hesitation makes sense. I can't deny it."

"I'll speak with Merlin, just not about that."

"But that's not the main part of your plan." She could read that expression of his. It was as if Draig was playing a game of three-dimensional chess and he was thinking ten moves ahead of his opponent.

"No, it's not."

"Then I'm afraid to ask," Riga said, because Draig's grim countenance suggested that he was about to place himself in harm's way. In her opinion, an all-too-regular occurrence.

"I'm going after Melissa."

"The Witch?" Riga lifted her eyebrows, her sharp look confirming that she was less than pleased by his decision.

"She's the best way for me to get to Typhon. He wants her, and she'll distract him for a time. It's as simple as that."

"Nothing is ever simple," Riga countered. "You know that better than anyone else."

"True. Let me rephrase. Finding Melissa will allow me to find Typhon. Hopefully I can catch him before he's ready and short-circuit his plan."

"It's quite a risk you're taking," Riga pressed. "One misstep ..."

"Can you think of a better approach? Because if you can, I'm all ears."

Riga pursed her lips together, angry with herself because no other options came to mind. "Unfortunately not."

It was his turn to reach out and grasp her arm warmly. "That's why I need to do it now. It's the only plan that I think I can make work. However, the window of opportunity is short."

"I hate it when you're right," Riga grumbled, kicking at an imaginary pebble on the pier. "The only positive is that you're rarely right, so I'll take some solace from that."

"And there's the Morrigan I know and love."

Riga stared sharply at Draig. She was quite familiar with that saying. Even so, she didn't think that Draig had offered it to her in just that way. She believed that there was more truth and meaning behind the words that he selected.

Still, with all that he needed to do, she decided not to pursue it. Not yet. "You're incorrigible, you know that?"

"So I've been told," Draig admitted. "And you've been visiting me quite a lot the last few days."

Riga shrugged. She didn't really know what to say, which was a rare occurrence for her. She was the Goddess of War and Battle, for the gods' sake. Blood, death, and pain were her domain. On the battlefield, no one could challenge her. Yet, there were times when Draig stole her tongue without even trying.

"You've been watching," Draig pushed.

Riga didn't bother to deny it. "Does that bother you? That I've been around more." She leaned in closer so that he could see nothing except for her eyes. "Watching over you as you say." Her smile widened.

Draig didn't hesitate with his response. "No."

"That's good to hear." Riga leaned in then, allowing Draig to move the finger's width required to bring their lips together.

They remained that way for longer than she planned. She didn't mind, however. And Draig didn't appear to mind either.

"While you're off saving the Teg, you can't assume that all will be well here. From what you said, the Teg in Kraken Cove are at risk, and not just from Typhon."

"I know," Draig replied. He didn't need to say anything, instead asking with his eyes.

Riga's lips curled into a cunning smile. "I will offer what help I can where there is need. Although I warn you, if it comes to it, I will not be gentle."

"You're talking about the assistance you're offering, right?"

Riga punched him lightly in the shoulder. "Now is not the time for your boyish humor, Axel."

"My apologies," he said. His smile made Riga smile as well. "Do what you believe is right. My thanks."

Riga already had a strategy in mind that she hoped would take some of the pressure off Draig so that he could focus on the real enemy and nothing else.

"Good." Riga nodded as if they had just reached a binding agreement. "There is one more matter we must discuss."

"I'm afraid to ask."

"The Witch." Riga didn't say it, yet there was some aspect to the woman that bothered her. And not just because she seemed to have an interest in Draig that was similar to her own.

"Any time there's another woman around it bothers you." Draig offered his comment as a jest.

Riga didn't take it that way. "You're right. But in this instance, my concern is something else entirely."

"Can you tell me any more than that?"

"I would if I could," Riga replied. "All I can do is offer you the warning I gave you before. Just like Merlin, she is playing a game. Don't allow her to play you. Beware the Witch."

"You think that she'll betray me?"

"Maybe. Maybe not." Riga shrugged, slightly angry with herself for not being able to provide any more detail than a vague concern. "The future is what we make of it. But this Witch?" Riga leaned up and gave Draig a kiss on the cheek, her lips lingering there before she breathed into his ear. "Listen to what I said. Be cautious. Exceedingly so."

Riga leaned back then. "Go do what you must do. We will talk when you get back. We have much to discuss."

She took several steps away from Draig. In a flash, she disappeared, a large raven in her place and already winging her way toward the southeast.

The ravens that had been circling above, focused on the three dogs below that were much more than dogs, pumped their wings furiously to catch up to her.

Riga had never been very good at waiting. And she hated to react.

She preferred to act.

Always.

Therefore, she would do what she did best.

She would make something happen.

4

RELEASING THE HOUND

"I had him, mother. I had him!"

Mordred stalked around his office, rubbing his hands across his cheeks, unable to contain the nervous energy running through him. He hadn't shaved that morning. He hadn't showered. He hadn't put on one of his several dozen hand-tailored suits that cost well over ten thousand dollars each.

Instead, consumed by the unjust defeat he had suffered and his all-consuming desire to challenge Draig once again, he wore a pair of shorts, a tank top, and trainers. All of which were distinctly out of character for him and a quite boorish selection by his mother's standards.

His servants had removed all the items that had been damaged or destroyed during his combat with Draig. They had cleaned as well, although they had yet to be able to remove the scorch marks that marred the stone walls in several places courtesy of Draig's use of the Grym. Also, it would take several weeks to replace the shattered stained glass in the top of the turret, tarps now covering the skylights to keep out the elements.

Morgase ignored her son. Taking the time to correct his perspective to one that was closer to reality was a waste.

Informing him that Draig had beaten him fairly, that Draig could have killed him if he desired but for some unknowable reason had left Mordred alive, wasn't worth the effort or the frustration that would result as her son challenged her every word.

Instead, Morgase let Mordred vent, knowing he'd tire himself out like he had done when he was a child. At least for as long as she could take it. Because she was losing patience quickly with Mordred's bellyaching. She needed to focus on more important matters, and he was getting in the way of that.

"If you had him as you say, Mordred, the Dragon would be dead, would he not?" Morgase shot her son a withering look, close to her breaking point. "And the Dragon most certainly is not dead. He is much too much alive and well and remains a threat to what we seek to accomplish."

Mordred's face, already red with rage, deepened to a bright purple. Before he could offer one of his several defenses for his lack of success, a woman dressed in running gear, long blonde hair flowing behind her, slipped through the space where the door was supposed to be. In fact, Mordred wouldn't have even noticed her if he hadn't been looking in that direction when she appeared.

"You failed me in Kraken Cove, Calypso."

"I did not fail you, Morgase," the woman replied in a respectful tone, stopping a few feet away from the large desk that dominated the space and behind which Morgase sat, demonstrating who really ruled the roost. "I had no choice but to leave when I faced not only the Dragon but also the Sorceress and some of his other friends. Once my Warlocks were removed from the fight, I stood little chance. I thought it better to return and let you know what happened rather than leave you wondering."

"Always an excuse," Mordred murmured, his lips twisting into a grimace as he shook his head in disgust and began his pacing again, unaware of the irony contained within his statement.

Morgase shot Mordred a look of warning. She knew what he was trying to do. Now wasn't the time. Nevertheless, he ignored her. "The Warlocks are your fighters, Calypso. They are your responsibility as are their successes and failures."

Calypso bit back the angry response that she really wanted to offer, choosing instead to concentrate on the real power in the room by turning her focus away from the son and back to the mother.

"Yes, your son is right. If I had known that I would face more than just the Dragon, then I would have brought more Warlocks. I was aware of some of the Teg who had gathered at his side. I did not know that the Berserkers Mordred hired had changed their colors and chosen to fight for the Dragon as well. I had no chance to prepare because I wasn't given accurate information. Critical information, in fact, that clearly affected the outcome."

She gave Mordred an angry look, pleased to see him flinch when her barb struck. It had been his responsibility to provide her with the particulars she required before she kidnapped the Witch from beneath the Dragon's snout. He should have told her that he had sent Berserkers just days before, but he hadn't, likely too embarrassed to reveal the mistake he made.

"My son's failings are none of your concern, Calypso."

Calypso pulled her eyes away from Mordred, then nodded respectfully to Morgase. "Of course, my apologies. I was simply trying to give you the full picture."

"I appreciate that, Calypso," Morgase replied. Then she leaned forward, forearms on the desk, hands clasped in front of her. "And in the interest of having a full picture, as you say, I hope that you are not now soft on the Dragon."

"What do you mean?" Calypso's eyes widened, though just briefly.

It was the only sign that Morgase had struck true, and it was the only opening that she needed. "I know the history between the two of you," Morgase murmured in a suggestive tone. "I worry that your time with the Dragon is coloring your decisions. That it is clouding your judgment. Worse, it is making you ineffective. And if you can't do the work assigned to you, well ... what use do I have for you?"

Calypso didn't respond right away, knowing that if she did she couldn't offer the more tempered response that was required for what had become a very dangerous conversation. Morgase's threat implicit. "Our history is no more than that. History. The Dragon means nothing to me."

Morgase studied the Sorceress for quite some time, waiting to see if Calypso would flinch under her gaze. She did not.

Finally, Morgase nodded. She couldn't say that she believed Calypso entirely. Still, she believed that the Sorceress would do what she demanded of her.

"I hope that is the case. Because if not, you will answer directly to me. Do we understand one another?"

Calypso nodded. "We do."

"Good." Morgase removed her forearms from the top of the desk and leaned back into the chair, crossing her legs. Clearly, she owned her son's inner sanctum. "You will take as many of your Warlocks as you deem necessary."

"The target?"

"Isn't it obvious?" Morgase didn't give Calypso the time to respond. "You will find the Dragon. If you cannot take him, you will kill him. Will that be a problem?"

"Will what be a problem?"

"Killing the Dragon if that proves necessary?"

Calypso responded immediately, shaking her head as she did so. "Not in the least." She had no qualms about killing the

Dragon even though a small part of her still loved him. In fact, it was because she still loved him that she wanted to kill him. The connection was a weakness, and she couldn't afford any weaknesses.

"Then get to it."

Calypso nodded and strode from the turret, although not before giving Mordred another angry look that held within it a promise. One that he couldn't disregard.

Nevertheless, he did his best to ignore it by glancing away quickly, afraid to hold her gaze, and he was quite glad when the Sorceress took her eyes from his own when she left the chamber.

"Why are we so concerned about the Dragon, mother? Should we not be focusing on our other target?"

"We are not concerned about the Dragon, Mordred."

"But you just ..."

Morgase cut him off. "Think before you speak, Mordred. It has been a failing of yours for far too long."

Mordred's eyes flashed in anger. Of course, he knew better than to release it. Though it was close to boiling over. Instead, reluctantly, he did as his mother demanded. It didn't take him long to figure it out. "Draig will lead us to the Witch." He smiled deviously. "Oh, that's very, very good."

"I'm glad you approve, because that's all that matters, Mordred. Find the Witch and we can use her against the Dragon."

5

KILLING CURSE

"Some more tea, dear?" Hestia asked. She stood poised to pour a hot stream into Medusa's empty cup, her frown revealing her increasing worry.

Medusa nodded weakly. "Thank you." She held out her mug, her hand shaking slightly.

"I hope that the herbs and other natural supplements that Peggy Rose provided are offering some comfort."

Hestia said it more to make conversation, already knowing the answer and suspecting that Medusa was going to lie.

The Gorgon appeared drawn, tired, almost lifeless. Her movements were slow, almost forced, as if she had to think for a time before she attempted them. Her eyes, known for their inescapable brightness, were filled with a teeth-clenching pain. And her hair, usually vibrant, alive, and having a mind of its own, was dank and lank, hanging limply down to her shoulders.

"Yes, they are. Thank you." Medusa nodded to Hestia before bringing the cup of steaming tea to her lips, needing to use two hands to keep it steady, then scarcely taking a sip before setting it down on the table, a great deal of focus required to do that simple task without spilling.

Hestia shook her head with worry. No appetite either. What was ailing Medusa was working its way through her body at a mind-boggling rate. What bothered Hestia even more was that there was nothing that she could do to help her, which went against her very essence.

"Perhaps there is something else I can get for you?"

Hestia's inn was named for what it was meant to be.

The Safe Haven.

For all Teg.

Free of danger and threats. Pain and discomfort.

A place to rest, recuperate, heal ... mind and body.

Yet at that moment Hestia, one of the most powerful of the Teg, felt powerless. Medusa, who had appeared tired though strong just the afternoon before when she checked in, was fading away at an alarming rate. Her pallor now a light grey that Hestia feared would soon turn a deathly white as her strength drained out of her.

Hestia likened what was happening to the Gorgon as being eaten alive from the inside out. A truly horrendous and cruel end.

Medusa reached out a cold hand, patting Hestia warmly and giving her an encouraging smile. Or at least as much of a smile as she could manage, that simple movement causing a spasm of pain that made her hiss softly. "I appreciate what you are doing for me, but there is nothing more you can do, Hestia. I'm sorry."

Hestia's eyes flashed. "There is always something more that I can do, and there is no need for you to apologize."

"Not in this case," Medusa murmured, needing to pause between her sentences to regain what little vitality remained to her. "I respect your power and your skill, that of Peggy Rose as well, but there is only one who might be able to help, and that is a longshot at best. Because even with him I have my doubts."

"Be careful, Medusa," Hestia said with a smile that she fought to keep on her face, a mix of anger and sadness -- anger at her inability to help and sadness at Medusa's fate -- making it difficult to keep up the facade. "If you tell him that, he might get a big head. And he already has more than enough confidence in himself."

"I'll remember that." Medusa took a few shallow breaths. She closed her eyes, trying to hide her resignation.

She was deteriorating even faster today than she was yesterday and the many days before when the affliction first struck, as if the disease was picking up speed by the hour. Worse, even with her skill in the Grym, there was nothing that Medusa could do to stop it. She hoped with all her heart that might not be the case, but she knew the truth. And that wasn't what she wanted to focus on then.

"Did I ever tell you what Draig did for me and my daughters?"

"Not in detail, my dear," Hestia replied. "I would certainly like to hear it."

Medusa offered a slight nod of thanks, knowing that Hestia likely already had the gist. And she did, because what Medusa told her over the next few minutes was much like the stories told by every other resident of Kraken Cove.

Draig defied his father and at great risk to his own life helped the Teg escape the King Teg's wrath rather than being the one to inflict it.

The hardest of the Teg proving that he had a good heart.

"Yes, he does have a habit of doing what's right," Hestia commented, "and not always what's best."

"I was exceedingly grateful for that," Medusa replied before she was overtaken by a rib-rattling cough. When she could breathe again, she wiped a sweaty strand of hair from her forehead.

"And as you probably discovered, he's not as tough as he tries to make himself out to be." Hestia said the last knowing that she and Medusa were no longer alone.

"Thankfully, I did learn that," Medusa confirmed. "If not, I and my daughters would be dead."

"Please don't start telling everyone I'm a softy, Hestia," Draig requested as he strode into the inn's dining room. "They would lose all respect for me and that would make my life immeasurably more difficult than it already is."

"Speak of the Dragon," Hestia grinned. She patted him warmly on the shoulder as he sat down across from Medusa. "And it's too late, dear. All the Teg in Kraken Cove know that you're just a big softy at heart."

"Wonderful," he grumbled. "That would explain why they push back at every little suggestion and make getting anything done around here more of a struggle than it needs to be."

"That it would," Hestia confirmed. "Although I think they do that just because they like to have a little fun with you." She pushed herself up from the table. "I'm going to leave the tea with you Medusa. I want to speak with the garden gnomes about a few things, so I'll give you two some privacy."

"Melissa?" Medusa asked once Hestia stepped into the foyer.

"We'll get to your daughter soon enough," Draig promised. "Let's talk about you first."

"I'm dying," Medusa said without a hint of blame or anger. "It's obvious, don't you think? And there's little to be done about it."

"Hestia and Peggy Rose have already studied the malady?"

"They have, along with Cerridwen. None of the three can do much more for me other than make my passage more comfortable."

Draig nodded, expecting as much. "Would you like me to give it a try?"

Medusa stared at Draig for several seconds. She knew how strong he was in the Grym as well as his several other talents. But she had never heard that healing was among them. "You think you can help me?"

Draig sighed and frowned, refusing to be anything other than completely honest. "No, I don't. But it seems that I'm your last chance, and I'm willing to try if you'll allow me."

"Is what you're proposing risky?"

"Yes, it could kill you."

"Then why would you suggest it?"

Draig didn't sugarcoat his answer. "Because as you just said you're dying anyway, so I see little risk if I hurry the process along."

Rather than being angry at what some might view as a callous response, Medusa snorted out a laugh despite the pain and the fit of coughing that followed. "Blunt as ever."

"There's another reason as well." He leaned forward then. "I might not be able to heal you, but I might be able to figure out what ails you. If I know that, then ..."

"You might be able to do something about it."

Draig nodded. "Exactly."

"You do realize that time is short?"

"In more ways than one," he replied.

Medusa thought about Draig's proposal, though not for very long. She had little to lose. She leaned in toward him once she made up her mind. "Whether you kill me now, whether you identify the cause of what ails me, will you still go after my daughter?"

She knew that making the request was likely asking too much of him. Still, she had to. Medusa would do anything she could for Melissa, and if she couldn't, as was the case now, she would seek the aid of someone who could.

Melissa had gotten stuck between a rock and a hard place, and though she was very good at wriggling herself out of difficult situations, Medusa didn't believe that she could do that now on her own.

Draig didn't hesitate. "I will, but I make no promises that I can save her. Know as well that there is a larger threat brewing who has a guiding hand over what your daughter is dealing with. If there is a choice to be made, I will seek to deal with this greater threat to the Teg even at the risk of your daughter losing her life."

"The many Teg before the one." Medusa smiled thinly, barely more than a crack in her visage to avoid the pain. "I appreciate your honesty." She nodded. "I would expect nothing less from the Dragon." She leaned back into her chair. "Do what you will."

Draig nodded. Feeling the clock ticking down in his head, he reached for the Grym, allowing it to surge through him. Then he took the next step, the one that he hoped would aid him in healing Medusa's illness. He called upon the power contained within *The Book of Whispers*, linking it to the Power of the Ancients.

Although that artifact was now in the Dragon Vault under Fafnir's watchful eye, the distance between them didn't matter. The energy of the ancient artifact was at Draig's service thanks to his mother inscribing the primer within him. Because of Tiamat's foresight, Draig was the key to unlocking the primal magic contained within *The Book of Whispers*, giving him and only him access to its secrets, and so it would remain until his death.

The effect upon connecting with *The Book of Whispers* was intense. Sparks of energy danced along Draig's skin and a golden luminescence framed him. His eyes, usually a fiery reddish orange, burned like an inferno and were too much for

Medusa to look at directly. She raised her hand, needing to protect her vision.

Taking a few seconds to grow accustomed to the potent energy surging through him, Draig started slowly. Not wanting to push. Just wanting to explore.

With that goal in mind, he reached out and placed his fingertips on Medusa's forehead. Thin, delicate tendrils of magic jumped out and drifted steadily into the Gorgon.

Draig had hoped that what he would discover lurking within Medusa was what he had come up against several times before. The Twisted Grym, the same power that he and so many of the Teg used, only corrupted by the intentions of the users, becoming over time and through its continued application a poison instead to the user and to anyone struck by it. That was an affliction that he knew how to address.

Feeling more comfortable with what he was doing, Draig sent more of the energy that he controlled into Medusa, continuing his search for what he hoped would be there. Unfortunately, he discovered quickly that it wasn't, the sick feeling in the pit of his stomach confirming the truth. He was wasting his time and effort.

"What is it?" Peeking through her fingers, Medusa glimpsed Draig's flash of worry.

"Usually, it's a matter of finding the source of the contamination and removing it. Much like a surgeon with a scalpel, though in this case the scalpel is the Grym. But I can't identify the specific source of your malady. The only thing I know for certain is that it's not the Twisted Grym."

"What do you mean?" A cold fear shivered through Medusa, only adding to the chills that she was experiencing because of her illness.

"The tainted power that is killing you is everywhere, not just in one place and spreading out from there. It's in your blood. In your cells. It is a part of you." Draig shook his head in annoyance and disappointment. "It's a part of who you are." He had never seen this before. He hadn't even known that it was possible.

"Can you do something about it?"

Draig didn't reply right away, needing time to think as he studied what the strands of energy he had sent into Medusa revealed to him. "I don't know."

"But you're willing to try?"

Again, Draig didn't reply right away. And when he did, he did so reluctantly. "I can. Though I don't know what the result may be." His ominous words hung in the air between them.

Medusa didn't hesitate. "Then get to it."

Draig smiled. That was the voice he remembered when he aided Medusa during her escape from his father more than a decade before. "As you command, but this is going to hurt."

And it did.

Medusa groaned as she leaned back into the chair, Draig calling upon more of the Grym linked with the magic of *The Book of Whispers* as he searched for some imperfection that would allow him to latch onto the taint that was rooted within the Gorgon.

It took him longer than he anticipated, and when he finally did, he tried to grasp that tiniest of anomalies with a gentle touch.

That was a mistake. His attempt at delicacy did nothing more than increase Medusa's pain, the Gorgon arching her back and moaning, tears streaking from her eyes.

"Medusa, I ..."

"Keep trying," she ordered through clenched teeth.

Draig obeyed. Still holding onto that irregularity in what was a masterful latticework of tainted and lethal magic, he settled on the only approach that he thought might work to unravel the rotten web.

He had always believed that when it was time to remove a

Band-Aid, it was always best to do it fast. There was no reason to allow the pain to linger.

Since he knew that trying to take his time to ease Medusa's suffering wasn't going to work, he did that now. With the magic he controlled, he pulled on the anomaly with a strong grip, seeking to rip free from the Gorgon the corruption that was killing her.

No joy.

All he succeeded in doing was lose his grip on the hitch he had been holding onto while also earning a sharp gasp of agony from the Teg he was attempting to aid.

Draig gave up on that approach in an instant, releasing his hold on the tainted energy coursing through Medusa's body.

He gave her a few minutes to recover from his ministrations, worried that he might have tried to do too much. She was struggling to breathe a bit more, and he could hear a phlegmy sound in her lungs that hadn't been there before.

"Are you up for one more try?"

Medusa nodded, gritting her teeth, sweat pouring off her. "Quickly. Before I lose my courage."

Draig feared that this, his last attempt, was going to fail just like the first two. Nevertheless, he wanted to try a different tack.

Pulling in even more of the power gifted to him by *The Book of Whispers*, he sent stream after stream of energy into Medusa in short bursts in which he targeted different parts of her body. He sought to burn away the blighted potency that had worked its way into her every pore.

At the very beginning, it worked. Barely. But at least it was some small amount of progress.

Draig burned away the corruption at the very edges yet gained no more success than that. Much to his dismay, the taint did something he had never thought possible.

It shielded itself, the corruption ensuring that he could no longer touch it whether with the Grym or the power contained within *The Book of Whispers*.

Glimpsing how Medusa was deteriorating, the Gorgon screaming silently, her back arching more violently, he released his hold, allowing the magic to dissipate.

He could have kept going, but there would have been no purpose in doing so. If he did, he would only succeed in killing Medusa all the faster.

Still, that brief moment of success, when he burned away the corruption plaguing her at the very edge, gave him hope.

A very faint hope, admittedly, but hope, nonetheless.

Unfortunately, he couldn't eradicate what ailed Medusa. But now he understood what caused Medusa's affliction.

During his last attempt, Medusa had reached across the table and grasped his hand to steady herself. It was still red from the intense pressure of her squeeze. And when she was finally able to push herself back into her seat and release her hold on him, her nails had cut into Draig's palm, leaving bloody streaks in their wake. A small price to pay for the knowledge Draig gained.

"I'm sorry I couldn't do more."

"You didn't kill me," Medusa replied quietly in between gasping breaths. "Although I almost wish you had. Then I wouldn't feel as if every part of my body was on fire."

"It wasn't wasted effort. I promise you."

Medusa didn't say anything until she could lift her head and rest it against the back of the chair. She was drenched in sweat, her clothes sticking to her, and she appeared to be completely drained of whatever energy she might have left.

"How do you mean?"

"I know what's killing you."

For just a second, Medusa wasn't sure if she wanted to know. Then she told herself that she was a fool for even hesitating. Of course she wanted to know. "Tell me."

"It's not the Twisted Grym. It's a curse, but one so ancient and so insidious that any attempt to remove it as I have been doing will kill you."

"Why?"

"Because it's linked to your spirit. If I actually succeeded in drawing forth the curse set upon you, and that would be a very big if, I would take your spirit with me."

"And send me to Tartarus as payment for the cure."

"Exactly right," Draig nodded. "However, that tells us who cursed you."

"I should have assumed as much," Medusa whispered, barely having the strength to do that. She tried to reach for the tea, but she couldn't. Draig helped her, holding the cup for her so that she could take a few sips, the warm liquid soothing her parched throat.

"The Ancient who hired Melissa?" Draig prompted.

"More like extortioner."

Draig opened his mouth to ask a question then closed it just as quickly. He already knew the answer.

Melissa had made a deal with Arthur, then betrayed him because of Morgase. She had then stolen *The Book of Whispers* from Mordred with the intention of giving it to Typhon.

Not for her own gain but rather for her mother, Melissa trading the artifact to the Ancient in exchange for lifting the curse that he had placed on Medusa and set all this in motion in the first place.

Clever in its simplicity. Heinous in its design.

"You see now why my daughter did as she did."

Draig nodded. "I do, and I can't say that I blame her. I likely would have done the same if I were in her position."

"Thank you for understanding," Medusa said, a great deal of relief in her voice. "You like her. Just as you ended up liking me after all the hassle I put you through in New York City."

"I wouldn't say that," Draig replied with a sparkle of amusement in his eyes. "She's grown on me a bit. That's as far as I'm willing to go."

"She's helping to open your heart just as I did."

"Your daughter is more like a fungus actually."

Medusa couldn't stop herself from laughing softly at Draig's sarcasm. It was the fit of coughing that quickly followed that did. When she could speak again, she let Draig know where matters stood between them.

"You owe my family nothing."

"I don't, you're right."

"But you're still going after her."

"Yes."

"Why?"

"Because it's the right thing to do."

"And ..." Medusa prodded, having little doubt that there was more to it than just that.

Draig didn't attempt to hide the truth. "And because it serves my purposes."

Medusa studied Draig for a moment, putting the pieces together. "You'll use her to get to the one forcing her to do this. To the one who did this to me."

"I will," Draig nodded. "Will that make you think poorly of me?"

"Why would you care?"

"In the past I wouldn't have cared," Draig admitted, "but as you said, you helped to open my heart." He held his thumb up not too far away from his forefinger. "If only a little bit."

Medusa smiled then. And not a warm smile. A cold smile. One that told Draig she understood what he was about to do and the lengths that he would go to achieve his objective.

"You are the Dragon. Try as you might, you can be nothing else. Now, for me, for my daughter, for the Teg, you must be who you are. Heart and soul."

6

A FRIENDLY WARNING

"What's the matter?" Draig asked.

Deep in thought, worried about Medusa, focused on what he needed to do not only for her but also for the Teg, it took Draig longer than usual to interpret Cerridwen's expression when he walked into Tia's Bakes.

She was waiting for him behind the counter, as there were only a few people at the register rather than the line that routinely snaked out the door. The early morning rush had ended a quarter hour before, the brunch rush about to begin soon.

"There's a blast from your past waiting for you in the kitchen who just can't seem to stay away these days." She nodded toward the swinging door that led into the back.

"I can't say that I'm surprised," he replied, walking through the shop.

"You should know that he's not here because of the cranberry orange scones that he can't seem to get enough of, right?" She adopted a tone of mock disapproval. "He put away four already, and he wants a full box to take with him."

"I assumed as much," Draig said with a smile. "At least some things don't change."

"And I assume that it will all be on the house?"

"You know me too well, Cerridwen."

"That I do." Cerridwen's brow furrowed as she studied Draig. He was smiling, but his eyes weren't. He had a look about him with which she was quite familiar. "Why do I get the sense that you're about to do something dangerous?"

Draig's smile broadened. "Because I am." Before she could ask him a clarifying question, Draig pushed his way past the swinging door and into the kitchen.

Because Draig was not only of the Teg, but also of the Draca on his mother's side, he could sense all magic and all those who could use the Grym -- Teg, monsters, gods -- within several leagues of him unless the individual or creature was strong enough and skilled enough to hide from him.

A rare and unlikely occurrence.

Even rarer, he could identify the magical signature, much like a magical DNA, of any Teg or monster.

Just like a bloodhound, once he had the scent, it stayed with him forever ... or until the Teg or monster died.

A unique and critical skill which ensured that Draig's target couldn't evade him, because no matter how strong the Teg or monster might be in the Grym, they couldn't change their magical signature. It was ingrained within them. Meaning that Draig could follow the trail anywhere. Even to places that weren't a part of the Natural World.

Thus, one of the reasons Draig was so successful at the task his father gave him. Hunting Teg who didn't want to be found ... or who did want to be found because they wanted to battle it out in a blaze of glory.

It was because of this ability and his experience as a hunter that he knew he had little to fear from the man waiting for him in his bakery.

"You look as you did when you swallowed the sushi I asked you to try the last time we celebrated my birthday together."

Gaheris, the older Knight of the Round leaning back against the counter, arms crossed in front of him, paled at Draig's comment. "You made me eat that because you knew what it was going to do to me. It was purely for your enjoyment and not mine."

Draig smiled, relishing the memory. "I just thought you might like to try something new."

Gaheris, grey hair cut tight to his scalp, held in a laugh. "Why would anyone enjoy eating raw fish?"

"Careful. You're insulting a very large segment of the world's population with a comment like that."

"Then let me rephrase. As we both discovered, eating raw fish isn't for me." Gaheris pushed himself off the counter and strode toward Draig, embracing him in a hug before stepping back. "It wasn't the taste of the sushi that got me. It was actually quite good. It was having to sit on the can for several hours afterward since something from that meal didn't agree with me."

"Was it the sushi that got you or that mead you had stashed away?" Draig asked. "I only had a sip because I thought it had turned. You ignored me and just kept going."

"Are we really going to have this argument again?" Gaheris asked with a weary sigh. "I was under a lot of stress at the time."

"No, we're not," Draig confirmed with a shake of his head. "I need to get going and you're here for a reason. Also, I need to have some pastries left for the lunchtime crowd, and you'll eat me out of house and home if you stay much longer."

Gaheris ignored the lighthearted jab and got right to the point. "Your father has reinstated the kill order. I have no doubt as well that your father will send out a few squads. And, of course, every Knight is required to challenge you on sight, no questions asked."

"Yet you're not challenging me."

Gaheris grinned at that. "I'm not. Then again, I'm not just a Knight of the Round."

Draig studied his friend and mentor for a few heartbeats. Despite his flinty expression that revealed little, Draig knew Gaheris better than anyone else and was able to peel off a few layers. "You're the messenger. Merlin sent you."

Gaheris nodded. "He did, although I would have come even if he didn't. We didn't want you to be caught by surprise."

"And you wanted a few scones."

Gaheris laughed softly. Leave it to Draig to make a joke right after being told that several thousand very dangerous Knights would be coming for his head. "I willingly admit that I do enjoy your scones. The oatmeal and cranberry cookies as well. But I didn't come here just for that. You need to take what I just told you seriously."

"Have no fear, I do," Draig replied. "After my last encounter with my father, I assumed that this would be his next move. Will the Knights be coming here in force?"

"I don't know," Gaheris replied, irritated with himself because he couldn't provide a better answer. "Knowing your father and his predilection for the application of overwhelming force that isn't beyond the realms of possibility or logic. Although I'll certainly counsel against that strategy."

"True enough." Draig offered Gaheris a shrewd look even as his eyes sparked with amusement. "Have you finally decided that enough is enough? Are you seeking sanctuary?"

Gaheris didn't offer Draig the immediate flippant response that he had all the other times his friend had asked that same question. Instead, Gaheris gave the query serious consideration, something that he had never done before. "Is that a legitimate offer?"

Draig nodded, surprised by Gaheris' serious expression. "A standing offer."

"I appreciate that," Gaheris said. "But no, not yet. I still feel like I can do some good while serving in the Knights of the Round."

"You mean do your best to temper my father's bad and increasingly bloody moods?"

"Something like that," Gaheris admitted, "at least for a little while longer hopefully."

"And when you can't?"

"Then I'll come on by for a coffee and some of those scones I like so much, maybe a few of the cookies as well, and we can discuss my options."

"Fair enough."

"Before that, however, you need to deal with this, Draig." Gaheris shook his head both in sadness and frustration. "Morgase is problem enough. You coming back into the world ... that's a recipe for disaster for your father. You know where he'll focus his attention. He believes that you slighted him in a way that your aunt has never come close. He'll ignore her and focus on you."

"You're afraid he'll kill me?"

"No, I'm afraid you'll kill him," Gaheris grumbled. "Not intentionally, of course, but he's not the man he used to be. He'll do something that he shouldn't. That's what I fear. He'll put you in a position where you won't have any choice. Then once he's gone all hell will break loose among the Teg."

"I'll deal with it, just not now. I need to deal with something else first."

"Something more important than your father, arguably the most powerful of the Teg, wanting you dead?"

"Remember, he's wanted me dead for quite some time." Draig shrugged. "I've gotten used to it."

"Yes, but Draig, you ..."

"You mentioned all hell breaking loose among the Teg," Draig cut in.

"I did."

"If I don't deal with what I need to first, then all hell will be unleashed *upon* the Teg. That worries me more than my father wanting me dead."

Gaheris studied Draig for quite some time. He knew him better than anyone. He had played a hand in raising him. He had also trained him as a Knight of the Round.

He didn't doubt what Draig was telling him. Nor did he doubt Draig's commitment and determination once he took on a task that he deemed essential, because he only did so if he truly believed that it was essential.

"I'll keep the Knights off your back for as long as I can," Gaheris promised with a sharp nod.

"Thank you. The more time you can give me, the better."

"Just one request?" Gaheris headed toward the swinging door, not wanting to keep Draig any longer than he already had and needing to get back before he was missed.

"That would be?"

"Try not to get yourself killed."

Draig gave Gaheris the smile that had irritated him when he was training to become a Knight. One that combined a hard resolve with a youthful confidence that bordered on arrogance. "I can't make any promises."

After Gaheris left wearing a bemused expression, Draig took a few minutes to think about what his friend revealed to him.

He had anticipated that despite his warning to his father, the King Teg wouldn't let go. He couldn't let go. Not after how Draig had embarrassed him. Again.

At least that's how his father would interpret what he had done in the Dragon Vault. An insult rather than the warning that it was intended to be.

And the same likely applied to his aunt. Morgase did what Morgase wanted to do, just like her brother.

Both were so used to getting what they desired that both likely rationalized his demonstration of power with *The Book of Whispers* as just another obstacle they needed to overcome to achieve what they both craved. Not surprisingly, they had missed or chose to ignore how Draig's demonstration had changed the battlefield upon which they had fought each other for so long.

That was not the result he intended. However, it wasn't entirely unexpected.

Therefore, it was definitely a good thing that he got out ahead of that problem.

He smiled at that thought. Hopefully Riga didn't have too much fun with whatever she had planned.

Although Gaheris was right. Neither he nor his father could coexist as they were now with the weight of a kill order hanging over Draig's head.

What Draig put in play would only work for so long. He was going to need to confront his father. And he could only hope that they could approach one another as reasonable men, because his father had demonstrated little in the way of reasonableness ever since Draig had started questioning Arthur's motives and decisions.

That was a worry for later, however.

Now, he had a Witch to find.

Because he was certain that she would lead him to the real prize.

7

ON THE ROAD

"Don't stop believin'. Hold on to that feelin'. Streetlights. People. Oh, oh, oh, ohhhhh."

"Crap," Melissa growled, turning the wheel sharply to the right and messing up her groove. This was one of her favorite Journey songs, and she had been carrying the tune like she did in the shower while beating out the rhythm on the steering wheel.

But she had allowed herself to be distracted for just a split-second while she checked her rearview mirror. Searching for any cars that had been trailing behind her for too long.

Swerving back into her lane, she narrowly avoided getting rear-ended by the eighteen-wheeler that was barreling down the interstate. She told herself that it wasn't her fault because the truck shouldn't have been in the far left lane to begin with. Then again, what she thought didn't really matter since truck always beat midsize SUV.

Breathing again, even as her heart continued to race at a breakneck pace, Melissa took some solace from the fact that she hadn't seen anything during her quick check that gave her any cause for concern. She seemed to be in the clear.

Two hands now on the wheel of her nondescript Toyota Highlander, she continued down I-95 South, the long expanse of the Delaware Memorial Bridge that would take her out of New Jersey and into Delaware coming into view.

Then, from there, onto Route 1 and the reason that she had snuck out of Kraken Cove.

She turned the music up, needing a distraction.

Once again, with too much time to think, Melissa was doubting her plan.

Should she have told Draig what she was going to do?

That question had been playing through her mind ever since she left Maine and entered New Hampshire.

She would be the first to admit that she could have used his help. Nevertheless, even if she had asked, she hadn't been certain that he would have given it.

He had helped her more times than she cared to remember in just the last few days, but what she would have asked of him

...

No, he had little cause to aid her in the manner required. And it wouldn't have been right for her to ask him that.

Melissa pounded the steering wheel with a bit more vigor, seeking to snap herself out of her circular thoughts.

She needed to stop thinking about Draig and what she could have done.

What's done was done.

She had made her decision.

There was no going back. Not now.

And there was no way that she was going to give him a call. Besides, she couldn't. She had left her phone in her purse in the back seat as a deterrent.

Besides, he was probably more than just a little angry with her, and she had no desire to deal with that.

The Dragon was scary enough.

The Dragon in a rage?

No, that wasn't for her.

"I can do this on my own," Melissa said softly. A mantra that she had been repeating to herself every few hours. A reminder of sorts whenever her nerves threatened to get the best of her.

She had been in many hairy situations in the past and escaped them all with scarcely a scratch. So why not again?

She had stolen the artifact from right under Mordred's nose, fought and escaped a werewolf, fought and escaped three Berserkers, fought and escaped a pack of werewolves, survived being kidnapped by Mordred, escaped him and Morgase, come up against Arthur Pendragon, and ...

Dammit!

She had done all of that, but she had only stolen the artifact and escaped a single werewolf on her own.

Draig had been there for her for all the other life-threatening experiences that had bombarded her as soon as she reacquired the item she had stolen for Mordred.

She hit her steering wheel again. The hard smack made her grunt.

Bruising her hand wasn't going to give her the peace she sought. Nor was it going to help her achieve her primary objective.

She couldn't trust that Draig would help her. It was as simple as that. Her objective didn't necessarily mesh with his objective. She hadn't asked him because she feared he might try to stop her.

Good decision.

She had to put the needs of the person who meant the most to her above her own.

Good decision.

To do that, she had to address this challenge on her own. She needed to hand over what Typhon required from her and then hope that he lifted the curse he had placed on her mother. Then, after that, she had to find some way to escape before he or that green-haired always angry daughter of his realized that she had played them. All of that was why she needed to do this all on her own. Draig would just get in the way and make her life more difficult.

Good …

Melissa sighed in frustration.

Maybe that last really wasn't a good decision. Nevertheless, that was the decision that she had made, and she needed to see it through.

She had no choice. If she didn't succeed, her mother died.

"Get out of your head and do what you need to do."

One of her mother's lessons while she was learning the family business. Good advice. Growling at herself for vacillating, she tried to apply it.

Melissa looked in the rearview mirror again. There was no vehicle behind her that stood out.

At least she had that working in her favor.

If Typhon had sent Jinx after her, either to make sure she got where she needed to go or to take the artifact herself before Melissa could deliver it to her father, thereby earning the credit and mitigating the need for Typhon to meet his promise to her, then she had to assume that he sent several of his other servants after her as well. If for no other reason than to be certain that he obtained what he most desired.

Reaching the bridge that would take her over the Delaware River, she slowed her speed, not wanting to draw the interest of the state trooper parked on the side of the road.

The call of nature striking her, and the need for Starbucks following right behind it, she hit her blinker as the sign for the exit to Route 1 appeared. Once she was off the interstate she would meet both her needs.

Then, she would get her head straight.

She needed to remind herself that this wasn't just another of her jobs that she was driving toward.

This was a battle.

"SHOULD WE TAKE HER?"

"Not yet, Walter," Burgess said wearily, tired of having to answer the same question ten times in the same amount of minutes. "We've been over this."

"You're always in a rush, for blaze's sake," Jack added. "For once, keep your pants on."

"I just want to get this done," Walter grumbled. "The sooner we do, the sooner we get paid."

"And you've got some bets to make," Jack nodded. "Is that it? Seeking to recover from your earlier losses?"

"I've always got some bets to make," Walter confirmed, "and I've got some sure winners, yes."

"Of course you do," Burgess said in a soothing tone, knowing full well how Walter could lose control of himself when he burned through what little patience he had. He didn't have time for his brother's theatrics. Not with so much riding on this job. "You have nothing to worry about. You can get on your app as soon as we've got her and we're on our way."

"And when will we be done?" Walter demanded. "Like I said, I've got some sure winners."

"We'll be done when we're done," Burgess replied, his voice calm though unyielding. Walter's constant griping was becoming more than just a little tedious. Burgess knew that wasn't entirely unexpected since the three lived together in such close quarters, so he tried to ignore his initial instinct to smack his brother a few times and remind him who was in charge.

The three Teg stood in the front of the semi-trailer staring through the two-way mirror set at the top of the wall that allowed them to look out over the tractor.

Their work required them to travel a lot. Preferring to stay away from hotels, they had come up with another solution that worked quite well. Most of the time.

In addition to the perch upon which they stood, they had modified the inside of the trailer into a comfortable apartment just big enough for the three of them.

Although they still had to share one bathroom and one shower, which had become a point of contention between them during the last few days.

When there wasn't much to do, Walter gave in to his desire to gorge on ice cream. That wasn't a problem except for the fact that he refused to eat soy, oat, or lactose-free ice cream, even though he was lactose intolerant. His more and more frequent blowouts and the resulting stench that pervaded the trailer threatened to send Jack and Burgess fleeing for the hills. It didn't appear to affect Walter at all. In fact, he seemed to relish inflicting his unique form of torture upon them.

They had been on the job for more than a month now. In addition to the monotony and the overwhelming stench of Walter's frequent visits to the bathroom that permeated their living space, they were tired of each other.

Jack, Walter, and Burgess all were looking forward to gaining some space for themselves for a few weeks once they captured the Witch and delivered her to their boss. Until then, however, they were stuck with one another and they needed to make the best of it.

"Any sign of her?" Walter asked.

Jack bit back the sharp remark that he really wanted to share with his brother, understanding that it wouldn't do either of them any good. "No, not yet. She went into the Starbucks and she's still in the Starbucks. Nothing has changed since you asked me that same question two minutes ago."

"I just want to make sure," Walter protested.

"Stay quiet and stay focused," Burgess urged. "It won't be long now. We'll grab her when she comes out."

Burgess wasn't worried. From what he could see, it would be an easy snatch.

The Witch's car was parked at the back of the parking lot and away from the shop. She didn't know that he and his brothers had been tracking her ever since she entered Massachusetts. And she hadn't been in the coffee shop for long. Four minutes now as he glanced at his watch again.

It would take a few minutes more for her to use the restroom and grab her order because the line at the register was fairly long.

Once she had her food, they would make their move. With her hands occupied, fumbling for her keys as she went to her car, the Witch's first thought wouldn't be to defend herself. It would be to try not to spill her coffee. Those few seconds of indecision were all that Burgess and his brothers needed to ensure she couldn't work the Grym upon them.

"I'm taking the Knicks over the Bucks."

"Walter, I don't care," Jack replied, keeping his eyes focused on the coffee shop across Route 1. "And we've been over this before. Not taking the Bucks is a bad bet. Never bet against the Greek Freak."

"Even the Greek Freak can have a bad game, and our friends in New York tell me that when he steps onto the court at Madison Square Garden, he will have a very bad game."

Jack lifted an eyebrow. "They're hexing the court?"

"They are," Walter confirmed. "I'm going to make a killing."

"I really hope so," Jack grumbled, "because I'm really tired of you begging me to buy you dinner every time you lose big, which seems to be every time you pick what you say is a sure winner."

"That never happens," Walter growled, shoving Jack in the shoulder. More than just a shove, actually, because Walter had a hard time managing his remarkable strength. Even so, Jack didn't budge an inch.

"It happened last week," Jack replied with a touch more heat in his voice, not appreciating Walter pushing him. His own temper rising.

To make a point, in turn Jack shoved his brother. Hard. Sending the very large Walter back up against the trailer wall that set their living quarters shaking.

With another growl that was more a roar, Walter was off the side of the trailer in an instant, reaching for Jack with his meaty paws.

He didn't take more than a step before Burgess placed himself between the two. "Now isn't the time for your crap. When the job is done, we'll find a mud pit and you two can settle your disagreement the way we did when we were kids. Clear?"

Walter and Jack didn't respond as they stared at one another as if they were participating in a WWE smackdown. Scrunching their fingers together, knuckles white. Eager to get to it, though neither was willing to challenge their older brother.

"Clear?" Burgess repeated, this time in a very quiet voice that drew both pairs of eyes. They both were all too familiar with that tone and understood what would happen if they didn't calm down.

Jack and Walter nodded. Scowling at one another, they returned to their work.

Burgess shook his head in resignation. Why did it seem like he was the only level-headed Troll in his tribe? All the others, just like Jack and Walter, would be set off at the slightest insult, real or imagined. Flying into a rage and pounding whatever angered them, object or Teg, into dust.

Turning back to the window, Burgess glimpsed his true reflection in the mirrored glass. His long, wild hair that hung below his shoulders and resembled meadow fescue along with his large bulbous nose and muscles that grew atop muscles marked him for one of the most dangerous and ferocious of the Teg.

Most other Teg assumed that Trolls were slow and dimwitted. That was just what the stories said, however, which was fine with Burgess. He was more than happy to take advantage of that common misconception.

The Teg also believed that Trolls were quick to employ violence. That was true. Walter and Jack were prime examples of that fact. But they were also clever, devious, and they had a great deal of skill in using the Grym to mask themselves.

To anyone who looked at them now, including other Teg, Burgess, Jack, and Walter would appear to be nothing more than heavy-set truckers with long, scraggly hair who favored jeans and stained t-shirts. Very large truckers, admittedly, but truckers, nonetheless. Unless the Teg knew what they were looking for.

That was why Morgase had selected Burgess and his brothers for this assignment. Their ability to get in close to their targets and stay in the background -- Morgase not trusting her son's planning – until it was time to take matters into their own hands if it proved necessary or the opportunity presented itself.

And it had, the Sorceress' concern proving valid when the Berserkers Mordred hired reneged on the contract and switched their allegiance to the Dragon.

The brothers found that decision somewhat odd, never having heard of Berserkers ever backing out of a deal. The blonde bastards were so bound by their honor that the Trolls had never thought it possible for their competitors to break an oath.

It didn't bother them in the least, however.

Trolls hated Berserkers with a vengeance.

"Maybe it would have been better if she hit you when she drifted into our lane," Jack said to Walter, offering an olive branch to his brother.

Trolls were quick to anger and just as quick to forget ... for a time.

While following the Toyota Highlander, they had never gotten too close. Always making sure that the Witch wasn't aware of their presence. And with so many rigs on the interstate, it was a fairly simple task.

Then, certain as to the Witch's route thanks to the information Morgase provided to them, they had decided to get ahead of her. They believed that it would be easier to take her if she came to them.

"Maybe it would have been," Walter agreed. "We could have grabbed her on the highway. No one would have paid much attention."

"That doesn't matter," Burgess said with the authority he had earned as the oldest of the three. "There are only a few people left in the Starbucks, and she'll be coming out soon. We'll take her now and be done with this. I need to breathe some fresh air. I can't take the stench any longer."

All three excited to get out of their dank and foul-smelling apartment, Jack and Walter jostled with one another to pull open the side door. Knocking both of his brothers out of the way, Burgess hopped out, Jack and Walter behind him and forcing their way through the door at the same time.

The Trolls made it no more than a step before they were forced to stop cold.

Two men stood in front of them, blocking their path.

They were dressed in neatly pressed grey suits and starched white shirts. Much like any other businessmen.

They looked familiar to Burgess. Although for the life of him, he couldn't place them. And that bothered the Troll because the fedora hats should have given the two men away.

"Gentlemen, we need to talk," the one on the right said.

"WHO THE HELL ARE YOU?" Burgess demanded.

"We could ask you the same thing," Tom said, "but we don't need to."

"What are a trio of nice Trolls like you doing this far south?" Harry asked. "Usually you keep to colder stomping grounds, yet you're not too far from the Mason-Dixon line."

Tom and Harry saw through the illusion the three Trolls had crafted around themselves with the Grym because they knew exactly who they were looking for.

"How do you know we're Trolls?" Walter demanded.

Burgess flicked his hand at his brother, quieting him to just a low growl. It didn't matter how these two Teg knew they were Trolls. What mattered was that they did. "I'll ask again. Who are you?"

"The Three Brothers," Tom replied.

Burgess, Jack, and Walter gave Tom a blank look. Burgess thought he should know these two. He did know them though the memory was slow to return, at least he thought he did. Maybe too much rough housing in the mud pit.

"You don't know who we are?" Harry asked. He wasn't the least disappointed by that finding. He and Tom had succeeded so long in their chosen profession because of their discretion.

"Should we?" Jack asked.

"We're well known for our work in certain circles," Harry replied.

"Not in our circles," Jack replied.

"And that's probably a good thing," Tom confirmed. Before he could get to the reason why he and Harry had put themselves in front of three quick-tempered Trolls, Jack interrupted him.

"If you're the Three Brothers where's the other one? Hiding away somewhere so that he can jump out at us? Take us by surprise?"

"He's dead," Tom said, offering no more of an explanation than that.

It didn't stop Jack from following up, his curiosity getting the better of him. "If he's dead, then why do you still call yourselves the Three Brothers?"

"Because in certain circles, not your circles of course," Harry explained, offering the trio of Trolls a nod, "that's how we're known. Besides, we like to remember our dead brother."

"He was a good brother?" Jack gave Walter a look when he asked the question that suggested that in his opinion Walter was not a good brother.

Walter ignored him, having eyes only for the two Teg who stood in their way.

"No, he wasn't. He was an ass."

Burgess frowned. Having grown tired of what he viewed as a useless conversation, and not wanting to miss his chance with the Witch coming out of the coffee shop in the next few minutes, he tried to move matters along.

"I suggest you step aside."

"Or?" Tom asked.

"Or we will crush you into the asphalt," Walter rumbled, flexing his hands that more resembled catcher mitts. "We will stomp on your bodies until we break every bone and your flesh is nothing more than a disgusting paste."

"You can try," Harry replied with a calm that came across as menacing even though he was smiling when he said it.

"You two little men are strange," Jack said. He didn't quite understand what was happening. These two Teg obviously knew that they were challenging three Trolls, yet going against form they didn't appear to be the least bit concerned. And they didn't seem to care about provoking them. It was almost as if that was their goal.

"That's one way to put it," Tom admitted.

"What's another way?" Burgess asked.

"We're also dangerous."

Before Jack could ask the next question that came to mind, Tom and Harry moved with a blinding speed. Two-foot-long metal spikes, hammers on the back end, seemingly appeared out of thin air and in their hands.

They started with Walter, recognizing him as the greatest threat since he was the one most prepared for a fight.

Before Walter could even blink, he looked down, a bloody hole punched in his knee, the damaged joint making him sag. He dropped to the ground just an instant later, Harry smashing him in the back of his head with the hammer side of his weapon.

"Walt ..."

Jack got no more than that out before he gasped, a hammer striking him in the forehead. Reaching up to the wound, blood sheeting down his face, he dropped to his knees heavily, then collapsed face first to the pavement because of the hard smack to the back of his head.

"I know who you are now," Burgess claimed as he stepped back slowly toward the door that led into his trailer. "You work for King Arthur."

The Troll was trying to earn some time so that he could figure out what to do. He would aid his injured brothers later, assuming he could get out of this mess.

"We did," Tom confirmed as he stepped to the left so that he could come at the last Troll at an angle.

"You did?" Burgess didn't understand. He had never heard of anyone working for King Arthur and then not. Once you were in with the King Teg, you stayed there.

Burgess' back hit the closed door. Dammit!

Jack had been paying attention for once. His brother had a habit of leaving the door open, Burgess reminding him time and again to shut the door behind him. And, just as luck would have it, when Burgess most needed to have that door open so that he could scramble inside before these two assassins were on him, Jack had closed it just as Burgess had requested.

"We did," Harry confirmed. He shifted a few steps to his right, advancing on the Troll from that angle.

The Troll could try to break past both of them, but he wouldn't get far. He couldn't protect both his sides at the same time.

He was trapped. Just the way Tom and Harry intended.

"Who do you work for now?"

Burgess understood the challenge he faced. Worse, he understood that he had few options left to him.

He smiled thinly to himself. Strange how life often worked out. He had been grumbling to himself just that morning that he couldn't wait to get away from his brothers, tired of Jack and Walter arguing incessantly and their irritating and disgusting habits. More than happy if they would disappear. Permanently.

Now that he faced two men who demonstrated an incredible martial prowess, he wished that his brothers were still by his side.

"We work for the Dragon," Tom replied, a hint of pride in his voice.

"The Dragon?" Burgess asked. He was surprised to hear that. "I thought he was dead."

"He was," Harry confirmed.

"The Dragon has come back to life," Tom said, taking a step closer to the Troll before stopping, recognizing the danger of getting too close before he attacked.

Despite their immense size and seemingly ponderous movement, Trolls were exceedingly fast. If this Troll got hold of

Tom's neck, he could snap it like a twig. In fact, if he got both of those paws around his waist, the Troll could break him in half.

Burgess licked his lips. He had been thinking about making a play for the Teg who had taken a step closer to him. But the Teg hadn't gotten close enough. If he made a grab for him now, the other Teg could finish him with a stab in the back.

He had only one option now. Burgess had to make a break for it between the two assassins.

If he was quick enough, he could kill one if he was really lucky – although he didn't place a lot of faith in luck -- or more likely knock one of them to the ground. The other Teg would catch him with that nasty spike that glowed with the Grym, but that was the price he would have to pay.

If the wound he took wasn't too deep, his plan just might work.

Knock one of the Teg to the ground, assuming he could catch his target by surprise.

Pivot and hope the unavoidable wound he suffered from the other Teg wasn't mortal.

Knock the other Teg down.

Then climb into the cab and get the hell out of there.

A lot of ifs, Burgess mused. He didn't like ifs. But that was all he had.

"How is it that the Dragon somehow ..."

Burgess sagged against the trailer, then slid down to the pavement, Harry easing him on his way.

"The Dragon is the Dragon," Harry said as he pulled back his hammer, the weapon's imprint marring the side of Burgess' head. Losing consciousness, the glamour that had been hiding the creature faded then disappeared entirely, just as had been the case with the other two.

"You want to help me with this one?" Tom asked.

Harry nodded, leaving Burgess where he was to aid his brother. They lugged Walter over to the unlocked door, then bundled him through. They did the same to Jack and finally Burgess, each one heavier than the last.

"We should have done this in the truck," Harry murmured. He was straightening his shirt and readjusting his jacket. He didn't like it when even the tiniest item was out of place. "It would have made it easier for us."

"Now we know for next time," Tom replied.

"There's going to be a next time?"

"We're working for the Dragon now."

"Good point," Harry admitted. In the space of just a few days they had fought Warlocks and then Vipers. Not what they had anticipated, although they couldn't say they didn't enjoy the challenge.

"Come on," Tom said, watching as Melissa left the Starbucks and made for her car. "We need to get going."

"Do you think she saw us?"

"No, but who can say? She is a Witch after all."

MELISSA TOOK a sip from her caramel macchiato while she waited for the light to change. With all the sugar she was consuming, she believed that she would be able to make it almost all the way to her next destination before she crashed and needed a nap.

Her brow quirked.

That was strange.

Looking across Route 1 as the traffic sped by, there was a truck parked at the far end of the gas station near the carwash. It looked like the rig that had blown past her right before she turned off I-95.

Not surprising in and of itself, but still ...

Before she could think more about that, she caught a hint of movement near the back of the cab. Two men ...

What were they dragging?

She had to be mistaken. The sugar was already affecting her.

Wait. Were those ...

No, they couldn't be.

The honk behind her pulled her gaze from the men and whatever they were carrying. Slightly startled, she pressed down on the gas a bit too hard, her car jumping forward as she sped through the green light and turned south down Route One.

Before the gas station was out of sight, she glanced behind her, wanting to check, but she couldn't see anything.

Strange. Very strange.

Melissa thought she glimpsed the Three Brothers by that truck.

But that couldn't have been them, could it?

No. Definitely not.

Still ...

If it was them, were they working for Typhon or for Draig?

Melissa knew only one way to get the answer to that question, and she was certain that she was better off not knowing.

8

POOR PEP TALK

"Where do you head next?"

Draig smiled, just a curl of his lips, not looking up from where he sat on a bench in Central Park near the Untermyer Fountain. He moved the newspaper he had placed next to him, nodding for Merlin to have a seat.

"That will depend in part on this conversation," answered Draig.

Merlin offered a cunning grin and gripped Draig's shoulder warmly, revealing a surprising strength for a man who appeared to be well past his prime. "You sound like me. I'm glad that at least some of what I taught you rubbed off."

"More than I care to acknowledge," Draig admitted. He looked up, giving his friend and mentor a wider smile. He always enjoyed spending time with the Sorcerer, even though doing so could be just as frustrating as it was exhilarating.

"Don't worry. Gaheris hasn't mobilized the Knights of the Round yet. He's taking things slow and giving you some time as he promised." Merlin sensed Draig using the Grym to search around them. He should have been offended, but he wasn't.

Best to be careful even with someone you trusted to ensure that several companies of Knights weren't bearing down on you.

"Once this is over, I'll owe him a great deal for taking that risk." Draig's father wasn't a forgiving man. If Arthur Pendragon learned that his second in command wasn't implementing a direct order as quickly as he desired, to say nothing of his aiding and abetting a Teg condemned to death, insubordination would be the least of Gaheris' concerns, a centuries-old friendship be damned.

"I know you're a bit under the gun, so why did you reach out to me?" Merlin crossed his legs and leaned back, enjoying the warm sunshine playing across his craggy face on what was a cold day. "What couldn't Gaheris give you that I can?"

"Information."

"Then you came to the right place. About?" Merlin's impish smile suggested that he already knew the answer to his own question.

"Typhon."

"I was afraid that you were going to say that." Merlin placed his hands behind his head, stretching out his long length. "A blast from the past that I would prefer stayed there."

"You don't think I can take him?" Draig asked the question not as a challenge, but rather because he wanted an honest answer. He needed to know what he was up against.

Merlin didn't respond right away, frowning slightly as he thought about how he wanted to reply. "You can ..."

"But what?"

"If the stars align."

"Really? That's what you're going to give me with all that's riding on this?"

Merlin added a bit of mystery to his features, an expression he had perfected over the centuries. "Sorry, I couldn't help myself. Old habits die hard."

"You need to put that one to bed," Draig growled. He

never enjoyed when Merlin equivocated. The Sorcerer preferred not to answer if he didn't know the answer, so he often cloaked his response in a way that protected him from being wrong.

"Noted," Merlin replied. "The best I can offer you is that I don't know that even if you defeat Typhon – and I do believe you can defeat him so long as all works in your favor – that you come out on the other side."

Draig nodded, not surprised or put off by Merlin's perspective. "Not much of a pep talk, Merlin."

"When have you ever known me to give you a pep talk," Merlin replied, slightly irritated, that irritation disappearing when he glanced at Draig and recognized that his former pupil was playing with him. "Even with this hanging over your head you feel the need to push my buttons?"

It was Draig's turn to apologize. "Sorry, old habits and all that."

"I can't imagine where you picked up a bad habit like that."

"Neither can I," Draig replied with just as much sarcasm. "Although it does help to relieve the stress."

Merlin snorted at that. "When have you ever felt stress?"

"When I was working for my father."

"I'll give you that." Merlin studied the Conservatory Garden for a time. Collecting his thoughts, he castigated himself silently for not stepping in when he could have so many times in the past. If he had, he might have been able to derail Arthur from turning his son into a weapon. "What do you know of Typhon?"

"A basic knowledge. I've been doing some reading. Online and from some other sources."

"Not on Wikipedia, I hope?"

"What's wrong with Wikipedia?" Draig asked with an absolute innocence.

Merlin's eyes bulged. The crowdfunded and crowd-developed online knowledge database offered useful information, but only that provided by those not of the Teg.

It didn't contain all that there was to know about the monster and his exploits. And how could it? The same could be said for *Bullfinch's Mythology* and a variety of other classic and classical resources that dated back to the times of antiquity.

The histories written about the Gods and monsters of the various mythologies were written by humans. They knew virtually nothing of the Teg world. Only the Teg knew what happened among the Teg.

How could Draig even think ...

Merlin's eyes narrowed, his expression darkening. "Must you get under my skin whenever you can? I admit, from time to time it was amusing when you were younger. But now you should know better."

"You always said that if you couldn't have a little fun in life, then life really wasn't worth living."

"I said that?" Merlin demanded. "That doesn't sound like me at all."

"It was right after you had me place that nest of scorpions in Gwennie's room."

Merlin drew a blank for just a moment. When it finally came to him, he gave Draig a broad smile. His former pupil had caught him out. "Yes, I remember that. Probably not the best decision I ever made. Still, I can't say that I regret it."

"How could you?" Draig prodded. "You got what you wanted when Lancelot came hopping out of her suite in her bathrobe."

"You've got the right of that," Merlin confirmed with a nod of satisfaction, "and that really was quite a sight. The greatest Knight of the Round jumping about with the air blowing up his robe as he tried to avoid those stingers." He chuckled softly then. "We were quite a team."

Merlin had required proof of the Queen Teg's many indiscretions with the man sworn to serve her husband. Draig's action at Merlin's prompting had given him that and much more, specifically, and most important, breaking the strange hold Guinnevere had on Arthur Pendragon.

"Now back to your question about what I know." Draig leaned forward, forearms resting on his knees, his eyes sweeping around them constantly to make sure that none of the walkers and joggers making their way along the various paths were paying any more attention to them than they should have. "Seshat gave me access to some of the texts that are thought long lost."

"*The Forgotten Histories of Gods, Monsters, and Men?*" Merlin asked. He assumed that's where Seshat had started with Draig. When it came to obtaining obscure or purposely obscured information – or desired artifacts that were difficult and sometimes all but impossible to acquire – Seshat was the Teg to speak with.

"That one and several others. Thanks to her, I have a good sense of how Typhon came to be and why he sought to destroy the Greek Gods. Also how Zeus defeated Typhon and banished him to Tartarus. What actually happened, not the stories meant to hide or distort key pieces of information."

"*The Record of the Oracle?*"

"Yes."

Merlin nodded, pleased to hear it. He wouldn't have to start from the very beginning. "That's an important point you mentioned. Zeus defeated Typhon in an epic battle, he deserves credit for that, but even he, the king of the Greek Gods, couldn't destroy Typhon. All he could do was lock away that monster so that he would be a problem for someone else at a later date."

"Someone like me?"

"That seems to be the case," Merlin confirmed. "Of course, your father had the pleasure of dealing with Typhon not long after you were born, so I guess it's a part of the family legacy."

"What happened? Seshat found little about that duel in her usual sources. All that I've been able to piece together suggests that my father fought like Hercules against the Nemean lion." Draig shook his head in amusement at that. "Not even the Oracle could provide more than that. All well and good, but based on experience, I have no doubt there's more to it than that ... as well as quite a bit less."

"No one fought like Hercules," Merlin replied. "I can promise you that. That Teg was a force of nature. The only resemblance between him and your father was the mean streak."

Draig nodded sagely. He knew exactly what Merlin was talking about. His father would do whatever was required to win a combat. Yet winning was rarely enough for him. He also needed to ensure that the men and women he defeated understood their place in his world and the utter foolishness of provoking him.

He was the King Teg.

He would always be the King Teg.

To challenge him risked not only death, but also humiliation and the strong likelihood that your name and legacy were wiped clean from the Teg history books.

"We'll get to your father's duel with Typhon. Before that, though, you need to be aware of the threat that Typhon truly presents to our world because of the power that he can wield."

"How so?"

"Typhon doesn't employ the Grym like most of the rest of the Teg. Rather, the Grym is an offshoot of the power that he exercises as an Ancient."

"Thanks for the uplifting news, Merlin." Draig understood what his friend was implying, his smile souring at the thought. The Ancients, meaning the various pantheons of Gods and monsters from which all the Teg derived, exercised a power very close to that of nature itself. Most of the Teg employed no more than a tiny stream of that power. The Ancients could put into play a tidal wave. And for some a tsunami. As a result, to think of challenging any of them was suicidal at best.

"I'm here to help," Merlin replied, ignoring Draig's sarcasm and offering some of his own. "When it comes to Typhon, remember that he has the strength to cause earthquakes, volcanic eruptions, monsoons, and floods that can reshape the world. With barely any effort at all, in fact, he could destroy whole continents."

"Then why didn't he when he had the chance?" Draig wondered. "And how do we know that he won't if he's free from Tartarus?"

"The only truth that we can be certain of is that Typhon wants to rule. He's wanted to rule ... actually, that's not entirely correct ... I should say that Typhon has wanted to dominate ever since he came into being. But he doesn't want to reign over a broken world. He understands that would only make his life more difficult. So though he has an almost uncontrollable urge for hegemony, he's not stupid."

"Not all that surprising considering his background," Draig acknowledged.

"Very true," Merlin admitted. "However, we need to keep in mind that there's more to it than just that. He also wants his vengeance. He will subjugate the Teg world if he can, but he won't destroy the Teg world to gain it unless that proves absolutely necessary. At least I hope he won't."

"I really don't like placing a lot of faith in hope."

"Neither do I," Merlin admitted. "We can have faith that Typhon also wants to destroy those he believed wronged him."

Draig thought about that. If that was the case, then Typhon had a long list. "And what of the Twelve Olympians? I'm assuming he would start there."

Merlin didn't reply right away, leaning forward on the bench, hands on his knees, and sighing. Sometimes, on days like this when it felt like the fate of the world was in balance, teetering on the brink, he felt his years.

"What of them?" The Sorcerer shook his head more in frustration than anything else. "Even with all my eyes and ears, I haven't been able to figure out where they might be. Retired atop Mount Olympus? I don't know because no one can get beyond the wards protecting the symbol of their power."

"You have heard nothing at all from any of them? They must know what's going on with Typhon."

Merlin shook his head. "Not a peep and not for a very long time. Maybe they lost interest in playing around in human affairs. Maybe they want to leave Typhon to us fearing failure on their part. Maybe they retired. Maybe they just ..."

"Faded." Draig finished Merlin's thought for him.

"That thought had crossed my mind," Merlin admitted. "Although I was hoping that wasn't the case. Any chance Medusa might know?"

"Medusa?"

"Yes, Medusa," Merlin repeated. "I don't have a great many sources in the Greek pantheon. I was hoping that perhaps your newest guest in Kraken Cove might be able to provide more information than I've been able to dig up."

Draig was about to ask the foolish question of how Merlin knew Medusa was in Kraken Cove. He stopped himself, not wanting to give Merlin the chance to offer a smart-ass comment.

Just because Merlin didn't have many good sources remaining among the Greek pantheon didn't mean he still wasn't connected in many of the other pantheons and throughout the rest of the Teg world. To think otherwise would be folly.

"She's not in a position to talk about it, unfortunately."

"Why not? I thought she was staying with Hestia. With her ties to the Greek Gods, she could provide us with a perspective that I can't gain elsewhere."

"I understand, but Typhon already has taken her from the board." Draig explained briefly what ailed the Gorgon as well as his failure to aid her. And, perhaps most important from Merlin's perspective, why Typhon had cursed her and what was now in play.

"That's quite disappointing," Merlin murmured, "although I can't say that I'm surprised. Most Teg viewed Typhon as a brute. A monster who relied solely on his remarkable power to gain what he wanted. But he is much more than that. He understands the different types of power and how to apply them all. That's why he was such a formidable opponent for Zeus."

Draig got the sense that Merlin's disappointment didn't come from the fact that Medusa was dying, but rather from the fact that she couldn't be of assistance. In that respect, Merlin and his father were much alike. They often viewed other Teg as resources to be used, not as individuals to be valued.

"So the challenge becomes even more difficult," Draig said, "because we can't rely on the Twelve Olympians for assistance."

"We can't," Merlin agreed. "Although I wouldn't have relied on them even if we could still reach out to them."

"Why not?"

"Only Zeus had the strength to take on Typhon the first time, and that was a close thing."

"You don't think he can do it again now?"

"Honestly ..." Merlin shook his head as he weighed the odds. "Probably not. And even if all twelve of the Olympians combined their power ... maybe. I certainly wouldn't want to place the fate of the Teg world on their shoulders. The last time I interacted with a few of the Olympians, they weren't what they had been."

Draig didn't bother to ask what Merlin meant. Just like any

religion or pantheon, the Greek pantheon depended on believers for much of their strength and power. At one time, the Greeks and the Romans believed in them. Faithfully. Without doubt. Without fail.

That belief augmented the Greek Gods' natural strength in the Power of the Ancients, making them almost invincible. But that belief faded over time as the world changed, and it seemed that the Greek Gods, like so many others from millennia past, had faded as well as their magical power diminished.

"For all we know, Zeus and his brood might not even be on Mount Olympus. They could be hiding away on a Greek isle with little interest in what's going on in the Teg world. In fact, they might even be hiding away because they know what would happen if Typhon found them."

"A distinct possibility," Merlin admitted. "There's just no way to know." The Sorcerer placed his forearms on his knees. "Because of the power that circulates in the Teg world, there are few absolutes."

"So we're back in class now," Draig mused, remembering many sessions just like this one where Merlin prepared himself to begin a lecture that could run for a few minutes or a few hours. There was no way to know until he was done.

"I was just going to say that no age stays the same," Merlin explained in a slightly miffed tone. "Ages come and go. That is an absolute. To survive, you must be able to adjust. Some can't. Others can."

"Just as my father has done."

"Exactly. His power just like so many others in the Teg world doesn't rely so much on belief. That was a mistake made by many of the early Gods that might have seemed like a good idea when they were in their prime but has cost them dearly once belief faltered."

"Assuming we can't connect to Zeus and those who used to hang with him on Mount Olympus ..."

"Typhon simply will shift his focus to those who remain on his hit list," Merlin concluded. "That scenario actually works in his favor, because going after your father allows him to kill two birds with one stone."

"Not just to gain the Teg throne," Draig prompted.

"No, that's only a part of it. Typhon wants your father out of the picture since he was the one who stopped him from escaping Tartarus the first time."

"I'm afraid to even ask how he did it."

Merlin offered Draig an expression of shock. "You don't remember your lessons while training to be a Knight of the Round and the strategy your father implemented to achieve his great victory?"

"Careful, Merlin, your sarcasm is dripping down to the concrete."

Merlin laughed at that. "Fair enough. You never believed all the lore that was developed around your father."

"You mean the lore my father developed for his own use."

"Point taken," Merlin said, "and you're right to doubt. Your father is one of the strongest Teg in existence. Few can challenge him with respect to his martial ability or with the Grym. Yet even he struggled against Typhon."

"Then how did he ensure the monster remained in Tartarus?"

"He didn't," Merlin stated with a wink and a hint of mystery, although not with enough mystery to keep Draig in the dark.

"You helped him, and you two have kept it a secret this whole time," Draig concluded.

"That fight along with many other matters. Combats. Schemes. A host of happenings the truth of which should never see the light of day."

"Why am I not surprised," Draig murmured, leaning back into the bench. His father's primary goal always had been to stay atop the Teg throne, and Merlin's primary goal had been to keep him there. Both would do whatever was required to make that happen. Success constructed upon success, strengthening the foundation of his rule, maintaining the myths built up around Arthur Pendragon, and thereby preventing any cracks in that foundation.

"Why would you be?" Merlin smiled, obviously quite pleased with himself. "In fact, I would have thought that you would have doubted that and many other stories well before now."

"I did," Draig admitted. His father had a unique ability to twist history for his own purposes. "I guess there was a part of me that still hoped that there was more fact than fiction to my father."

"There is, I promise you that," Merlin said.

"I'll believe it when I see it," Draig replied, the disappointment in his voice thick.

"You're being unfair, Axel. You know as well as I what's required of the King Teg." Merlin leaned in close to Draig, making sure that he caught his eyes. "You better than anyone else I would think."

Draig had several choice responses to Merlin's comment. He kept them to himself, none of them useful. In large part because he didn't like the look that Merlin was giving him. One of anticipation. Why Merlin was doing that, he didn't know, and he really had no desire to find out.

"You would expect nothing less from him?" Merlin chuckled, although not with a great deal of mirth. Strangely, there was a hint of anger in the sound. Almost resentment. "He saw an opportunity to burnish his own image, and he took it. Just as he has done many times before and I'm sure he'll do many times in the future."

"Yes, he has mastered that skill, hasn't he? If you want me to give him credit for something, I'm happy to give him credit for that."

"You can't really fault him for it," Merlin replied. "Though it might rankle at times, the tactic has proven useful in his efforts to maintain his hold on the Teg throne." Merlin reached over and patted Draig on the knee. "We don't always like having to do what we must to maintain our positions in life, but still we do what we must if we want to stay there."

Draig ignored the comment, in large part because he didn't want to fall down that rabbit hole, but also because Merlin was right.

Although he didn't want Merlin to be right. He wanted the Teg world to function in a less dysfunctional way.

However, there was little that he could do about that from where he was sitting, and he had no desire to pursue the hint of a question that he saw in the back of Merlin's eyes. "How did you and my father beat Typhon and send him back to Tartarus?"

"Your father kept him busy. I came at him from his blindside."

Draig snorted. "One of his favorite tactics even to this day."

"Because it works, Axel. You should know that better than most."

"Fair enough," Draig admitted, not needing to be reminded of the most recent time he and Merlin had used the exact same tactic to their advantage … against his own father, no less.

"You really have to give your father credit. He took quite a beating before I could knock that monster from his perch and back through the gates of Tartarus."

"We can discuss my father and his tactics later."

Merlin held back what he was going to say. Draig was testier than usual this morning. Probably because of the topic of their conversation. Not Typhon, but rather his father.

Arthur had quite a bit to answer for, so Merlin could understand. Axel had every right to blame his father for what he had become. However, if he was being completely honest, and judging by the pained expression that briefly passed across his face he was doing just that, Axel needed to blame himself as well.

But now wasn't the time for deep introspection. Now was the time for action. Draig could punish himself later.

"Distinct from your father's tactics, there's something important you need to know about the end of that combat that no one else knows."

That pulled Draig from the dark thoughts that threatened to drag him down. "That might actually give me a chance of success?"

Merlin nodded, then leaned in close again so that their heads were almost touching. "Typhon is an opponent to be feared, and rightfully so. That monster has no equal in our world. But he can't come back fully to our world. Not until he figures out some way to free himself from Tartarus."

Draig's frown shifted to one of irritation. "Speak plainly, Merlin." He didn't have any patience left for his friend's often drawn-out explanations. "Isn't that what we've been talking about?"

Merlin patted Draig on the knee again. "Sorry, my apologies. Yes, you're right. We can and should assume that Typhon is back in the Teg world, hiding away somewhere, biding his time until he's ready to make his move."

"Then what do you mean he can't come back fully into the Teg world?" Draig worked hard to keep his rising frustration out of his voice, beginning to wonder whether visiting with Merlin was a waste of time when he still had one more visit to make before he could make a play for the monster that sought the Teg throne.

"Typhon couldn't escape again from Tartarus on his own. He's not strong enough."

There was almost glee in Merlin's voice. Draig didn't understand why, his former mentor and instructor reminding him as to why he often left their lessons together in a bad mood. Still, he fought hard to stay patient.

"How could Typhon not be strong enough?"

"When Zeus first locked him away, fearing what would happen if Typhon broke free and came for him again, he enlisted the help of his brother Hades. The two of them working together – I know, strange to even think that ..."

"Merlin," Draig said sharply, not interested in the sidebar.

"Right, sorry." Merlin's expression was more of amusement than contrition. "Hades tied Typhon's spirit to Tartarus. Typhon can escape as he's proven, but he can't stay free for long before he begins to lose his strength. Until he finds some way to untie his spirit from Tartarus, he must return to rebuild his strength or risk defeat as his potency fades."

Draig smiled then. He had assumed that Merlin kept an important part of the story to himself, wanting to reveal it in his own time. "You and my father took him on when Typhon began to weaken."

"Of course we did," Merlin admitted. "We wouldn't have stood a chance otherwise."

That revelation got Draig thinking. Why did Jinx propose a partnership with her father? Typhon could stand against the Twelve Olympians and barely break a sweat. Yet the monster who put more than doubt in the minds of arguably what for a time had been the strongest of all the pantheons wanted to do a deal with him?

It didn't make sense.

Unless ...

"Based on what you've told me, I might actually have a chance," Draig murmured so quietly that Merlin needed to strain to hear him.

"You exercise a power against which few of the Teg can stand against." Merlin reached out and gripped Axel's arm, wanting to make sure that his former pupil was listening. "Even so, you must remember that Typhon is one of the Ancients. He exercises the Power of the Ancients on a scope that most Teg can't comprehend."

"Are you saying I can't stand against him?" Draig asked.

"I'm saying that you can stand against Typhon. You're the Dragon. It takes a great deal to kill a dragon." Merlin pulled away from Draig and shrugged. "Then again, if anyone can kill a dragon, it's Typhon."

Draig snorted and then chuckled softly. Leave it to Merlin to ensure he stayed grounded even while the Sorcerer was praising him. "This has been a slightly tedious though useful conversation, Merlin. Thank you."

Merlin smiled and gave Draig a wink. "I aim to please."

9

BRIGHT LIGHTS

"This is where you chose to set up shop?"

Jinx couldn't hide her surprise as she surveyed the elegant though slightly gaudy display that greeted her eyes. A lot of shiny, expensive objects with three white leather couches positioned around a monstrous television.

She did hide her disdain, her tastes quite different from his. She didn't want to anger her father. It didn't take much to set him off, though she could understand why after the fate forced upon him.

"After spending so much time in Tartarus, I need to be somewhere different in every respect. Here, it's all an illusion, and I can do with some of that after the reality of the last however many centuries." Typhon spoke in a deep, gravelly voice that matched his large frame. More than seven feet in height, he towered over his daughter. "I also need to have a little fun, and I can do that here without drawing too much attention."

"You mean before the real fun begins."

"I do."

Typhon had taken up residence in a suite atop the Bellagio.

The bright and always shining lights of Las Vegas streaked the floor-to-ceiling windows.

"And this is your attempt at staying under the radar?" Jinx nodded toward her father, giving him a raised eyebrow. He wore white pants and loafers, a pink shirt, and a neon blue blazer.

"This isn't appropriate?" Typhon rumbled. He didn't take offense. He had been away for quite a long time.

"No. Not unless you want to look like you're playing the role of Don Johnson in a remake of the *Miami Vice* TV show from the 1980s."

"And this is a bad thing?" Typhon didn't understand the reference.

Jinx pursed her lips. She chose to respond diplomatically. Her father's temper tended to be short and could be as explosive as Mount Vesuvius with just as lethal consequences. "Maybe something a little less eye-catching. It's hard to fear a Teg dressed like you are right now."

Typhon didn't reply, considering his daughter's comment. Harnessing the Power of the Ancients, he changed his clothes in an instant. His ghostly white hair was still slicked back, but now he looked like an older man with money to burn. Black pants. Open collared white shirt. Black leather loafers.

"Better," Jinx confirmed with an appreciative nod.

"Glad to hear it. I wouldn't want to disappoint my daughter." He turned back toward the window, enjoying the play of the lights and the fountain that had just come to life far below. Even more the sense of licentiousness that permeated the city. His kind of place. A place where there were few rules. A place where chaos could reign and he could be at the very center of it all. "Just as I know my daughter doesn't want to disappoint me."

Jinx didn't miss the menace in her father's words. The threat contained there.

She refused to show any fear, however. Her father would

view that as a sign of weakness, and her father abhorred weakness.

"Of course I don't, father," Jinx replied with a confidence that was more feigned than real.

"Good." He turned back toward her, his eyes a deep black that swirled like a whirlpool, pulling her in and refusing to let go. "Now tell me of your encounter with the Dragon."

She did. Quickly and concisely. She had learned from a young age the penalty for taking more of his time than he believed was required.

Once she was done with her report, Typhon turned back toward the glass, watching the end of the fountain show as he considered this dilemma that also was wrapped in opportunity.

"Do you believe the Dragon will recognize the value of the partnership I offer him?"

Jinx didn't hesitate with her response. Her father preferred precision and certainty in all things. "No, he won't."

"Despite knowing that I could squash him like a bug? That I will if he remains recalcitrant?"

"I believe that he assumes you will squash him like a bug regardless of whatever decision he makes. He likely believes that partnering with you now only would delay the inevitable."

Typhon chuckled softly at that, a deep resonance that echoed throughout the suite that encompassed three floors. There had been little to laugh about in Tartarus. "Finally a worthy adversary." He smiled, the expression visible to Jinx in his reflection off the glass and quite unsettling. "He's right, of course. I will. All I offered him was a bit more time. Little more than that. And he was perceptive enough to understand that yet still resist."

"You seem almost impressed by him," Jinx hinted, not understanding her father's good humor.

"Aren't you?"

"Because he has chosen to stand up to you?" Jinx scoffed. "That suggests arrogance mixed with a large dose of stupidity."

Typhon didn't reply right away, although his expression, still visible to Jinx in the reflection off the glass, changed. Hardened. His eyes swirled even faster.

He was no longer amused. Far from it. Rather, he was disappointed and a hair trigger away from anger.

"Of all my brood I held out the greatest hope for you, Jinx. Yet it seems that my hope was misplaced. You have not learned all that you should have."

"Father, that's not fair. I was simply saying that ..."

Typhon turned in the blink of an eye, his unyielding gaze bottling up the words in his daughter's throat. "What you say is irrelevant, Jinx. All that matters is what you do. For me."

"I do whatever you require of me," Jinx protested. She tried to control the tremor of unease that ran through her. She had seen her father in this mood many times before. It never ended well for the Teg interacting with him.

"Best that you do, and best that you not think more than is necessary. Best that you obey. Do you understand?"

Others might have wilted under Typhon's harsh gaze. Jinx refused. She understood that if she did she might provoke him into a fit of rage. He demanded and expected strength at all times.

"Of course, father."

Typhon glared at his daughter, his rage building. His desire to lash out became almost unbearable.

In a flash, that drive vanished. As if it had never been there. He nodded. "It would be best if you remembered that the Dragon is neither arrogant nor stupid."

"I understand, father, it's just that ..." Jinx stopped herself, then nodded in apology. "I'm sorry, father. I overstepped. It won't happen again."

Typhon hadn't said anything. He had simply stared at his

daughter. Not realizing that the shift had begun until he caught the look of fear in Jinx's eyes.

Jinx hadn't missed it, however. A mist of black seeping out from his eyes and forming around him as her father's massive frame began to lengthen and broaden, the true Ancient appearing.

Typhon growled. He had been imprisoned for so long that the desire to give in to the urge surging through him was almost too much to hold back.

In Tartarus, he was a king. Even so, a king with limited power. There in the depths far below the underworld, he could sense only a trickle of the potency granted to him as an Ancient.

But here, finally back in the Natural World where he truly belonged, he could feel all that the Power of the Ancients offered to him. All that it promised.

He was confident in all that he could do with that power.

And he would.

Just not now.

Just not yet.

Realizing what he had been about to do, Typhon took several deep breaths while he closed his eyes. Regaining control over himself and the energy that begged to be released.

"As I said, daughter, the Dragon is neither arrogant nor stupid. He is smart. He seeks to provoke me."

"Provoke you? But how could that be smart if ..."

"Do not make the same mistake twice, daughter. You have overstepped once. I will not allow it again."

Jinx gulped. Her father had halted the shift, returning to the form he had selected for the Natural World. Nevertheless, the sense of power that radiated from him was so intense that it threatened to take her breath away. It was like watching a wavy heat rising up off the highway, though in this case it came from the monster that even the Greek Gods feared.

Not trusting herself to say anything, she simply nodded.

Typhon nodded as well, offering his daughter a small smile. Though not one of reconciliation. Rather menace.

He believed that fear was the most powerful of all the emotions. Therefore, it was always his first choice for ensuring that those who served him did as he demanded of them.

"The Dragon seeks to provoke me because he seeks to distract me. I will not allow it."

"Do you want me to eliminate the Dragon for you?" Jinx asked, hoping to get back into her father's good graces by making up for her lack of success in Kraken Cove. Having little doubt that if she didn't, one of her brothers or sisters might be given the chance to take her place.

Typhon considered his daughter's question for several seconds. "You will be given that opportunity. You will have to wait a little while longer, however."

"You have another task for me?" Her eyes brightened with delight. She had not fallen too far in the eyes of her father. Not yet.

"I do. The Dragon is cutting at the edges right now. We will allow him to do that. I want you to go right to the heart of the matter between us."

Just as was his way, Typhon provided Jinx with a succinct set of instructions that brooked no questions or argument.

"Once I'm done with this, I can have a little fun with the Dragon?"

"Yes, I will allow it. But not too much fun. Because if anyone is going to feast on the Dragon, it will be me."

10

DINNER DATE

"No plans with Professor Dennison tonight?" Chandra asked.

Kassandra didn't reply right away, frowning and pursing her lips. This wasn't a topic she wanted to discuss. She just wanted to enjoy a quiet dinner at her favorite restaurant in Williamsburg.

She had invited her friends to the Blue Talon Bistro rather than the professor she had been seeing for a reason.

"Wait, don't tell me?" Riley gave Kassandra a playful grin. There was a sparkle in her eye that suggested she was enjoying the conversation that seemed more interrogation a little too much. "You did what you usually do."

"What do I usually do?" Kassandra asked, trying to profess a confusion and innocence that fell flat.

"After a few dates you start looking for faults," Riley explained with a knowing grin. "And you find them, whether real or imagined. It's one of your unique talents."

"I do not do that," Kassandra protested. Even she recognized that it was a half-hearted attempt to defend herself.

"You do. Every time," Chandra confirmed. She leaned

forward, putting her elbows on the table. "Tell us. We have to know. What was the problem this time?"

"It wasn't a problem …"

"Come on, Kassandra," Riley prodded. "We know you better than you know yourself. In matters of the heart, you follow a very clear pattern."

Kassandra was about to protest again. She stopped herself. She didn't want to waste her breath.

"Fine, I'll tell you." She leaned forward and put her right elbow on the table, cupping her chin in her hand. Enjoying the cool breeze that played across the outdoor patio with her left hand she moved a few strands of her long, silky black hair behind her ear.

"Finally we get to the reason we're here," Riley said with a great deal of pleasure. "Spill."

"There was nothing wrong with Denny," Kassandra began.

"There didn't seem to be," Chandra confirmed with a suggestive nod and a predatory smile. "A fine specimen in my opinion. And how many young professors that good looking are teaching in the same department as you are? It seemed like a match made in heaven."

"That was the problem right there," Kassandra explained.

"What, that he was good looking?"

Kassandra snorted, giving Riley a sharp look. "No, that's never bothered me before."

"That he's a rising star in his field?" Chandra asked. "I hear that he's negotiating a contract for his first book."

"No, it wasn't that," Kassandra sighed. She leaned back into her chair, feeling deflated. Her friends were right. She had a unique ability to identify what she perceived as faults in the men she chose to date. Always looking for the smallest of reasons not to become too involved even when a few seemed like they could be a good fit.

Chandra's eyes flashed as she gave Kassandra a sly look.

"Were there problems of a more intimate type? In the bedroom maybe?"

Riley almost choked on the water she had been drinking. "Was he not very good in bed? That would be so disappointing."

"No," Kassandra replied quickly, flustered, not expecting her friends to get to this topic so swiftly, although she should have assumed that they would. "Or rather I don't know."

"What do you mean you don't know?" Riley demanded. "When it comes to sex, you either know what you're doing or you don't."

"What I'm saying is that I don't know because our relationship never progressed that far."

"Your relationship never progressed that far?" Chandra demanded with a questioning eye. "You're serious? You were dating him for what? Two weeks? Three?"

Kassandra laughed then, some of the stress of her breaking up with Denny finally leaving her. "You might be willing to jump into the sack with a guy on the first date. I'm not."

"Well I never," Chandra's pretense at offense shifted to amusement, "like to wait. That's just the way it is. If a guy can't demonstrate much prowess in bed, I don't want to waste my time on him. So why put in the effort until I've made that critical initial discovery."

"I'm just saying that we have a different perspective on matters of the heart."

"This isn't a matter of the heart, Kassandra," Chandra corrected. "This is a matter of ..."

Before Chandra continued farther down the road that Kassandra had no desire to travel, she cut off her friend. "I liked Denny. I did. Most of the time. It's just that ..."

"Something about him bothered you," Riley prompted, wanting the dirt.

Kassandra nodded a grateful thanks to Riley. "Yes." She

sighed. "He's smart. He's good looking. Accomplished. And he's probably good in bed, though I never found out."

"But ..." Chandra pushed.

"But he is also incredibly arrogant."

"There we go," Chandra sighed, leaning back into her chair.

Riley mimed the striking of a bell. "The death knell."

Kassandra laughed softly. "I'm sorry. I'm sorry. It's just one of my peccadilloes. I can't get past a guy who is arrogant. It pinches a nerve." Nor could she get past a man who liked to talk down to her as if he knew more about their same areas of study than she did.

After just a few discussions over coffee, she had learned that though Denny seemed like a nice guy, he was so full of himself and what he thought he knew that she would never get past it because he listened only to himself and to little of what she had to say.

"Did he challenge your theory regarding the Morrigan and her role in Irish folklore?" Chandra asked. She knew that this was a hot button issue with Kassandra, much of her dissertation focused on the Irish Goddess of War and Battle.

Kassandra bit her tongue for a moment before shrugging. "He spent ten minutes telling me everything I supposedly didn't know about the Morrigan. Then he spent another ten minutes telling me why my thoughts on the Morrigan were incorrect."

"You gave him twenty minutes?" Riley asked, impressed. Usually Kassandra demonstrated little patience for anyone wasting her time.

"We have to work together in the same department, so I needed to let him down easy."

"Fair enough," Chandra said. "As my mother likes to say, there are always more fish in the sea." She nodded toward Prince George Street and where a small crowd was waiting for tables. "Maybe that one, in fact. He can't seem to keep his eyes off you."

Riley looked where Chandra nodded, eyes widening in delight. "A bit older, maybe, though it's hard to tell with the shadows. Still, dark hair. Intriguing eyes. Obviously fit. Even a sense of danger radiates off him. I like that. A little weird with him carrying a walking stick, but I can get past that."

"Come on," Kassandra huffed. "I'm not in the mood for this."

Wait. Walking stick. Kassandra hadn't really been listening until she heard that.

"In the mood or not," Riley said, "he's coming over."

Kassandra looked over her shoulder, then sighed. She shook her head, not knowing whether to be pleased or resigned.

"What's the matter?" Chandra asked. "He can't be any worse than Denny."

"He's not."

"Then what's the problem?"

"Because the man coming over here is my father."

"Hi, Kassie," Draig said with a warm smile, offering nods of greeting to Chandra and Riley, both of whom seemed quite taken with their new dinner guest. "I thought I might find you here. Do you want to introduce me to these two lovely ladies?"

"YOUR FRIENDS DIDN'T HAVE to leave," Draig protested. He took the last bite of his roasted cod. He hadn't realized how hungry he was until he sat down.

"They did need to leave," Kassandra replied. She had picked at her food to start, spending most of her time trying to figure out why her father stopped by. Her own hunger finally got the better of her when her friends made their excuses.

"There are certain parts of my life that I need to keep distinct from others."

He had visited just a week before. And only because she had invited him. That's the way it was supposed to be. They had agreed that he wouldn't appear in Williamsburg unannounced.

But here he was without a word of warning.

She didn't know whether she should be aggravated that he had ignored the rule she had put in place or pleased.

When she was younger, Kassandra hadn't wanted to have anything to do with her father. It was only after she began her doctoral program that she opened the door just a little bit for him. Not all the way, but enough so that she could get a better sense of who he was rather than having to rely on what her mother or other Teg had to say.

"You haven't told me why you're here."

"You haven't asked," Draig replied as he leaned back, clearly satisfied with his meal.

"Really? This is how we're going to do this?"

"Do what?"

"This is the first time you showed up without me inviting you." Her eyes flashed. When the light struck them in a certain way, they resembled Draig's reddish-orange orbs.

"I know. I'm sorry." Draig offered his daughter a contrite smile, or at least as contrite as he could make it. There was a steeliness to him that he just couldn't get past. "It's just that I enjoyed our last visit together and I was coming through town. I hoped you might be free for dinner. And I called but it went to voicemail."

"You enjoyed our last visit together?" she asked, giving her father a raised eyebrow. He did leave her a message. That was true. She was certain, however, that there was more to his visit than just his passing through.

"I did. I enjoyed you showing me the campus and then dinner at the Fat Canary. It was just as good as dinner here."

Kassandra nodded to herself as she studied her father. She could tell that he wasn't being entirely truthful with her. But he would be. She would dig it out of him. "Dinner was good last week. I'll give you that. And how was the after-dinner entertainment?"

"After-dinner entertainment?" Draig adopted his best expression of innocence, even though from the suspect look his daughter was giving him he assumed that she saw right through him. He had never been good at innocent.

"You can't try to cover it up," she said with a pleased smirk. "I was tracking you and then Mom filled me in."

"Of course she did," Draig grumbled. He leaned forward, catching his daughter's eyes. "That wasn't my fault. Just bad luck really."

"It's never your fault." Kassandra crossed her arms. "And you don't believe in bad luck."

Draig had an immediate reply not only to Kassandra's response but also to the sharpness of her tone. He restrained himself, however.

His daughter had him there. She was right.

He didn't believe in bad luck or any kind of luck. Not after spending so much time with the Fates and learning how the universe really worked.

Luck had nothing to do with it. It was all about choice.

And, admittedly, she had a right to be angry with him. He understood as well that on occasion that anger was going to spill out. He needed to handle this delicately if he could. Not one of his strengths, unfortunately.

"I was simply trying to say that I had no idea that a fist of Daemons would decide to take a shot at me in Colonial Williamsburg."

"Why should I believe you?" Kassandra demanded.

Draig's eyes sparked and locked onto hers. His expression hardened. He didn't like being challenged. He spoke in a quiet, reasonable tone, taking a deep breath before doing so, an acknowledgment that Kassandra had every right to question him. "Because I'm telling you the truth."

Kassandra examined her father for quite a while before she nodded and released him from her own unyielding gaze. "You had to destroy them all?"

Draig smiled softly. The fact that five Daemons had come looking for him, and that they were shadowing her for a time as well when he was with her, didn't seem to bother her in the least. Good for her.

"I didn't have a choice."

"You always have a choice," Kassandra countered with a raised eyebrow.

"No, you don't." Draig's tone was strong, but not strong enough to offend his daughter. He actually was quite pleased that she was testing him. Even more so that she remembered some of what they had talked about regarding luck, fate, and choice. "I talked with them first and tried to defuse the situation. I couldn't. As soon as the first Daemon attacked, their intentions were clear. I did what I needed to do."

"Just as you always do."

Draig looked at his daughter for a time with a very sharp eye. She was putting on a brave face, but he could see the hurt in the back of her fiery orbs. "Meaning?"

"You do what you need to do, unless you don't see the need to do so."

Draig let Kassandra's words sit there between them. For a time at a loss.

He sighed, clearly disappointed in himself and not knowing how to explain to her what he was feeling. "You have every right to be angry with me. I don't blame you for that in the least."

Then he leaned forward on the table, clasping his fingers together in front of him. Struggling because the topic of the conversation had shifted. "I did see the need to do so, Kassie. But I couldn't do what I wanted. I couldn't do what you wanted me to do. I know you don't believe me, but it's the truth."

"Because you were a hunted Teg," Kassandra prompted. "Yes, you told me that before."

"And I'll keep telling you that because it's the truth. I won't ever lie to you. When you were born I didn't visit as much as I should have because of what was required of me. I didn't want that world to touch yours. As you were getting older ..."

"Enough," Kassandra said, lifting a hand and stopping her father from continuing with his explanation. Although she didn't do it in a nasty way. She seemed more tired than anything else, not wanting to delve too deeply on that topic. At least not right then. "Why did you decide to visit again so soon?"

"Like I said, I was coming this way and I thought that I would check in."

"Sure you were."

His daughter's expression and tone told him that she didn't believe him. Draig didn't think she would. Still, he pressed on. Not yet ready to get to the real reason he was there.

"How's your doctorate going? Do you have a date yet?"

Kassandra decided to play along for the moment. The last time her father had been there, she had told him that she was almost done with her dissertation. "I'll be defending in April."

"Great news," Draig replied. "Am I allowed to sit in?"

"You most certainly are not," Kassandra replied sharply, although she said it with a smile on her face. "Despite the fact that you have lived more history and mythology than the three professors on my committee. I don't need the additional pressure."

"It was worth a shot," he replied, giving her a warm smile. "I have no doubt you'll do great."

"Now let's get past the small talk," Kassandra said, refusing to allow her father to sidetrack her any longer. "What are you really doing here?"

Draig's smile broadened. They were alike in many ways. They both preferred to be direct, Draig only taking a roundabout route to the topic he was about to raise because he was still trying to figure out how best to interact with his daughter.

"I need your help."

"My help?"

Draig nodded. "Your work passed the test."

"My work?" It took Kassandra a moment to figure out what he was talking about. Her eyes widened in delight when she did.

Her father had asked her to craft an exact replica of *The Book of Whispers*, the most powerful artifact in the Teg world. Well, not an exact replica. That was impossible. Rather a forgery that would pass more than just a cursory inspection, the trick being ensuring that the item radiated the necessary magical signature that would suggest it was the real thing.

"You're serious?" She couldn't keep the excitement from her voice.

Draig nodded. "You should be proud of yourself. I don't know another Teg who could have done what you did."

Kassandra was proud of herself because she heard the truth in her father's words. "And you came here to tell me that?"

Draig didn't miss the skepticism lacing her voice. "For that and another reason. I need you to give me a link so that I can follow the signature to your creation."

Kassandra nodded as she considered her father's request. The link functioned much like a magical AirTag, but it was delicate work. If not done correctly, whoever had the item could discover that they were being tracked then break the connection. And clearly her father didn't want that to happen.

"Peggy Rose can't do it for you? Or Cerridwen? Brigid?"

Draig shook his head. "They could, but not with the skill that you can. Besides, it's best if the creator of the item does it. Less chance of the link being discovered."

Kassandra was both surprised and pleased, her smile revealing both emotions. Her father's acknowledgment made her feel needed in a way that nothing else ever had before, and she relished the feeling.

More important, it was an acknowledgment of her skill in the Grym, and that's what thrilled her the most.

"Why?"

"I just told you," her father replied. "Because you can do this a lot better than anyone else can."

"Yes, I understand that. I want to know why." She leaned forward so that there was no more than a foot between them. "Why did you want me to create a forgery of *The Book of Whispers*?"

Draig balked at telling her. "It's best that you don't know."

"Why? Because you're worried about me?"

"Yes, actually I am. If I mess up, I don't want this to blow back on you. The less you know, the better."

Kassandra drew back just a little. She hadn't expected such an honest response from her father. Still, he needed her assistance, so she was going to make use of that advantage. "Tell me, or I don't do it."

Draig gave his daughter a hard look. Not because he wanted to but rather because she expected him to. Secretly, he was quite pleased that she refused to back down.

He nodded and began. "The Daemons who came for me last week wanted *The Book of Whispers*."

"I gathered as much."

"I assumed that you did."

"So the Daemon King wants the artifact. That's not all that surprising considering the power that whoever can make use of the artifact can call upon."

"Not just the Daemon King."

Draig didn't say anything else besides that. Waiting. Watching as his daughter worked through the puzzle on her own. It didn't take her long.

"Grandfather as well." His desire to obtain *The Book of Whispers* was more than obvious if the Daemon King wanted it. The two were sworn enemies. Neither could allow the other to obtain the artifact, because either could control the other with *The Book of Whispers.*

Draig nodded, then motioned for her to keep going.

For a moment, Kassandra was surprised, believing that she had solved the puzzle. But she realized that she couldn't have, because if her grandfather wanted something, then so did ...

"Morgase as well." She smiled, pleased with her success. But her father was still giving her that expectant look of his, one eyebrow arched. "Not just grandfather and Morgase?"

Draig shook his head.

Then she understood. That's why he was worried.

Not so much about the Daemon King. She could deal with his spawn if necessary.

Nor with her grandfather or Morgase. They both knew what would happen if either made a play for her. They would avoid that risk like they would avoid the plague.

So another party. But who?

Kassandra considered the dilemma for several minutes, coming at it from a variety of different angles. The answer felt like it was right there in front of her. Yet always dancing around the edges of her reasoning and refusing to become clear.

She could think of only one possibility, though it seemed a bit farfetched. Her grandfather and Morgase were the two most powerful Teg next to Merlin, and her father of course. That would mean the only other player had to be ...

"An Ancient," Kassandra murmured quietly.

Draig smiled proudly, then nodded.

She didn't feel any better about her success, however. She understood what an Ancient wanting *The Book of Whispers* meant. Even more, the terrible threat presented by that truth.

Because there was no good way to challenge an Ancient. They were too strong. Too powerful. Too vengeful. Too intractable.

"Which one?" Kassandra asked, almost too afraid to ask.

"Typhon."

Draig almost whispered the name to her. And then he did something that he had never done before.

He told Kassandra all that had happened after his fight against the Daemons. How Peggy Rose, Cerridwen, Seamus, and a cast of new characters had become involved. And, of course, the Witch who seemed to have caught her father's eye and was the cause of all this.

Next her father did something that she never believed that he would ever do for her or anyone else. He explained what he had in mind. The strategy he had put in place. He even asked her a few questions, seeking her input.

And she had given it. Willingly. Loving the experience of speaking with her father in this way.

She viewed the challenge that her father had taken on as another of the puzzles that she so enjoyed completing. Jigsaw puzzles were a favorite of hers when she was younger, and she still did them from time to time now that she was older because they helped to calm her brain that never seemed to want to turn off.

Through it all, as she and her father discussed his plan for going after Typhon, a strain of thought teased her. Confused her more than anything else.

For most of her life she had been angry with her father. In large part because he hadn't been there when she needed him to be there, her mother's excuses for him falling on deaf ears.

But also because while growing up among the Tylwyth Teg she heard stories of who her father really was. She learned about what he did for her grandfather. What was demanded of him. How the Teg perceived him as a result.

That had hurt her just as much, not believing that it was fair that so many of the Teg didn't want to interact with her or looked at her in fear because of her father.

The man sitting across from her had constrained her world in a way that no one else could have.

Yet, sitting across from him now, having a real discussion about matters critical to all of the Teg, she was having a very hard time painting a real picture as to who her father really was.

The stories about her father didn't mesh with reality. She knew what her father had done to the Teg for his own father. She knew what he had done for the Teg after faking his own death.

And now he was taking the latter to an entirely new level. He was talking about what he planned to do to protect the Teg from the most vengeful of all the Ancients. A monster who exercised a power that none of the Teg had a ghost of a chance standing against.

But he was going to do just that.

He was going to risk his life for the Teg even though many of the Teg would have preferred that he stay dead.

More unsettling, it didn't seem to faze him.

Although she enjoyed engaging with her father in such an open dialogue, she was having a very hard time making sense of it all.

"You all right, Kassandra? I'm not throwing too much at you?"

Kassandra didn't reply right away. She frowned instead, eyebrows furrowing. "No, I'm just trying to understand."

"How so?"

"You're the Dragon."

"I am."

"You're the guy grandfather sent to manage the really hard cases among the Teg."

"That's how your mother put it?"

"She did."

Draig nodded. He was glad that her mother told it to her straight. "I was."

"Most of the Tylwyth Teg are scared to death of you."

"That seems to be the case, yes."

"And those who aren't are either sociopaths or fools."

"A fairly good assumption, yes."

"Or they want to make a name for themselves by challenging you."

"Another good assumption, though it never works out well for them." Draig didn't say that with pride. Simply as a fact.

"Then why are you doing this?"

"What do you mean?"

"Most of the Teg either hate you, want you dead ... actually, most of the Teg probably hate you and want you dead with the same level of intensity."

"No argument there," Draig confirmed with a sad smile.

"Then if that's the case, why would you put yourself at risk for them?"

Draig looked down for a moment, needing to gather his thoughts. Needing to ensure that his daughter understood. "Because someone has to."

Kassandra snorted, pushing back from the table and shaking her head in disbelief. "You're the hero of the story now?"

"Far from it," Draig replied.

"Well, it seems to me ..."

Draig lifted his hand, asking for a few seconds from his daughter. She granted them.

"After all that I've done, I'm far from being a hero. I'm doing this because someone needs to stand up to Typhon."

"Why?"

"I don't like bullies."

Kassandra snorted, not missing the hypocrisy. "You were a bully. One of the worst."

"I was," Draig admitted, refusing to run from the truth no matter how much it pained him. "I have a lot to atone for."

Kassie thought about that, not yet sure what to make of either her father's guilt or contrition. "And grandfather won't deal with Typhon?"

Draig shook his head. "No. He's more concerned about your aunt and the Daemon King. And even if he wanted to, he wouldn't stand much of a chance."

"Why not? I thought he beat Typhon once already."

"So did I."

"What do you mean by that?"

"Merlin told me what really happened."

Kassandra's gaze sharpened, beginning to understand. She decided to challenge him. "You feel the need to do one better than he did? Is that it?"

Draig bit back the response that he knew if he said aloud would ruin whatever progress he had made with his daughter during the last few years. "No, I'm trying to get away from your grandfather's shadow, but it seems that every time I try it still falls upon me."

"Then what is it? Why do you feel the need to make a play for one of the strongest of the Ancients?"

Seeing the look Kassandra gave him with her question, finally he understood what was driving her. Concern. For him. He hadn't expected that.

"I thought I was serving the Teg when I was serving your grandfather," Draig explained in a very soft voice that forced Kassandra to lean in so that she could hear him. "I realized that more often than not, I wasn't serving the Teg. I was serving your grandfather. That didn't sit well with me. Once I realized that – and I admit I should have reached that conclusion sooner than I did -- I've tried to help the Teg whenever I can. In my own way. That's the primary reason I turned Kraken Cove into a safe haven."

"You're trying to make amends just as you said," Kassie suggested.

"I can't make amends," Draig stated bluntly. "Not after what I've done. Not after all the Teg I've hurt in so many different ways because I didn't have the courage to ask the right questions. For too long I did what I was ordered to do. I didn't ask why. Now, I'm just trying to do what I should have done when I first became a Knight of the Round. I'm trying to do what's right."

"Even though it could cost you your life?"

Draig understood how asking that question hurt his daughter. She was worried about him. There was a time when he thought that might not ever be possible.

He nodded. "Even that." He reached over the table and grasped her hands with his. She didn't pull back as he feared she might. "I believe that sometimes there's a difference between doing what's right and doing what you must. With respect to Typhon, doing what I must and doing what's right are one and the same."

Kassandra stared into her father's fiery eyes. Asking her to trust him. Identifying as well his resolve. He was going to do this whether she helped him or not. Because that's who he was. She couldn't fault him for that. "If I do this for you, Dad, you'll be careful?"

"I will."

"Good, because I expect you back here for dinner next week."

Draig smiled, both pleased and surprised. Kassie had never called him dad before. He nodded. "I'll see you then."

"It had to be here?"

Draig stepped out of the shadows, a slightly bemused expression on his face rather than the usual grimness. After dinner he walked Kassie back to her apartment. They had another long talk along the way. He left feeling as if the matters between them were moving in the right direction, and he knew that he couldn't ask for more than that. Because there still was a great deal they needed to work through.

"This is the best place," Aleck explained, shrugging his shoulders as if to say the selected location for their meeting was obvious. "The Peyton Randolph House is the most haunted spot in all of Colonial Williamsburg. The tour guides refuse to go near it at night."

"And I can see that doesn't bother you."

"Why would it?" Aleck shrugged again.

Draig realized that was a good question as he studied the young man standing before him, seeing him just as clearly in the darkness -- there being very few streetlights in Colonial Williamsburg -- as if the sun were shining down brightly. Short dark hair that curled at the edge. Glasses with wider rectangular lenses than were currently stylish. A trimmed beard with a premature streak of white down his chin.

Even though he was a decade or more older, he looked like many of the other grad students walking around the William and Mary campus. Except for the fact that there was an incisiveness and curiosity to his strong gaze that was lacking in most every other Teg. Likely because he had seen things and done things that most every other Teg hadn't done and had no desire to do.

"How's business, Aleck?"

The young man smiled, although it clearly was a tired smile. "Good. More than I can handle actually."

Draig expected no less. Few could provide the service that Aleck did. In fact, he couldn't think of anyone else among the Teg who could at that moment, the other two passing to the other side within the last few years.

A not entirely unexpected result, as Aleck and his former colleagues had a unique skill that made their line of work exceedingly dangerous. The slightest mistake often proved fatal ... or worse.

Draig had reached out to Aleck because he was a hunter of sorts. He found items of value to the Teg that they couldn't find or acquire on their own. Teg as well, though those requests were fewer.

At least that's what most of the Teg knew about the unassuming young man who didn't demonstrate the least bit of concern meeting the Dragon on a dark street with not a soul to be seen well past midnight in front of a haunted house.

Draig knew better. Aleck was very good at what he did because he was one of the few – now likely the only -- Teg with the ability to communicate with spirits. But that wasn't the only work that he did for the Teg. Or rather for Draig. Because Aleck had other unique skills that only a handful of the Teg were aware of.

Aleck didn't exactly try to hide those skills. But he didn't advertise them either.

Which Draig believed was a good move on his part. There were some among the Teg who no doubt would look to make use of Aleck's unique abilities for their own purposes and much to his own detriment.

Just another reason why Draig liked to keep an eye on

Aleck. Not just because Aleck seemed to have an eye for his daughter ... and his daughter for him, though she had yet to acknowledge that fact.

"Anything you've been hearing that I need to know about?"

"I hear a lot, Draig. And you have me listening for a lot. You need to be more specific."

Aleck spoke the truth. In fact, that's why he couldn't keep up with the demand for his services. He gained a huge amount of knowledge from the spirits of the dead because many of them preferred to drift through the Natural World. They didn't want to stay in the Underworld, still having a connection to the living that they didn't want severed. A connection that would be cut the longer they spent in the Underworld. And once cut, never to be mended, leaving them with no way to return.

Those recalcitrant and often wandering spirits formed their own ghostly Internet. And of the living Teg, at that moment it seemed that only Aleck Geist could tap into it.

The spirits saw everything. They heard everything. And if they didn't, usually they could find another spirit who did.

However, there always was a price attached to the information that Aleck sought. Often it involved sharing a message from the spirit with someone in the Natural World. It also could involve completing a task that the spirit had failed to accomplish before going to the other side.

Sometimes the price was higher. Riskier.

Aleck had learned early upon interacting with the spirits that he needed to be careful about what he traded in. Some of the deals he made put his own life at risk, and he had no desire to become a spirit anytime soon. He understood as well that if he failed to meet the terms of an agreement made with a spirit that there were consequences that could be worse than death.

Therefore, he only took jobs he believed that he could accomplish. And he never failed to complete a deal as promised.

Draig valued that. That's why he sought out Aleck.

His lips almost curled into a smile. He enjoyed speaking with Aleck because he was one of the few Teg who treated him like he would anyone else. The fact that he was the Dragon didn't resonate with Aleck.

To Aleck, Draig was just another customer. Albeit a very powerful one.

"Any word on Typhon or his children?"

Aleck tended to reveal very little. Spirits, in addition to dissecting words with the skill of a surgeon, picked up on the slightest of movements, even nothing more than a fleeting facial tic or a raised eyebrow, there than not. That made negotiating with them all the more difficult.

But mention of the Ancient's name gained Draig a spark in the back of Aleck's eyes that Draig couldn't miss but he couldn't interpret.

"You certainly do like to live dangerously."

"One of my failings," Draig replied with a dry humor.

"I'd hate to think that you viewed it as a strength."

Draig snorted. Amused. Allowing Aleck a leeway that he rarely gave to any other Teg, except perhaps for Seamus and a few of his other friends in Kraken Cove. "Funny at this late hour?"

"Funny all the time," Aleck said with a grin.

"Once a smart ass ..."

"Always a smartass," Aleck completed for Draig. "Yes, I know. We've had this conversation before."

"I still don't know why I put up with you."

"Because I can give you the assistance you require that no one else can," Aleck said with complete confidence. He enjoyed the give and take with Draig, but he understood that he was there for a reason. Moreover, Draig wasn't known for his patience. So Aleck didn't want to keep him any longer than necessary. "And I have heard rumblings in the Spirit World."

"About Typhon?"

"Not specifically, no."

"Then why do you have that look on your face?"

Aleck smiled. Talking with Draig was like speaking with a spirit. He didn't miss a thing. "Because I was speaking with a spirit on another matter right before this meeting and something that he said stuck in my mind."

"How so?"

"A breakout."

Draig nodded. That kind of reference linked to Draig's interest could mean only one thing. "Typhon is free from Tartarus." It was as he suspected and feared.

Aleck shrugged. "I can't say for certain. You know how it is with spirits. Information goes from one to the next and it can get garbled just as if you were playing telephone with string and a soup can."

"But you can say it with enough confidence to raise the issue with me."

Aleck nodded this time. "This spirit is well connected. It was one of his unique abilities while he was alive. Ferreting out useful information."

"I'm almost afraid to ask."

"Cardinal Richelieu."

Draig nodded. He had to agree with Aleck's assessment. A French statesman known as the Red Eminence – he was a cardinal in the Catholic Church after all, his goal while he was alive to make France the most powerful nation in all of Europe. To do that, he employed a network of spies, acquiring information that he used against his rivals and enemies all to great effect.

Draig couldn't say that he was surprised that the Cardinal continued to employ the same skills in the Spirit World.

"A source we can trust then."

"I certainly would," Aleck agreed.

"What did Cardinal Richelieu have to say?"

"He's still trying to get to the bottom of it all, and that's going to take time, but from what he said, and as I confirmed with a few other spirits, there was a breakout from Tartarus. As you know, that, in itself, is extraordinarily unusual. More interesting, perhaps, because an escape from Tartarus rarely occurs, you would expect a lot of chatter about it."

"Not much?"

Aleck shook his head no. "It's too quiet. Almost as if the powers that be in the Spirit World don't want word to get out. Only those spirits who are well connected are providing much information and even then they're hesitant to do so."

Draig nodded in understanding. "Tartarus is supposed to be impregnable. Once in, never out."

"But we know the truth," Aleck said. "Impregnable except for the most powerful of the Teg if they can get all the necessary pieces in place."

"The other Ancients aren't happy," Draig mused. "That's why they're trying to keep it quiet."

"Far from it," Aleck confirmed. "They don't like that a Teg escaped Tartarus. They're also nervous, because ..."

"They're worried about the Teg who escaped. About whether they can stop the Teg if the Teg decides to come after them."

Aleck nodded. "Correct. All that leads to only one conclusion."

"Typhon found a way out."

"We have to assume that, yes."

Draig thought about what Aleck had just provided him. He had assumed Typhon was free or would be soon enough. Gaining confirmation, at least of a sort, only strengthened his resolve. "Thanks Aleck, I appreciate your work on this. What does Cardinal Richelieu want in return?"

"Exactly what you would expect."

Draig smiled. He should have assumed as much. "Information."

"There you go. Some of the information I can provide. Some I can't. I'd need to speak with Hestia and Cerridwen. Would that be all right with you?"

"Of course. I'll let them know you'll be paying Kraken Cove a visit."

Aleck nodded his thanks. "Now what else do you need from me? I know you didn't come here just for that. I could've relayed all this to you as I normally do."

"I'm concerned."

It didn't take long for Aleck to figure it out. Typhon wasn't the only Teg in play in whatever scheme had sucked in Draig. He nodded. "About Kassie."

"I am," Draig confirmed.

"You know she's quite skilled in the Grym. She can handle herself."

"I do. But considering who I'm dealing with now, I just want to make sure that she isn't caught by surprise if a Teg decides to try to use her as a bargaining chip."

"More than understandable. Once we're done here, I'll speak with the spirits in Williamsburg. They'll be happy to keep an eye out. Many of them are colonial soldiers, so this is right up their alley. They'll appreciate the assignment."

"Thanks Aleck. If you get any more information about Typhon, Jinx, or any of his other spawn, pass it on."

"Right away."

Draig took a few steps back into the shadows when Aleck called after him.

"I'll keep an eye on Kassie as well," he promised. "Stop by once in a while just to check on her."

Draig turned then, locking eyes with Aleck to ensure that there was no mistake between them. "Not too close, Aleck. You understand?"

Aleck nodded quickly, having no desire to antagonize the Dragon. "Of course. No worries there."

11

STOPPING FOR A BLIZZARD

Melissa told herself that she wouldn't do it. That it was a bad idea. That it would only hurt her in the end.

But she couldn't help herself.

When she walked out of the Dairy Queen on Route 1 not too far north of Lewes, Delaware, she had in hand a Blizzard mixed with Reese's peanut butter cups.

A treat that she rarely had the willpower to resist. Especially when she was so stressed, and that stress was intensifying as the miles to her final destination ticked down.

Besides, she was starving. She hadn't eaten since New Jersey.

And she was exhausted. She couldn't take another drop of caffeine, but the sugar would help. Until she crashed from that as well.

That was a worry for farther down the road, however. And by then, she'd be at her hotel and she could take a nap before going to the meeting that she had been dreading for the last week. The encounter that would determine her fate and that of her mother.

For a time she feared that she wouldn't even reach this point. That she wouldn't be able to complete the deal that she hadn't wanted to make in the first place. That all the work and worry that she had put in over the last few months would be for naught.

But she was almost to the finish line. In large part thanks to Draig and his friends.

Draig!

Why did she keep thinking about the Dragon?

She had gone over her reasoning time and time again. A constant refrain as she drove south. She had made the right decision to leave him out of this. She was sure of it.

Melissa couldn't afford to involve him. Not with all that was at stake.

This was her fight. Not his.

She had spoken with Medusa the night before, and she could tell that her mother's health was worsening. She was only getting sicker. And she would die if Typhon didn't remove the curse he had placed upon her.

That fear driving her, she needed to manage the hand-off with Typhon on her own. This was her problem. She needed to be the one to solve it.

Only she could ensure that Typhon met his end of the bargain. And if the deal went sour, she didn't want anyone else, especially Draig, to be caught in the crossfire.

Melissa shook her head in amusement as all those thoughts cycled through her head once again, an almost never-ending now very annoying loop for the last few hours.

Who knew that she would start thinking of others at a time like this?

Doing so went against all that her mother had taught her. But that was a topic for another day and likely for her next session with her therapist. Assuming, of course, that she was able to make her weekly appointment.

Stuck in her head as she walked toward her Highlander, she stopped short in surprise, spoon still in her mouth.

"What do you want?" she muttered through soft ice cream, chocolate, and peanut butter.

Melissa wasn't happy. She didn't like Jinx. There was something ominous about the woman that always made Melissa more uncomfortable than she already was when the monster appeared. She only worked with Jinx because Typhon hadn't given her any other choice.

What she liked even less, however, was that this engagement wasn't a part of the agreement. She was supposed to meet with Typhon that night, and she certainly didn't need an escort to get to him.

"I would think that you would be more grateful."

"Why would that be the case? I've got some place to be and you're slowing me down."

"Be careful, Witch," Jinx warned. "If you insult me, you insult my father."

Melissa chuckled at that, licking the last of her Blizzard from the spoon before responding. She was attempting to display a confidence that she really didn't feel. There was no good reason for Jinx to be there. At least not a reason good for her. "You're going to play that card? Really?"

"You don't believe me?"

"I believe that your father cares little about whether I insult you. The only thing he cares about is what I can give him." Melissa added a pinch more heat to her voice. "So if you don't mind, get away from my car so I can get going. I don't want to be late."

Jinx didn't move, still leaning against the driver's door, her expression more amused than anything else. "Always so testy."

"Wouldn't you be?" Melissa challenged.

Jinx ignored her. "I am here at my father's request. To get from you what you owe him." She shrugged as if it was only a small matter. "I'm just trying to speed things along. Give me the artifact and I give it to him. Your agreement with him will be concluded."

"That wasn't part of the deal." Melissa was less than pleased with this new development. It didn't feel right to her. And she didn't like last-minute changes.

"Contracts change, Witch. You know how my father is."

Unfortunately, Melissa did know how Typhon was, having to deal with him more than she would have liked. Although there was one truth that she had learned as a result. With Typhon, the deal was the deal. There were never any changes. Ever. For any reason.

His daughter was trying to play her. Melissa was certain of that.

Studying Jinx's attempt at giving her an expression of innocence, Melissa could only assume that the monster had found her here because she wanted to be the one to give Typhon the artifact, thereby raising her standing in the eyes of her father. After all, Jinx had to worry about her brothers and sisters seeking to take her place by his side.

Melissa understood the concept of sibling competition. She had five sisters of her own. Although their contests, schemes, and betrayals were on a much smaller scale compared to those of an Ancient's spawn.

But that mattered little to her now.

Jinx wasn't going to get what she wanted. It was as simple as that.

Melissa had made the deal with Typhon. It was too important to let it go. She couldn't take that risk.

She had started all this. She was responsible for this mess. Even more, she was responsible for what happened to her mother.

Therefore, come what may, she would see the agreement through to the end.

"I do know how your father is. No deal. Now get out of my way so I can get this done."

Jinx glared at Melissa, less than pleased by her decision. Uncrossing her arms, she took a step closer to the Witch.

Melissa responded by taking a step backward.

"I've lost patience with you, Witch. Hand over the artifact. This instant. I won't ask again."

"Go to whichever hell you prefer." Melissa was terrified of taking on Typhon's daughter. Even so, her ire was up. And she was worried about her mother. That gave her a courage she held onto for all that she was worth.

She refused to allow this last obstacle to get in her way. Reaching for the Grym, Melissa prepared herself for a fight that she wasn't sure she could win.

A little of her fire waned when she noticed the half-dozen Vipers appear around her, Typhon's soldiers releasing the Grym that they had been using to hide themselves in plain sight.

Each stood a head or more taller than she was. That didn't bother her, however. The size of her opponent never concerned her.

The number of her opponents did. As did the weapons the Vipers had brought to the party. In addition to their fangs and their ability to spit venom, each Viper held a chain-link whip with inch-long spikes on the metal head, poison drops glistening on the steel.

Her breath caught in her throat. She should have assumed that this was a possibility as soon as Jinx appeared. Of course Jinx would seek to push her way into the deal by employing the creatures Typhon's wife Echidna had created as their own personal army.

What to do now?

She tried not to cringe as the Vipers' split tongues flickered out from between their fangs and tasted the air.

She didn't like snakes. But she could deal with them.

Vipers were a different threat entirely.

A more lethal threat that offered a certain death.

She couldn't take on Jinx and six Vipers. Not with any real expectation of surviving the encounter.

Could she run?

Could she catch Jinx by surprise with the Grym, get into her car somehow, and make a break for it?

"You know, Harry, I can't remember the last time I saw a Viper out of its glass cage. They look a lot different when they're out in the wild."

One of the Three Brothers appeared behind the Vipers, standing to the right of Melissa.

"You've got a short memory, Tom," Harry answered, the second of the Three Brothers appearing behind the Vipers and to the left of Melissa. "It was in Kraken Cove just the other day."

"That's right, Harry. Thank you for reminding me. How many Vipers were there? I can't recall."

"Now I'm beginning to worry," Harry murmured with feigned concern. "Thirteen Vipers, Tom."

"That's right, Harry. Thank you. Thirteen dead Vipers in Kraken Cove. Six more about to join their brethren."

"You two? Again?" Jinx snapped.

"You're not happy to see us, Jinx?" Tom asked.

"I don't know about you, Tom, but I'm insulted." Harry shook his head sadly.

"You'll be more than insulted," Jinx hissed. "I'll send you and your brother to Tartarus if you don't get lost. Now. The Witch belongs to me."

Tom and Harry appeared to seriously consider Jinx's demand, though their eyes never left the Vipers. Typhon's killers had turned toward them, spreading a bit farther apart so they'd have more room to maneuver.

No matter what Jinx might say, the Vipers anticipated a

fight with these two men who appeared to have walked out of the 1950s. And they were looking forward to it. They didn't like being insulted. And they had the chance for revenge on two of the Teg who had sent so many of their comrades to the other side.

"We don't work for you, Jinx," Tom said, almost apologetically.

"If you work for my father, then you work for me," Jinx growled in a very quiet, very threatening voice, her green dreadlocks beginning to sway behind her just as a cobra rising up to strike might.

"It doesn't work that way, Jinx," Harry clarified. "You know that."

"You two are wasting my time. As I said, the Witch is mine."

"We can't allow you to take her, Jinx," Tom said almost apologetically.

"We won't allow you to take her," Harry confirmed, following up on his brother's statement.

"You won't allow?" Jinx demanded. "Vipers, you will bring me the heads of these two ..."

She never had the chance to get out the rest of her order, the Three Brothers launching themselves at her assassins with the speed of stinging wasps.

Before the Vipers could even raise their whips to strike at Tom and Harry, two of Typhon's assassins lay dead in the gravel parking lot, their throats cut.

And Tom and Harry were far from done with their gleaming spikes crafted of the Grym.

Another Viper fell, clutching at his chest. Tom had thrown his spike as he would a dagger, the sharp point striking true and burying itself in the creature's chest. The Grym infused within the weapon swiftly burned through the Viper's flesh and bone, leaving a pile of ash on the ground. The spike appeared back in Tom's hand just a heartbeat later as if he had never thrown it.

Harry did his brother one better. He gripped his spike by the end with the hammer, then threw it in a sideways motion. The spike resembled a circle of energy as it curled through the air, striking the first, the second, and then the last Viper.

All in less than a second.

All of the Vipers most definitely dead, the energy contained within the weapon ripping through the creatures' chests. The spinning spike came to rest in Harry's hand once its task was complete much as if he'd thrown a boomerang.

"You were saying something about my brother and me dying?" Tom asked, turning his attention toward Jinx. He gave her a curious expression.

Jinx's face was a mask of rage -- six of her Vipers gone just like that, she could barely contain herself. Wisps of green and black curled around her hands, the Twisted Grym at her beck and call.

"You would dare to defy me!" she shrieked.

"We don't dare, Jinx," Harry corrected in a deceptively calm voice.

He and his brother glided toward her from both directions, effectively trapping her against the car. Unconcerned about Jinx trying to come at them now that Melissa had called upon the Grym as well. Three against one.

Harry liked those odds. "We do. We do defy you, just as you've seen."

"Why don't you come out and play, Jinx?" Tom suggested.

For just a moment, Jinx appeared to be considering the request, her nostrils flaring, the greenish skin of her cheeks flaring purple with fury. But rather than letting her emotion rule her, she allowed her reason to reign. Taking on three Teg, especially the Three Brothers, was not a recipe for success.

A sphere of the Twisted Grym forming in her hand, she

threw the energy down at the ground. The explosion forced Tom, Harry, and Melissa to look away for just a heartbeat.

When they turned back, Jinx was gone. Just as the Three Brothers assumed would be the case.

"A pity," Tom said.

Harry nodded in agreement. "I was looking forward to killing her."

Both of the Three Brothers shaking their heads in disappointment, they shifted their focus to Melissa, who had viewed the brief distraction as an opportunity to creep by them and get into her car before they could stop her.

Rather than reaching for the door handle, she tried to make it seem like she was just pushing a strand of loose hair back behind her ear. She didn't think the Three Brothers fell for it. So she attempted to take control of the conversation before they could ask her about her intentions.

"Do you work for Typhon?"

"On occasion," Tom replied.

"What about Draig?"

"On occasion," Harry admitted.

"Who are you working for now?" Melissa asked, needing to know her options if she was going to find a way out of this new mess.

Both brothers smiled, but they didn't answer.

Instead, Tom motioned for her to follow him to their car. A Toyota Prius. Later model. Just like hers, completely nondescript.

"Come on," he said. "Jinx knows your car. She's probably been tracking it."

"We need to get out of here," Harry added, placing a hand on her elbow and gently guiding her away from the Highlander. "Jinx isn't known for her mercy. She'll be back, and she'll want blood. Yours to be exact."

12

A FAIR TRADE

Draig stepped out from the Dragon Door right in front of the Daemon King's front stoop, his mode of transportation blinking out as soon as he was through.

The villa sat atop a steep hill. Grape vines trailed down the slopes in all directions, a large crag with conifers running intermittently along the broad expanse visible to the north.

He could have gone in search of his host. He decided against taking the initiative, knowing how testy the Daemon King's servants tended to be.

Besides, he doubted that it would be long before he was discovered.

While he waited, he couldn't help but think of how impressed he was with his daughter. Kassie had done excellent work, not only in crafting a forgery of *The Book of Whispers* out of the Grym that was all but undetectable, but also in giving him a link so that he could follow the connection directly to the fabricated artifact ... and to Melissa.

Draig frowned. He was more than just impressed with the quality of Kassie's work. He was proud of her. In fact, looking back, at her age he didn't have the patience or the precision to do such delicate work with the Grym.

He should have told her that before he left.

And he would. Next week when he met her for dinner. Assuming he didn't die beforehand, of course.

"You again?"

"Good to see you as well," Draig replied as he looked up.

The same Daemon as the last time he visited stood at the top of the steps. However, on this occasion, he was dressed like a bouncer at a cowboy bar, minus the hat.

His pure black eyes revealed his true nature. Five more of his brethren lined the porch railing.

All of them stared down at Draig with a mixture of contempt and curiosity.

They knew who he was. They knew what he could do. What he had done to their kind. Yet despite that they all seemed quite anxious to test themselves against him.

"Maybe you'd like to stay in the guest house since you keep coming here so frequently." The Daemon stared menacingly at him, appreciating his own humor more than his ilk, who couldn't take their eyes off Draig. A few even inched toward the steps, their natural belligerence pushing them forward.

"Something to think about," Draig replied with an amiable nod, unconcerned by the Daemons' itchiness. "I've heard that the accommodations are quite nice."

"For a prison, yes," the Daemon replied. He was less than pleased with his Master's circumstances and his own, and he sensed an opportunity with the cause of those circumstances standing before him. "The more the merrier, of course."

"I guess it's all in how you look at it."

"What do you mean?" The Daemon appeared to be slightly confused.

Draig shrugged. "You and your ilk are stuck here with your

Master. That's true. But it's also true that if you weren't here, you most likely would be back in the Daemon Realm."

The Daemon growled, large fists shifting quickly into claws. "And you would be the one to send us back?"

"If I had to," Draig replied evenly. "But I didn't." He added a little more heat to his voice, wanting to ensure that the Daemons understood that they were playing with fire. "Though I won't hesitate to do so now if there's a need."

The Daemon's dark eyes flashed dangerously. "You think that you could send all of us back to the Daemon Realm?"

"I don't think," Draig replied with an almost unnerving calm. "I know." He gave the Daemon a grin that bordered on arrogance. "If you doubt me, then you should ask the several hundred Daemons I've already returned to your home world. A fist of them just last week, in fact."

"You insult me in my home?" growled the Daemon, who strutted a few feet closer to Draig, putting him in shadow.

"Actually, I'm just telling you the truth. You just don't want to hear it."

"The truth is that you're no match for me or my brethren. Perhaps you'd like to test yourself against us. Show us if all the stories about the Dragon are fact or fiction."

Draig didn't take the bait. He sensed that the Daemon and his friends were just looking for the excuse they needed so that they could have an alibi for their Master. Although he really wouldn't mind the diversion, he didn't have the time for it. "I'll think about that. After I speak with the Daemon King."

"We'll decide whether you see him or not." The Daemon walked down the steps, boots clomping on the wood and coming to a stop right in front of Draig. "And in what condition you're in if we allow it. Because the time for words has come to an end."

Draig nodded. He should have assumed this would happen.

Daemons were aggressive by nature. Even more so when

they held a very strong dislike for you that trickled well beyond hate.

Attempting to defuse the tension rapidly building around him, Draig tapped his blackthorn shillelagh on the stone walkway. Not very loudly, but loud enough to pull the eyes of the Daemons seeking to antagonize him.

He kept the walking staff's true essence hidden for now. He just wanted to offer them a gentle reminder that they were messing with the wrong Teg.

He had sent more Daemons back to their own realm than he cared to recall. He doubted that these six would offer him much in the way of a challenge.

"Do you really want to do this again?" Draig asked, shaking his head from side to side in disappointment. "If I send you back to the Daemon Realm, do you really think the Daemon King will bring you back here? That he'll ever trust you again?"

"No, he won't," a deep voice said from right behind Draig. A voice that explained why the Daemon who hoped to taunt him into a duel had glided back toward the steps, the other Daemons looking like they wanted to be anywhere else but there right at that moment.

The Daemon King walked around Draig. Dressed in jeans, a t-shirt, and sandals, he appeared to be nothing more than the successful owner of a winery, except for the machete strapped to his belt and the bodies of four rattlesnakes that he carried in one hand, a few of them still twitching.

Draig nodded with appreciation at his haul. He was clearing the vineyard again. One of the Daemon King's favorite pastimes since it also usually led to a tasty dinner.

"Master, the Dragon just ..." The large Daemon who sought to challenge Draig didn't get very far with his attempted explanation.

"Leave us," he ordered. The Daemon and his friends hustled away, grateful to escape their Master's wrath. At least for a time. "And don't forget to put the new barrels in place. Within the hour. Or I will send you back to the darkness I took you from and leave you there for eternity."

Satisfied that the Daemons would do exactly as he instructed, the Daemon King turned and offered Draig a smile that was only slightly marred by the bright fires burning in the place of his eyes. He held up the snakes.

"Interested in staying for dinner?"

"Tempting," Draig replied, "but I can't. I already have an engagement tonight that I can't get out of."

"That's too bad. The fatter snakes are quite tasty." The Daemon King hadn't expected his visitor to accept his offer. Draig always was on the move and he couldn't fault him for it. "I didn't think I'd see you so soon after our visit to the Dragon Vault."

"Neither did I. But this works out for the best as I didn't want to raise this when my father or aunt could overhear, much less Fafnir. A few of my Draca would have informed my mother, and I don't need her looking over my shoulder right now with what I've got in play."

"That I can understand. Since you're pressed for time, let's get down to it. I assume you need something." The Daemon King motioned toward the front door and then passed through the veranda, leading Draig up the steps. He left the snakes in the sink by the outdoor kitchen on the shaded patio. He would clean them later.

"I do. An introduction."

The Daemon King turned, giving him a curious look. "I'm almost afraid to ask. An introduction to whom?"

"The Frost Queen."

The Daemon King didn't say anything right away, staring at Draig, his expression one of incredulity. He had to give the Dragon credit. He certainly had a pair on him.

"You do understand what you're asking for, right?"

Draig nodded. "I wouldn't ask if it wasn't necessary."

Draig was well aware of the risk he took in seeking a meeting with the Frost Queen. It couldn't be avoided, however.

Though whether he could actually get a meeting with her was a matter of debate. Because she never gave access to any of the Teg who were not on her very small list of guests. And Draig knew that he wasn't on the list and likely never would be. All for good cause he would readily admit.

Those seeking a meeting with the Frost Queen who were not on her list required an introduction. Because there was no other way to find her otherwise.

She was very secretive. Very private. And she would be very, very angry if he appeared unannounced, although he doubted that he could even find her without the Daemon King's assistance. To even attempt it would be harder than finding a needle in a hundred haystacks.

"Are you sure there isn't another way to get what you require?" The Daemon King frowned, almost as if he was concerned about Draig. "She's tetchy at the best of times. You should know that."

"I'm sure," Draig nodded, appreciating the warning. "There's no other way. I wouldn't be bothering you otherwise."

The Daemon King shook his head, more in disbelief than anything else. "I always thought that you were slightly insane. What you want now confirms it for me."

"I'm glad that I could oblige," Draig replied with an uneven grin. "Can you help me?"

"I can," the Daemon King confirmed, "but you do understand what you're asking? The Frost Queen may or may not help you. That's for her to decide."

"I'm well aware of that."

"And are you aware that if the Frost Queen doesn't kill you, she may decide to keep you just because she desires to add you to her menagerie. If she does the latter, there is nothing that I can do to help you. You'll be just another of her pets. And for her, I'm sure the Dragon would be quite the prize."

"I understand," Draig replied with a sharp nod. "I considered all that before coming here."

"And just so we're clear, you going to her, if she decides to kill or keep you, you probably won't be able to defend yourself. You'll be in her territory. I know you're one of the strongest of the Teg, but that might not matter once you're in her domain."

"I understand that as well."

"And you really want to do this?"

"I didn't say that I wanted to do this." Draig shrugged, as if to say that he had little choice in what fate had proscribed for him. "I need to do this. You know how it is."

"With you, yes, I know how it is," the Daemon King sighed. "And I was just getting to the point of liking you. Or at least not hating you as much as I did before."

"I appreciate that," Draig smiled. "The feeling is mutual. Now can you help me?"

The Daemon King gave Draig one more hard look, then nodded. "It's your funeral."

Stepping around the kitchen counter, he pointed toward the floor with his hand. Using the magic of the Daemon Realm, he burned a pentagram into the tile and ensured that the seal around the outer boundary couldn't be broken by anyone but him.

"Sorry about that," Draig said, nodding toward the pentagram that was also a portal.

"You mean you making sure I can't skip out this way?"

"Yes, exactly that."

"Don't worry about it," the Daemon King replied. "You did what you needed to do. And you showed me mercy when no one else would. I can't fault you for the restrictions you put in place."

Draig nodded, then stepped toward the pentagram that

flashed with a mix of white and black misty energy, sizzling where it had been carved into the stone.

"You're going to owe me another favor," the Daemon King warned.

"Should I be worried?"

"Maybe. Though with you gifting me *The Infernal Dictionary*, I feel as if I'm the one who owes you."

"Then we'll call it even," Draig suggested, about to step across the whitish black border of the portal. "Any advice?"

"Don't get killed," the Daemon King said with a noncommittal shrug. "You can mention my name, though I don't know that it will do you any good where you're going. I haven't visited the Frost Queen for quite some time ... for obvious reasons, of course."

"Good enough," Draig said, pulling a small item from his pocket and handing it to the Daemon King.

He looked down. A small gold key. "What's this?"

"Your get out of jail free card."

The Daemon King's eyes widened when he looked back down at what he held in his hand, understanding what this truly meant. "Why are you doing this?"

"You earned it."

"So you trust me?"

"As much as you trust me."

Then with a nod and a grin, Draig stepped past the pentagram's border and disappeared.

13

AN ULTIMATUM

"Are the Knights ready, Gaheris?"

Arthur Pendragon sat in his spacious office in one of the four towers of his Westchester County estate. If he bothered to look out the window, he could glimpse the edge of the training ground just beyond the gardens.

He had moved his operations from New York City, at least for the time being, worried that there were too many leaks feeding information to his son. Here, he could exercise more control over that ... and identify more easily who the mole might be. Although he did have his suspicions.

"Ten squads just as you ordered, Arthur." Gaheris was afraid to ask, already guessing at what the King Teg had in mind. Still, he needed to. "The assignment?"

"The Dragon, of course."

Gaheris grimaced, taking a moment to think about how to say what he believed he needed to say. "I respectfully request that you delay that command, my King."

"Delay?" Arthur snorted. "Why would I delay?"

"Because there's more in play than just what happened in the Dragon Vault, my King. You know it just as well as I do.

Delaying just a few days won't hurt us, and it even might benefit us."

"In the Dragon Vault my son, who should be dead but didn't have the good sense to remain so, decided to challenge me, Gaheris. Again." Arthur's cold gaze could have frozen the koi pond that was the centerpiece of the garden. "I am the King Teg. That can't be permitted, Gaheris. You know it just as well as I do. Challenges must be addressed swiftly and with over-whelming force to ensure the Teg throne remains secure."

To ensure that you remain secure on the Teg throne, Gaheris corrected, although he chose not to put that thought into words. "In the Dragon Vault your son, who you and I both trained, did what he believed he needed to do because he sees a peril that is beyond what we have faced in quite some time. A peril that threatens all of the Teg. Therefore, I suggest with all due respect that we delay and gather more information before we initiate our strategy."

Gaheris took a step toward Arthur, hoping to convince his friend and liege to adjust his approach. But he took only that step, held in place when the King Teg's unyielding glare locked onto him. "Arthur, there is no harm in taking a little time so that we can make a more knowledgeable decision. The kill order remains in place. I simply ask for a few more days so that we can address this situation with our eyes completely open. That's all."

"It is not *our* strategy, Gaheris," Arthur replied in a brittle tone. He seemed to have not heard any of Gaheris' argument. Or if he did, he chose to ignore it. "It is *my* strategy."

Arthur pushed himself up from his chair, placing his hands on the hand-carved table taken from an offshoot of Llangernyw Yew, said to be the oldest tree in Wales. When he leaned forward, his eyes smoldered with an unquenchable rage.

"The Dragon should have stayed dead, Gaheris. Yet he has been reborn, and just as he did in his first life, he has challenged me in a way that puts at risk all that I have built. I can't allow that, Gaheris. The Dragon will die once more. By *our* hand. And he will not rise again. Do I make myself clear?"

"My King," Gaheris began, his eyes challenging and pleading both at the same time. He feared what would happen if he continued to press Arthur, but he couldn't allow this to go on. Not without getting his liege to understand that allowing his animosity to rule his decision making was a recipe for defeat if not complete disaster. "Respectfully, I believe that this is a mistake. I request again that you delay, if only for a few days, so that we can seek to confirm reports that ..."

"Arthur shouldn't delay what he's put in motion," an exceedingly frigid voice offered from the shadow of the doorway. "Arthur should rescind the order entirely. The kill order as well. Neither does anyone any good. Except Arthur, of course. A balm to his wounded ego. No more than that."

Gaheris stared into the gloom, unable to see even the dim shape of the woman who had interrupted him. Until that woman peeled herself from the shadows and stalked into the office.

"The Morrigan," Gaheris said, taking a step back and offering her a nod of respect.

"Sir Gaheris. It is a pleasure to see you again after so long a time."

"The pleasure is mine, my Lady. It is good to see the Phantom Queen well."

"If you two are done with your trip back to the Middle Ages, and before you start talking to one another in thees and thous, you owe me an explanation, Battle Goddess," Arthur interjected.

The raven-haired woman with mesmerizing black eyes glided more than walked to a position right across from the King Teg, who stared at his new and unwanted arrival with a questioning and slightly worried glance.

"What explanation would that be, Arthur?" the Morrigan asked. She tapped one long fingernail on the yew. Each time it made contact a white spark shot out, a charred mark on the wood left behind.

"Why are you here, Morrigan? Why have you invaded my home without seeking my permission?"

The Morrigan snorted more in disbelief than humor. "You forget yourself, Arthur. You may rule the Teg realm, but you do not rule all the Teg. To make that assumption would ensure a very painful fall."

"You dare to threaten me?" Arthur asked in a dangerously quiet tone. "In my own home, no less?"

"I dare nothing, Arthur. I simply tell you a truth that you don't want to hear. Just as you didn't want to hear the truth in Gaheris' words. You have gone deaf to reason. You are allowing your emotion to reign. If you continue to do so, it will cost you in the end. And more than just your throne."

"Is that why you have intruded, Morrigan? To offer me this warning?" He pressed down harder onto the wood, desperate for some outlet to his boiling anger. Yet knowing all the while that directing his anger toward the Irish Battle Goddess would be a very bad idea. "I can only assume you are here at your lover's instigation. That being the case, you have no right to be here. The personal cannot be allowed to taint the political."

Riga ignored the barb thrown her way as well as the hypocrisy. "I have every right to be here, Arthur, if it means stopping you from making a stupid mistake."

"Stupid mistake?" Arthur almost choked on the words. "How dare you? I'll ..."

"In this instance, of course I dare," Riga said with a snort of derision. "Your strategy ensures your own defeat. Gaheris is correct. As I just said, if you allow your emotion to continue to guide you, you are in for a fall from which you will never recover. I suggest you heed what I have to say rather than ignore it."

Arthur's knuckles turned white as he pressed even harder into the top of his desk, imagining for just a second the wood bending and then cracking from his efforts. His rage demanded that he lash out. However, a quick glimpse to his right stopped him.

Gaheris was pleading with him with his eyes and shaking his head, trying to warn him as well. His building rage was nothing compared to the power exercised by a Goddess.

That tiny bit of reason finally breaking through, Arthur contained the explosion of fury that he was only a heartbeat away from releasing. "Since you know so much more than I do, great Goddess of War, please explain it to me." He leaned back. Crossing his arms over his broad chest, he motioned with his hand for her to proceed.

"It's really quite simple and obvious, Arthur," Riga said, crossing her arms as well. "You're so focused on Morgase. Worried about what your sister might do. Yet even after all this time, neither you nor she have come to realize what many of the Teg have come to understand."

"And what would that be?" Arthur asked, a hint of worry creeping into his voice, as if he feared the answer the Morrigan was about to provide him.

"That you two are in many respects irrelevant."

"Irrelevant!" Arthur exploded, pounding a fist onto his desk. "How could you possibly say that I ..."

"You have not told him this, Gaheris?" Riga asked, fixing her hard gaze on the Knight for just a few seconds. "Is that not your responsibility? To tell your commander the truth even when it's not the truth that he wants to hear?"

Before Gaheris could reply, and before Arthur could interrupt, Riga continued. "Oh, right. You were attempting to do just that. You were attempting to get the King Teg to see reason. But apparently his head is as hard as his desk."

"You go too far. I will not allow you to ..." Arthur spluttered.

"We've been through this, Arthur. Of course I dare. I must dare because you must see." She leaned forward onto his desk then, lightning fast, her eyes catching Arthur's. "You and your sister are irrelevant. Not in the sense that you both don't exercise power. You both do. I won't deny that. Rather, you two negate one another and the power that you both wield."

"Negate?" Arthur asked, not understanding the comment, forgetting his anger for just a moment.

"Negate," Riga repeated. "You two are always scheming against one another. You to keep the throne. She to take the throne. In all that time, nothing has changed. Other than the fact that the Teg have gotten weaker because of the incessant warfare between brother and sister."

"You have no idea what you're talking about," Arthur huffed, beginning to feel uncomfortable because the truth in her words was hitting a little too close to home. "Do you have any idea, Gaheris? Because clearly she doesn't know what she's talking about."

"I do know of what the Phantom Queen speaks, Arthur," Gaheris replied in a firm tone, never afraid to offer his unvarnished perspective to Arthur, even if it wasn't what his friend and liege wanted to hear. "And she speaks the truth. We are weaker now than we ever have been in the past."

Arthur's eyes widened in disbelief. "Gaheris, I cannot believe ..."

"We have spoken of this for several years, Arthur," Gaheris interrupted, though he did so gently, keeping his own irritation and frustration under wraps. He understood that to release it now would do more harm than good. "Or at least I have."

"Gaheris, be very careful where you tread. I made you my second in command. You do not need to stay in that position."

"And I do not want to stay in that position, Arthur, if you so willingly ignore the challenges that we face. The real challenges. Morgase is a threat, I won't deny it. But we have focused so much attention on her and then on the Dragon that we have lost sight of the other threats that face the Teg."

Riga was impressed with Gaheris. Speaking his mind despite the King Teg's threat. However, she expected no less from the Knight of the Round. He had trained the Dragon after all.

"Listen to Gaheris, Arthur, if you will not listen to me. Your centuries-old war with your sister is nothing compared to the war that approaches."

"How could you possibly know that a war ..."

"I am the Goddess of War," Riga said in a sharp tone that shut up Arthur in an instant. "You said it yourself. I know more of war and battle than you ever will."

Arthur did not respond right away, his gaze shifting from Riga to Gaheris and then back again. His initial instinct was to relieve Gaheris of his responsibilities and order the Morrigan to leave his office. But he concluded that neither would be the right decision.

He realized then that he needed to hear what the Morrigan had to say. Whether at Draig's instigation or she had come here on her own, he had to at least give her that.

"Tell me."

"You saw an opportunity to defeat your enemy once you gained control of *The Book of Whispers*."

Arthur nodded, not bothering to deny it. "I did."

"And that plan has gone up in flames because Draig refused to give you the artifact."

Arthur nodded. "He has caused a great many problems for me these last few decades. My son has much to answer for."

"Just as you do, Arthur," Riga replied. Shaking her head, her disappointment was almost a tangible thing.

"How so?" Arthur clearly didn't understand what Riga was talking about.

"You and your sister both made a play for the most powerful and dangerous artifact ever crafted by a Teg."

"And with good reason," Arthur argued. "With *The Book of Whispers*, I could have removed my sister as a threat. Thereby protecting all Teg and my rule."

"Perhaps," Riga said, not sounding entirely convinced, pushing off of Arthur's desk and giving him a sad look, as if she saw nothing more than a petulant and overbearing child standing in front of her who refused to listen to reason. "But you never considered the possibility that another player would identify an opportunity once you put your plan to obtain that artifact in motion."

"Another player?" Arthur scoffed. "I have no idea what you're talking about."

"And that's the problem right there, Arthur. That's why you're holding on to your throne by a thread."

"You have no idea of what you speak," Arthur hissed. But he did know what the Morrigan was talking about. Because it was much the same as what Gaheris had been telling him for years that he had chosen to ignore.

His position among the Teg was not what it used to be. And it wasn't because of his sister.

There was another force in play, biting at the edges, looking for a weakness. Searching for an opportunity just as the Morrigan suggested.

Arthur was sure of it. Though he couldn't pinpoint the source, and he refused to speak of it. Almost as if doing so would bring that threat down upon him all the faster.

"You see it now, don't you, Arthur?" Riga asked, although she already knew the answer to her question. She could recognize it in the King Teg's eyes.

"It is a whisper, nothing more," Arthur replied.

"It is more than a whisper, Arthur," Gaheris said, sensing an opportunity. "It is real. And that is why I beg of you. Please delay. Give me a few days to confirm what I fear. Then, once we know, we can make a good decision. The right decision."

Arthur did not reply right away, staring off into the distance, not seeing anything. Trapped in his own fears and concerns. Reverting to what he was used to since it was so much of a struggle to shift his thinking, which had been in place for so long and was so deeply entrenched within him. "Nothing either of you have said gives me cause to change what I have in mind."

Riga shook her head sadly once again. She was dismayed, although clearly she wasn't surprised by his reaction. "And there is the cause of your current circumstances. Once again you rely on a short-term and simplistic view of the battlefield. That has always been your Achilles' heel."

"Simplistic," Arthur choked. "How could you ..."

Riga rode over the King Teg before he could offer a more thorough defense of himself and his thinking. "Simplistic. You don't see the larger picture. Because of that, you can't see what's really going on. You choose to ignore your real enemy, focusing instead only on what is right in front of you. And, by the time you realize your mistake, the blade will be in your side, and there is nothing that Gaheris and all your other Knights will be able to do to prevent that from happening."

"Really," Arthur snorted, nodding his head as if he were amused. Not sure how to defend himself, because once again the Morrigan's words were hitting very close to a truth he preferred to ignore, he sought some time to think. "Then tell me why you believe that. Tell me why I am so focused on keeping my throne, since that seems to be what you're implying, isn't it?"

"You don't trust your son," Riga said in a very quiet voice that threatened to take Arthur's breath away.

"He betrayed me," the King Teg whispered.

She nodded. Though not in agreement. Rather in understanding.

The King Teg looked at the world in a certain way, and clearly he didn't have the capacity to adjust his perspective. If for no other reason than the fact that his perspective had served him so well for so long.

Comfortable in that reality, why would Arthur bother to explore other perspectives when they would only complicate his own?

Arthur didn't understand what Riga really was saying and he likely never would. "How did Draig betray you?"

"You know exactly how he betrayed me," Arthur grumbled. Strangely, all the fire had left him. He stood there facing off against the Morrigan as if the battle between them had been lost because he didn't want to face up to the truth that she was trying to present to him.

"How did Draig betray you?" she repeated.

"He didn't do as I ordered," Arthur explained. "He didn't obey me as he should have. Instead of helping me as he had sworn to do, he helped I don't know how many Teg escape the sentences they deserved."

Riga shook her head wistfully. She feared that Arthur was a lost cause. Still, she had no choice but to continue to try. "Draig didn't obey you because your orders were not just orders."

"That's impossible. Every order I issue is a just ..."

"Arthur, we do not have the pleasure to continue as we have been. Time is short. When your time to go to the other side comes, you can speak with your God of the Underworld about what a just order is and is not. That conversation will determine where you will go. Right now, attempting to justify your decisions is a waste of time."

"You make it seem like my demise approaches," Arthur challenged, although his usual fire had yet to return. His thoughts were still on matters that he had no desire to devote his energy to though he couldn't seem to escape them.

"I know not when your demise comes. All I know is that if you continue along your current path, your demise will come sooner than it is deserved."

"So now you can foretell the future, Morrigan? I did not know that was within your skill set."

"I do not foretell the future, Arthur. Other Tegs do that, and when they speak, I listen. Because I do understand fate and foretelling at the time of battle. And make no mistake, whether you see it or not, whether you acknowledge it or not, the Teg are at war. A war in the shadows for now, but a war nonetheless."

That response was like a shot to Arthur's gut as he tried and failed to pull his eyes away from those of the Morrigan. Once again there was a truth contained within her words that he had no desire to recognize even though a small part of him understood that he couldn't deny that truth. "Regardless of what you say, Morrigan, my son betrayed me. He helped those Teg escape my justice."

"Arthur, you know it as well as I, but still you refuse to admit it. Draig protected the Teg he helped."

"And he betrayed me," Arthur replied, the words coming out in a grate that sounded much like a chainsaw biting into wood.

"He protected you as well, Arthur. You just never saw it. You didn't want to see it."

"Me?" Arthur scoffed. "Who was Draig protecting me from?"

"Yourself."

"What in blazes are you talking about?"

"Think about it, Arthur. You're a smart man. Misguided more often than not but still a smart man. You'll figure it out."

Arthur frowned then grimaced. This conversation was

proving to be a more painful experience than seeing his son come back to life. Wanting to get out from under the burden that was pressing down upon him, he attempted to push his duel with the Morrigan back to safer ground.

"I didn't take you for a lowly messenger, Morrigan."

"I'm more than that, Arthur. Much more." Her eyes flashed dangerously as her patience ran out. "Remember who I am, Arthur. I came here out of respect for Draig, not you."

She leaned in again, hands on the desk, exercising a dominance that Arthur was quite unused to. Wispy smoke appeared from where her fingers pressed into the yew. "I am a Goddess of War, King Teg. Of retribution. Of revenge. Do not forget that, because my loyalty is not to you. It never has been. It never will be. My loyalty is to the Dragon. Leave the Dragon be. He knows what he's doing. He can't do what he needs to do with you breathing down his neck. Because unlike you, he understands who the real enemy is. And he's not afraid to take on that enemy."

"Are you threatening me?" Arthur demanded, although there was little strength in his voice. The Grym radiated off the Morrigan in waves, released by her anger, and it was a power that not only matched his own, but exceeded it.

"Yes, I am Arthur. Best to heed this one warning. I won't give you another." Riga pushed off the desk then, her power more muted now, though still there. "Now if you're done acting the child, I need your help with something."

"You're going to ask me for my help after what you just did and said? Seriously?"

"I am," Riga replied with a confident nod, "and you're going to give me the help that I need. You're going to give me Gaheris and those Knights."

"Why in all the Gods would I do that?"

"Because it involves Morgase."

14

FRIGID WELCOME

Draig was more than just a little surprised when he stepped through the portal the Daemon King created with the pentagram. He assumed that he would be entering a bone-chillingly cold environment. Snow would be falling to add to drifts yards high. Tearjerkingly frigid gusts of wind would threaten to knock him from his feet. And there would be a fortress made of carved ice beckoning to him in the distance.

He never thought that instead he would find himself on what he assumed was a private Caribbean island. The warm sun shone down brightly. The surf pounded in a soothing rhythm against the beach that was only a hundred yards away in any direction he looked. The palm trees swayed invitingly in rhythm with the gentle breezes.

A land of relaxation and recovery rather than one that could turn him into an icicle in seconds. Draig certainly wasn't one to complain about his unexpected circumstances.

With the clock ticking, rather than waiting to be found, he stepped onto the path made of crushed seashells and followed it toward the white stucco mansion situated atop a small rise that was shielded by palm trees.

Draig was almost to the portico when he spun on his heel, his blackthorn shillelagh adopting its true form as he brought the weapon up in a sweeping arc and knocked away the huge mace made of jagged ice that had been cutting down toward the back of his head.

He kept moving, gliding across the crushed shells, Excalibur flashing blindingly bright even in the Caribbean sunlight when Draig blocked the mace, the sharp sound ringing out across the small island with a frequency that the giant who wielded the weapon hadn't anticipated.

Clearly, Draig's attacker had assumed that a single blow would crush him just like the shells they stood upon. And why not? The huge fellow's mace more resembled a battering ram.

Draig smiled at the giant's brief flash of consternation, glad that he was making his opponent's life more difficult than he wanted it to be.

As Draig had learned while training hour after hour with Gaheris and the other Knights of the Round, it was dangerous to make assumptions in a combat.

Continuing to move up and down the path, Draig spun and dodged with an inhuman fluidity. Bringing Excalibur into play, he warded off the heavy-handed blows from the several more giants who burst out of the undergrowth, their strikes so potent that their maces crafted of clear ice with just the hint of blue sang through the air with a power that mimicked the blustery wind.

Most missed him with space to spare, only a few slices and slashes close enough to give him any cause for concern. Those few that connected created an uneven rhythm of fiery steel cutting into hardened ice.

Draig smiled. He was definitely in the right place. He never should have doubted the Daemon King.

Frost Giants.

Jotun.

The same size as most other giants.

Two times larger than a man.

Although they tended to have nastier dispositions than other giants, and that was saying something.

Their appearance made sense. Jotun were used to the colder climes. Their skin a bluish white, their hair and the whiskers of their long beards resembled icicles. And their eyes were a blue brighter than that of the sky. All five of the Frost Giants wore clothing that would have allowed them to fade into invisibility within the frozen landscape of the northern climes, whites, blues, and a little grey in a dizzying pattern that was difficult to fix on.

But here, on this small cay, the Frost Giants stood out like five sore thumbs. And clearly they weren't enjoying their exertion in the tropical heat, water dripping off their heads and down their beards, sweat making their clothes, more suited to a winter climate, cling to their massive bodies.

Or perhaps their rising aggravation resulted from the fact that they had yet to earn a clean hit on their target.

Draig moved with a deceptive grace among the battle-scarred Frost Giants, unconcerned when one Jotun after another tried to come at him from behind or from the side while he was engaged with one of their peers.

The Frost Giants were strong. Determined. Relentless. And they were fast. Remarkably fast for warriors so large. But they weren't as fast as Draig.

The Frost Giants spent just as much time trying to kill Draig as they did trying not to kill one another. More often than they cared to, they were forced to hesitate during their attacks. Fearful that they were about to harm one of their brothers rather than the interloper who had appeared on the island they were tasked with guarding.

And it was that hesitation that cost them the most and Draig masterfully employed for his own benefit.

Unwilling to kill one of their peers even if it meant finally connecting with the intruder's flesh rather than his steel, they had no chance to kill the Teg dancing around them.

Draig knew it, which was why he was more than happy to weave his way through the melee and create as much chaos as he could. Using Excalibur to defend himself when that proved necessary. Spending even more of his energy on evading his opponents rather than fighting them. Smiling as he earned curses and grunts of frustration from his partners in the dance as they failed time and time again to inflict a killing blow ... or a blow of any kind for that matter.

If he wanted to, Draig could have ended the fight.

Swiftly and with a lethal finality.

But killing these Jotun wasn't why he was there and would likely complicate his efforts. He believed that if he remained patient he would gain what he wanted.

The Frost Giants became so enraged at their failure to even nick him that their fabled discipline wavered. They gave Draig a multitude of opportunities to finish them, all of which he chose not to capitalize on.

He could have left all five Frost Giants bleeding out on the path of crushed white shells.

He refrained, however.

Despite that being the easiest solution for bringing the clash to a close.

Instead, he chose to be careful. Defending himself and not seeking to harm the Frost Giants, and doing it in a way so that they didn't realize what he was doing. Their fury at their failure helping to mask that reality from them.

Trusting in his intuition, Draig understood that the climax of the combat was fast approaching.

And he was grateful for that.

Because he needed to be somewhere at a specific time. And this wasn't the place.

To force the issue, the next time one of the Frost Giants – he didn't know which one because there were very few differences between them other than battle scars and a bit more white in their hair rather than blue – swung his mace toward his head, rather than stepping out of the way as had been his habit since the clash began, Draig advanced. Excalibur sang through the air, shining blade targeting the Jotun's neck.

The Frost Giant recognized the danger immediately. He tried to counter the attack, arresting his swing and striving to raise his mace before the deadly blow struck.

So distracted by the swift turn of events and the lethal steel streaking toward him, the Frost Giant forgot for just a moment the fragility of the crumbly surface upon which he fought. Already in a precarious position because of the shells beneath his feet, in his frantic effort to defend himself, he overextended, thereby putting his balance at risk, his front foot sliding too far forward.

With a deft kick of his right foot, Draig ensured the Frost Giant couldn't recover, knocking his adversary's foot even farther forward. And painfully so ... for the Frost Giant.

The Jotun gasped as his legs split farther apart, the muscles in his groin protesting, straining, threatening to snap as he dropped toward the ground.

Everything stopped then.

Even the breeze that gusted across the island with a welcome regularity.

When the injured Frost Giant looked up, he assumed that he would be doing it through eyes that only had a few seconds of vision left as his head rolled a few feet away to watch his slumped body bleed out on the pristine trail.

He almost breathed a sigh of relief when he realized that his head was still attached to his shoulders.

But he didn't.

He couldn't.

The Teg who had appeared uninvited on his Mistress' island home stood above him, shining blade pressed against his throat. Despite his perilous posture, the Frost Giant wanted nothing more than to adjust his position. The searing pain in his groin demanded it. He was scared to do so, however. He didn't want to risk that glowing steel biting into his neck.

Not moving his head a hair, the Frost Giant looked for his fellow warriors.

They were there. Watching him. Unwilling to make a move.

He appreciated their concern for his life.

But they had forgotten a key lesson.

They were Jotun.

Jotun did not fear death.

Jotun welcomed death.

Better that he die so that his brothers could kill this invader without them having to worry about him.

The Frost Giant was about to tell his brothers just that when a melodic voice right behind him drew the gazes of his warrior brothers.

"I would really prefer if you didn't kill Orsoo. He has been with me for quite a long time. And though he likely believes that he deserves to die because he did not defeat you, he would be wrong."

"Why would Orsoo be wrong?" Draig asked. He remained where he was, Excalibur still held to the Jotun's throat.

"Because it would be more than foolish for any of my Jotun, even five of them, to assume that they can defeat the Dragon in battle."

"An enlightened perspective," Draig said.

"A perspective based on reality. To lose to the Dragon is not a matter of dishonor. It is simply a hard truth. One that grants enlightenment farther down the road so long as no one loses their head."

Draig smiled at that as he took in the young woman who

stood on the path just beyond the small battlefield. She wore a bright pink bikini, a thin sarong tied around her hips, and a floppy white hat to protect against the sun.

He appreciated what she was doing, trying to stave off any foolish actions on the part of her guards.

"But Mistress ..." Orsoo attempted to protest. He could say no more, having a difficult time pushing out the words with the steel pressed against his throat.

"No buts, Orsoo. I have need of your services, and I will not allow the honor of the Jotun to ensure your needless death. Dying at the hands of the Dragon does not serve me. Do you understand?" The young woman's eyes flashed with a coldness that sent a shiver straight to Draig's heart and seemed to wake the Frost Giant under his blade from his delusion of sacrificing himself for the benefit of his mistress and his brothers.

Orsoo nodded, just barely, after struggling with his conscience for a few seconds more, but enough for Draig to remove Excalibur and step back a few feet. He then offered the Frost Giant a hand, needing to lean back so that he didn't get pulled to the ground when he hauled the Jotun back to his feet. Much like Berserkers, Frost Giants were honorable to a fault. Orsoo's nod just as good as a contract struck in hardened ice.

Orsoo hobbled over to where his brothers stood, grimacing at the pain that burned through his groin muscles. Rather than an expression of hate or a spark in his ice-blue eyes that promised vengeance, Orsoo offered Draig a nod of respect that was mimicked by the four other Jotun.

They made no move to assist their brother warrior. To do so would dishonor Orsoo.

Nodding with satisfaction, the young woman turned her gaze toward Draig. Studying him. Smiling when with the use of the Grym Draig once again hid Excalibur behind the image of a blackthorn shillelagh.

"I must admit that I never expected the Dragon to appear at

my doorstep. And if he did, I assumed it was for the worst possible reason. Your father does not forgive. Ever. As you know better than most."

"Which is why the Jotun attacked." Draig nodded, now understanding the reception that he received.

He should have anticipated it, in fact. But his mind was already farther down the road he still needed to travel.

"I must do what is necessary to protect myself," the Frost Queen replied. "I hope you can understand that."

"It makes perfect sense," Draig answered agreeably. "My apologies. I just came here to talk with you, and I didn't have time to send word."

"And how did you locate my secret hideaway?" The Frost Queen appeared more curious than angry.

"The Daemon King offered me passage."

"The Daemon King? Really? Another enemy of your father who apparently is not an enemy of yours. I must say, you keep strange company, Dragon."

"My father has a very limited view of the world," Draig replied with a knowing grin. "My perspective is broader. I have learned that to succeed and survive among the Teg, seeing the grey and valuing the differences among our kind offers greater value than the black and white that rules my father's perspective."

The Frost Queen didn't respond right away to Draig's explanation, instead continuing her study of him. Then she nodded, her gaze keen. "You said that you wanted to talk." Her tone suggested that she assumed that it would be more a negotiation than a dialogue.

"I do," Draig confirmed.

"And we can, so long as you promise to leave my Jotun still among the living so long as they don't provoke you."

"The best deal I've heard today."

"Good," she replied in satisfaction. "Why don't you join me for a drink." It wasn't a request.

The Frost Queen stepped past him, her sarong sliding silkily against his hip, and walked down the trail toward the terrace at the back of the mansion, Draig right by her side. "You seem a little surprised," she said.

"Surprised?"

"You have that look in your eye."

Draig realized that he needed to do a better job of hiding his questions, the Frost Queen more than just a little perceptive. "It's just that ..." He didn't know how to put it without insulting her.

The Frost Queen smiled and then laughed softly. "My appearance, I take it?" She waved her hand in front of her when they reached the back deck. "Were you expecting someone more like this?"

In an instant, she was no longer a beautiful young woman spending the day at the beach. Instead, she had taken on the appearance of an old hag. Sans the wart on the end of her nose, still she wore heavy black robes. Her long, white hair was scraggly and unkempt, and her skin was pulled tightly over her bones, giving her a skeletal appearance.

The Frost Queen shifted back to the younger, less world weary woman before she sat down, motioning Draig to take the seat across from her.

"Which is the real you?" he asked in as respectful a tone as he could manage. He knew just how testy the Frost Queen could be. Vindictive as well. He couldn't afford to have this conversation start out on the wrong foot ... especially after putting one of her Jotun under the blade.

"It depends on the need," she replied, reaching for the pitcher between them and pouring the iced liquid into the tall glass in front of him before serving herself. "Really no different than you, Dragon, wouldn't you say?"

"I would indeed," he confirmed. Draig took a sip, the cool drink refreshing in the steamy heat. An Arnold Palmer. "How did you know?"

"I know more than most give me credit for." She leaned forward then, offering Draig a bright smile. "You're wondering now why I'm here rather than where you would expect me to be."

"That thought had crossed my mind. When I first arrived, I feared the Daemon King had made a mistake."

"A fair assumption," the Frost Queen replied. "The truth is that though I will never be able to escape the winter entirely, and the winter will never be able to escape me, I need the sun and the warmth of hotter climes at least for a few months out of the year. Otherwise, I get too depressed."

"That makes perfect sense, though it doesn't seem like your Jotun enjoy this time away as much as you do."

"You noticed that during the clash." She smiled, then shook her head in amusement. "That was quite impressive, you know. It will take them some time to realize that you showed them mercy. My Jotun are proud, often more constrained by their honor than they should be, but they will understand eventually."

"No blood vendetta to worry about?"

"Not with my Jotun. They are not as hot-tempered as some of the other Giant folk. They reason before they act. Their usual environment gives them a hard and cold calculation, which is critical to my work. But here ..." She waved her hand to the swaying palm trees and the turquoise ocean that was all around them. "They are not comfortable just as you assumed. They tolerate my being here, and for that I am thankful."

"Obviously, you inspire a great deal of loyalty. The Jotun do not trust easily."

The Frost Queen laughed at that, tilting her head back, her

eyes sparkling in delight. "Flattery will get you everywhere, Dragon. You are quite the charmer."

"Just speaking what I see," he replied.

"For that I thank you. And from what I understand, you inspire a great deal of loyalty as well."

Draig lifted a hand as if to say that it wasn't for him to determine if that was the case. "I like to assume no more than I deserve. Though probably more than I deserve actually."

"A humble Dragon," the Frost Queen mused. "I never would have thought it possible." She leaned forward again, her ice-blue eyes catching his fiery orbs. "You've got quite the fire in you, Dragon. It intrigues me."

"I don't know how to take that, but thank you."

"Take it however you like. How ever far you would like as well."

Draig caught the mischievous glint in the Frost Queen's eye, then he smiled. "You're enjoying this quite a bit, aren't you?"

"And what is this?" She was curious as to how he would define it. Whether he would take the avenue she had left open to him.

"Trying to make me uncomfortable."

"And am I succeeding?" the Frost Queen continued, more than just intrigued as she waited for his reply.

"I was uncomfortable the moment I first saw you." He said it with a devilish glint and then wink that brought a spark of color to the Frost Queen's pale cheeks.

She leaned back in her chair and laughed again, clapping her hands together as she did so. "Oh, you are quite the charmer, aren't you, Dragon? And in a way in which your words can mean many things all at once." She shook her head in pleasure. "I must admit that when you first appeared I didn't know what to think. Now I'm glad I didn't try to kill you the moment you set foot on my island."

"I'm glad about that as well."

The Frost Queen laughed again before she leaned forward, arms resting on her crossed legs. The humor gone from her eyes. The cold and hint of ice returning. She was all business. "Now enough with the fun, Dragon. You came here for a reason, and I'm only allowing this conversation because you ignored your father's order."

"I did," Draig confirmed.

"Did he ever tell you why he wanted you to kill me?"

Draig shook his head. "He was never specific. He only said that you defied him in some way and that he had good cause to eliminate you."

"You never came for me, though. Why was that? You took a great risk by not doing as the King Teg ordered?" Her eyes narrowed, deeply interested in what he had to say.

"Actually, I did come for you."

"You did?" The Frost Queen didn't bother to keep the surprise from her voice. "Really? I would have known."

Draig nodded an apology. "Fifteen years ago at exactly this time of year. You were on holiday in Ibiza, so perhaps you had yet to claim this island as your own."

The Frost Queen's eyes widened. "You were there?" For the first time in a very long time she felt a stab of fear shiver through her body.

"I was."

"How did I not know this?"

Draig shrugged almost apologetically. "I was very good at my work. Too good, in fact."

"I won't dispute that." She smoothed out her sarong, working to get past the feeling of being slightly flustered. She didn't blame herself for her unease. Any other Teg would experience much the same reaction if not worse if they discovered that the Dragon had been so close without even realizing it. "You were there, I didn't know it, and you didn't try to kill me."

"I didn't."

"Why not? Your father gave you that order."

"Because I didn't believe that you deserved to die," Draig replied matter-of-factly.

"Why did you believe that?" the Frost Queen asked, intensely curious despite the fact that she was talking about how close she had come to her own death. "I've done some terrible things during my long life."

Draig nodded. "So have I."

"That's not an answer."

"It's part of an answer," he suggested. Then he shrugged. "I didn't trust my father, so I did some digging on my own. Just as I had started to do then every time my father gave me an assignment."

"And what did you discover?"

More than he wanted to know about his father he could have said. But he didn't. There were some things that didn't need to be shared.

"Enough to start me on the path that allowed me to leave the Knights of the Round. In short, I discovered that the information my father gave me was inaccurate."

"And that's why you didn't kill me?"

"As I said, you didn't deserve to die. At least not by my hand."

"Yet you were in a position to carry out your father's order. Watching you fight with my Jotun, it would have been quite easy for you."

"It would have been, yes."

"Yet still you stayed your hand. You disobeyed your King's order. Your father's order."

"I did," Draig confirmed.

"Then why did you go to Ibiza if you didn't have any intention of killing me?"

"I wanted my father to believe that I was still on task. I couldn't help it if I got there too late to kill you. Once you left

Ibiza, you were in the wind and out of my reach."

The Frost Queen smiled at him then, beginning to appreciate who Draig really was. Not just a sharp weapon. Clever as well. Thoughtful. Calculating.

Which only made him more dangerous than he already was.

"Even with all that you've told me, why would I want to help you?" The Frost Queen believed that she might be pushing the Dragon too hard. Nevertheless, she felt the need to do so.

"Why not?" Draig replied.

"You're the Dragon. You did some things for your father that I didn't appreciate and that I'm not sure that I can forgive. And, honestly, if not for my curiosity, I'm well within my rights to kill you here. In fact, I probably should have the second you set foot on my island."

"Then I'm glad you're still curious." Draig leaned in, placing his forearms on the table. "You're right. I did some things as a Knight that I regret. For which I've tried to make amends, continue to try to make amends, knowing that no matter what I did and what I do it will never be enough."

"I've heard of some of what you've done," the Frost Queen said as she nodded her head judiciously, valuing his honesty. "Particularly what you're doing in Kraken Cove."

Draig frowned slightly. He was a little concerned that word was spreading so rapidly among the Teg about his enclave. But there was little that he could do about it. "As I said, trying to make amends."

"I'll help you on one condition," the Frost Queen promised.

"Even though I didn't kill you when I could have?" Draig's eyes burned a bit brighter then. Not a warning, just a reminder that didn't go unnoticed.

"If you didn't spare me I would have more than one condition."

Draig didn't reply right away. His expression hardened for

just a heartbeat, but only because he knew that the Frost Queen needed to have a victory, small though it may be. "What would that be?"

"You allow me to visit Kraken Cove."

"Done." Draig had guessed this might be her requirement.

"And if I like the town I'm free to buy a property."

Draig thought about that request. Studying the Frost Queen, he could tell that this was important to her. She had quite the reputation. And not really the best reputation. Then again, he had a reputation that rivaled hers, and he needed to focus on Typhon. "Done."

"Just one more thing."

"I'm afraid to ask."

"When I visit Kraken Cove, you have dinner with me."

Draig didn't hesitate. "Done."

"What do you need from me, Dragon? It seems that I'm in your debt."

15

NOT SO OLD FRIEND

"Does the ocean bring back good memories?"

Draig didn't turn at the voice. He didn't have to. It was all too familiar.

The woman slid up next to him without making a sound as he stared out at the gentle waves of the Delaware Bay.

"A couple."

He had hoped for a few more minutes of peace and quiet before the real fun began. But there was little space for hope in his world.

This confrontation was inevitable. In fact, that's why he was waiting there.

He thought it best to deal with her now so that she didn't interfere with the business he needed to conduct later that night.

That's why he wandered down the Lewes public beach all the way to the channel breakwater. Out in the open for all to see. Leaving a trail with the Grym that a very powerful Sorceress who was quite familiar with his magical signature would have little difficulty following.

Killing some time.

Before Calypso tried to kill him.

"Just a couple? Really?" Calypso scoffed at that. "Don't you remember the many months we spent in the Greek isles? What we did on beaches much nicer than this one?"

"That would be hard to forget," he murmured, a faint smile curling his lips for the briefest of moments.

"It was good to be home," Callie recalled. "It was good to be there with you. The sun. The ocean. And very little clothing." She turned toward him. Her kaleidoscopic eyes fixed onto his. "You seem less enamored of those memories than I am. Why is that?"

"Because I've always wondered about the time we spent together."

Callie grinned like a Cheshire cat. "You're thinking about whether ..." She nodded. "I guess that's only to be expected."

"Thank you for understanding," Draig replied.

"But you won't ask?"

Draig didn't reply at first, losing himself in the flashing colors of Callie's eyes and the memories they awakened within him. He had always wondered whether Calypso had used her powers of persuasion against him while they were together. After she left him, he never really was certain whether he loved her or she was using her magic to make him believe that he loved her.

Clouding his thoughts.

Confusing him.

Putting him in a position where she could take advantage of him when the time was right.

It was certainly what she was known for.

And though he wouldn't put it past her, he didn't think she had.

At least not all the time.

At least some of the time they spent together was real ... he hoped.

"No, I won't ask."

"Why not?"

"I'd prefer to leave those memories in the past. The good and the bad."

Back then, Callie had been working for his father. She provided support on some of his more difficult assignments while performing other tasks for the King Teg that Draig wasn't supposed to know about.

They had worked well together. On the job and off it.

He hadn't gone into their relationship blind. He knew what she was capable of. What she had done in the past.

Yet with everything else that was going on in his life then, he didn't care. He needed to escape from the challenges and pressures of being the Dragon, and she helped him do that.

For a time.

Until their final mission together.

His father sent him to kill the Chessmaster. Callie was there to assist him.

She was to make sure their target didn't get away. Draig didn't realize until the very end that Callie had two targets that day.

The timing of the hit was good since they were already in Greece. It was just a matter of them making their way by boat to Vulcano, one of the Aeolian Islands. A trip of no more than a few hours from where they were staying.

Cy Polyphemus was on his father's hit list.

When Draig asked his father why, he hadn't received anything more than his usual response.

Cy was a threat to all the Teg. The Chessmaster had to go.

Feeling uncomfortable with the charge, Draig spoke with Merlin, seeking more information because his intensifying doubts about his father's decisions were dominating his thoughts.

When Merlin couldn't give him any additional data that

justified the kill order, Draig did what he believed was the right thing to do.

He got word to Cy, warning the Chessmaster to make himself scarce. The son of Poseidon had done just that, not needing to be told twice. Especially considering from whom the message came.

Cy didn't die when Draig and Callie made it to his island home.

Although Draig almost did.

Because though Callie couldn't complete her first mission with Cy in the wind, she could try to complete her second.

"You know I still love you, Draig. And I have no doubt you still love me."

Draig didn't reply right away, finding it hard to pull himself out of his memories.

His eyes were still locked onto Calypso's, the multicolored orbs flashing in the darkness more than just mesmerizing as he remembered what had happened when they reached Cy's small home with their target nowhere to be found.

"I love you, Draig. That's why I need to kill you."

That's what Callie told him when he turned back toward her after searching the immaculately kept villa. He had looked down at the glowing steel punched between his lower ribs.

The shock of Callie's betrayal numbed the pain.

She guided him down to the tile floor when his strength fled, his blood pooling around him. He had seen the truth about them in her eyes when she leaned over and kissed him one last time on the lips before she left him there to die.

But he hadn't died.

Because though Cy made himself scarce just as Draig had told him to do, he had forgotten his most prized possession. An item he couldn't live without. An item that was more important than his own life.

After hiding in the hills above his villa, waiting for Draig and Callie's boat to leave, Cy had returned to his home, wanting to grab his favorite chess set before he disappeared for good.

Instead, he found Draig and saved his life.

Just as Draig had saved his.

Draig had lost his lover, but he had gained a lifelong friend.

A fair trade, as he had learned over the years.

And during those years Draig had wondered about that last fateful encounter with Callie.

The Sorceress was skilled with a blade.

She had never failed to kill her target before.

Yet she had failed to kill him.

Had she made a mistake?

Or had she done the deed reluctantly, perhaps seeking to give him a little extra time to save himself if he could?

He didn't know. And he wasn't about to ask her.

Best to leave the past in the past. He needed to focus on his present.

"You think I still love you?" His tone was wistful, a little sad.

"I know you do," Callie replied. "Deny it all you want. I know the truth."

He didn't bother to. But he didn't want to continue down the road Callie had started them on. "And how is Morgase doing these last few days? I assume she's in a bad mood."

"That's an understatement," Callie murmured in a soft chuckle. "She is not pleased with you."

"I can't recall a time when she was pleased with me." Draig smiled knowingly. "She's still angry because I didn't die in the Chessmaster's villa."

"Among other reasons," she confirmed. "Those reasons seem to be piling up even faster these days. You have a knack for irritating her."

"And that's why you followed me here. Morgase sent you after me again."

"She did."

"To take me or kill me?"

"To kill you."

Draig nodded. That made sense.

Morgase wanted *The Book of Whispers* just as much as her brother did. During his last encounter with his aunt and uncle, they had learned that the artifact no longer was of use to either of them because of its link to Draig.

Yet even after that discovery, he doubted that either of them would accept their spanking and leave him be. He had assumed that Morgase would attempt to cut her losses, just as his father was doing with his kill order.

After experiencing the power that Draig could exercise thanks to the artifact, neither wanted to experience it again. Neither believed that they could appear weak. Beholden to another Teg. Even if it was the Dragon.

Thus, Morgase's desire to eliminate entirely the power accessible through *The Book of Whispers*.

There was only one way to do that.

She needed to eliminate the only Teg who could employ that power.

That meant Draig had to die.

"She still trusts you after the last time?"

Calypso nodded, although it was more feigned than real. "She wouldn't have sent me otherwise."

"And this time you're going to do the deed? Leave me dead here on the sand?"

She gave him a sad nod. "I love you, Draig. That's why I need to kill you."

He smiled, a melancholy creasing his usually grim countenance for just a heartbeat. The same words as she used last time.

Although this time he doubted she would demonstrate the mercy she did while they were still besotted with one another. If indeed it had been mercy.

"It was good to see you again, Callie," he said.

"It was good to see you too, Draig." She frowned, not understanding his bemused expression. "But you know how it is. Love is love. Business is business."

"I'm all too well aware," Draig confirmed with a nod.

Before Callie could say anything else, he was moving. While spinning around he used the Grym to craft a magical buckler that blocked the spikes of energy shot at him by the Warlock to his left.

He continued to move in that direction, wanting to put some space between himself and Callie, wary of the many daggers she carried on her. Some visible. Most not.

Draig ducked. A whip crafted of the Twisted Grym snapped just above his head.

Before the Warlock could pull it back, Draig reached out with a hand protected with the Grym and snatched the length out of the air, giving it a sharp tug.

The Warlock should have just released the power that he controlled. But he didn't. Doing so never crossed his mind. Worse, he wasn't ready.

Draig's action taking him by surprise, the Warlock stumbled a few feet forward and right onto Excalibur. The gleaming blade punched right through the man's gut and out his back.

Draig didn't have time to admire his handiwork. He turned swiftly, knocking away with his buckler the spear of energy thrown at him by another Warlock.

Then he turned again, ducking and shouldering into the Warlock who attempted to attack him from his blind side, magical short sword sliding innocuously through the space where Draig's neck had been just a second before.

Rising swiftly, Draig launched the stunned Warlock over his shoulder.

Perfect timing.

At exactly that instant, the Warlock so enamored with

spikes sent another swarm of missiles blasting from his palms and headed right toward Draig.

Draig didn't need to move. The Warlock tumbling over his shoulder proved to be an effective shield, absorbing the full brunt of the strike and dropping dead in the sand.

Draig grinned, pleased with his work. Two Warlocks removed from the fight in just a handful of seconds.

Yet when he scanned around him, the breakwater at his back, he realized that his work was far from done.

At the outbreak of the clash, Callie positioned herself toward the west. The only direction that Draig could go to make his escape unless he decided to test the waters of Delaware Bay.

The seven Warlocks who were still alive had set themselves in a semicircular pattern around him.

They had decided to wait before attacking him, unsettled by the ease with which he dispatched two of their number.

Draig had never known Warlocks to exercise such common sense. Even so, he understood that their hesitation wouldn't last for much longer. Not with Callie leading them.

He believed that he could manage seven Warlocks. He feared that if he attempted to do so, however, Callie would make a play for him while he was engaged.

Just as she preferred to do, attacking from the shadows.

Therefore, he decided to seize the initiative while he could.

Besides, he needed a little more space to do what he had planned.

With that in mind, he flicked his wrist. A spray of glowing orbs no larger than marbles shot out from his palm.

Ensuring that his left side was protected while the Warlocks defended themselves, or didn't, from the orbs he crafted of the Grym that burned right through flesh and bone, Draig advanced with a stunning speed on the three Warlocks positioned on his right.

Two skipped backward quickly rather than stand against him. The third, who glimpsed an opportunity with Draig charging toward his comrades, came at him from the side. Not realizing much too late that the opportunity presented to him actually was a trap.

Draig pivoted faster than humanly possible, Excalibur already slicing through the air and targeting the onrushing Warlock's neck.

The Warlock tried to defend himself, raising above his head the quarterstaff he had formed with the Twisted Grym to catch the glowing steel.

Just in time as well.

Unfortunately, the Dragon was a great deal stronger than he was, both physically and with the Power of the Ancients. Excalibur sliced right through the staff and then into the kneeling Warlock's collarbone, cutting down toward the man's lungs before Draig pulled his weapon free.

The Warlock stared in shock at his split staff, the energy powering it flickering and then fading away for good when he slumped to the ground to breathe his last.

Draig could have continued with his attack. The surviving Warlocks to his left had drifted back a good ten yards. And the two who danced away at Draig's initial advance had not rushed back into the fight, eyes still wide at how he had dispatched their friend so easily.

For just a breath, he considered finishing the Warlocks. He thought better of that idea only an instant later, catching Callie's cold expression and the seething anger just beneath.

He didn't fear taking on Calypso in a combat. However, he did fear being delayed.

Gliding away from her until the rocks of the seawall were at his back once more, he gave Callie a predatory smile followed by a wink.

Then he crouched down swiftly, smashing Excalibur's pommel onto the stone right by his foot.

A massive wave of blistering white energy erupted.

The blast was so bright that the resulting shadow at his back gave him exactly what he needed.

A path of escape.

Using the magic gifted to him by the Daemon King, he slid back into the darkness and disappeared, uninterested in the final conclusion of his work.

The blast was so powerful that the rush of air knocked several of the Warlocks from their feet.

To prevent being flung onto her back, Callie employed the Grym to craft a shield to her front.

"Draig!" she screamed when he disappeared in the shadow he created.

She gave up any thought of going after him, forced to remain behind her shield and turning away as she crouched down, hoping that her handiwork held.

Because the blast was so hot that the sand around Draig melted and reformed in a flash, long shards of glass shooting down the beach.

When the rush of heat and wind finally ended, Callie slowly pivoted back around. She released her hold on her shield only after she was certain that Draig was gone.

More frustrating, the magical trail that she followed to find him here was nowhere to be found.

Cut.

Nothing of his magical signature with which she was so familiar remained for her to grasp.

Not after what he had done to escape, the magic of his blast still pulsing up and down the beach and overwhelming any trail that might remain.

Closing her eyes for just a moment, she worked hard to

control her warring emotions. Most powerful was her anger. At Draig. At herself. But it would do her little good now.

When she opened her eyes again, she stared in disbelief at the sight that greeted her.

Her Warlocks were dead. The practitioners of the Twisted Grym lay broken and bleeding on the beach, those Draig hadn't killed before the explosion ripped apart by the thousands of shards of glowing glass that took shape thanks to the blast.

What was she going to do now?

Draig was in the wind once more.

She needed to ...

Her eyes widened as the realization struck the Sorceress.

She hadn't found Draig here.

He was too smart for that.

Draig had lured her here.

He had wanted this combat.

He had wanted this distraction.

But why?

She could think about that later.

A shiver of fear ran through her.

An uncomfortable feeling.

An uncommon one as well.

She had failed.

Twice now.

Thirteen of her Warlocks were dead as a result.

She shook her head, having a hard time believing that truism.

She never failed.

Ever.

Except when it came to Draig.

And if she couldn't find him again, she would need to make a decision.

Explain what happened to Morgase ...

Or run.

16

MOMENT OF TRUTH

The only good light came from the full moon that lit up the night in an ethereal glow. The few floodlights in the parking lot below the dune upon which the gun emplacement had been built did little to dispel the dark that draped itself over the decommissioned military base that served as the anchor to Cape Henlopen State Park.

Fort Miles.

A few of the concrete artillery observation fire towers that lined the shore west to the edge of Lewes and south down the coast to Rehoboth were visible just off in the distance, ghostly silent sentinels still standing strong. The lookouts stationed atop the towers during World War II hunted for any sign of the U-boats that preyed on shipping along the Atlantic Coast, ready to relay that information to the gun batteries centered around the fort.

Several of the old guns used during that time sat dormant below what had been the largest bunker. The National Park Service had turned the emplacement into a museum. And it was in front of those doors that Melissa stood now, the Three Brothers right beside her.

She was anxious, which was an unusual feeling for her. She had been on more jobs than she could remember that required her to put her life at risk, yet she had approached them without the twinge of a single nerve upsetting her.

This job was different, however, so her unease was understandable. On this job she wasn't risking just her own life. She was risking her mother's as well.

"I'm sorry," Melissa said. "I never thanked you for what you did for me at the Safe Haven or earlier today at the Dairy Queen."

"We were happy to help," Tom nodded.

"Thanks to you, we get to test our skills against Teg we rarely have the chance to encounter," Harry added, "which is saying something considering our line of work."

Melissa laughed softly at that. She couldn't dispute Harry's claim.

Warlocks.

Trolls.

And Vipers before the Trolls.

All in a matter of days.

"Aren't you coming in?" she asked after taking a few steps toward the main door, realizing that neither of the brothers took a step to follow her.

"No, we can't," Tom answered apologetically. "Typhon was very specific. We were to bring you to the door but take you no further."

"Don't worry, though," Harry said, hoping his voice helped to buttress Melissa's flagging confidence. "We'll be close."

She nodded. Disappointed. Not surprised.

She could have used a couple allies with her for what she needed to do next. But that would have been unfair of her. This wasn't their fight.

"You don't think he'll meet his end of the bargain?" Melissa already knew the answer to her question. Still, she felt the need to ask it.

The Three Brothers shook their heads no in unison.

"You think Typhon will try something?"

"Without a doubt." Again the Three Brothers replied in unison.

She nodded again. She expected as much.

Yet there was nothing for it now. She had played the game deep into the late innings. Now she needed to find out if she could close it.

Melissa walked up to the main door and grasped the handle, pulling back. Unlocked. Just as she had been told it would be.

Before she stepped inside, she looked back over her shoulder. "Did Draig put you up to this? Watching over me as I made my way here."

"Be smart," Tom said with a mysterious smile.

"Be careful," Harry added.

Neither answered her question.

With a slight nod and a nervous smile, she stepped into the shadows of what had once been a bunker but was now the Fort Miles Museum.

Melissa wasn't much of a history buff, and she didn't have the time to explore her new surroundings. Taking a deep breath with the hope of gaining a little more control over her anxiety, she strode down the main hallway, ignoring the counter on her left and the pictures and other memorabilia hanging from the wall that marked a different era when the distinction between good and evil was crystal clear.

Following the instructions given to her, she walked into a conference space at the end of the hallway. The glass doors along the far wall allowed her to look out on a concrete deck set with rows of chairs and a lectern at the far end.

She gave it no more than a fleeting glance, having eyes only for the circle burnt into the floor. Various runes and sigils that she couldn't make out clearly in the gloom marked the boundary of the portal.

Understanding that time was short, she stepped across the charred lines. Setting herself in the portal, she whispered the incantation the monster she was supposed to meet made her memorize.

Upon uttering the very last syllable, the space within the circle glowed with an unearthly light, becoming brighter and brighter until Melissa had no choice but to close her eyes.

For just a few seconds she felt as if she were moving. A strange sensation since her feet were rooted to the concrete.

When the light that flashed through her eyelids dimmed to a manageable level, she opened her eyes.

Melissa hadn't known what to expect, but certainly not this.

It looked like she had entered the Hall of Hades, or at least what she imagined Hades' sanctuary might look like. Behind her, streams of lava flowed through wide rivulets cut into the rock, following an indecipherable pattern toward the far side of the vast rough-hewn chamber. Sheets of steam blasted into the air where the magma met the handful of small waterfalls that flowed down the far wall.

Through those clouds of steam she could just make out what appeared to be a black granite throne that shot up out of the ground. It was too large even for one of the Berserkers to sit in. If Ragnar or one of his brothers tried, they would look like a child, feet swinging off the edge.

Just above the throne, stalactites reached down, points sharpened to a razor's edge. The display reminded her of the fangs of a Viper.

Having no desire to walk deeper into the cavern yet having no other choice, she stepped out of the portal and steeled herself for the negotiation that would decide whether she and her mother lived or died.

"You're cutting it close, Witch. The sand in the hourglass is in the last hour."

The deep, rumbling voice that greeted her out of the gloom sounded like an earthquake and sent a bolt of fear straight through her heart.

17

COLLEGE VISIT

"Do you know where she is?" Mordred demanded in a plaintive voice.

He had arrived in Williamsburg a few hours before with his mother. Starting at the girl's small house on Lafayette Street and finding it empty, they continued their search on the William and Mary campus with a hundred Paladins in tow.

Mordred was dressed like one of his soldiers. Two short swords were strapped to his back and black tactical gear allowed him to blend more effectively into the darkness. The use of the Grym strengthened the illusion, ensuring that anyone passing by saw nothing more than a shadow a bit darker than the many other shadows of the night that smothered the very dark grounds of the second oldest institution of higher learning in the United States. Although the dim glow of the lampposts could be seen every so often on the walkways that wound through the college, they did little to dispel the darkness.

Morgase ignored her son's question for a few seconds more. Her thoughts were on the challenge that they had set for themselves.

She had given Calypso and her Warlocks the task of finding Draig. Then, assuming they did, because that was far from a given, killing him.

Not an easy assignment as she well knew, which was why Morgase was worried. She wouldn't be surprised if the Dragon evaded the Sorceress, in large part because of the history between the two. Calypso's failure to kill the Dragon the first time Morgase gave the Sorceress that same responsibility not filling her with much confidence.

Thus, Morgase's decision to put an alternate plan in place and jab at Draig's weakest point with the hope of gaining some leverage just to be safe.

If she could capture Draig's daughter, then she would be able to exercise more influence over him if he survived Calypso. Even though she couldn't make use of *The Book of Whispers* herself, she could compel him to use the power offered by the most potent artifact ever crafted by a Teg for her own purposes. Almost as if she were exercising that power herself. Not the optimal solution but a solution, nonetheless.

Admittedly, an approach with more complications and the potential for a great many mishaps. Still, an approach worth pursuing with all that was at stake.

And if Calypso succeeded in killing Draig, then Morgase still would make use of the daughter, because the girl employed a unique power of her own that also could prove quite beneficial to her efforts to seize the Teg throne from Arthur.

"You asked me that just a few minutes ago, Mordred. Why do you believe I would have the answer for you now when I didn't then?"

A sharper reply was on the tip of her tongue, Morgase wanting nothing more than to snap back at her son. She restrained herself, however. The resulting argument only would slow down their hunt.

Mordred was not himself. He hadn't been, in fact, since his latest confrontation with his half-brother.

Although it wasn't really a confrontation with the Dragon, now was it?

It was a combat. A very one-sided combat at that.

The Dragon had beaten Mordred.

Again.

Badly.

With an embarrassing ease.

Confirming once again that the man who viewed himself as the true successor to Arthur Pendragon's throne -- once Morgase obtained it for herself, of course, and then deigned to relinquish it to her progeny when she deemed the time right -- was no match for the Dragon.

Worse, Draig could have killed Mordred during their last encounter.

Several times, in fact.

However, for reasons of his own he had chosen not to.

Instead, he ensured that Mordred wallowed in the shame of his defeat, which was likely a more painful outcome than a sharp and bloody end.

Mortifying.

Mostly for her son, but for her as well.

More than that actually as Morgase thought about that sad defeat a little more.

Degrading.

Draig was a half-breed.

Her son was a pure Teg.

Yet the mongrel had defeated the pure breed just as he had done every other time Mordred challenged him.

And it was always Mordred challenging Draig, not the other way around. It was almost as if her son required a beating every so often. As if he had grown used to it and couldn't go without a good shellacking now and then.

Morgase rolled her eyes and shook her head ever so slightly.

She couldn't allow this to continue.

The Queen Teg needed to appear strong at all times. As did all those by her side.

Weakness could not be tolerated.

Especially not within her own son. For his failures reflected poorly upon her.

"This has to work," he pleaded. "It has to."

Morgase sighed heavily. Never believing that she would ever need to hope this, but still she did.

She hoped that Mordred regained the confidence that was so much a part of his personality and so frequently drifted into the realm of arrogance. Because the frailty he radiated now made her clench her teeth in disgust.

It was woeful.

Sickening.

Unbecoming of a child of the strongest Sorceress of the Teg.

"It will," she promised him.

At the same time the stray thought that kept gaining more of a foothold in her mind returned.

Could she trust Mordred to do what was required?

Much depended on him.

And seeing him now …

She didn't know.

Morgase let that distracting thought go for the moment, lifting her head past the Wren Building and toward Colonial Williamsburg, which was just on the other side of the V-shaped intersection that linked Richmond Road to Jamestown Road.

One of the Paladins had just reached out to her through the Grym.

"Come on," Morgase said, striding deeper into the darkness. "She's been sighted."

~

"WE ARE STANDING BEFORE ARGUABLY the most haunted house in the United States. Built in 1715 by William Robertson and purchased by Sir John Randolph in 1721, this original house in Colonial Williamsburg is plagued by a host of ghostly sightings and supernatural perils. Noises. Voices. Objects moving. Otherworldly breaths in the ear and touches on the arm. In fact, with the witching hour almost upon us, most tour guides won't stand as close to the home as we are right now."

Kassie gave the twenty people in her tour group a devilish smile as she held the colonial-style lantern closer to her face. "And don't even think about entering the home after the sun has set. At least not on your own. Why?"

She waited a few seconds to allow the tension to build, every eye fixed upon her. "Because here on this very ground more than thirty people have died – adults and children – because of accidents, strange illnesses, and ... murder. And many of those people remain in the house and on the surrounding property, their spirits unable to gain the peace they desire."

"That's not strange, though. It's an old house. You just said so. Of course people have died in it. So what's the big deal?" a cracking voice interrupted.

Kassie turned toward the voice. A teenager. The acne on his cheeks and the all-knowing sneer confirmed it for her. "You're right. I won't deny it." She stepped closer to the young man. "It only stands to reason, doesn't it? However, there's more to my claims than just words. Real evidence supports all that I've said."

The teenager scoffed. "Evidence of ghosts? I don't think so. And don't tell me your evidence comes from one of those TV shows where they chase after the spirits of the night. That's all made up."

"Not that, no," Kassie replied. "Eyewitness experiences from people we can trust."

"Really?" the teenager snorted in disbelief. "Who would that be?"

"The Marquis de Lafayette, one of the heroes of the American Revolution, for one. He wrote about it in his diary." Kassie spun around slowly, pleased to see that every eye remained locked onto her, even those of the skeptical teenager. "And I quote, 'Upon my arrival, as I entered through the foyer, I felt a hand on my shoulder. It nudged me as if intending to keep me from entering. I quickly turned, but found no one there. The nights were not restful as the sounds of voices kept me awake for most of my stay.'"

"That's real?" the teenager frowned. "You're not just making it up?"

"You can look it up," Kassie said. "I should note as well that the hauntings are not limited to the house. The tree right over there is said to be haunted because a young boy climbing it fell to his death ... or was pushed by a mysterious force. The true cause has never been discovered."

Several of the people on the tour glanced quickly at the tree just over their shoulder that was barely visible in the dark before returning their wide-eyed gazes back toward Kassie. Several who stood on the outer edges of the group took a few steps closer to their peers, not wanting to be so far away from human contact.

A heartbeat later, the teenager shrieked, stumbling back into the older couple standing behind him. That set off a chain reaction. Everyone moved away from the teenager, even his parents, while at the same time those wide eyes, now a touch fearful, scanned around them, seeking and failing to penetrate the surrounding darkness. The only point of safety was the small lantern that Kassie carried.

"It touched me! It touched me!" The teenager spun around,

looking for something that wasn't there. "A hand. A hand gripped my shoulder and shoved me."

Kassie smiled, ignoring him. "And I should have said hauntings here are not limited to the home and its grounds. Participants on this tour faint regularly when they reach this point or experience other ... just as unexplainable events." She waited almost a minute to let that sink in, enjoying how the sense of trepidation built quickly within the small group, the teenager the worst of the lot, as the silence deepened. Even the crickets deciding to go quiet.

"Now if you'll follow me," she said, giving the teenager a wicked smile as she walked by him. "We'll head back the way we came."

All of the tour's participants followed closely behind her, including the teenager who no longer doubted the existence of ghosts and threatened to flatfoot her because of his fear.

Kassie enjoyed leading these tours. She earned a little extra spending money and, as had just been demonstrated, they offered some unexpected fun from time to time.

Although her other side business, providing certain services to the Teg, was a great deal more lucrative, it was also a lot more serious and potentially lethal.

She stopped a few more times along the way and offered some fast facts as she led the tour back down Duke of Gloucester Street and toward the Merchant's Square, the lack of lighting only adding to the frightening ambiance that had settled over the group after the teenager's supernatural encounter.

"This ends tonight's tour." She stood in front of Bruton Parish Episcopal Church. "I hope you enjoyed it as much as I did." She stared pointedly at the stunned teenager who was still shaking slightly. "The only words of wisdom I can offer you is that when it comes to what you cannot see, better to believe than not."

After a long round of applause and several murmured thanks, as well as a few tips, once the tour participants had disappeared Kassie shifted her focus to the graveyard on the church grounds.

"You can step out of the shadows, Aleck. No point in continuing to hide away."

She gave him a raised eyebrow when he emerged from the gloom at the back of the small cemetery and joined her on Duke of Gloucester Street. The red tinge on his cheeks revealed his embarrassment at being discovered. "How long did you know?"

"As soon as you started tracking me at the Governor's Palace."

He shook his head in anger. At himself.

He should have done a better job of following her. No, actually that wasn't the right way to look at his failure.

He should have assumed that Kassie would know that he was there. It would have saved him some of the discomfiture he felt now.

"I take it you had a hand in what happened in front of the Randoph House?"

Aleck shrugged. "Well, it wasn't my hand ..."

"Aleck ..."

"Right, sorry." He smiled, clearly pleased with himself. "I may have asked one of the spirits to offer a helping hand to prove what you were saying."

Kassie didn't respond right away, giving Aleck a hard look, not enjoying what he likely perceived as dry wit that from her perspective only masqueraded as a bad pun.

They had been friends for a long time. Ever since they came to William and Mary and lived in the same dorm during their first year as undergraduates.

Their academic interests and their unique skills as

members of the Tylwyth Teg had pulled them in different directions.

Yet still they felt a bond after some of their more harrowing experiences when they were younger.

A bond that continued to pull on them now.

A bond that Aleck valued.

A bond that Kassie continued to struggle against.

She knew that it would be easy to give in. There were times when Kassie wanted to give in. More times than she cared to acknowledge, in fact.

Aleck worried her, however, and in a way that most people would not understand. Except perhaps for her father. And there was no way she was going to talk to him about that topic. Not yet anyway. Not until she was certain her father wouldn't knock some sense into Aleck with his blackthorn shillelagh.

"Thank you," she said, a broad smile replacing the frown after she believed that she had made her point. "Perfect timing."

Aleck smiled, relieved. "I'll relay that to the spirit. She'll be quite pleased to hear it."

"Now tell me why you're here."

Not a question. Aleck nodded knowingly. It was never a question with Kassie unless she had no other choice. It was simply an expectation on her part of a response.

So he hesitated. Then waited some more. Understanding that any delay irritated her.

Kassie's eyes narrowing confirmed it for him. Although he didn't wait long enough for her to give her temper free reign, the brunt of which he had experienced more times than he cared to remember.

Aleck shrugged, trying to make it seem like his answer wasn't a big deal, though he didn't doubt that it would be. "I promised your father that I'd keep an eye on you."

"Really?" Kassie snorted. "An eye on me?"

She should have been angrier than she was. In the past she would have viewed her father's request as an invasion of her privacy. But now, understanding what was at stake within the Teg world?

She wasn't angry. Rather, she was pleased that her father was looking out for her. Though Aleck didn't need to know that. And she would be speaking with her father so that he understood that if he felt the need to do something for her they needed to talk first because she was more than capable of taking care of herself.

"That's what he asked."

Kassie offered him a raised eyebrow. Her turn to make a point. "Do you believe I need someone to look after me?"

Aleck didn't miss the trap she had just set for him, and he had absolutely no intention of becoming ensnared. "No, of course not. But we could all use an extra set of eyes on occasion."

Instead of being angry with him, as Aleck assumed she would be, Kassie laughed softly, amused. She knew that Aleck was interested in her. He had been since their freshman year.

She also knew that if her father asked Aleck to keep an eye out for her, he would have sensed that and likely wouldn't be happy. Yet still her father had made the request. That got her thinking. "You sure that it was my father? The guy with the reddish-orange eyes and the bad temper?"

"He was concerned about you," Aleck explained. "And it's not like I was going to say no to him, considering who your father is." He shrugged again. "I was concerned as well."

"You were concerned about me?" Kassie's tone suggested that he didn't need to be.

"Only because your father is concerned about you. I figured that if he was worried about you ..." Aleck left the rest unsaid, having learned that it was better not to say too much when speaking with Kassie about certain matters that in the past had aggravated her. He breathed easier when she dropped her initial inquiry.

"You joined the tour tonight."

"I did," Aleck confirmed.

"You're worried."

Aleck sighed. She hadn't dropped her inquiry. She had decided to come at him from a different direction. Typical. With her personality, a dogged and relentless determination one of her key characteristics, he always thought that Kassie should have gone to law school rather than pursuing her doctorate in history and mythology.

"Not worried," he replied cautiously, curious as to where she was going to go next. "More concerned." He hoped that she recognized the distinction between the two, slight though it may be.

"Spill it, Aleck. You've never been good about keeping things from me. Even things that you should keep from me."

Aleck frowned. He hated how she could read him so well. Hated as well that she was right. "I'm sorry, I just didn't want to upset you."

"Aleck ..." Kassie's temper, which was much like her father's, built swiftly.

"At least not until I needed to. Not until I was certain."

"What's going on?"

"Why don't we head back to my place?"

"Aleck, we talked about this. After what happened the last time, we shouldn't ..."

"Could you please get your mind out of the gutter," Aleck growled, though he said it with a smile which she returned after a few seconds passed. Thankfully, she fell into step beside him as he walked back toward the Capitol and away from the William and Mary campus.

"I wasn't ..."

"I know you weren't. Sorry, couldn't resist. I'm trying to get you to the safest place I know."

"What's going on?"

"I got word from several of the ghosts on campus."

"About what?"

"Scores of men searching the college."

Kassie thought about that, frowning. If that were true, such an occurrence would have captured many unwanted eyes. Then again, maybe not.

It was close to midnight and most of the students were away on Fall Break. The campus would be dead, in a manner of speaking. And if these visitors were using the Grym to cloak themselves ...

"What did they look like?"

"Black tactical gear. Maces and short swords strapped to their backs. The ghosts they passed by said they could sense the Grym in the steel as well as around the hunters, so they're attempting to hide themselves."

"Paladins."

"My thought exactly."

Reaching Spotswood Street, they turned left. From there, a quick right onto West Nicholson Street, past the Compton Oak, and then they would be safe behind the wards of Aleck's home that was hidden beneath the Peyton Randolph House.

Most people, Teg included, preferred to stay away from spirits. But when you could communicate with spirits, and often felt more comfortable with the spirits than in the company of other Teg, Aleck's unique living arrangement made a great deal of sense.

"Thank you," Kassie said as she hustled beside Aleck.

"For what? I haven't done anything yet."

"Because you cared enough to get involved. You didn't have to. Knowing who we're dealing with. Most other Teg would have steered clear."

Aleck blushed at the comment, thankful that his red cheeks were invisible in the gloom. Not knowing what to say, he scanned around them quickly.

He stopped abruptly, reaching out and grabbing Kassie's arm before she could take a step beyond him.

"What's the matter?" she whispered, although she already had a sense of what it likely was.

Aleck didn't say anything, instead nodding toward his home that was just a hundred yards farther down the street.

Shadows flickered on the street.

Shadows within the shadows that didn't belong there.

Likely Teg hidden by the Grym.

His fear was confirmed just a few seconds later by the spirits that Aleck connected to with the Power of the Ancients.

"What do we do?" Kassie asked.

"The goal remains the same," Aleck replied.

Kassie's eyes widened slightly as she watched the transformation come over him. Usually quiet and unassuming, Aleck had a shy way about him that always had appealed to her. Ever since the first day they met.

The strong and silent type.

Her type.

She had been able to resist him ... for the most part ... off and on.

But now, the silent part of his personality fading away and the strong part intensifying, gaining dominance, sent a subtle charge of electricity through her, reminding her of her attraction to him.

"Back to your place?"

"Yes."

A glow caught her eye. When Kassie looked down, she saw that Aleck held a dagger in each hand. A curved shining blade a foot in length stuck out from each end of the grip.

"Are you sure about this?" She interpreted what he

intended to do from the deadness of his eyes. They were flinty now. As sharp as the blades he held.

Aleck nodded. "They know we're here. Instead of waiting for them to find us, I think it's time to say hello. Come on."

He trotted toward the group of Paladins standing near the base of the Compton Oak, Kassie right behind him. She wondered if this was how her father felt – adrenaline surging through her, senses sharp, the world around her clearer, more alive – right before a battle.

"Any other great ideas?" Kassie asked as she sent a fireball crafted of the Grym toward the three Paladins sprinting down East Nicholson Street toward her and Aleck.

The Paladin in the lead couldn't miss what shot his way. He tried to stop abruptly, sliding across the slick pavement instead. Unable to keep his feet, he ended up on his ass.

His clumsiness saved him from taking the brunt of the strike, the power screaming right above him. Singeing him. Burning off a large swathe of the hair from his scalp and leaving a reverse mohawk in its wake along with angry scalded flesh.

His two compatriots weren't so lucky. They didn't see the attack in time. Their views blocked by their comrade, they suffered the full impact of the blow. The energy smashed into them with bone-crunching effect, the Paladins flying backward twenty yards farther down the street. Landing badly. Unmoving. Definitely broken. Maybe dead.

Yet despite her small victory, she and Aleck still faced dire straits.

Aleck enjoyed some early success against the Paladins as well.

Before the men loyal to Morgase and Mordred even knew

that they were under attack, he had maimed two of them. Quick, precise swipes of his blades across the back of their legs, severing a hamstring and then an Achilles tendon, ensured that they were done with the fight before it even really began.

He removed two more while he was in among the black-clad soldiers. The large number of Paladins attacking him hampered their efforts more than anything that he was doing as he ducked, dodged, cut, and slashed. Not seeking to kill. Not unless he didn't have any other choice.

Kassie had given him a few seconds of breathing room when she fired a few blasts of the Grym into the midst of the Paladins. That shock attack allowed him to step back and set himself alongside her.

But her efforts weren't enough.

There were too many Paladins, and they were coming too quickly.

Their path blocked, Kassie and Aleck's only choice was to carve out a space beneath the massive Compton Oak, using the tree's monstrous branches that spread out close to the ground to protect their backs and their flanks.

A good decision against so many opponents. A limiting one as well.

Because they had nowhere to go. The safety of Aleck's home, a mere fifty yards away, seemed no more than a faint hope now.

Aleck surged forward.

One of the Paladins to his front overextended. The soldier, who stood a head taller than Aleck, swung down with his mace, making the bad decision to try to brain him even though Aleck clearly was much faster than he was.

That fact was confirmed when Aleck smashed the hilt of his dagger across the Paladin's jaw. Likely breaking it. Definitely knocking him out.

Even better, when the Paladin dropped to the ground like a

puppet off his strings, he took two more Paladins with him, his body getting tangled with their legs.

For just an instant, Aleck considered killing the two men while they were trapped beneath their injured friend.

The thought didn't stay with him, however. He didn't want to provide the Paladins on either side of the scrum with the chance to come at Kassie from either flank. He didn't want to disrupt her since she was using the Grym quite effectively to keep the mass of Paladins around them from doing anything more than feint and then flee backward. Most of them preferring to be cautious rather than play at hero.

"You're not going to like it," he grunted at the same time he caught a Paladin's mace with his daggers crossed above his head.

Holding the weapon in place as the man tried to push Aleck's arms down, the Paladin's eyes widened upon realizing that the Teg engaging him was stronger than he was.

Aleck used his adversary's surprise against him.

Bringing his knee up swiftly, the Paladin grunted first in shock and then soul-crushing pain, his knees coming together slightly when that first wave of agony swept through him, starting in his groin and then rushing out to his extremities. Black spots appeared at the edge of the Paladin's vision when Aleck brought his knee up again. Those spots became a hazy cloud the third time Aleck rang.

Barely conscious, the man's eyes rolled into the back of his head as he choked out a gasp and fell to the ground, his hands grasping at his damaged and aching groin, all thoughts of the fight fleeing him.

"Try me," Kassie ordered.

Aleck smiled as he stepped back closer to Kassie. Another command from her. Not a question. Even now when they were fighting for their lives.

"You're going to make a run for it."

"What in all the hells are you talking about?" Kassie demanded.

With a quick flick of her wrists, sparks of energy shot from her palms. For the next few seconds, the space in front of her resembled a small fireworks display.

The Paladins turned away to protect their eyes. A few even danced backward, the sparks touching their armor setting it on fire and scorching any unprotected flesh.

Three of the men sprinted away from their peers and then dropped to the ground, rolling in the dirt and grass before the sparks had a chance to burst into flames.

"You're their target," Aleck said as if it was obvious. "Not me."

"I'm well aware. What's your point?"

Both Aleck and Kassie held their ground as the Paladins stepped back a few feet. A temporary truce that both sides welcomed.

"I don't matter."

"You don't matter?" Kassie scoffed. "What do you mean ...?"

"Think, Kassie," Aleck replied in a sharp tone that he rarely used with her, yet when he did it was always for a good reason. As a result, Kassie almost always listened to him.

"You're going to take all these shitheads on by yourself?"

"If I have to," he shrugged. "You need to get away."

"I will *not* leave you," Kassie said with a hard determination. "We're in this together."

"Instead of focusing on what's right in front of us, focus on what's coming toward us. Why do you think these Paladins stopped attacking us?"

Kassie's initial thought was to offer Aleck a flippant response about their remarkable skills as fighters. She didn't.

Aleck didn't act this way unless he believed that there was a need to do so. And he raised an excellent point.

The Paladins were less interested in attacking them and more interested in keeping them in place.

On the one hand, that was a good thing. It gave them a chance to recover and prepare for the next round. On the other hand, that was a bad thing, because the Paladins only would be hesitating for one reason.

She identified that reason just a second later when she searched around them with the Grym.

"You understand now?"

"I do," Kassie grumbled, hating the fact that he had caught what she had missed.

She had believed that they stood a good chance of maintaining their defense against the Paladins and perhaps even slipping past them and gaining the safety of Aleck's home if they could force a mistake from their attackers.

But not now.

Not with Morgase about to join them on the battlefield.

She'd be there in only a few minutes. Even with Aleck's unique abilities and her strength in the Grym, they stood little chance against her aunt. She was too strong and too vindictive.

"When I tell you to go, you go." His tone was gentle but unyielding.

"Aleck ..."

He cut her off, his voice harder than the oak at his back. "When I tell you to go, you go. Please."

"And where am I supposed to go?" she sighed in frustration, having a great deal more to say to Aleck but understanding that now wasn't the time. "There are too many Paladins. Even if I get out from beneath the tree, they'll be after me quickly."

"Leave that problem to me. Just follow your guide. She'll get you somewhere safer than here."

"My guide?"

Kassie understood in a flash when a spectral figure took shape just behind her shoulder. She appeared to be no more than a young girl. Her essence was misty, distinct then not. There but not there.

The spirit smiled and Kassie smiled back. Clearly, her guide was looking forward to the game to come.

"Follow Clarabeth. She'll get you out of here."

"And what are you going to do?" Kassie demanded, irritation mixed with guilt creeping into her voice along with a deep-seated concern that bordered on ... Kassie chose not to think on that. She knew what Aleck was offering her. Though she appreciated it, she didn't like it. "A heroic last stand?"

Kassie shook her head as her annoyance increased. At herself for allowing so much venom into her voice. She had never understood why men felt the need to risk themselves when they didn't have to. It was such an archaic concept and one that she didn't believe was necessary.

Yet in this instance, Paladins penning them in, the greatest Sorceress of the Teg about to appear, she had no chance if Aleck didn't take that risk. Because he was right. She understood what would happen if Morgase got her claws into her.

What really got her goat was that he was more than willing to do it.

For her.

Despite all the baggage between them.

"No, not that if I can avoid it. But I am going to have a little fun before your aunt gets here."

Aleck turned away from her then, a menacing grin now gracing his flinty features. Setting his feet, he held his hands out to the sides, glowing daggers still gripped strongly between his fingers.

A wispy grey mist trickled out from his palms. That trickle intensified quickly. Becoming a steady flow and then a deluge, the wispy grey thickened into a musty fog that smelled like an open crypt as it spread out swiftly from where he stood at the base of the Compton Oak.

And with the fog came something else.

Or rather someones.

The spirits of the dead.

Dozens of them.

Men. Women. Children.

Called from their nightly wanderings.

Called from their graves.

All of them eager to once again feel the touch of warm flesh.

All of them willing to assist the Teg known in the Spirit World as the Lord of Whispers.

"Go!" Aleck urged when Kassie was no more than a shadow next to him.

Then he was gone, sprinting through the fog, racing toward the Paladins, joining the spirits who were a few steps ahead of him.

18

THE NEXT ACT

"Where are you taking me?" Kassie sprinted after Clarabeth, her spirit guide drifting swiftly just above the cobblestone paths that wound their way through the William and Mary campus.

Clarabeth didn't reply. Instead she motioned with her hand for Kassie to stay with her, the spirit's dark eyes promising that they were close.

Kassie growled in frustration.

She felt like she was abandoning Aleck, knowing all the while and hating the fact that he was right and she had no choice.

Aleck could speak with ghosts. She couldn't.

The fog billowing up around them, the spirits answering Aleck's call, he charging at the Paladins like a damned warrior of lore, while Kassie followed Clarabeth over and around the large tree limbs that threatened to touch the ground until they broke out from beneath the massive oak.

The Market Square greeted her. Thankfully, it was covered in a thick gloom thanks to the grasping grey.

Kassie had shivered at Clarabeth's light touch, the spirit

nodding in the direction that they needed to go. Past the court-house and back toward the college.

After that, all Kassie worried about was staying as close to her guide as she could.

The fog didn't start to clear until they were well past the Wren Building and beyond the Sunken Garden, the Paladins late to the fight completely unaware of their presence as they raced silently in the other direction.

When they reached the far side of the campus and were on the backside of the School of Business, Kassie thought Clara-beth's ultimate goal was the woods around Matoaka Lake. Certainly an excellent place to hide, and she knew the trails there quite well thanks to her daily wanderings.

Yet Clarabeth didn't stop once they were within the wood. She continued along the trail behind the business school until they reached the Briggs Amphitheatre, the lake behind her and the woods all around.

"Why here?" Kassie asked.

Clarabeth didn't reply. She did offer Kassie a cunning smile with a hint of menace in her gaze. Then, just as quickly as she appeared, the spirit faded away.

"What the ..."

Kassie's words got caught in her throat when she heard the voice coming from the trail and drawing closer to the amphitheater.

"There is nowhere for you to run, rabbit. Nowhere to hide."

A shiver of fear swept through Kassie as she stood on the stage, the only protection the darkness that surrounded her.

Yet even that was failing. An ethereal light that mimicked the dusk illuminated the space around her.

In the dim glow, Kassie caught the movement in the trees on each side of the outdoor theater. Preferring to keep her distance as the voice gained shape at the top of the steps that led down past the benches to the stage, she stepped back a few feet into what little shadow remained. All the while she knew that it was wasted effort.

Why did Clarabeth take her here?

To offer her up like a sacrifice?

This didn't make sense. Kassie was certain that the spirit was seeking to aid her escape. Aleck wouldn't have requested her assistance otherwise.

And perhaps the spirit was.

Perhaps it was just a matter of her pursuer being too strong in the Grym.

And because of that Kassie was trapped.

Her hunter had found her. Quickly at that.

Really not all that surprising considering who her hunter was.

Morgase materialized out of the gloom, striding imperiously down the steps. Her son was at her back, and behind him came a host of Paladins who spread out across the first few rows of the theater. Ensuring that Kassie had nowhere to go if she sought to escape the snare except into the lake at her back.

"What did you do to Aleck?" Kassie demanded.

"I didn't do anything to that pest," Morgase replied with a snort of derision. "The ghost whisperer isn't worth my time."

Kassie didn't believe that Morgase was lying. If the Sorceress had gotten to Aleck, then she would have used him against her.

Aleck was smart and quite skilled in the Grym. Perhaps not strong enough to challenge Morgase directly, but his unique abilities certainly would allow him to stay free of the Sorceress' clutches, assuming he could extract himself from the Paladins.

"And I am?"

"For more reasons than you know, my dear. Now come along." Morgase motioned for her to step off the stage, a squad of Paladins marching down the steps to take her into custody.

"You've had your fun. Best not to irritate me any more than you already have."

"You don't scare me," Kassie replied, grimacing at what was a very unoriginal response. She should have done better and offered more of a threat than weak bluster that lacked conviction, but she was more flustered than she cared to admit.

"You should be scared, my dear. I thought that you were smarter. More clever. My mistake in that regard. Or perhaps it's just the fear talking."

"I am not afraid of you."

"You are afraid of me, child, because you are not a fool. Even more, I can smell the fear coming off you." Morgase chuckled softly. "Still, I will give you some credit. You are definitely your father's daughter. An ingrained defiance even when you know in your heart that it would be better just to acquiesce."

"That's not all I gained from him."

"Really," Morgase said, a flicker of amusement in her tone that was more heavily weighted toward annoyance. "What else might that be? A disrespect for your betters?"

Kassie smiled then, thanking Clarabeth silently. "Knowing when a few seconds of delay will prove useful."

"You dare to attack my daughter?" The harsh, brittle voice preceded the raven-haired woman who glided out of the shadows at the back of the stage.

The Morrigan.

Riga came to stand next to her daughter. The resemblance unmistakable. Both stared at the Sorceress. Riga with the cold determination of a veteran warrior. Kassie trying to mimic her mother as best as she could despite her lack of experience.

At the same time, a series of loud squawks rang out. Several ravens alighted atop the stage and gazed down with cold eyes at the soldiers gathered below.

"And you dare to stand in my way, Battle Goddess?" Morgase asked.

The Morrigan replied in kind. "When it comes to my daughter, Sorceress, I dare anything."

Morgase studied the woman who opposed her. Beautiful in a dark sort of way, the scent of death followed her.

She knew of the Morrigan all too well. Although she did not know her well.

The Morrigan preferred to be on her own. She only interacted with the Teg when she deemed it necessary then retreated to wherever it was she hid away.

Though Morgase didn't know the Morrigan well, she did know of her power. And clearly the Battle Goddess seemed to have little concern about facing off against her, the Morrigan's disdainful look suggesting that she was less than impressed by the Sorceress.

"We mean her no harm, Morrigan," Morgase explained. "We simply wish to work with her. Once the girl does what I ask her to do, she will be free to go."

"I'm supposed to believe that?" Riga scoffed, nodding toward the soldiers to her front. "Your words do not match your actions. Several hundred of your Paladins seek to kidnap my daughter in the middle of the night and you expect me to step aside?"

"I expect that you will do what you believe must be done. But I warn you that you do not want to challenge me. I am playing nicely now. I will not if you push me too far. After just dealing with your former lover, I have little patience left in me."

The Morrigan laughed throatily at that, clearly pleased by Morgase's admission. "Did the Dragon take a bite out of you again?"

"The Dragon wouldn't dare," Morgase hissed.

The Morrigan laughed even harder. "Dare he would. Yet he would do more than just dare. He would do." She caught

Mordred's scowl, Morgase's son standing a few feet behind her. "Not you, not yet. Not until he must." The Morrigan nodded her head sagely. "Mordred instead. Why am I not surprised?"

"He did not ..." Mordred began to protest, his face swiftly turning red.

"That's a lesson for you, Kassandra," Riga said, turning toward her daughter, "and one that Mordred has yet to learn. Poke the Dragon and you get his claws."

"You would think he would learn by now," Kassie replied, enjoying how her mother had irritated Mordred with such ease and more than willing to pile on.

"Indeed. But there are some who simply refuse to learn."

"Draig did not defeat me," Mordred almost screamed, spitting out the words.

"Tell yourself whatever you need to if it gets you through your humiliation," the Morrigan replied with another sharp laugh that sounded like the caw of a raven. Before Mordred could offer another rejoinder, Riga continued. "You will leave now Sorceress. Take your good-for-nothing son and your Paladins with you."

"We will not leave without the one we came for," Morgase responded, her tone as hard as her expression. Her anger, which boiled just beneath the surface, was less for the Morrigan and more for her son who had felt the need to insert himself in a dialogue in which he had no part to play.

"I will not make this offer again, Sorceress, so decide wisely. Leave now. Do not come back here. Ever again. Do not be so foolish as to come for my daughter and think that I would allow you to take her."

"And if I don't leave?"

"Then you will confirm that you are the fool that I always believed you were."

A long silence descended then, Morgase's pale face becoming splotchy with red at the insult. Her son and the

Paladins at her back couldn't quite believe that any of the Teg would dare to antagonize a Sorceress with a power such as hers.

"You would dare to insult me?" Morgase demanded in a dangerously quiet voice.

"I did more than dare, Sorceress. Just like Kassie's father, I do."

"A bold choice, Morrigan." Morgase lost whatever patience remained. She already had spent too much time in this college town seeking the one she wanted, and she refused to spend any more time than necessary. She strode toward the stage, wisps of the Grym drifting out from her palms.

Before she could do as she planned, however, Mordred interjected himself into the confrontation once again. "Enough! Step out of the way, woman. You may be the Morrigan, but you do not have the strength or the power to take on so many of us. So save yourself the grief and the embarrassment. Your daughter comes with us." He pulled the sword from the scabbard on his back, infusing the steel with the Grym to emphasize his point.

"Mordred, this is not your ..."

The Morrigan interrupted the Sorceress once again, clearly unconcerned that Morgase and her son held the Grym in hand. "You are a fool to anger me, cub. You're lucky the Dragon couldn't join us. From what I understand, the last time you were stupid enough to challenge him he thrashed both you and your mother."

Seeing how Mordred's face shifted from a bright red to a purple, the Morrigan pressed forward as she hoped to push Mordred deeper into his own shame. Understanding that to succeed in a battle, you needed to control your emotions. You needed to make your emotions work for you. And clearly, Mordred did not have that capacity.

A good thing for her. Because a battle was coming. The

Morrigan had guaranteed that result. It was one of her special skills, after all.

"I'm sorry I couldn't see that," the Morrigan continued. "But I warn you now, whatever the Dragon did to you won't compare to what I will do to you."

"Strong words," Morgase murmured, calling on more of the Grym, the swirls of energy around her palms growing in size, flaring every now and then. "You and your daughter are here alone, Morrigan. To take such a risk is the mark of the real fool."

"The mark of the real fool is seeing what you want to see rather than seeing what is," Riga replied. She barked out a keen laugh at Morgase's witless thought. "I didn't come here on my own as you believe." Her black eyes sparked in the shadows, relishing that the fight she craved, the fight she lived for, the fight that was so much a part of who she was, drew inevitably closer. All she needed to do was give it one more nudge in the right direction. "I brought a few of the Dragon's friends with me."

"What in the blazes are you ..." Mordred began. He turned toward his mother when several figures draped in shadow pulled themselves free from the gloom. He whispered to her sharply. "You said this would be a simple job."

Morgase gritted her teeth, holding back the several expletives she wanted to let fly. "No job is simple when it comes to the Dragon. You of all people should know that, Mordred. Focus on what must be done."

From one side of the stage, the Three Little Bears emerged. The Berserker brothers looked even more imposing in the darkness, their size exaggerated by the murk. The bars of steel that each one held, the weapons glowing in the dim light, added to their already quite substantial menace.

"Best not to wake the Dragon," Ragnar grumbled, his deep voice sounding like a landslide.

"Right you are my bearded friend," Peggy Rose agreed. She didn't look like much. Petite. Hair askew. Owl-like glasses perched on the end of her nose. She wore a sundress despite the chill of the night.

Yet her eyes sparked with a worrisome energy. And the St. Bernard who trotted out beside her looked like quite a handful.

"Are we done with the talking?" Peggy Rose directed her question toward the Morrigan.

"We are," Riga confirmed, her lips curling into a wicked smile.

"Good, because I didn't come here to talk." Peggy Rose pointed toward Mordred. "Pinkie, bring me that one's arm so I can beat him with it."

With a deep growl that could have cracked the gates to the Underworld, Pinkie fixed his gaze on Mordred, bent his legs, then launched himself from the stage.

In just a breath, the dog grew to the size of a monstrous bear. His canines lengthened into fangs and a dozen sharp spikes appeared on his long tail, having eyes only for the one who fashioned himself the next King of the Teg.

Peggy Rose chortled with glee as a streak of energy shot from the diminutive Sorceress' hand.

She didn't have the chance to see if she hit her target. Instead, she danced to the side to avoid the Paladin who sprinted toward her and sought to smash her into the ground with a single swipe.

Even so, she heard a terrible scream from the direction that she was aiming. The smell of burning meat that drifted her way just a second later confirmed her success. Whether she hit the soldier she targeted or another of the men loyal to Morgase, she didn't know.

She didn't really care either.

She did know that she had taken one of the Paladins out of the fight … permanently.

Usually she didn't enjoy applying her skill in the Grym to the martial arts. Against these thugs, however, she savored every second. Because she hated bullies.

Pivoting to avoid the Paladin's backhanded swing that was aimed for her hip, her eyes gleamed with delight. If nothing else, she wouldn't need to get in her steps tomorrow morning. She was taking care of her exercise right then.

"Stand still you crazy witch!" grunted the Paladin.

The man towered over her. Grinning wickedly, mace infused with the Grym raised above his head, he prepared to bring it down once again.

Peggy Rose shook her head in mock sadness. "Have you not learned anything?"

"What are talking about?" the Paladin demanded. He swung with his mace again, seeking to take her across the jaw.

Yet once more he missed. The old woman wasn't there. She was too fast. Stepping to the side with the grace of a dancer to avoid the blow, she didn't even bother to defend herself.

"Don't bring a mace to a magic fight."

Before the Paladin could deliver a clever rejoinder, Peggy Rose gestured with her hands. Wisps of energy streaked from her fingertips and latched onto the Paladin's mace.

The Paladin brought his weapon down from above his shoulder, looking at it in consternation as if it might try to strike him on its own. Confused for just a heartbeat, he laughed. "That's the best you can do?" His weapon appeared to be no different than it had been before, his concerns misplaced.

"Wait for it," Peggy Rose replied with an unnatural calm.

It didn't take long. With a flicker of her fingers, the threads of energy on the Paladin's weapon flared, burning through the ensorcelled steel and leaving a molten heap of metal at the soldier's feet.

The Paladin watched it happen in shock. Stunned. Then fearful. And that hesitation mixed with disbelief proved to be his fatal error.

He should have let go of his mace when he had the chance. But he didn't. And those threads weren't done.

The magic leapt from the steel to the Paladin's arm. Burrowing beneath his flesh, his skin smoked and then began to sizzle.

The Paladin's face became a rictus of pain as the magic raced through him. Setting his blood to a boil, his flesh burned from the inside out while his bones charred.

It all happened so fast that he didn't even have the time to scream.

Peggy Rose turned away from the Paladin, not having any desire to watch the man's gruesome demise. His flesh began to flake away, pieces of ash drifting to the ground. Then his entire body pulsed with an all-consuming energy. The unstoppable process, once initiated, wouldn't come to an end until the Paladin was no more than a pile of cinders right next to what had once been his weapon.

Sensing the movement just a few feet behind her, she whipped around and sent a burst of energy streaking through the air.

Right on target.

The power she released slammed into the Paladin who had hoped to take her from behind.

No such luck.

The man flew back through the air to land atop some of his comrades. His chest was missing, flesh and bone smoking.

When the battle began, Peggy Rose had wanted to challenge Morgase. They had a rivalry that went back a millennium.

She held back instead.

Morgase had gone after the Morrigan's daughter. Therefore, Morgase belonged to the Battle Goddess.

Peggy Rose would have to make do with the leftovers. And there were quite a few left that required her attention.

"THIS IS NOT WHAT I EXPECTED," Thorsen grumbled, disappointment plain in his voice.

With a quick flick of his wrist, the Berserker parried the Paladin's swing. Having lost his balance because there was no give in Thorsen's strong arm, before the man could recover Thorsen kicked down with his boot.

Catching the top of the Paladin's knee, the man shrieked in pain. He crumpled to the ground, losing all interest in the combat with his kneecap shattered and his leg bent at a horrifying unnatural angle.

"Nor I," agreed Urs. Thorsen's brother swung his glowing three-foot bar carved with runes in a wide backhanded arc with such strength that when he struck the Paladin's mace, the steel bounced back into the man's forehead, cracking his skull.

Leaving the Paladin where he fell, Urs jumped over the body and kicked with his right leg. Catching the chest of the Paladin sprinting toward him while yelling at the top of his lungs, Urs grunted in satisfaction as the unlucky fellow flew back through the air in a pained silence, unable to do anything more than groan and fail to take a breath when he hit the ground. Urs had hit the soldier with such force that he crushed the man's rib cage and in the process shredded his lungs.

"You thought these Paladins would offer more of a challenge," Ragnar grunted. He was surrounded by the bodies of the soldiers foolish enough to challenge him. A few were piled on top of one another. None of them would be joining the clash again.

"A foolish hope, I know," admitted Thorsen. He lifted his bar a split second before a Paladin's mace smacked him across the back of his head, not even needing to look to know that his attacker was there.

Holding the man's weapon in place, Thorsen turned to face his attacker, blowing the Paladin a kiss.

Taken aback, the Paladin was unprepared when Thorsen knocked him senseless with a headbutt.

"Yes, these Paladins are no better than those we faced at Mordred's estate a few nights ago," Urs grouched.

It was for that reason that none of the Berserkers saw any value in shifting into their true form.

As Werebears, they could tear through these soldiers with even greater facility. Yet the energy the shift demanded of them would be wasted on these opponents, and they wanted to conserve as much magic as they could in case there was a need for them to join the fight against Morgase.

"We can't always get what we want, brothers," Ragnar explained in a reasonable tone, even though he was just as frustrated as they were. "Well done, Urs." He watched with pleasure as his younger brother spun through the air, bar of light flashing as he knocked three Paladins to the ground before his feet touched the earth again. "Therefore, we do what we must."

Ragnar slashed with his bar, knocking away a Paladin's mace. The Berserker recovered faster than the stunned man, swinging in a tight arc from his left to his right and crushing the Paladin's ribs, breaking each one as he sent the man soaring back above his comrades to lie in a broken heap.

"We can't," Urs agreed, "and we do what we must."

Thorsen nodded. "But we fight for the Dragon, and that is what we want."

"That we do," Ragnar agreed, a frightening smile gracing his features. "Hail the Dragon."

MORDRED BARELY ESCAPED THE HELLHOUND. He only succeeded because he pulled a few Paladins in the way as he scrambled back from the monster soaring toward him, claws extended for the kill.

The trio of unlucky Paladins saved his life.

At the cost of their own, but he didn't care about that.

It was more important that he was alive than them.

What in all the hells was the spawn of Cerberus doing padding along beside a dainty old Teg? That made no sense!

Mordred didn't have the time to ponder that question. Raising his sword, he prepared to fight for his life.

The hellhound, whose shoulder came to the top of his head, growled hungrily. Snapping his teeth as he advanced, the monster offered Mordred a grin that turned his blood cold.

Rather than launching himself at Mordred, the hellhound swiped at him.

Mordred knocked the paw away.

His gleaming steel sword was of little concern to the hellhound, unable to cut through his thick hide.

For just a second, Mordred thought the hellhound snickered at him. Then he danced back from another swipe, the beast's claw missing his leather armor by little more than a hair.

Mordred's eyes widened. He couldn't believe how fast the hellhound was, especially for a creature of such size, his claw streaking past him a blur. Yet mixed with his astonishment was a stunned incredulity.

The monster was testing him.

Mordred growled to himself in an anger meant to hide his embarrassment.

Not testing him, he realized. The hellhound was playing with him.

Unable to resist his rage, Mordred swung with all the strength that he could bring to bear.

He spit out a curse at the same time he pulled his sword out of the dirt.

Despite its size, the hellhound glided to the side, not bothering to attack even though Mordred had left himself exposed.

"You think you can best me?"

The hellhound didn't reply. Surging forward, the monster slammed into Mordred with his shoulder and knocked him up and over the Paladins crowding at his back.

Mordred coughed silently as he struggled to lift his head off the ground, the air knocked from his lungs.

It took several seconds before he could breathe again, and even then only a few shallow breaths. Cracked ribs, he believed. Thankfully none broken. He hoped.

Finally able to push himself up to his feet, he chortled softly despite the pain in his ribs.

The hellhound had made his point.

Mordred couldn't stand against him. Not if all he employed was his sword. He should have used the Grym as well, though he remembered vaguely that hellhounds had some natural protection against the Power of the Ancients because of who their creator was.

None of that mattered now, however, because the hellhound was no longer his concern. In fact, the hellhound had done him a favor.

Flinging him backward over his men had put several dozen Paladins between them. And though the monstrous hound was a true terror, sweeping Mordred's soldiers out of the way with his spiked tail while his paws batted away Paladins like they were no more than bowling pins, there were always more Paladins to take the place of those who fell.

Just then a Paladin landed right at Mordred's feet. The man gasped out the last of his life, his chest punctured in five places by the hellhound's tail, the bloody ooze from his wounds puddling around Mordred's boots.

Yes, definitely a good thing he brought so many Paladins with him. Even more so that so many were willing to die for him.

Looking up once the Paladin's eyes glazed over, Mordred nodded to himself.

This might be the opportunity that he was looking for.

His Paladins had little chance of harming the hellhound. But the hellhound had little chance of breaking free from so many of his Paladins.

At least for the next few minutes, so time was of the essence.

If he could get the girl under his blade all the fighting would stop.

He would be victorious.

He would be the hero.

But first he needed to eliminate the Morrigan. And he believed that now was his chance since his mother had the Battle Goddess' full attention.

Grinning in expectation of what he believed would be his most remarkable triumph yet, he slid farther to his left and stayed behind his Paladins as they struggled futilely against the hellhound. Reaching the far edge of the stage, he pulled himself up.

The Morrigan's back was turned.

Now was his chance. And this time he wouldn't use his sword. He would use the Grym.

"You would attack my mother like the coward you are?"

The Morrigan's daughter stepped out from the shadows, her eyes burning a fiery reddish orange just like her father's.

19

A SURPRISE GUEST

"I came just as I promised I would."

Melissa shifted from one foot to the other. Willing herself to stop, somehow she gained control over her nerves and stood still, holding her head high as she sought to pierce the gloom that greeted her.

It didn't help that the stone throne and the two stalagmites made it seem like she was staring into the maw of a frightening beast. The deep rumble of the voice that emanated from the back of the cavern only added to the illusion of terror.

Although perhaps she was staring at a frightening beast.

A monster better left to the depths and the darkness of Tartarus that had somehow managed to claw its way free from its centuries-old bonds.

"The thief who is also a Witch finally appears," the shadow said without bothering to turn around. "I've been waiting for you. Time is short. Or rather your mother's time is short."

Melissa stared harder at the gloom hoping to identify the source of the voice.

No luck.

"That's why I'm here. I have the item I promised you."

Melissa steadied herself. Pleased that when she spoke her voice remained strong, not cracking as she feared it would. "I've met the requirements of our agreement. I ask that you do the same."

Her request was met with silence.

A silence that deepened and became more alarming as it dragged on.

A silence that worried her more than the voice that set the entire cavern trembling.

She continued to stare into the gloom, seeking to pierce the veil.

Finally the shadow turned around. A giant of a man coalesced out of the darkness, walking around the stone throne. Stopping just a few feet in front of Melissa, he put her in his shadow.

The figure standing before her terrified her. She wasn't embarrassed to admit that. The menace mixed with the hate that radiated from him made her want to crawl under a rock and hide.

But she didn't.

She was stronger than that.

She would control her fear.

She would see this through to the end, whatever that end may be.

She had done a deal with the devil.

In this case an Ancient.

Typhon.

A monster who nearly defeated Zeus. Who should have defeated Zeus. If he had, he could have destroyed the Greek Pantheon.

Yet Typhon had lost. Banished to the depths of Tartarus.

Now he was back. And he wanted something that only she could give him. Even so, it didn't feel like she exercised any leverage.

She wasn't a contractor, signed to complete this one assignment. In Typhon's eyes, she was nothing more than a servant.

She had been a fool to do the deal. She had known that going into it.

But she didn't have a choice. She didn't do a deal with one of the most potent of the Ancients because she wanted to.

Rather, understanding the potential consequences, she did it because she had to.

Her mother was at risk.

Her mother was dying.

Because of the Ancient towering above her.

It was Typhon's turn to speak, so she used the few seconds she had to study her adversary. Clearly he was powerful. Not only his physique, but also the incredible energy that radiated off him.

His face was as craggy and hard as the rock of the cavern, his frame looking as if it had been built from that very same rock.

Melissa frowned. Just for a second. She didn't want to give anything away as Typhon studied her as well.

He was dressed in a white shirt, black pants, and loafers. The outfit made her think of a waiter at a high-end restaurant. Although she would keep that thought to herself.

"Is that it?" He motioned toward the small package she held that was wrapped in brown paper.

She nodded. "As promised. Do what you need to do to remove the curse and it's all yours."

"All in good time," he rumbled.

"That was the deal." The sense of urgency that Melissa experienced since leaving Kraken Cove had only intensified as she made her way to this meeting. Joining it now was a jolt of fear. She hated the fact that she needed to trust a creature not known for being trustworthy. "You remove the curse that is killing my mother. I give you *The Book of Whispers*. That's what we agreed."

Typhon ignored her. "Why did it take so long for you to bring this to me? I would think that you would have wanted to get here sooner because of your mother."

Melissa tried to demonstrate a confidence that she wasn't feeling. Usually, she went into a meeting like this with something safely stored in her back pocket that ensured the other party couldn't double cross her.

Now?

She had nothing. She hadn't had the time to find anything that she could use. And even if she had, she doubted that it would have mattered to an Ancient.

"I had to steal it from the Dragon. You think that was easy?" She nodded toward the shadows behind the stone throne. "Just ask your daughter. She's had to deal with him. And with a lot less success than I've had, since I have what you want and she doesn't."

Eyes narrowed, lips puckered, Jinx stepped out of the darkness, less than pleased at having been discovered. Even more so at the slight Melissa offered her that was wrapped in the truth.

"The Dragon is a bit of a challenge," Jinx admitted with a shrug, trying to play off how easily the Witch had identified her even though she had been hiding herself with the Grym. "And I would have gained the artifact if you hadn't gotten in the way."

"It took a bit longer than I anticipated." Melissa ignored the challenge in Jinx's voice, pleased that she had put Typhon's daughter on the defensive. Anything she could do to knock Typhon or his daughter off balance could help her with what now felt like more than just a negotiation. It seemed a test with only one possible result. "Nevertheless, I acquired the item in the agreed-upon time frame. I have met the requirements of our contract. I ask that you meet your end of the bargain. As you said, time is short."

"Of course," Typhon said, his eyes never leaving Melissa. "You have met the terms of the contract."

She could almost feel his contempt like it was a physical thing. Although she understood that it wasn't directed just toward her. Rather, it was directed toward anyone he viewed as being beneath him, which meant all of the Teg -- monsters, Gods and Goddesses, and the many other creatures of their realm. So at least she was in good company.

"Then please remove the curse from my mother and I will give you the book. Then you can do with it what you will. That is all that I ask. Please meet the terms of our agreement."

Melissa feared that it would come to this. That she would need to take more drastic action.

She had learned as much as she could about Typhon. Or at least as much as she could since he had spent centuries locked away in Tartarus.

He was known for being a merciless opponent. For exercising a power that few could match. For holding grudges. For doing whatever was required to gain what he wanted.

Not for being truthful or doing as he promised.

Because there were few who could call him on it.

And Melissa wasn't one of them.

"I gave you my word when we made this arrangement. You have nothing to fear. Before all else, I keep my word. Always."

She nodded. Not challenging him, though she had little doubt as to what his word was worth. "Remove the curse from my mother and the book is yours. Please. Then we can put this business behind us."

She had reached the point in this negotiation that she feared would come to pass. Typhon had all the leverage in this arrangement. He could do what he wanted. He didn't have to do what was required of him, and when push came to shove she had no good options for pushing him.

It wasn't like she could challenge him directly.

Although she would have.

If she could have, she would have come here without the artifact and refused to give it to him until the terms were met. Just as she had done so many times before on other jobs.

But this wasn't like her other deals. This wasn't about getting paid. This was about saving her mother's life.

With time counting down, she couldn't do what she wanted. And she realized then, for the first time in fact, that she was going to lose on a deal.

Typhon had gotten what he wanted from her. He didn't need her anymore.

Her mother was going to die. So was she.

"Just kill her and be done with it, father," Jinx said. The Hydra stood off to the side, bringing her hand to her mouth to cover her yawn. She was getting tired of the conversation and wanted to move matters along.

Typhon smiled. Just like one of his spawn to end every confrontation with death and blood. "Can you sense the power within it?"

"I can," Jinx confirmed. "Let's take it from the Witch and be done with her."

"Is that your solution to every challenge?" Typhon asked, his bottomless black eyes swirling slowly, as if the burnt essence of Tartarus had come with him when he escaped. "I thought I taught you better."

"You taught me this," Jinx replied in a soft chuckle. "The Witch has what you want. She's served her purpose. Take the artifact. Kill her. Simple. Then we move forward. We gain the revenge that you deserve. We make the Teg pay for their insolence."

Typhon nodded as he thought about what his daughter said, relishing the fear that the Witch tried to hide but was all too obvious to him. A fear that he savored and from which he gained sustenance.

"We will take the artifact, but we will not kill her," he said finally. "We will wait."

"Why would we do that?" Jinx asked. Frowning, she didn't understand her father's reasoning as she viewed the Witch as no more than a loose end. "The Witch is nothing more than a complication now."

"Perhaps, but she's still a chip to be played. Insurance of a sort, and likely necessary because of the Dragon. He has a habit of involving himself in business that doesn't concern him."

Jinx's expression became one of confusion.

Typhon ignored his daughter. Instead he looked beyond the Witch toward the far end of the cavern. "Isn't that right?"

"In this matter," Draig said, striding toward Melissa and Typhon with his blackthorn shillelagh tapping against the rock, the Dragon Door winking out behind him, "I do have a legitimate interest."

20

THE CLOSE

Morgase cursed softly under her breath. Nothing that she tried had worked, and it seemed like nothing would. An uncommon result for her.

Another of her attacks with the Grym slammed against the Morrigan's shield with little effect. The latest flash of energy she blasted toward her adversary, just like all the others, shimmered brightly against the Battle Goddess' gleaming barrier, yet it did no more than that. The magic against which few Teg could stand limply fizzled out as if the power was scarcely any better than children's fireworks.

More than unsatisfied with her results, her whiplash anger taking hold, Morgase set herself on the stage. She was done playing nice.

When the combat began, she sought to overpower the Battle Goddess with a few deft maneuvers. A demonstration of skill and power that would put the Morrigan in her place.

Her approach served as a way for Morgase to confirm her legitimate standing among the Teg. An opportunity to show the Battle Goddess that she occupied a position several rungs below her. That the older Teg had no place in what would be the new order.

Morgase's strategy failed miserably.

Nothing she tried gave her the victory she desired. The Morrigan blocked every one of her attacks, her damnable shield consuming the magic Morgase sent her way, thereby strengthening the Morrigan's own defense.

Staring up at the sky, hands out to her side, Morgase brought them together, a clap of thunder echoing within the wood as a blazing torrent of power spun faster and faster within her palms. As she pulled her hands apart, that torrent expanded into a tornado of fiery power that grew bigger than she stood tall, a whirlwind of compressed energy that she was certain would force the Battle Goddess from the fight.

With a devilish smile, Morgase flung the tornado at the Morrigan. When the Morrigan released her shield crafted of the Grym, Morgase was sure of her success. Her opponent clearly understood that against this latest of Morgase's creations, she didn't stand a chance.

The energy swept across the stage, the gusts of power knocking anyone within twenty feet of the raised platform from their feet.

Settling over the Battle Goddess, the tornado consumed her. Blanketing the Morrigan in crackling energy, Morgase left her latest weapon in place until she was certain that her work was done.

That she had vanquished her opponent.

The whirlwind wasn't designed to destroy the Morrigan.

That would have been too simple and created complications for her farther down the road.

Rather, the tornado was designed to bind the Battle Goddess and prevent her from using the Grym. Once ensnared, Morgase would have two levers to use against Draig.

But the scene she so craved didn't play out as she expected.

The tornado began to slow, then fade, its power weakening, even before Morgase manipulated her creation to release its hold on the Morrigan.

What was happening?

This shouldn't be possible.

Taking a page from her son's playbook, Morgase applied more of the Grym, seeking to exert greater control over her creation.

She couldn't.

A brief moment of shock ran through her when her new dreaded reality became all too real.

She no longer controlled the tornado of energy.

The Morrigan did.

That belief became truth just a few heartbeats later. The charged whirlwind continued to slow, continued to fade, to deflate and diffuse, until it was little more than a dancing flame atop the Morrigan's palm.

Morgase's creation blinked out of existence the instant the Morrigan closed her fist.

Perhaps most disconcerting for Morgase wasn't her adversary's demonstration of skill. It was the fact that the Morrigan's expression hadn't changed as she stared across the stage, her dark eyes fixing the Sorceress in place.

There was no smirk at Morgase's failure. No smart comment or challenge.

There was only the Morrigan's look of grim determination and a promise that Morgase did not want to think about.

A challenge as well.

The Battle Goddess questioned with just the lift of a single eyebrow whether that was the best that Morgase could do.

Yet unlike her impetuous son whose first thought when faced with a similar circumstance was to attack. Immediately. Without considering other avenues. Morgase didn't.

Instead she studied the Morrigan. Thinking. Plotting her next move.

Morgase had never come up against an opponent like the Battle Goddess before.

Despite all the skill and power she employed, none of her attacks had broken through the Morrigan's defenses. The Battle Goddess faced off against her with ease as if every attack Morgase attempted she had seen before and many times over at that.

And the Morrigan had just offered Morgase a hint that she had been holding back. It was almost as if the Morrigan was testing her rather than the other way around as it should have been.

A shiver of concern passed through Morgase. An exceedingly rare and unwanted reaction.

She never anticipated this possibility.

Yet it was the only possibility that made sense.

She was beginning to understand what the Morrigan was doing.

The woman had yet to come at her directly.

Not because Morgase wasn't giving her the opportunity. Not because the frequency of her own attacks forced the Morrigan to fight from her back foot.

No, the Morrigan was allowing Morgase to attack her.

She wanted Morgase to attack her.

The Morrigan was more than happy to concentrate on defending herself and only defending herself, because just as much as Morgase wanted to make a point to the Morrigan, the Morrigan wanted to make a point to Morgase.

A point that was undeniable.

A point that Morgase dared not acknowledge for if she did it would shatter the image she had constructed for herself.

Growling in rage at her adversary's temerity, Morgase shifted her approach in an instant. She would still bind the

Battle Goddess, but she would bruise her first. She would give her a lesson that even the great Morrigan would never forget.

To that end, Morgase pulled in as much of the Grym as she could hold without destroying herself, relishing the immense amount of magic surging within her and begging to be released.

Yet before she could, her flash of concern became something more tangible. She realized that she had been too slow. Letting go of any thought of attack, for the first time Morgase worried about defending herself.

Because the Morrigan was done with giving Morgase her lesson.

Morgase saw it in the woman's eyes. How they changed. Sparking for just a heartbeat, her black orbs shimmered with an otherworldly power that Morgase had never witnessed before.

With a flick of the Morrigan's hand, a spike of energy shot across the space between them.

Morgase manipulated the Grym she had called upon without thinking, forming a shield of her own.

When the Morrigan's spike struck, it felt like a hammer blow. It was so potent that it forced Morgase to stumble back several steps in order to stay on her feet.

And then again when another spike slammed against Morgase's shield. And another. And one more after that.

It was then that Morgase realized just how badly she had underestimated the Irish Battle Goddess.

Just how much alike Morgase and her son were.

Just how lethal their arrogance – in her hidden, in him oozing out -- could be on the field of battle.

A field of battle mastered by the Morrigan long before.

KASSIE SMILED when she sensed the power being used behind her. She would know that surge of magic anywhere.

Her mother.

The Morrigan was fully engaged.

She almost felt sorry for Morgase.

Almost.

"You sure you want to risk your reputation against the Dragon's daughter?" Kassie challenged with a raised eyebrow.

Mordred stood no more than twenty feet away from the young woman, unable to miss the scorn in her voice and her goading expression. He had sheathed his sword, instead seizing the Grym so that he could use the Power of the Ancients against the Morrigan. His plan ripped apart before he could put it in play by the whelp who dared to get in his way.

"You're the one taking a risk, girl," Mordred replied with more heat than he intended. He had been going for cold resolve but his new adversary had plucked from his grasp what he thought would be a decisive victory.

His decisive victory.

Even so, Draig's daughter foolishly choosing to stand in his way was another opportunity for him to end this battle with a triumphant flourish. "I have trained with Merlin," Mordred bragged. "I have trained with Morgase. Two of the greatest Sorcerers to ever touch the Grym. I doubt that you can say the same."

"Why would I need to?" Kassie replied, thickening her voice with as much sarcasm as she could and loving how it rankled Mordred. "I trained with the Dragon and the Morrigan. I believe that's more than a match. Now if you're done trying to compare the size of ... you know ... perhaps we could get to your spanking and be done with it."

Growling softly to himself in anger, Mordred took a few steps closer toward the girl. He halted when he saw the sparks of energy begin to dance across her palms, those sparks becoming threads of magic that swirled around her hands and then her forearms.

"Being able to use the Grym is quite different than using the Grym in battle," Mordred warned. "There is no time to think. There is no time to decide. There is only time to move. To allow instinct to guide you. Learning how to use the Grym while being bounced on your father's knee can't compare to what it's like to use the Grym against someone who is using the Grym against you at the very same time."

He took a few more steps toward his quarry, trying to push her into a rash decision. Offering her a very unpleasant smile, he continued. "Are you ready for that, baby Dragon? And against someone like me? Someone with knowledge and skill that you have no hope of ever claiming? Someone who will not grant mercy when you beg for it?"

Kassie ignored Mordred's attempts to throw her off her game. If he thought his words would make her nervous, he was mistaken. She had dealt with men like him before, and she knew exactly what to do to make him doubt himself.

"You're taking quite a risk, Mordred. Spanked first by my father. How many times?" She shrugged, giving him a much too sweet smile. "So many times you've probably lost count. And now I'm going to hit you even harder. Just a girl as you said." She shook her head, giving him a mocking look that was designed to anger him, and it did. "I don't know how you'd be able to live that down. Defeated by the baby Dragon. Unless, of course, that's what you're into. Getting spanked by a girl."

Mordred's eyes flashed red with rage. Even so, despite the struggle, he kept his temper in check. Although just barely.

He saw over the girl's shoulder how the combat between his mother and the Morrigan was playing out. Evenly matched for now, though it didn't seem as if the Morrigan was exerting herself as much as his mother was.

Growing slightly concerned, he went against character.

Rather than launching himself at his opponent as was his usual approach, he chose caution instead.

He didn't believe the girl could beat him. That was inconceivable.

But if the Morrigan could offer his mother a worthy challenge, then he needed to be wary of the Grym the girl wielded. He couldn't allow Draig's daughter to distract him or take him by surprise and get in a lucky strike.

"Thank you for your concern, girl. But have no fear. This is a combat that you cannot win."

He took a few steps closer to his target, now only ten feet away. For just an instant, he thought the Morrigan's daughter was going to attack him with the Grym, and he was ready for it.

She didn't. Instead, she used the Grym swirling around her to craft a quarterstaff that gleamed a bright white and was a foot taller than she was. She hefted it easily, clearly enjoying its feel in her hands.

"There's only one way to find out, Mordred," Kassie said with a confidence born of experience. She had spent a great deal of time in the practice ring with her mother. Mordred didn't know that, but he would soon enough.

"You're challenging me?" Mordred chuckled, finding it hard to believe.

He didn't have a chance to say anything else because she was already on him. Forced to hustle backward, he pulled his sword free and raised it just in time to prevent the girl's quarterstaff from knocking him senseless.

And then back a few more feet, the girl demonstrating a tenacity that didn't surprise him considering her parentage. Her gleaming quarterstaff slashing and slicing, chopping and jabbing, was just as dangerous as a steel blade as she sought to force him from the combat before it even really began.

A smart move on her part. Not allowing him to dictate how the combat played out.

He was physically stronger than she was. If she allowed him to seize the momentum, then she would be fighting from a distinct disadvantage.

"You can't keep this up," Mordred gloated as he parried her every strike, refusing to give ground now because if he did he'd fall off the stage. "I can see that you're already tiring."

Chopping down with her quarterstaff while aiming for where Mordred's neck met his shoulder, Kassie didn't reply. She couldn't. Because the bastard was right.

She was tired. After just a few minutes.

She had been spending more time at her desk working on her dissertation than in the gym. A weakness that she would need to remedy, assuming she survived this combat. Because she sensed that Mordred was about to make his move.

Mordred parried her strike with just his wrists, twisting his blade just so to turn away her weapon.

She took a half step back then so that she could reset herself before she attacked again. But at the last second she hesitated. Worried.

He had shifted his feet, spreading them farther apart to improve his balance, also placing his right foot in front of the left a little farther than he had before.

Mordred was preparing to lunge. She was sure of it.

Her mother had taught her what to look for, testing her in such a way many times before.

"Perhaps I am tired," Kassie replied, seeking to buy herself just a few extra heartbeats. "But at least I don't quit."

Mordred lunged, sword targeting his opponent's hip. A glancing slice would not result in a mortal wound, but he was certain that the first touch of his blade would force her from the fight then and there.

He missed just by a hair, the Morrigan's daughter swiping down with her quarterstaff and knocking his steel away.

"I never quit," Mordred almost shouted. Continuing his

motion, he spun quickly, bringing his sword around in a backhanded blow. A smack across the back of her legs with the flat of his blade would end the duel with the girl face first on the stage and his blade at the back of her neck. The Dragon's daughter would be his captive, the victory in the amphitheater his to claim.

"Really?" Kassie asked. She pivoted away from him. A deft move, but sweat was pouring down her brow. She was breathing more heavily now, her face turning red because of the effort required to prevent Mordred from getting in too close and using his greater size against her. "That's not what I heard. In fact, by all rights you should be dead. The only reason that you're not is because you do quit when you come up against someone more skilled than you. You don't have the guts to see a combat through if you're not sure that you're going to win. Like when you fail time after time to tame the Dragon."

"Be careful, girl," Mordred growled. "You speak of what you don't know."

He slashed at her. A vicious, less precise strike this time. His anger was beginning to affect his technique.

Kassie ducked the blow and glided away from him, not bothering to respond with her quarterstaff. Seeing what she needed to see. Learning what she needed to learn.

"I know that you've fought my father several times," Kassie continued. "How many times have you challenged him now?" She frowned slightly. "I can't recall. Let's just say too many times." She swung a lazy blow at Mordred's head. He knocked it away easily. She didn't expect it to connect, however. She hoped only to solidify in his mind the sense that she was done physically. "And you haven't beaten him once." She snorted out a laugh. "Not ... a single ... time."

Mordred slashed at Kassie. A blow more ragged than the last, his rage was replacing his reason.

She brought her quarterstaff up just in time, knocking away

the strike, though not escaping the attack entirely. A slash of red appeared on her forearm. Thankfully not deep, though still painful and a distraction if she allowed it to be.

"I told you not to speak of what you don't know," Mordred ground out through clenched teeth.

"You say you've never quit, yet you've lost to my father every time you have challenged him. Every time."

"Your father ..."

Kassie cut him off. "What do you do? Beg him when he has his blade at your throat? Is that why you're still alive? Because my father rarely shows mercy. Especially to Teg he considers fools and bullies."

Mordred growled louder than the hellhound who just a dozen yards away was tearing through the Paladins who were doing all they could to keep the beast away from him. He stalked toward Kassie, his face twisted into a demonic glare.

"You will regret your words, girl. They will be the last you ever speak ..."

So focused on taking the girl's head from her shoulders, sword already raised above his shoulder, about to swing with a deadly grace, he didn't notice when she smashed the butt of her staff down on the wooden floor.

The blast of energy that erupted sounded like a mallet striking a church bell and sent Mordred flying from the stage.

WHEN MORDRED LANDED hard on his back, stunned, his surviving Paladins circling protectively around him, a natural lull settled over the clash, the immense power Kassie revealed bringing a brief moment of reason to a chaotic battle.

Morgase glared at the Morrigan. Eyes narrowed. Frown deepening. She was beginning to understand that there was much that she didn't know about the Battle Goddess, concluding as well that what she didn't know could cost her more than she was willing to pay.

Mordred cursed under his breath as he struggled back to his feet. Slowly. Sore in places he didn't think he could be sore. His ribs and back aching, he knocked away the hands of several Paladins who sought to assist him. Despite his injuries, he couldn't appear weak now.

Pinkie snarled, a deep rumble, licking his chops to get rid of the blood of those he already had vanquished as he trotted over to Peggy Rose. He stopped in front of the stage, still towering over her despite the Sorceress standing next to Kassie.

The Three Little Bears stepped back from the pile of Paladins at their feet. Placing themselves in front of the stage on the other side, they stood ready for the next round. Their hungry expressions suggested that they were looking forward to it.

And no one in the amphitheater had any doubt that there would be another round.

In less than a quarter hour, the Berserkers, Peggy Rose, and Pinkie had removed half the Paladins from the clash. Their success confirmed by the broken and battered bodies scattered around the long rows of benches that staggered up to the top of the hollow.

But there were more Paladins coming. Several hundred more. The reinforcements clad in black leather armor rushed down the trail and circled around to each side of the stage to ensure that there would be no open avenue of escape for the band of fighters called to protect the Dragon's daughter.

Kassie assumed that these were the rest of the Paladins who had been hunting around the campus for her.

Fewer than she anticipated. Likely because of Aleck.

Kassie cursed softly under her breath. Aleck better not have done anything foolish on her behalf. He better be all right. She hadn't asked for his assistance, yet still he had given it without a second thought.

She pursed her lips, shaking her head slowly from side to side. He should have refused her father's request.

But she knew him. She knew that he would never refuse. Not when it came to a matter involving her. A matter that put her at risk.

Draig as well, although she was certain he didn't give that fact much thought.

He had only been thinking of her.

"That pain in the ass better still be alive," she muttered under her breath.

"What was that dear?" asked Peggy Rose. She appeared to be completely unconcerned by the hundreds of soldiers trapping them against the stage. Her smile curled up much like a cat about to pounce.

"Nothing," Kassie grumbled, embarrassed by her show of emotion.

"Worried about the young man who helped you?"

"How could you ..."

Peggy Rose gave her a mysterious grin. "Have no fear. He is well. Though I doubt he will make it here in time."

"In time for what?" Kassie could only assume that Peggy Rose meant the resumption of the battle. Yet the Sorceress' expression hinted that she might be referring to something else entirely.

"You will see."

Kassie shook her head again as her anger rose. Why did Peggy Rose always have to be so obtuse?

Kassie loved her, but sometimes she hated how the Sorceress preferred to offer tidbits and teases rather than actual explanations.

She snorted at her complaint. She should be used to it by now. Her father was much the same way.

Aleck as well.

Aleck!

Why did he keep popping into her mind with several hundred Paladins standing across from her and Mordred giving her a stare that made her think that now he wanted nothing more than to drive his sword deep into her gut and give it a twist?

She didn't have any more time to waste on that question. Her focus was drawn to the Sorceress standing off to the side on the stage, her mother squaring up to her.

"Give the girl to me and she will be returned whole and none the worse for wear," Morgase promised in a strong voice. She spoke with a confidence that was quite impressive for someone who had discovered the Battle Goddess to be more than a match and was cut off from her son and her Paladins.

"Once you are done with the Dragon," the Morrigan murmured, her black eyes somehow flashing even darker.

"Yes, I swear it. Your daughter has nothing to fear from me."

"Your word means nothing to me, Sorceress," the Morrigan replied without a moment of hesitation. "My daughter and I will not betray the Dragon."

"Look around you, Morrigan. See the truth. Better the Dragon than you and your daughter."

Riga didn't need to take her eyes from Morgase to observe all that was going on around her. Instead, she relied on the eyes of her ravens perched atop the stage and circling in the sky above.

The last of the Paladins brought to Williamsburg, two full companies in all, had joined the Paladins already in the outdoor theater, more than replenishing those of their comrades lost.

Her daughter and her protectors were outnumbered.

They were surrounded.

They stood little chance of success.

Even so, she was the Battle Goddess.

She understood how quickly a fight could turn, and for the smallest of reasons.

A slip at the worst possible time.

A mistake born of arrogance.

A surprise over which no one had any control.

A twist in luck or fate.

"The truth, Morgase, is that you will never gain what you want, whether you take my daughter or not. You cannot kill the Dragon."

Kassie reset herself, magical quarterstaff gripped firmly in her hands. She sensed that the battle was about to begin again and that when it did they were in for a tough go of it. Their initial success would mean little against so many more Paladins.

"The truth, Morrigan, is that we will take your daughter," Morgase hissed with greater vehemence. "You cannot stop us. If you continue to resist, you and your friends will pay for your obstinance with your lives. Better to admit defeat and fight another day."

"You will take no one, Morgase. You will leave my grand-daughter be."

The deep voice that echoed around the outdoor theater was accompanied by a bright flash of light. At the back of the stage, a portal of pulsing energy solidified into a gateway to another location that was masked by darkness.

Arthur Pendragon walked through. Merlin by his side. Gaheris followed with several companies of Knights of the Round, the soldiers swiftly spreading out around the stage and into the woods on both sides to serve as a counterbalance to the Paladins.

"Brother, you risk a great deal by involving yourself in this matter," Morgase growled with a heavy dose of spite. "You have no business being here."

"I risk nothing, Morgase," Arthur replied in a commanding voice. The King Teg stopped right beside the Morrigan, towering over the petite woman. Yet there was little difference in the power that radiated off the both of them. "Your undying enmity? I already have it."

"I seek only the services of your granddaughter so that I can remove a threat to us both."

"You've sunk quite low, Morgase. You seek to use her as a chip against her father."

"And what's wrong with that?" Morgase demanded. "You reissued your kill order for your son. You want him gone just as much as I do. And how could we not after what he did to us. The threat that he presents. He must be eliminated."

Kassie gave her mother a quick look, frowning, angry. Her grandfather reissued the kill order for her father? Why would he do that? Clearly, she didn't have the full story.

She was about to ask her grandfather that very question when a brief shake of Riga's head told her to stay quiet ... for now.

Listen.

Learn.

Then act.

Not the other way around.

A lesson taught to her by her mother. Her father as well.

"My son is my business, not yours. I have made that clear to you, yet still you persist."

"That undying enmity as you said," Morgase snorted, her disgust plain in her voice.

Arthur's eyes hardened in a flash. His voice grew colder. More authoritative. A reminder of who he was and the power he wielded. In fact, the power that he had wielded for well over a thousand years. The power that Morgase so desperately wanted. For herself first. Then for her son.

"I rule the Teg, Morgase, despite your best efforts to topple me from the throne. The Dragon will answer to me and to no one else."

"Arthur, you must ..."

"No one else but me." Arthur cut off his sister in a voice barely above a whisper. "Do I make myself clear?"

Morgase sensed the Power of the Ancients surging through her brother. She could tell as well that Arthur was looking for the chance to release the Grym, anxious for any excuse to have a go at her.

She did a quick calculation in her own mind.

The Knights her brother brought with him would negate her Paladins. A fight with even odds, though likely tilting in favor of the Knights if the Berserkers and the hellhound joined in. And she had no doubt that they would.

That would leave her facing off against Arthur. That appealed to her. She had wanted that combat for quite some time.

What didn't appeal to her was challenging Arthur at the same time she battled Peggy Rose and the Morrigan. The Dragon's daughter as well.

And then there was Merlin, who stared at her with an impassivity that sent a concerning shiver down her spine.

A Teg never defeated in battle.

Even with Mordred fighting by her side, the Sorcerer tipped the already weighted scales fully in Arthur's favor.

"You are making a mistake, Arthur," Morgase said in as reasonable a tone as she could manage in her current disappointing circumstances. "You cannot trust the Dragon."

"I do not trust the Dragon," he replied. "But as I said, the Dragon is for me to deal with."

All emotion left Arthur's face, the dead-eyed stare that he gave her then one with which she was more than familiar. It was the expression that fell across his features right before he went into battle.

"This will not end here, Arthur. I promise you that."

Morgase stepped back then, offering her brother a slight nod. The barest minimum of respect that was required to get her message across.

She would do as he wanted. This time. Under duress. But she would do it, nonetheless.

"I know what your promises are worth, Morgase." Arthur stared at his sister for a little while longer, the tension building until he nodded as well. Scarcely a dip of his head, he allowed her to stand down and lick her wounds. "So we will continue this another time. Not here."

"Not here," Morgase agreed, already walking away from her brother and the Morrigan toward the stairs that would take her down from the stage and to her Paladins.

"Not here?" demanded Mordred. His eyes flashed, an anger mixed with desperation. He may be battered and bruised, but he refused to give in so easily. To quit as the girl had taunted him. "My mother might acquiesce, but I do not. I will never give you what you want."

"You seek to challenge me, Mordred?" Arthur asked ever so quietly. The King Teg turned his steely gaze toward his son, though he seemed more amused than concerned. "Do you think you can best me?"

"Without a doubt," Mordred spat.

He pushed through his Paladins and approached the stage. Finally!

Finally he had the chance that he had been waiting for. The chance to challenge the man who had no right to sit upon Mordred's throne.

That's as far as he got, the stage still a few feet away.

He froze when Merlin stepped out from the shadows and stared down at him with his cold, remorseless eyes with which Mordred was all too familiar.

"Your mother has reached an agreement with your father.

You will abide by it. Now is not the time nor the place for this. Other more important matters must be dealt with first."

Mordred was impulsive. He allowed his emotions to guide him more than he should. He was arrogant. He was used to getting his way. And he was angry. A fury surged through him that he desperately wanted to bathe in.

But he wasn't a fool.

Merlin hadn't seized the Grym yet.

Mordred would know when he did.

If he gave Merlin cause to do so.

He wouldn't, however.

Because no one challenged Merlin. Not even his father.

Hissing with frustration, Mordred bit his tongue before he said something that he shouldn't. He stepped back reluctantly, hate-filled eyes starting with his father and ending on the Dragon's daughter.

"Leave now, Morgase, and take the whelp with you," Arthur ordered. "Know as well that any who seek to take my granddaughter will die. Painfully. Slowly. That is my promise. The King Teg has spoken."

21

MAKING HIS MOVE

"What might that interest be?" Typhon asked.

He had never met the Dragon before, most of the life of Arthur Pendragon's son stretching out over the time that he was imprisoned in Tartarus.

He had heard of the Dragon, however, even in the underworld's deepest pit.

And he had learned as much as he could about the Dragon. A powerful Teg.

And possibly a Teg who could be of use to him.

For a time.

Because just like him, the Dragon held onto his grudges.

More important, perhaps, there was bad blood between him and his father. And grievance was an emotion that Typhon understood better than most. An emotion that he could use as his own.

"To rescue the damsel in distress, of course," Draig replied with a sardonic grin. "Or rather in this case, the Witch."

"You can't be serious?" Melissa demanded.

She was going to say more, but the wink he gave her threw her off.

"I'm not," he replied, hoping that she understood. Stopping right beside her, he held out his hand. "Would you mind? I believe that belongs to me."

Melissa hesitated. "I need this to ..."

Draig's eyes flashed dangerously, a prickle of energy sparking off him. She had never seen him this way before, or at least not with her as his focus. She extended the package to him as her eyes widened in fear, realizing that now wasn't the time to challenge him.

He took hold, needing to tug gently before she released her grasp on the artifact. "Thank you." He turned toward Typhon, motioning toward him with the wrapped book. The Ancient had watched the exchange impassively, although one raised eyebrow revealed his curiosity. "As you said, she's a Witch but also a thief. I don't like it when Teg steal from me."

"You're not here to rescue the Witch?" Typhon's tone suggested that he was more amused than anything else.

"I'm not. You can do with her what you want."

"You can't ..."

Jinx cut off Melissa's protest. "Don't believe him. He's helped her I don't know how many times during the last few days. He's here because of her."

Draig gave Jinx a look that would freeze the blood of most any Teg receiving it, then shook his head sadly. His expression hinted that he was disappointed in her. "You're right. I'm here because of her. But not because of why you think."

"Explain," Typhon ordered in a tone that brooked no argument.

"I helped the Witch because she was helping me. Although she didn't know it."

"You used her as bait," Typhon rumbled. He lifted his head, a cunning smile curling his lips.

"You wouldn't have dared to ..." Melissa began to protest. Draig's words cut her off.

"I did. She wanted *The Book of Whispers*. I had it. I knew who she was stealing it for."

"How could you know that?" Jinx demanded. "No one knew that except for the Witch. I made sure of it."

"You really need to ask?" Draig frowned in disbelief. "You showed up at my doorstep. How could I not figure that out? Subtle isn't your strong suit."

Jinx's face turned red, an interesting contrast to her flowing green dreadlocks. A gesture from her father held her in place when she took a step toward the Dragon.

Draig continued. "The Witch had several deals in play. The most important one was the one that she had with you."

"You allowed her to come here."

"I did. I allowed her to steal the artifact knowing that she would bring it to you."

"And you followed her to me," Typhon nodded in appreciation.

"I did."

"Why?"

"We'll get to that. May I?" Draig motioned again with the package in his hand. Typhon nodded.

Draig ripped off the wrapping, revealing a book that was an inch larger than a paperback on each side. The essence that radiated from the text covered in a leather that resembled human skin pulsed with an almost uncontainable power.

"*The Book of Whispers*." Draig held it up so that Typhon could get a better look at the ancient tome. Then he broke the spine and flipped through the first few pages, angling the text so Typhon could see it.

Typhon frowned. "Those look like recipes."

"They are recipes," Draig confirmed.

"I don't understand." Typhon's flinty expression shifted swiftly. His remorseless eyes, sparking with a power that only an Ancient could wield, promised retribution if he were made to look the fool. "How could this be *The Book of Whispers* if it contains recipes?"

"That's why you need me," Draig explained. "It's an additional level of protection. When this artifact was created, there was a great deal of concern that a Teg or some other being, such as yourself, would use it for more nefarious purposes. Therefore, the creator of *The Book of Whispers* also crafted a primer."

Seeing Typhon frown, Draig provided more of an explanation. "A key if you will that allows you to unlock the mysteries hidden within this magical text."

"And where is this key?" Typhon demanded. He was losing what little patience he had. He was so close to achieving his objective. So close after centuries of confinement. So close to earning what he truly deserved. And now he had to climb over an additional obstacle?

"I'm the primer. The key." Draig shrugged. "I'm the only one who can translate *The Book of Whispers*."

Typhon thought about that. He hadn't expected that response and he wasn't sure if he should believe the Dragon. "If you're the only one who can unlock the power of this artifact, why would you place yourself in this position? I can do to you whatever I desire."

"We'll get to that."

Typhon studied the Dragon. There was a confidence and a calm within him that the Ancient found impressive. Although he wasn't concerned.

Typhon understood the power to be put in play through the artifact. How it could be used. How he was going to use it. But it couldn't be used against him. He was an Ancient. He was one of the few who could resist the power contained within *The Book of Whispers*.

"Prove it," Typhon demanded.

Draig smiled. Then he placed his right hand just above the

book and whispered an incantation, a stream of energy flowing from his downturned palm and setting *The Book of Whispers* alight. Once he was done, Draig turned the book toward Typhon so that he could see what he had done.

Typhon's eyes sparked with pleasure. The Dragon had spoken the truth. "Why not use the power contained within the book for yourself?"

"I am the Dragon, but even I don't have the skill or the strength to employ the power contained within *The Book of Whispers*. Not in the way it could be. The way it should be." Melissa gave him a sharp look at his lie. Draig hoped that Typhon didn't notice and that she kept quiet, relying on the wink that he had given her when he forced himself into the middle of these proceedings. If she challenged him now, they were both done for. "However, an Ancient can."

Draig turned toward Jinx, who continued to glare at him. Clearly, she had not forgotten his earlier insult. So there was no reason not to add another one to the first. "Your daughter didn't tell you about that? Really? I would have expected more from her, wouldn't you?"

Typhon's eyes blazed. Because he heard the truth in his words. He shifted his gaze toward his daughter, obviously less than pleased.

"I didn't know," she protested, scowling. "I had no way of knowing. This artifact has been in the Dragon Vault for so long that no one knows anything about it other than the few stories that still circulate among the Teg."

"You should have," Draig challenged, wanting to bury Jinx even deeper if he could while making her even angrier than she already was. "With a task so crucial to your father breaking free from Tartarus, I would think that you would want to do everything in your power to ensure his success. Leave no stone unturned. But apparently not."

Jinx took a step toward Draig, the Twisted Grym already

flaring above her palms. Ready not just to put him in his place for his insults, but also to put him in the ground.

She got no farther. Her father's raised palm held her in place.

"You will give me the power of this artifact?"

Draig nodded. "I will."

"Why?"

"Because despite all that I did for my father, he wants me dead," Draig replied in an incredibly cold voice. "I'd like to kill him before he kills me."

Typhon studied the Dragon for several seconds, not detecting a lie. He looked at Jinx, who continued to simmer in her rage. Even so, she nodded. "Arthur Pendragon has reissued his kill order."

Typhon nodded to himself as he studied the Dragon, not taking long to reach his decision. "I will happily kill your father for you. I have thought of little else since he tricked me back into Tartarus. But you must want more than just his death."

Draig didn't reply. He didn't feel the need to, his expression becoming harder at the exact moment a hint of greed flashed in the back of his reddish-orange eyes.

Typhon nodded again. Seeing it. Comprehending it. "Power."

Draig nodded. "I have some other scores to settle. Not just with my father."

That Typhon certainly understood. "The outcast seeks revenge."

"Something like that."

"Can I trust you?"

Draig smiled at that, then shrugged. "Why would you need to worry about that? You're the all-powerful Ancient. Not me."

Typhon's expression softened, although only a hair. Both amused and pleased by the Dragon's comment. He looked at his daughter, asking for her perspective.

"He will betray you," Jinx warned.

"If he didn't try to betray me then I would be disappointed," Typhon countered, shrugging off his daughter's concern.

Typhon understood greed just as he understood revenge. And at that moment both of those characteristics were driving the Ancient's thinking because both benefited him.

Typhon needed *The Book of Whispers* to stay fully in the Natural World. Only with the power contained within that artifact could he cut the thread that kept his spirit in Tartarus. To do that, he had only one path.

The Dragon was correct. He was an all-powerful Ancient. The Dragon didn't stand a chance against him.

So he would take the risk.

And he would be prepared to crush the Dragon when the time came, just as it inevitably would.

"We will work together, you and I," Typhon explained. "We will kill your father and take revenge on those others who have slighted us."

"What about my mother?" Melissa demanded, barely able to contain the anger flowing through her. The sense of betrayal made her feel sick to her stomach. "She's going to die if Typhon doesn't remove the curse."

Draig turned toward her, his expression just as harsh as his tone. "You used me to get this to Typhon." He held up the book. "I used you to get in front of Typhon. It's only fair. In the larger scheme of things, your mother doesn't matter."

Melissa stared at Draig. Thunderstruck. Not quite believing what she was hearing. Not understanding how he could be so callous. Not after all that ...

Before Melissa could throw a few choice curses in Draig's direction, the cavern began to shake, some of the smaller rocks crashing down from the ceiling, all because of Typhon's harsh laugh. "I will enjoy working with you, Dragon. I see that there is much to be gained through our partnership."

"As do I," Draig confirmed with a smile. "Although there is one other thing I need to note with respect to *The Book of Whispers.*"

"What is that?"

"It's notoriously fickle."

Before Draig had gotten the last word out of his mouth, a massive explosion erupted right in front of Typhon, forcing him to turn away. Dirt and rock blasted all around the Ancient, hiding him in a gritty, grey haze.

"Come on," Draig said, grabbing a stunned Melissa by the hand and pulling her back toward the Dragon Door that appeared just a dozen yards behind them.

They were only a few feet away from their escape hatch when Draig realized that he and Melissa were too slow. He skidded to a stop and turned, letting go of his hold on the Dragon Door.

Draig's distraction had proven less effective than he hoped. Typhon strode out of the gritty cloud, clearly intent on extracting from him blood and pain for the deception.

And *The Book of Whispers.*

Setting himself on the stone floor, legs just a few feet apart, Draig lifted his hands out to the side as he called on the Grym. When he slammed them together, a wave of energy flowed out in a broad arc.

Just in time.

The blast of fire that erupted from Typhon's mouth struck Draig's shield a heartbeat after it took shape.

Roaring in anger, Typhon spit another blast of fire. Hotter than the last. The flames more white than red and capable of burning through any substance in a flash. Nothing able to prevent the fire from claiming its victim.

Except for Draig's shield, constructed of both the Grym and the Power of the Draca. Draig's heritage gifted to him by his mother provided him and Melissa with the required protection.

Even so, Draig understood that he was experiencing only a temporary success. Even with the Power of the Draca woven into his barrier, he could stand against Typhon only for so long. Because he knew that Typhon was employing only a fraction of his own power against him.

Likely because Typhon didn't want to kill him. Not yet.

He still required Draig's services to make use of *The Book of Whispers*.

That was the only reason that he and Melissa were still alive.

"That was a trick?" Melissa demanded, more than just a little angry.

She stood at his back, the heat on the shield intensifying as Typhon invested in the task more and more of the overwhelming power at his command. Making it harder for her to breathe as the barrier began to warp. Bend. The edges melting.

A reality she had never seen before. A reality that she never wanted to see.

Draig nodded. "It seemed the best play." He glanced at her briefly. But only briefly. He needed to focus on Typhon. The Ancient stood across from him, a cunning grin breaking his usually grim visage as he continued his assault.

It was that grin that worried Draig the most, but he didn't have the bandwidth to think on that just yet. He had needed to call on even more of the Power of the Draca, directing it into his wavering shield. All the while he felt the strain of his efforts, which were draining him of both energy and will.

"What about my mother?"

"Typhon was never going to heal your mother. You know that just as well as I do."

Melissa wanted to dispute Draig's conclusion. She wanted to tell him that she had everything under control before he pushed himself into the deal. That his getting involved ensured her mother's death.

She couldn't.

She knew the truth.

She just didn't want to acknowledge it.

Because she couldn't allow her mother to die without her doing everything that she possibly could to save her.

Cursing softly under her breath at her failure and her naivete, Melissa caught a hint of movement at the very edge of Draig's barrier. His shield didn't extend across the full length of the cavern, and Jinx was about to sneak around and attack them from the flank.

Enraged, finally having a target for the fury surging through her -- because of Typhon, because of her inability to aid her mother – she reached for the Grym.

Melissa had watched Jinx in combat before. Typhon's daughter was fast. Preternaturally so.

Trying to strike her likely would be more hope than reality.

So she didn't.

Melissa decided on a more expansive approach.

She targeted the area around Typhon's daughter, a dozen spikes of energy shooting from her extended palm. Then another dozen just to be sure.

The weapons crafted of the Grym slammed into the cavern's floor in close proximity to the Gorgon, creating massive holes in the stone and sending rocks that were never smaller than the size of a human head flying in all directions.

Melissa nodded to herself in satisfaction.

Typhon's daughter actually yelped, caught by surprise as she scrambled back around the edge of the shield. Glowering at her, Jinx didn't come for them again. Instead, she moved closer to her father to avoid another attack.

At least that was one threat they wouldn't have to deal with.

As sweat poured from her body, the heat raging around them becoming unbearable, Melissa squinted at the magical barrier, needing to shield her eyes with her hand because of the intensity of the glow. She felt like she was in a furnace. Her clothes were sticking to her. Her hair was singed.

And there was no way out of their predicament.

They were trapped.

Playing the role of Draig's rabbit to the very end.

Deservedly so, she admitted to herself grudgingly. She should have told him the truth from the very beginning. But she hadn't, always thinking that she could manage on her own anything thrown at her.

Unwilling to admit the truth that sometimes she couldn't succeed on her own. Sometimes she needed to demonstrate a little trust.

And there was another truth that was bothering her as they faced the peril of being burned alive. The Teg who had saved her life once again hadn't had to assume the risk.

He didn't have to place himself in his current position.

He could have left her to her fate.

But he didn't.

He had come for her.

Just like the Druid had said, Draig seemed to have an innate urge to do good by doing what was right.

At least in part.

Because she was certain that Draig was exactly where he wanted to be. Right in front of Typhon, though perhaps not in the way he had hoped to be.

So, yes, he had used her. That couldn't be denied, because although she had known him only for a brief time, she had learned quickly that he was more Machiavellian than Machiavelli. He always had schemes within schemes.

"Is that the best you can do my little Dragon?" Typhon called from the other side of Draig's weakening barrier. The magic flared and flashed, dissolving along the edges as the center bulged backward toward Draig.

"It's all I need to do, Typhon. I don't have to show off as you do."

"You are weak, Dragon. Even so, I will grant you your father's death."

"That's very kind of you, but I think not."

Typhon had anticipated just such a response. "Better to surrender now, Dragon. Better to serve me. You know that you will in the end. You can't escape me, no matter what you might try."

"Again, very kind of you, but I think not," Draig grimaced.

The strain was becoming too much for him. Typhon was too strong. Draig could put more of the Power of the Draca into his creation, but it would only delay the inevitable. And if he did, he wouldn't have the strength to do what he wanted to do next.

Draig turned toward Melissa. "Are you ready?"

"Ready for what?"

Melissa had kept her focus on the flank, wanting to make sure that Jinx didn't make another attempt to sneak up on them.

She hadn't. Typhon's daughter had learned her lesson, although clearly she wasn't happy about it based on the scowl that marred her features.

When Melissa looked again at Draig, she almost took a few steps backward.

The color of Draig's eyes had changed. The reddish orange with which she was so familiar was gone, replaced with a golden flame.

Even more unsettling, his hair stood on end as if he was in the center of a thunderstorm. The crackle of electricity thick in the air between them.

When she nodded reluctantly, he smiled then turned back toward Typhon. Sparks of energy flashed all across his body, those sparks lengthening, expanding, surging with a breathtaking speed, until Melissa could no longer fix her eyes upon him, Draig at the very center of a blinding nimbus of magical energy.

She couldn't see what he did. She did feel it, however. And she heard it.

A deep chime rang out, echoing off the walls of the cavern, as Draig smashed Excalibur's hilt against the rocky floor.

The flash of light that erupted from his strike was brighter than the sun, forcing even Typhon to turn away as the wave of power that followed set the entire cavern shaking and rolling. Massive boulders crashed to the ground. Then the two stalactites, cracking and breaking apart, crushed the granite throne beneath them.

She was certain that even more destruction occurred, but she wasn't there to see it.

Already murmuring the words the Daemon King taught him, Draig pulled Melissa into the shadow at his back that lasted for only a split-second more.

Escaping Typhon, he left the Ancient roaring in rage.

22

THE BATTLE BEGINS

"You trust me to do that?" Melissa felt completely drained. Mentally and physically.

Her clothes clung to her. Her sweaty hair draped lifelessly on her head.

She felt like she had spent a week in a sauna and was only now exiting. A fair description after suffering through just a few minutes of Typhon's fiery attack.

Yet Draig, who had been in the same inferno with her for the same amount of time, appeared to be just fine. Refreshed even. What in all the hells?

Not a hint of exhaustion.

Not a drop of sweat on his forehead.

She would ask him about that if they survived the next few minutes.

"I do," Draig replied.

"Why not Fafnir?"

"Fafnir has his own task. Better not to complicate matters."

The Draca with eyes that resembled Draig's nodded to her, Fafnir's confident expression making her feel a little bit better.

They stood toward the back of the Vault where the light

fought with the shadow. A deepening gloom extended behind her. A gloom that despite their dire circumstances still beckoned to her.

She was curious about the many other treasures hidden within that darkness. Having glimpsed just a morsel of the artifacts contained within the Dragon Vault, she would have liked nothing more than to wander the aisles. Her fingers itchy.

That would have to wait, however. Because for the first time fear trumped her natural inquisitiveness. The battle begun in the cavern below the old military installation in Lewes was far from complete.

"I'll take care of it," Melissa promised. "Don't worry."

Draig smiled. "I won't."

Melissa called to him as he strode toward the front of the Dragon Vault and the stone wall that protected the stronghold from intruders, only those Teg with invitations able to cross through the magical illusion without experiencing a slow and painful death.

"Thank you."

Draig stopped, turning. Eyebrow raised. "For what? I used you as bait."

"True, and I can't say that I appreciated that part of it." Melissa smiled sheepishly. "Still, you came for me."

"Do you think I would have come for you if you weren't my way in to see Typhon?"

"I know you would have." Melissa replied with a confidence burned into her very bones.

Draig didn't reply. Not because he didn't want to. Rather because he couldn't.

Instead, he turned back around. Sensing rather than seeing the change in the entrance to the Dragon Vault. The shift in energy as what appeared to be solid rock became a more malleable substance. A shimmering mist that would solidify again once the visitors were through.

"You have been betrayed, Dragon." Typhon strutted through the barrier, Jinx right beside him.

"Hasn't been the first time," Draig replied, although he didn't appear to be concerned by that admission.

Draig looked past the Ancient. Eris blew him a kiss before she slipped back out of the Vault. He owed his sister now, but he would worry about that if he made it through the next few minutes with one of the most powerful of the Ancients.

"Did you really believe that I would not come for you?" Typhon shook his head. Mocking him. "There is nowhere you can go to escape me. Not even here."

"You think I was trying to escape you?" Draig shook his head in imitation of Typhon, even infusing just the right amount of disdain in his voice. Pleased that he earned a spark of irritation in the Ancient's eyes for his efforts.

"If you were smart, you would already be well away from here. Then again, if you were smart, you would have chosen to serve me rather than fight. But it seems that of your many intriguing qualities, knowing when to bow down to your betters is not one of them."

"Fair enough," Draig admitted. "Although it could be that I have yet to come across one of my betters."

Typhon's eyes narrowed, though he chose to ignore the barb. "You have the Witch and the Fish with you." He nodded toward Seamus and Melissa. They stood next to Fafnir, half in and half out of the light. "Good. That will make my job that much easier. Once I make you mine, I will kill the Witch. Payment for her betrayal. Then she can join her mother on the other side. I will leave the Fish to my daughter."

Jinx smiled broadly at that, clearly pleased with her father's gift.

"Kraken, for the love of the Gods," Seamus muttered, more than just a little miffed by the insult. "I'm the *Kraken*." Seamus had balked at joining Draig on this encounter until he learned he would have a chance to renew his acquaintance with the Gorgon.

Draig allowed his lip to curl. Leave it to Seamus. Still surly despite facing off against an Ancient. If nothing else, he was consistent. Dangerously so, in fact.

"You have made a mistake, Dragon." Typhon commanded his attention once again.

"What would that be?" Draig's lip turned down, his flinty mask back in place. "*The Book of Whispers* is safe here in the Dragon Vault. You can't take it now. The Draca won't permit it. And even you don't have the power to challenge the Draca." Draig's voice hardened. "You can't untether your spirit from Tartarus, so you can't attain your full strength in the Natural World. You're vulnerable. And you're in my playground now."

"Impressive speech," Typhon laughed. "The confidence of youth. The foolishness as well."

"Meaning?" Draig studied Typhon closely, sensing that something wasn't quite right. As if the Ancient had been waiting for just this moment.

Typhon was a creation of power. Brute force.

Yes, he demonstrated a cunning borne of experience. Yet Draig didn't believe that the Ancient had the ability to bluff. At least not well.

And why would he need to bluff? He likely never had to in the past. He could just do as he wished much like a bull in a China shop.

"I don't need the artifact any longer." Typhon's eyes widened in delight, smiling thinly as he watched the realization strike Draig. "That's right. I don't need the artifact when I have you."

The menace in the Ancient's voice was unmistakable. Yet that worried Draig less than the fact that Typhon had every right to be confident.

Draig had made a mistake.

A bad one.

One that could not only cost him, but also all of the Teg.

Typhon wanted *The Book of Whispers* because it would allow him to untether the last of his spirit from Tartarus. He would be completely and entirely free from his prison once and for all.

Whole.

Full of his potency.

As close to indestructible as an Ancient could be.

And he would not have to return to Tartarus.

Ever.

Draig's mistake was believing that Typhon needed the actual artifact to achieve his objective. To cut the rope linking him to Tartarus.

Typhon did still need the artifact, though not in the way Draig envisioned originally.

Because Typhon was a physical manifestation of power. And of all the truths regarding power, one stood out.

Power always sought more power.

One of Merlin's lessons that had stuck with him.

Believing that he had everything under control, that Typhon wouldn't see through his ploy, Draig had revealed to the monster that he was the primer. The key to unlocking the potency of *The Book of Whispers*. The magic required to do that inscribed within him.

Take the key …

Take him …

"Yes, you see it now." Typhon nodded his head in pleasure. "I didn't think that it would take you long. I have a great deal of experience in magical bindings. It comes after studying my own for so many thousands of years."

His grim visage broke into a rapacious grin. "I will not kill you, Dragon. Because then I will lose the artifact for good. Instead, I will bind you. I will use you, and you won't be able to resist. I will imprison you in Tartarus just as I was, and I will call upon the power of *The Book of Whispers* whenever I deem necessary. I will call upon you." He chuckled then, a dreadful sound. "You will not be able to do anything to stop me once you free my spirit. Because Tartarus is my playground. It may have been my prison, true, but still I ruled there."

Before Draig could offer what likely would be a useless denial, Typhon's words containing too much truth to be argued against, he dove to the side. Rolling across the ground, he came back to his feet.

The blast of fire that erupted from Typhon's palm missed him by no more than a hair, the heat rushing across his back.

"Run, rabbit, run," Typhon laughed. "As I said, you cannot escape me. I will make you mine. I will chain you much like Prometheus. He gave fire to man. You will give me all that is *The Book of Whispers*."

Once again, Draig didn't have the time to reply nor the opportunity to continue with his self-recrimination. Angry at himself for allowing his foolish pride to rule him, Draig formed a shield with the Grym that he fixed to his front.

Just in time.

Just not enough.

The blazing fire Typhon shot toward him from both palms blasted Draig backward, sending him sliding across the floor.

"As fun as this may be, better to surrender, rabbit," Typhon laughed, his deep rumble echoing in the darkness of the Dragon Vault. "You only delay the inevitable."

Draig pushed himself back to his feet feeling like he had been run over by a truck. And then the truck had backed up and run over him again.

He was angry.

He had been overconfident.

Too certain of his success.

Too sure of himself.

So focused on the plan that he was so convinced would

work that he hadn't spent enough time trying to poke holes in that plan.

His own arrogance had cost him and put him in this position.

Another of Merlin's lessons came to mind. One that he shouldn't have forgotten.

Get too big a head and you'd probably lose it.

He hated when Merlin was right.

Although perhaps it might help him now.

Arrogance might be the only option he had left.

But not his.

Draig dove out of the way again, not bothering to stand against the next streak of flames Typhon shot his way. Having no desire to be thrown backward again and put himself in an even more vulnerable position than he was already in.

He cursed under his breath as he rolled to the left before he even made it back to his feet, avoiding another strike by a hair. Then back to his right as the next blast scorched the stone where he crouched just a second before.

This wasn't how this confrontation was supposed to play out.

JINX COULD BARELY CONTAIN HERSELF, smiling in delight as her father played his game with the Dragon. Still, she was anxious. Chomping at the bit to make her play.

She bounced from one foot to the other. Her hands moved of their own accord, wisps of the Grym playing across her fingers.

She plotted out in her own mind what she would be doing if she were the one battling the Dragon.

Confident that if her father gave her a chance she would

demonstrate that she had the skill and the strength to enslave the Fallen Knight.

It was more than just a little frustrating that she couldn't get into the game. Yet. Still, she was enjoying watching the Dragon scamper about like the mouse he was as he attempted to avoid the full brunt of her father's attacks.

She just needed to exhibit the patience that so often was a challenge for her. The patience her father was looking for.

She would have her chance. He had promised her that. She just needed to look for the right moment.

And it had to be the right moment, because she couldn't afford to disappoint her father. She couldn't afford to make a mistake. She had been on thin ice with him ever since her failure in Kraken Cove.

Then she saw it.

The one opportunity that she had been waiting for.

Her father was doing her a favor by using his attacks to force Draig to the right side. A series of fireballs that Typhon sent the Dragon's way meant more to keep him in place than do him any real harm, thereby giving her a chance to blindside him.

Green eyes sparkling with delight, dreadlocks the color of seaweed swirling around her head in a rhythm all their own as she called upon more of the Grym, Jinx fashioned thick ropes that flashed the color of the ocean.

Fasten those binds around him and the Dragon would be helpless.

Her father could do what was necessary to enslave him.

She liked the sound of that, especially since she never thought such a thing was possible. The very idea too fantastic to contemplate.

The son of Arthur Pendragon made a slave?

That was just too rich.

And it would all be because of her.

With one stroke, she would solidify her place next to her father.

Her brothers and sisters would be jealous.

Enraged.

And impotent.

Just the way it should be.

Visions of her success already dancing before her eyes, she pulled back an arm to fling the first rope constructed of the Grym toward Draig's upper body. Just as fast the next rope would follow, targeting his legs.

She didn't need to hit him. She just needed to get the ropes close to him.

The magical construction would do the rest, slithering over the Dragon like sea snakes, tightening their hold as he struggled and weakening him by using his own power against him. Ensnaring him.

Jinx ducked right before she made her first throw. A blast of water shot right by her head and forced her to turn away.

The crafted energy was flung with such velocity that she had no doubt that if it had struck true, it would have decapitated her. Her belief was confirmed just a split-second later when the watery shard struck the stone behind her with so much force that it punched a hole into the rock that was three feet deep and just as many feet around.

Releasing a few choice curses, she turned to her right.

Blasted Fish!

He had cost her the best chance she had to ensnare the Dragon. And now Draig was on the move. Sensing the danger she presented, Draig glided over in the other direction, weaving his way around the jets of flame her father blasted toward him and ensuring that she didn't have another clean shot.

Seamus stood no more than thirty feet away from her. He had taken advantage of her complete focus on the Dragon to sidle along the cavern wall and come at her from her blindside.

The nerve!

Worse, clearly he was quite pleased with himself.

Calm.

Confident.

Small surges of water played across his hands and his forearms.

He stared at her with a condescending look. Then he smiled with that devilish grin of his and shook his head as if he disliked having to discipline an unruly child.

That snotty bastard!

Then he did something that Jinx hadn't expected and really pissed her off.

The Fish had the nerve to wink at her and then blow her a kiss.

She smiled then.

A vicious smile.

A smile made of anger but mixed in with it was a great deal of ... lust.

Jinx was pleased by the Fish's reaction. Seamus' eyes widened, revealing his uneasiness. Just as she wanted him to be.

"Do you think you can handle me, Fish?" Jinx demanded. Still desperate to get into the fight with the Dragon, she was certain that she would. She just needed to dispose of her former lover ... after she had a little fun with him.

"Kraken," Seamus growled. He hoped that he was misinterpreting Jinx's expression, all the while knowing that he wasn't. Still, it was time to find out which one of them truly ruled the sea. "And there's only one way to find out."

23

STREAMS OF FIRE

Draig rolled to the side, coming up in a crouch sword at the ready.

Habit more than anything else.

He had no use for the weapon. Not against the current onslaught. So he rolled again. Farther to the side.

The stream of fire followed him. Scorching the cavern floor, the flames transformed the stone to magma. The heat blistering.

Typhon's attack didn't end until Draig dove and rolled a few more times, putting on a display of agility and prowess that couldn't be matched.

The Ancient laughed heartily as he took a few steps closer.

Clearly, Typhon was enjoying the game as he made Draig dart about this way and that, obeying the Ancient's whim. Just as would be the case when Typhon chained him in Tartarus.

Draig's eyes flashed, revealing the fury he fought to keep in check.

He was more than tired of serving as the Ancient's plaything.

He knew what Typhon was doing.

The Ancient was trying to put him in his place. To demonstrate that Draig had little chance of success against him.

Cow him before Typhon subjugated him.

Break his spirit before he was imprisoned.

That didn't just make Draig angry.

It pissed him off.

His reddish-orange eyes blazed brighter as his fury intensified. Savoring it, Draig drew upon it.

Still, he needed to be smart.

No matter how much he hated Typhon's arrogance, that weakness gave Draig an opportunity.

Draig dove to the side, rolling out of the way as another stream of fire shot by him. Typhon's hearty laugh echoed in his ears, the Ancient sending that burst almost like an afterthought. Wanting to keep him on his toes. Reminding him that Draig would dance to his tune.

Enough was enough.

It was time to change the game.

When he came up in a crouch this time, rather than dodging to the side again as had been his habit, Draig set his feet on the cavern floor then sprinted forward.

Typhon's expression shifted for just a heartbeat as Draig charged him. From confidence to disbelief. Then the Ancient shook his head.

Who else would be witless enough to attack him other than the Dragon?

With a snort of amusement, the Ancient wanting to teach Draig a lesson, Typhon shot a fireball from his palm that grew in size as it streaked through the air until it was larger than a pickup truck.

Draig continued to advance, refusing to alter his path.

Not caring about what blasted toward him.

Draig needed Typhon to learn the lesson that he was about to offer him.

With a single swing of Excalibur he sliced right through the comet of flames.

Then again.

And once more as Typhon sent at him one blazing ball of fire after another.

Draig refused to be stopped. Slashing with Excalibur, he cut through the Ancient's attack until finally he was so close to Typhon that it disrupted the monster's assault and forced the towering Ancient to demonstrate an unexpected agility for a creature of his size.

Typhon danced backward, having no choice except to retreat as Draig's glowing blade sliced through the air in search of his flesh.

But he couldn't get away. Draig wouldn't allow it. Seizing the initiative from the Ancient, he forced the monster to think only of protecting himself.

A change of events both unexpected and disconcerting. And one that Typhon could do little to correct as Draig continued his incessant attack, slicing and slashing faster than a scorpion's sting.

Typhon avoided each assault, though often by just a whisker, his rage increasing as he glided about the chamber. Dancing to the Dragon's tune now and hating every second of it.

Before Typhon could even think about how to turn the tide of the combat, a blast of energy erupted at his feet, requiring the Ancient to turn away and shield his eyes.

When he spun back around, growling in anger, Draig was back where he had been when he started his assault. Towards the center of what appeared to be a large practice ring carved out of the Dragon Vault's stone floor.

"You think that you can defeat me?" scoffed Typhon. "Because of that little display of yours? Luck, no more than that."

"I wouldn't be here otherwise." Draig gave Typhon a shit-eating grin that quickly worked its way beneath the monster's skin, adding to the rage that was visible in the giant's remorseless eyes.

"You are more of a fool than I thought," Typhon proclaimed. "You are mine, Dragon, you just don't know it yet. The longer this goes on, the more pain you will experience before the inevitable happens. Better just to surrender. Avoid the pain. Accept your fate." He chuckled softly, the sound still a deep rumble. "Be a good little Dragon."

"I have never surrendered, Typhon. I will never surrender. And fate ..." Draig shrugged. "Fate can be a finicky thing. I choose to make my own."

Typhon nodded, a frown beginning to break through his grim though confident visage. He took a moment to study his quarry once again.

He was beginning to understand more of the Dragon.

He was beginning to understand why he was such a threat.

"I can see why your father wants you dead." The Ancient was done with his weighing and measuring. "Perhaps I shall just have to crush you. It matters not to me. You will serve me. One way or the other. Broken or whole."

"I will never serve you, Typhon," Draig replied in a deathly quiet voice. "I serve only the Teg."

"Not your father?" Typhon asked with another snort. "Because it seems to me that with the skill and power that you've displayed, you could have killed him already if you so desired and taken his place."

Draig shook his head. "Killing my father is not worth my time or effort. I no longer serve him. That is enough for me."

"So you lied." Typhon couldn't say that he was surprised. He was disappointed, though. In himself. For not sniffing out the falsity until now. "You don't want your father dead?"

Draig thought about that for just a heartbeat. Did he want

his father dead? "No, I don't. I want only to be left alone. I want only to ensure that the Teg important to me are safe and free."

"How magnanimous of you," Typhon snorted. "Thinking of others rather than thinking of yourself. A pity I don't believe you. You are no different than the rest of us, Dragon. You want what is best for yourself before others. That is the way of the Teg."

"The way of the Teg is what the Teg make of it. I don't care what you believe, Typhon."

"You should." Typhon nodded his head with absolute confidence. "Because what I believe becomes what is. I make the world as I want it. That's why Zeus banished me the first time. But Zeus and his cursed brothers and sisters are no longer here."

"Only me," Draig replied, clearly not worried by that concept.

"Only you," confirmed Typhon. "You will serve me, Dragon. Try as you might, you cannot resist me."

"You can tell yourself whatever you want, Typhon, if it helps you get through the day. What you believe doesn't matter. All that matters is what is."

"You will serve me, Dragon," Typhon repeated. "You will free me completely from Tartarus. You will help me kill Arthur Pendragon. You will help me claim dominion over all the Teg."

"Words mean very little, Typhon." Draig's voice dripped with contempt. "Only actions matter. You of all the Ancients should know that."

"Brave words, Dragon. You will pay for them. Because in your words I hear only insults. That cannot stand."

Draig understood that in the end their combat would come to this. Even so, he wasn't completely prepared when it began.

The shift.

Typhon began to change.

Taking his true form, flames burst out from his eyes. His mouth. His fingers. His entire body.

The giant became a figure of flame, the fire transforming the Ancient.

Much like the phoenix rising from the ashes. But in this case, what resulted would not be a phoenix. It would be a monster who specialized in only one activity.

Destruction.

It was time.

Draig couldn't wait any longer.

He couldn't finish the combat here in the Dragon Vault. Not if he was to have any chance of surviving the encounter much less escaping the bonds Typhon was so intent upon tying around him. Not if he was to send the Ancient back from whence he came.

Looking over his shoulder for just a heartbeat, he locked eyes with Fafnir. Based on the Draca's expression and his posture, standing on his toes, one foot in front of the other, he was desperate to join the fight. As were the handful of Draca standing behind Fafnir who were hidden in the gloom of the Dragon Vault, only their reddish-orange eyes giving them away.

But they couldn't.

They and Draig had spoken about it at length before the combat commenced.

They didn't like it. Nevertheless, they understood why. And they would adhere to his wishes.

Because though Fafnir could not go to Draig's aid directly, still he could offer some immediate assistance that would improve Draig's odds of achieving his objective.

Before he turned back to face Typhon, Draig nodded. Then he grasped Excalibur with both hands, one on the hilt, the other on the blade.

Holding the mystical weapon out in front of him, a mist made of flashing particles poured out from the steel. Forming a cloud around him, the particles began to swirl in a clockwise direction. Faster and faster with each rotation.

"Your parlor trick will do nothing for you, Dragon," Typhon proclaimed as he continued to grow larger. His massive shape covered in flames flexed, bones breaking and reforming, muscles tearing and reknitting, the shape of his body adjusting as his true form pushed its way to the forefront as the Ancient released his hold over his human shape.

Becoming something else.

Becoming something more.

A monster of indescribable power and fury.

"And you think yours will?" Draig replied.

The challenge in Draig's voice infuriated Typhon even more. Roaring in rage as he continued to shift, a thick stalk appeared on each shoulder. Shooting up swiftly. Growing. And just as fast each stalk split. Now four taking shape. And so it went. The necks lengthening, stretching, forming glowing scales, the heads. Typhon's human shape no more than a memory except for his single grotesque skull of melted flesh and eyes of flame.

The transformation complete in seconds, the hundred heads, some more formed than others, all fixed their sharp eyes on Draig. Those heads now the spiky skulls of dragons.

And from each one that was fully formed a white-hot fire blasted toward him.

Draig wondered whether Typhon's initial goal had changed. The Ancient no longer interested in chaining him. Now just interested in killing him.

He had no time to come up with an answer. Focused solely on adding more of the Grym to the swirling mist of particles to his front, the tornado expanded, changing its shape. Widening. Lengthening.

The vortex now spun with a demanding fury, blasts of scorching air swirling around Draig. His frame highlighted by a golden nimbus of light, his hair stuck straight up in the air. Sparks of energy danced across his body, his eyes now the color of the setting sun.

He was ready, and in the nick of time.

Typhon's streams of fire all struck at once. Yet rather than destroying Draig, the vortex sucked in the flames much like a black hole would.

Taking in the heat and energy.

Tempering it.

Dissipating the effect.

Protecting Draig.

For now.

"Any time now, Fafnir!" Draig called over his shoulder.

What he was doing was working. Yet already it was taking a toll on him, the strength required to fuse the Power of the Draca with the Grym placing Draig under an immense strain.

How long he could maintain his whirlwind in response to the potent force that Typhon was employing?

Draig preferred not to think about that.

He had chosen his path. Now he needed to stick to it.

"Are you ready?" Fafnir asked.

"Yes," Melissa replied, although she doubted that the Draca could hear her. The air around them crackled with the energy being employed, the tempestuous gusts of wind threatening to knock them from their feet.

"Do what you need to do," Fafnir shouted into her ear. The roar of the flames blasting through the cavern only added to the cacophony. At the same time consuming the oxygen and making it difficult to breathe. "I'll be ready."

Melissa nodded. Tearing her eyes away from Draig and his combat, she focused on the floor.

She wasn't a Druid.

She was a Witch.

Even so, when she was atop Druid's Peak while Draig was

cut off from the Natural World while in among the stone mono-liths, she had spoken with Leya about the Druid's Circle. How it functioned. The principles for its use.

She had learned an interesting fact then, and she meant to make use of it now.

However, she needed to do it right the first time, because she wouldn't get a second chance.

Or rather Draig wouldn't get a second chance.

With the potency Typhon was bringing to bear against him, she could tell that he wouldn't be able to hold off the Ancient for much longer.

That fear driving her, she called to the Grym.

Not a huge amount. Leya had been clear about that.

It wasn't the quantity of power that was important in waking up a Druid's Circle. It was the delicacy of the touch that mattered most. The individual's skill in the Grym.

Yet even that wasn't enough.

Because the trick was where you started.

Her focus sharpening even as it became harder and harder for her to breathe, the heat stifling, the gusts of toasted air tugging at her, Melissa touched the rocks set in the floor that were positioned at the cardinal points of the compass with four separate threads of energy, all at the same time.

The effect was immediate. The four smooth, shiny stones flashed brightly, lines of magic racing across the floor from each one in both directions, igniting the other stones along the way until the outer boundary of the Druid's Circle was illumi-nated. That complete, new lines of energy from each of the cardinal stones set along the edge raced in toward the center where Draig stood against the shifting Typhon.

Melissa breathed a sigh of relief. Not only because she had succeeded, the Druid's Circle awakened, but also because Draig was exactly where he was supposed to be. As was Typhon, the Ancient caught within the boundaries of the Circle.

"It's all yours!" Melissa shouted. She could wake up a Druid's Circle, but she couldn't make use of it. She didn't have the power needed to do that. However, the Draca did.

Fafnir didn't wait.

Calling on the Power of the Draca, he added the energy at his disposal to the Circle. The bright light became even brighter. The illumination so intense that it became painful to look at the two combatants caught within it.

Then it was done.

With a resounding crack and blinding flash, the light faded.

Only Melissa powered the Circle now.

The stones glowing dimly, the portal was empty.

Draig and Typhon were gone.

"Keep the Circle charged," Fafnir ordered.

He didn't need to shout, most of the power that had been sizzling through the Dragon Vault no longer a concern. The heat and noise with it when Typhon and the Dragon disappeared, the Druid's Circle one of the few portals that could manage the immense raw potency of the Ancient.

But still a threat remained.

"Why do you want me to ..."

Thinking about the request just a second more, Melissa nodded as understanding came to her. She shouldn't have been surprised. Like father, like daughter.

While Draig challenged Typhon, Seamus prevented Jinx from attacking his friend's blind side. Being a nuisance more than anything else. One of Seamus' unique skills.

And he seemed to be enjoying himself.

With each surge of water he fired toward Jinx -- sometimes liquid, sometimes ice, sometimes a scalding mist that threatened to smother her – Jinx got angrier and angrier. Her scowls no match for the stream of invective flying from her mouth.

Until she couldn't stand being pecked at any longer.

Done with Seamus' games, she was shifting just as her father had done, though into a different form.

Her body was growing in size. Lengthening. Her dreadlocks swirling more violently as she began to reveal her true shape.

Fafnir didn't want the fight that was brewing to take place in the Dragon Vault.

"Seamus!" the Draca called. "The Circle!"

Seamus nodded upon hearing the note of concern in Fafnir's voice though he didn't take his focus away from Jinx. Good thinking on the Draca's part. For what Seamus had planned, he needed more space.

He had been cutting at Jinx's edges ever since she tried to attack Draig while he was occupied. And fun though it was, he was losing patience.

Getting antsy.

His last fight hadn't gone well.

Then again, taking on Morgase, arguably the strongest Teg Sorceress, hadn't been his best idea.

He felt the need to redeem himself, at least in his own eyes.

To prove that he wasn't over the hill.

That he wasn't the Fish as Typhon had called him.

That he was the Kraken!

Smiling with a wicked intent, Seamus sent an unstoppable rush of water flooding to his front.

Directed right at Jinx.

And he came with it, surfing across the churning surface with a remarkable dexterity.

Catching Jinx by surprise, Typhon's daughter still in the midst of shifting, he dove and flung his arms wide, wrapping them around her sinewy and sinuous body covered in shiny green scales that was now four times longer than it had been before the conflict began.

As soon as he carried Jinx past the outer boundary, Fafnir acted. Sending the Power of the Draca into the Druid's Circle, the response was immediate.

Another flash of blinding light along with a resounding crack.

When the light dissipated, the combatants had vanished, Fafnir sending Seamus where he requested if doing so proved necessary.

"What do we do now?" Melissa released her hold on the Grym, the Druid's Circle blinking out as soon as the touch of the Power of the Ancients faded.

Turning toward her, Fafnir glimpsed the fear in the back of her eyes. He was worried as well, but there was nothing that he could do.

"We wait."

"We can't just wait!" Melissa yelled. "I can't help Draig against Typhon, but you can."

"I am not strong enough to challenge Typhon. That monster is an Ancient. He exercises a power that few if any can match."

"You and some of the other Draca then. If we don't help Draig, then we've sent him to his doom."

Fafnir shook his head, refusing her request and pained at having to do so. Yet he had no choice. "We cannot. The Queen does not permit it. She was quite clear."

"The Queen does not permit it?" Melissa was shocked. "How could she not permit it? Isn't the Queen Draig's mother?" It had never been said, though it hadn't taken much for her to figure that out.

"Yes, Draig is her son."

"She doesn't want to help her son?" Melissa lifted her arms, rolling her eyes, unable to understand what she viewed as selfish and myopic thinking. "That doesn't make any sense."

"She does want to assist Draig, but she cannot." Fafnir wanted to say more, but he didn't, knowing that doing so would only waste more time as Melissa would have more questions. "The Queen has made her decision. The Draca must abide by her decision."

"She can't help her son?" Melissa couldn't believe what she was hearing. "Isn't she the most powerful of the Draca? Isn't that why she's the Queen?"

Fafnir ignored Melissa's last few questions. "She cannot aid Draig, and Draig understands why. We talked before Typhon appeared. His mother's decision and reasoning make sense."

"He needs our help, Fafnir. He's fighting an Ancient for the Gods' sake! He can't take on this monster by himself."

"He must," Fafnir replied with a cold certainty. "For our sakes. For his own as well."

"Fafnir ..."

Fafnir shook his head, done with the conversation. "We would like to aid our brother, but we cannot. For reasons known to him and to the Queen, he must do this on his own. There is no more to be said."

24

THE HYDRA VS. THE KRAKEN

"Your Draca friend sent you to your tomb, Fish! You die here."

"Kraken," Seamus muttered even though he knew that it was wasted breath.

They were in the cavern deep beneath Cape Henlopen. Draig had told him about the hollow cut out from the earth, and it sounded like the space would be perfect for what he had in mind. Although Seamus couldn't say that he was impressed by the renovations made to the hollow by Typhon and Draig at the start of their game.

Massive stones littered the floor. The only piece of rubble that was still somewhat recognizable was the immense, partially shattered granite throne at the back where Jinx positioned herself. The stalactites that just hours before had hung above it sheared off and lying across the seat.

None of that mattered to Seamus, however. What mattered were the many small waterfalls that trickled down the stone behind Jinx.

"No more games, Fish," Jinx hissed, her shift into the Hydra complete. A monstrous, scaly green sea snake with nine heads, each maw was filled with razor-sharp teeth.

Seamus' immediate instinct was to correct her. He didn't have the opportunity, instead forming a shield of water that froze into ice the instant the magic struck the air.

Perfect timing.

One of Jinx's heads smacked against the frosty barricade, cracking it. The head that came right after the first finished the job, smashing the barrier into thousands of pieces.

But Seamus was already gone, moving with a speed that was incongruous with his appearance as a crusty old fisherman.

He formed another shield just like the first. Stronger this time.

Another of Jinx's heads smacked into it. This time it took two more strikes before that barrier shattered.

And once again Seamus wasn't there.

"Run, my pretty," Jinx hissed. The voice came from all of her heads at the same time, all of her heads connected to a single consciousness. "It will do you little good. I will snap you up just like the tasty little treat I know you to be."

Jinx lunged again, this time all of her heads shooting forward.

Recognizing that it would prove futile, Seamus didn't bother to form a shield. In its place, he used the Grym to create a large flow of water beneath his feet, surfing away from the Hydra, one of her heads grazing the back of his shoulder with a fang and nearly taking him to the ground.

Grateful that he had escaped with no more than a bloody scratch, Seamus curled around the chamber, riding the wave and avoiding the rocks that protruded out of the floor. He was far from being in the clear, however.

Jinx slithered after him, the monstrous sea snake demonstrating a dangerous dexterity for such a large creature in such a tight space.

Seamus jumped up from the wave the instant before one of her heads snapped down where he had been surfing just a breath before.

Jinx reared up, screeching in rage at her failure.

Seamus took full advantage of the chance that she gifted him.

Distracted by her miss, one of Jinx's heads was no more than a few feet away from him as he hung in the air. Without even thinking, he fashioned a headsman's axe out of ice that was as strong as steel.

With a single swing, he cut through Jinx's neck, her head falling with Seamus as he dropped down to the puddle-covered cavern floor, the rush of water he had called upon trickling away.

"Blast it!" For his sheer stupidity Seamus uttered a few more curses that would have made even the most callous sailor blush. He shouldn't have acted precipitously.

Within seconds, a growth appeared at the end of Jinx's bloody neck.

And not just one head.

Two.

The process was complete in seconds.

Seamus was quite familiar with the saying that two heads were better than one. In this context, with what he was dealing with right then, he disagreed.

He knew better!

Yet still he had done it, unable to help himself.

He knew as well that he couldn't fight Jinx in his current form when she was the Hydra.

He needed to shift as well if he was to have any chance against the now ten-headed sea snake.

And to do that he required more space.

A lot more space.

No more dancing around.

Before Jinx could make another play for him, he lifted both hands and sent two streams of water with a velocity that matched the energy of a laser blasting into the far wall behind the damaged throne.

Seamus was quite pleased with the resulting explosion.

The primordial rock had held back the ocean for millennia, and as time passed it was slowly losing that battle. The many waterfalls along its surface proof of that.

Seamus simply sped up that natural process of erosion.

The Atlantic Ocean rushed in with a bone-crushing force.

Seamus welcomed it, allowing its power to flow over him. To spin him around the chamber and throw him out into the ocean.

As soon as he was free of the cavern, he shifted into one of his favorite forms. A form that he believed would give him the greatest chance of success against the Hydra.

In seconds he stood as tall as Jinx was long, his body growing, reshaping itself. Armor stronger than titanium that resembled the shell of a lobster formed on his shoulders, forearms, chest, and thighs. His hair and beard became a thick green seaweed. While spikes formed on his back, ensuring that Jinx would have to think twice before trying to attack him from behind. And in his hands he held a massive harpoon crafted from the bone of a sperm whale.

"Come to me, lover," Jinx called, the ten-headed Hydra sidewinding through the water. "Time for our last embrace."

Seamus dodged out of the way a heartbeat before Jinx struck, not wanting to give her the chance to wrap her body around him and crush the life from him. And he was smarter this time.

Rather than surrendering to his initial instinct and slicing across one of Jinx's necks with his harpoon, he punched the bone into her back as she shot past him. Holding the harpoon in place, he allowed Jinx's momentum to do his bloody work for him.

Jinx shrieked, pulling away from him, the long gash leaving a bloody trail through the ocean. Before she could turn and try again, Seamus was on her. Avoiding her heads and her razor-sharp teeth, he jabbed at her wherever he could find purchase in her flesh.

His objective was to slow her down. Weaken her. All the while without him making the same mistake of removing a head and having to take on even more snapping maws.

For a brief time, Seamus relished the fight.

It was like he was acting out a scene from one of the Kaiju movies that he so enjoyed having on in the background when he was working a jigsaw puzzle on a rainy afternoon.

Godzilla versus King Kong.

Though in his current battle, he didn't know which role he preferred the most.

"Fight me, dammit!" Jinx roared, becoming more and more frustrated as she failed to strike him.

"I am," Seamus replied in a booming voice that traveled for leagues across the ocean, "and you're losing."

"That's only because you're a coward," Jinx hissed. "You won't stand and fight. You keep running."

Seamus agreed with her. About not standing in place. Not the running.

He wasn't allowing Jinx to get a fix on him as he dodged and jabbed, ducked and slashed. A fight of agility and cunning. Not strength and power, which was what Jinx craved because it played to her advantage.

"Be careful what you ask for, Jinx."

"Why?" Jinx demanded, curling back around for what seemed like the hundredth time since the combat began and once again finding that Seamus already had taken up a new position where he could poke at her with that damned harpoon of his.

"Because you just might get it."

When Jinx again whipped back around, seeking to get a bead on him, this time rather than moving around her he held his position in the ocean and in a smooth motion threw his harpoon.

Aimed right for Jinx's heart.

Or where her heart would be if she actually had one.

The missile sped so fast through the water that it appeared to be a blur, only its wake visible.

The harpoon never struck home, one of Jinx's heads shooting down and snapping the spear in two before it could slide between her shiny green scales.

But that was fine with Seamus.

Because the harpoon was only a diversion, and it gave him the few seconds that he needed to do what he really intended.

A flood of frigid water surged out from his hands, shooting across the space between them, swirling around Jinx, turning the ocean into a frothy, ice-capped churn.

Jinx struggled to break free.

She tried to lunge at Seamus with her heads.

But she couldn't.

The ice forming around her, spreading swiftly, instantly took hold and refused to release its grip.

Her growl of anger turned to a shriek of fear. Already she couldn't move most of her body, only a few of her heads still having any range of motion. And she could feel the cold grip of the ice creeping over her at an astounding rate. Beginning on her scales, the painful frosty touch worked its way inside her.

Chilling her blood.

Limiting her movement.

Freezing her in place.

"Seamus, I'm going to eat your heart with a ..."

His work complete, he never had the chance to hear what Jinx was going to do to him.

When Jinx could no longer move any part of her body, even her eyes fixed in place, the thick layer of ice that held her expanded outward. Becoming thicker. Harder. All but unbreakable.

Pressing in upon her, the Gorgon's prison tightened around her snakelike body and her ten heads so that she had no chance of breaking free.

Yet still the ice thickened. Making excellent use of the seawater, Seamus wanted to ensure that his creation would last for a good long while.

He didn't release his hold on the Grym until a massive iceberg floated before him, Jinx in the form of the Hydra hidden within.

He smiled in satisfaction. His work was done.

"Only one monster can rule the sea, and that's me," he grumbled.

Seamus grinned then, giving Jinx a wink.

She couldn't respond to him. She couldn't move. All she could do was stare at him with a venomous hatred through a hundred feet of ice that was stronger than the strongest steel.

He could taunt her for his victory.

Seamus chose not to do that. Instead, he offered her a reminder.

"This is why I'm the Kraken. This is why the ocean belongs to me."

He sighed then, pleased that after all these centuries he finally could get in the last word with her. But he still had one more task to complete.

Placing a hand in the ocean, he swirled the water with his fingers, a current forming that pushed the iceberg away from him.

That current would listen only to him. And it would

continue on its way, taking the iceberg with it, until it reached its final destination.

The Antarctica.

Seamus could have killed Jinx, freezing her until her blood vessels burst. That might have been the safer course.

But that would have taken a great deal more effort than he had expended already. And he didn't want to take that risk.

Besides, strange as it seemed, he still had a soft spot for her in his heart. Even though she had called him Fish. For a time, she had been what he needed her to be.

Once Jinx reached the bottom of the globe, she could enjoy a long winter vacation. Until the ice melted of course. Which would happen. It was just a question of when.

But what he had done should keep her out of commission for a good long while.

Unless her father killed Draig and decided to free her.

A possibility that he didn't want to think about.

25

AT THE GATES

"How did you find this place?" Typhon demanded.

The Ancient believed that after all this time and after all his efforts to erase the location of Charon's Cave from the collective memory of the Teg, the primary gateway to Tartarus should have been wiped from history.

"I have a very good librarian," Draig replied.

"A librarian?" Typhon didn't understand the reference.

"A librarian," Draig confirmed with a twist of his lips.

Seshat deserved all the credit for finding this immense cavern deep within the earth and far below Yellowstone National Park. When she told him what she had dug up from resources long thought lost, he hadn't doubted her. Yellowstone sat atop the largest caldera in the world, so it only made sense. Besides, the Egyptian Goddess of writing, knowledge, and wisdom was never wrong. Ever. And woe to any who dared to question her.

"You make a mistake by bringing me here, Dragon. It means only that you are that much closer to your doom. That tunnel leads to Tartarus." Typhon nodded toward the large opening in the rock wall that was just off to their right, wispy threads of grey mist twisting out of the ground right in front of the gloom. "You have made my task that much easier."

Draig nodded, not replying right away. Instead he used the time that Typhon was giving him to get a better sense of his surroundings. Never having been here, he never had the chance to survey the ground to prepare for this combat after Seshat gave him the information he needed.

Rivers of flowing magma crisscrossed the cavern floor and ran down the walls in more than a dozen places, illuminating the darkness. Some of those rivers met in large, bubbling pools of molten rock. The largest, which seemed more underground lake than pool, was behind him. Maybe a quarter mile distant, which gave him a good sense of just how large Charon's Cave was.

The name was a misnomer. It should have been called Charon's Canyon.

In several places along the floor, noxious plumes of scalding fog blasted into the air. And with a frightening frequency massive geysers of boiling water shot out of the earth, releasing for a time the pressure beneath.

"Perhaps," Draig replied. "Then again, perhaps I made my task easier."

"You presume too much, Dragon." Typhon drew closer, moving out from the shadows at the back of the cave.

Thanks to Seshat, Draig knew what to expect. Still, it was quite breathtaking to take in for the first time the monster towering above him, Typhon having completed his shift into his true form just seconds after arriving in Charon's Cave.

The Ancient was known for many things in history and mythology.

The God of volcanic forces.

The father of typhoons.

A Titan, said to be even stronger than Kronos.

An enemy to Zeus and the entire Greek pantheon of Gods.

An enemy to any who dared to stand in his way, Typhon's greatest desire the complete subjugation of the Teg.

And a monster who thrived in the chaos and destruction that only he could generate.

It was as a monster that Typhon appeared before Draig now. A colossal, serpentine giant whose head was said to touch the clouds. Clearly an embellishment although the Ancient was at least two hundred feet in height. What was not exaggerated were the one hundred dragon heads sprouting from his scaly shoulders, all of which spewed fire. Huge wings affixed to his spiked back would do him little good in the confines of Charon's Cave, although the coiled serpents' tails in the place of his legs should allow him to move with a good deal of dexterity for a monster of such great size.

A nightmare come to life. Draig couldn't deny it.

Worse, Typhon was said to be indestructible. Hence Zeus' inability to kill him, having to settle for banishing him to Tartarus, a place of Typhon's father's creation. The irony of that not lost on the Greek pantheon who rejoiced upon Typhon's imprisonment.

Draig's father also had defeated Typhon the first time the monster tried to escape his prison, Zeus and his brothers and sisters nowhere to be found. The stories about that threat to the very existence of the Teg conveniently ignoring the fact that Merlin played a large role in that victory, which wasn't all that surprising to Draig. He knew how his father liked to spin events, often thinking more about the public relations value of an act rather than the actual result and the consequences to follow.

Yet despite the immense power that Typhon exercised, Draig believed that the Ancient had a weakness that he could exploit.

And it didn't have anything to do with his employing *The Book of Whispers*.

Because it would have been foolish to believe that he could make use of the power contained within that artifact against Typhon in his current form. To do so only would ensure his death and disaster for the Teg.

Typhon was an Ancient.

Not just one of the Tylwyth Teg.

The Grym of the Teg came from the power that was physically a part of the Ancient.

Therefore, Draig would require something more, an angle, if he was to have any chance of success against the monster staring down at him, the eyes of one hundred dragon heads fixed upon him.

"Maybe, because I presumed that bringing you here you'd have the inescapable urge to return to Tartarus," Draig suggested with a shrug. "Your father did create it after all. After making it your residence for so long, I would think it feels like home."

"You are overconfident, Dragon," Typhon boomed, his deep voice that sounded much like the roar of a hurricane creating a heavy ripple that ran through the pool of lava separating them.

"Just hopeful."

"Hope will not help you now, Dragon. For you, all hope is gone."

Draig didn't bother to respond, not having any desire to continue the conversation.

He was already moving, sprinting above the pool of bubbling magma on the path he created out of the Grym. So fast that he was no more than a blur.

Before Typhon could react, Draig was on the monster.

Slashing and cutting at Typhon with Excalibur, his glowing blade sliced with little resistance through scales alleged to be impregnable. Blood and the hiss of burning flesh followed in his wake as he danced around the monster's tails.

Racing around erratically, he left no pattern or rhythm for Typhon to discern.

Typhon's needing to guess, not knowing where Draig would be, made it difficult for the century of dragon heads that snapped at him from above to find their mark. More often than not the heads got in each other's way as each one strove for the kill.

Through it all, Typhon roared and cursed with frustration. Unable to escape the little dog nipping at his tails.

Normally he wouldn't have cared.

It would have been an annoyance. No more than that.

But with the Dragon, it was much more than annoyance.

Every bite of the Dragon's sword sent a scorching flame shooting through Typhon's body.

Not enough to kill him.

Nothing could kill him.

He was an Ancient after all.

But those wounds burned in a way that nothing else quite could, the fire only intensifying.

Typhon had no one to blame but himself as his dragons struggled vainly to catch up to their quarry. He shouldn't have underestimated the Dragon.

"You will not last!" Typhon roared as he slithered this way and that across the cavern floor. He even drifted back into a pool of lava, thinking that he could escape the Dragon's assault in the molten rock and finding much to his chagrin that he couldn't. The Dragon followed him out over the magma, crafting those blasted paths of energy to continue to harry him. "You will pay for your insolence! Chaining you in Tartarus is not the worst that I can do to you!"

Draig ignored the Ancient. Focused on the task he set for himself, he strove to inflict as much pain and injury upon his opponent as he could before he needed to adjust his strategy.

The Grym alone would have done nothing against Typhon's

armored scales, which was one of the reasons the Ancient was such a frightening opponent for most of the Teg.

The Grym coupled with the Power of the Draca was another matter entirely.

Infusing his steel with both potent magical energies, with every slash, every score across Typhon's scaled flesh, Draig opened a bloody gash that burned at the first touch of the steel and then flashed with an even greater intensity. The Draca fire that never went out flared deeper into Typhon's body. The wounds expanded, the blackened flesh flaking away and the charred scales useless, brittle, and vulnerable. Worst of all, Typhon had no way to end the sizzling torment as he burned from the inside out.

Typhon's rising concern became more apparent as he struggled to evade his attacker, his movements becoming more rushed and uncertain.

The dragon heads smashed down with greater freneticism. Missing. Ripping apart stone. Crushing boulders into powder. Sending large swathes of lava flying into the air. But always missing their prey.

Typhon was stronger than he was. Draig would never dispute that. Typhon always would be stronger.

But Draig was faster.

Both in movement and thought.

And he put that speed to use in a way that Typhon had never experienced before.

All the while Draig stayed in tight to Typhon. As close to his two tails as he could as the monster slithered this way and that, seeking to escape him.

That made it that much harder for one of the dragon heads to snap him up. And it made it that much easier for Draig to do his bloody work. Earning the enmity of the Ancient for his efforts and hopefully setting the stage in his favor for the climax of the combat.

While serving his father he rarely had cause to employ the Power of the Draca.

Now, free from that constraint, free to do as he needed to do against the deadliest adversary Draig ever had faced, he relished the feel of the unique energy coursing through him that was gifted to him by his mother's bloodline. And he had no doubt that without it, Typhon already would have chained him in Tartarus.

Thanks to the blood of the Draca running through his veins, Draig was faster than most other Teg. He enjoyed greater endurance. Greater strength. And even more important, he had at his disposal the tool required to wound one of the Ancients.

And that would have to be enough, because Draig had little doubt that no matter what he did, he had little chance of killing Typhon. Still, he would take what he could get.

Because his goal wasn't to kill Typhon.

It was to annoy the Ancient.

Peck at him.

Distract him.

Make him feel pain.

Make him experience worry.

Force him to rethink his strategy.

Drive him toward a bad decision.

Push Typhon into a mistake.

And constant movement and instinctual thinking were the keys to that.

Gliding.

Slashing.

Diving.

Stabbing.

Sprinting.

Cutting.

Draig moved with grace, power, and determination.

Refusing to be denied, he bit through Typhon's scales and

into the flesh beneath. The Power of the Draca infused within Excalibur scorched the Ancient's scales and burned his flesh, offering the monster a torturing pain that flashed with a greater severity with each passing second.

Until Draig's luck ran out.

Just as he feared that it would.

One of the dragon heads sideswiped him more by chance than by design, sending Draig sprawling to the cavern floor right up against the cusp of a pool of lava that extended off into the darkness.

Draig pushed himself up as quickly as he could, feeling a little unsteady on his feet, at the same time wary that another of the dragon heads already was streaking down to snap him up.

But he had nothing to fear.

It had gone quiet in Charon's Cave.

Typhon glared down at him. His hundred dragon heads spread all around Draig to his front, glittering eyes staring at him intently. The pool of lava at his back.

He was trapped.

"Your game is done, Dragon," Typhon's deep rumble of a voice echoed through the cavern, the lava behind Draig rippling. "Well fought, I will give you that. But your fight is over. Because you never considered one key fact."

"I'm afraid to ask," Draig replied, trying to incorporate as much indifference and disrespect into his voice as he could.

"Even now you seek to annoy me," Typhon grumbled. "Though I should not be surprised after your display." Typhon shook his head sadly. "The wounds you have caused me will heal, Dragon, once you are gone from the Natural World. And the pain you have caused me ... that has sealed your fate."

"Tartarus, yes, you were quite clear." Draig was trying to draw out the conversation for a few seconds more, hoping that he might be able to find some room to maneuver. "I take your place in the chains that once held you."

"Tartarus, yes," Typhon agreed. "But the one key fact that you failed to consider is that for me to chain you in Tartarus, I don't need your body. No, that's a myth. I just need your spirit."

Draig had no time to consider the true implication of what Typhon revealed, a hundred streams of white-hot fire blasting toward him.

The Dragon disappeared within the flames, all of the fiery streams joining together to form a giant pyre that was hot enough to burn through any substance in the world ... and certainly one Teg.

Yet still the dragon heads spewed their flames. Typhon gave in to his need for revenge. Already caught up in what he viewed as his most important victory.

Because once he imprisoned the Dragon's spirit in Tartarus, the Dragon would be there for eternity. Doing Typhon's bidding, the Dragon's first task would be to cut the cord that kept Typhon's own spirit locked within the depths of his father's underworld.

More than a minute passed, the dragon heads atop Typhon's shoulders continuing to spew their fiery venom.

Typhon wanted to make sure.

And he needed to release his rage, enjoying every second of his vengeance.

Until, shockingly, despite his immense bulk, Typhon was flying through the air, knocked from his tails, falling hard to his back, as a colossal explosion rocked Charon's Cave. Several massive stalactites sticking down from the ceiling, many of which were hidden in the gloom, broke free and crashed to the floor, sending up great gouts of magma when they struck the lava pools.

Typhon pushed himself up slowly, not quite believing what

he was seeing. Unable to take his eyes from the one who waited before him.

The Dragon stood there.

Not the son of Arthur Pendragon, King of the Teg.

Rather the son of Tiamat, Queen of the Draca.

Although for some inexplicable reason that Typhon didn't quite understand, the figure seemed more than just the Dragon.

A creature beyond Teg or Draca.

A creature of legend.

Rarely spoken of.

More dreaded than welcomed.

A good thing, then, that Typhon planned to kill the Dragon. Because clearly he was more of a threat than the Ancient ever could have imagined and, more enticing, the additional power that Typhon would have at his beck and call upon chaining the Dragon's spirit would prove quite useful when it came time to conquer the Teg.

Typhon watched as the Dragon, who stood half as tall as he did, unwrapped his huge wings. Reddish-gold scales that matched his eyes had replaced his skin. Spikes ran from the top of his head to the tip of his barbed tail. And his hands were now claws not only made for shredding flesh, but also strong enough to crush bone. Excalibur remained within his grasp, the sword growing in relation to his size.

Yet despite the many changes in the Dragon's appearance, the eyes were much the same. The faint hint of mockery as the Dragon stared at his adversary. The promise that their combat was not yet over.

"So this is the real Dragon," Typhon rumbled. "I can't say that I'm impressed."

"The feeling is mutual," Draig growled, making sure that Typhon couldn't miss the contempt that leaked from his voice.

"You have put on a good show, Dragon. I give you credit for that. But you are no match for me. You will die here."

"You're so certain of that?"

"I am," Typhon intoned, as if any statement he uttered was the truth.

"Then how is it that I'm still alive even after your own good show?" Draig offered Typhon a raised eyebrow, enjoying how it rankled his adversary.

"Even now you seek to push me." Typhon shook his head, not quite believing the Dragon's audacity.

"I seek nothing. I do. I do push you, Typhon. And I will continue to push you until the very end."

"You will answer for your arrogance!" Typhon hissed, the hundred dragon heads swaying and snapping on his shoulders adding to the sibilant noise. "You cannot defeat me. No one can defeat me." The Ancient completely missed his own arrogance in making such a statement.

Draig chuckled then, certain that his doing so only would enrage his adversary all the more. Just as he wanted. "You know, Typhon, there's a lesson in every myth."

"What's the lesson in this one?" he demanded.

"Don't be a dumbass," Draig replied with a shrug. "But I guess you just can't help yourself."

Before there was time for Draig's words to sink in, he launched himself at Typhon. After just a few flaps, his massive wings lifted him into the air and sent Draig hurtling toward the Ancient.

Before he slammed into the towering monster, Draig dipped to his left and curled around Typhon, avoiding the massive fist that sought to grab him out of the air. At the same time, he slashed with Excalibur in a tight arc, the glowing steel slicing through the necks of more than a dozen dragons and sending the heads to flop in their death throes around Typhon's tails.

Draig ignored the Ancient's roar of rage, anguish, and pain, focusing on what he needed to do. Because even in this, his true form, even with the power that he controlled, killing Typhon was more than he could ask of himself.

Still, that didn't mean that Draig couldn't give the Ancient a good fight.

Just as he did at the beginning of the combat, he relied on his speed. Forcing Typhon to move constantly, he never allowed the Ancient to get in a good strike whether with fist or flame from his own maw or that of the dragons on his shoulders. The number of those dragons decreasing, Draig took a particular pleasure in slicing through their swaying necks whenever he could.

For his efforts, Draig picked up a dozen different wounds. Bloody slashes across his body. Aching bruises when Typhon's fists connected. Rips in his wings when the white-hot fire from Typhon's maw struck true.

Even so, Draig gave as good as he got. Even better than he got in his estimation. Though he knew in the end that would not be good enough.

More would be required if he was to have any chance of surviving this encounter.

"You cannot escape me, Dragon!" Typhon roared. He spun around on his wounded tails more slowly than he would have preferred, trying to track Draig as he flew and sprinted around him, Excalibur gleaming brightly, covered in the Ancient's blood. "You only delay your death! You do not prevent it!"

Finally Draig saw his chance.

A pile of broken stalactites lay just off to Typhon's left.

Landing deftly right by the pile, he swung down with Excalibur. The blade infused with the Grym, energized by the Power of the Draca, crushed the stone, sending millions of pieces of razor-sharp rock flying through the air in an explosion that rivaled the eruption of Mount Vesuvius.

The attack did not harm Typhon badly. The stone frag-ments smacked harmlessly off his scaly flesh, the only real damage inflicted upon a few of the dragons still swaying atop his shoulders that were struck in the eye with a shard.

But it did distract the Ancient, Typhon pivoting away from the blast for a split-second and missing the large hole in the cavern floor that Draig's strike created. The instant one of Typhon's tails dropped into that hole, sending the Ancient crashing to the ground, Draig struck.

With a single swing of Excalibur, he sliced clean through the trapped tail, taking more than fifty feet off its length.

Typhon roared in agony, never anticipating or experiencing such a blow. Never believing that the Dragon would put him in such a position.

Yet despite the grievous wound, Typhon did not fear. He was still stronger than the Dragon. In spite of the power the Dragon brought to bear, it did not compare to his own.

Which was why Draig wasn't satisfied with his latest attack. An attack that was really just a precursor to his main play.

Reaching beneath his shirt, he pulled out the necklace he had placed there. Ripping the leather strap from around his neck, he threw it toward Typhon. The Ancient had yet to rise from the ground, finding it difficult to balance his gigantic frame on one working tail.

Then, Draig did as the Frost Queen instructed.

He called upon not only the Grym that was so much a part of him, but also the Power of the Draca, relying on the ancient magic of his mother's family to bolster his effort and intensify the potency of what he was about to do.

Satisfied that he had pulled in as much of that natural magic as he possibly could without bursting at the seams, the sizzling power scalding him from the inside out, he pointed with his hand toward the snowflake crafted of what appeared to be clear glass that was floating in the air.

When the snowflake was lined up with Typhon's chest, Draig released the magic building up within him, that threatened to rip him apart, experiencing a welcome relief as the stream of power shrieked through the cavern and hit the snowflake dead center.

The effect was instantaneous and heart-stopping.

A monstrous wintry storm erupted that was centered around Typhon. The strength of the blizzard so great that the heat of Charon's Cave, the lava running along the cavern floor and around the Ancient, did nothing to assuage the intense power of the tempest.

In fact, the lava began to cool and harden, the screaming wind blasting the Ancient with ice and snow as a thick layer of frost formed swiftly all over the monster's body.

Typhon fought back. Refusing to be defeated, blazing fire erupted from his mouth. The dragon heads that remained on his shoulders joined the effort.

All to no avail.

Even here in Charon's Cave, the power of the Frost Queen proved too potent.

The frost turned to ice.

The cold seeped beneath Typhon's scales and into his many wounds, all the injuries Draig gave him at the start of the fight designed to provide the debilitating cold with more and faster paths into the Ancient.

That bone-chilling cold slowed him.

Distracted him.

Incapacitated him.

It formed a cocoon of frosty white all around him that thickened as one wintry blast after another struck.

Draig didn't wait to land the second of his one-two punch.

He called upon the power that only he could employ.

The power that had brought him to this place.

That had led to this confrontation.

The power contained within *The Book of Whispers.*

A power that wouldn't allow Draig to control Typhon. But he didn't want control over the Ancient. He wanted something else.

The potency of the ancient tome that was linked to him thanks to his mother latched onto Typhon with a shocking greed.

Feeling that first touch of the artifact, the Ancient struggled even harder to break free from the icy storm swirling around him. Recognizing what was happening, Typhon realized in a heartbeat that much to his horror his efforts would gain him little.

Because in just seconds *The Book of Whispers* did as Draig wanted.

The artifact drained Typhon's remarkable power from him, stealing it for a time, borrowing it and weakening Typhon even further.

"You can't take from me what only belongs to me!" roared Typhon, even as he felt himself flag. His body, curling in upon itself, grew cold. Nonresponsive. His body temperature dropping as if he was being placed in a deep, frozen slumber.

"I'm not taking it from you," Draig said. Never losing his focus, he continued to call upon *The Book of Whispers* to do the work required. "I'm using your own power against you. Ironic, don't you think?"

Typhon could only mumble an incoherent response, his energy fading rapidly as the artifact drained him, making the impact of the magic granted by the Frost Queen that much more effective.

Pleased with his success, all the while understanding that time was short, that the gift granted to him by the Frost Queen would last for only so long, he used the Grym to lift Typhon and move him across the cavern floor, the storm wrapped around the Ancient the entire time and keeping him in a weakened state.

A good thing, because for Draig next came the most worrisome part of his entire strategy.

Having maneuvered Typhon right in front of the gloom that led down to Tartarus, he didn't know what he needed to do next to send the Ancient back to where he belonged.

Give him a shove?

No one had been able to help him answer that question. Not Seshat. Not even Merlin.

And then as the seconds ticked away his worry began to increase, because the intensity of the icy storm that allowed Draig to use *The Book of Whispers* against the Ancient was dying down. It wouldn't be long before Typhon freed himself. And when that happened ...

Draig didn't want to think about that.

Thankfully, he didn't have to.

As soon as Typhon's frozen body touched the very edge of the gloom where the wispy grey threads spun into the air, those tendrils reached out with a sinuous grasp and wrapped around Typhon's massive frame, the darkness just behind beginning to spin.

Slowly at first.

Then more rapidly.

And faster still until the swirling gloom resembled a whirlpool.

Seconds later, the black flashed and darkened.

"We can be allies, Dragon," Typhon shrieked, slowly coming back to himself as the power of the Frost Queen waned, though not so fast that he could do anything about his plight, the grey tendrils drawing him through the entrance to Tartarus too strong and too intent on their purpose. He would need to rely on the mercy of the Dragon for that. "We can kill your father. We can claim the Teg throne. We can make all those who have wronged us pay for their actions in sorrow and blood."

"There can never be a we, Typhon. With you, there is only an I. Besides, what I want isn't what you want. I don't want revenge. I don't want to subjugate the Teg. I want to ensure that *you* can never threaten the Teg again."

A blast of musty air erupted from the misty whirlpool. Then, just as fast, that wind reversed itself, circling around the chamber and back through the gloom, taking Typhon with it.

Draig couldn't see past the swirling waves that now resembled a black hole, the vortex framed by gates made of black steel affixed to ancient pillars of stone. Those gates opening as Typhon drifted deeper into the tunnel. Welcoming him. The pull of the darkness of Tartarus too much even for an Ancient.

"No, you can't do this!" Typhon screamed. "You can't do this!"

"I just did," Draig replied. "Welcome home, Typhon."

Though it seemed Typhon missed Draig's last comment, the Ancient's focus on what he was moving toward, not what he was moving away from.

"You're not supposed to be here. You're not supposed to ..."

Draig heard the terror in Typhon's voice, never believing that he could. But he never heard who Typhon might be speaking to.

Because at that very moment, the gates of Tartarus swung closed with a thunderous crash.

26

DIFFERENT PATHS

"She'll be all right?"

Draig stepped out onto the Safe Haven's porch. Melissa was leaning against the railing, arms crossed in front of her, her worry plain. He nodded.

"She will. It's just going to take some time for her to heal. She's lost a lot of her strength."

Before Typhon slipped through the gates of Tartarus, Draig kept to himself just enough of the Ancient's power to break the curse the monster had placed on Medusa. It hadn't been easy, but with Hestia and Peggy Rose's assistance, he was able to extract the poison that had been killing the Gorgon by consuming her spirit.

"Thank you," Melissa sighed with relief. Finally free of the guilt that had been plaguing her ever since she got wrapped up in schemes built upon schemes that began at Mordred's mansion by the sea and ended here, farther up the eastern coast, in Kraken Cove. Well, not entirely free of her guilt. But she would be when her mother was back on her feet. "I'm in your debt."

"You're not," Draig said, waving her off, as if what he did, what he risked, wasn't of any consequence. Ever uncomfortable in situations such as this one, he leaned back against the side of the house and tried to change the topic. "I understand your mother will be staying in Kraken Cove. Cerridwen said she helped her find a nice old Victorian that she plans to fix up. Something about practicing homeopathic medicine, though she didn't know all the details."

"She is," Melissa nodded. "It makes sense for her. She has friends here, and I think she's tired of living on the edge."

"But you won't be joining her here?"

Melissa shook her head no.

"Why not?"

"I was the bait," she said flatly.

Draig didn't reply right away, knowing that there was more to Melissa's reluctance to stay than just that. "Not you so much as what you had in your possession."

"That doesn't matter," she stated again with more heat. "I was the bait."

"You were the bait," Draig confirmed, "but the Three Brothers stayed close to you the entire time until I could catch up to you."

Melissa frowned, crinkling her lips to demonstrate her displeasure. "I'm still not happy about being the bait."

"I can understand that." Draig wasn't going to apologize. He did what he needed to do. Using Melissa was the only way to put his plan into motion and get close to Typhon.

"But I have to admit that it was a good strategy."

"You're still not happy though," Draig confirmed with a small smile.

"I'm not."

"Fair enough."

Melissa studied Draig for several seconds. The Dragon stood only a few feet away from her. Before all this had begun the thought of being so close to him terrified her. Now, the thought of being this close to the Dragon appealed to her. She almost wanted him to make her another homemade dinner in recompense. Almost.

"My mother asked me to work with her on her business. She wants me to be a partner."

"But ..." Draig prodded after a long silence.

"How did you know there was a but?"

"I don't get the sense that you're used to being in one place for a very long time. And not just because of the pressures of your work."

"How can you tell?"

"Because I used to be the same way. I needed to move to feel alive."

Melissa smiled then. "I have some unfinished business."

"I figured as much."

"Perhaps you'd like to join me? We'd make quite a pair. The Dragon and the Witch." She smiled again. "See, I'd even give you top billing."

Draig hadn't expected the offer, not after what he did to her. Then again, it was only fair after all that Melissa had done to him. When he looked into her eyes to try to determine what she really wanted, he could see that she already knew how he was going to respond.

"I have some unfinished business here."

Melissa's smile dropped a bit. Then she nodded. "I thought as much." She stepped forward, placing her hands on his arms and kissing him softly on the lips. Briefly. When she pulled back, her eyes were wistful.

"I'll see you soon," she whispered as she opened the door and walked into the inn.

Draig watched her go.

Doubting that he would once she left Kraken Cove.

27

LOOKING AHEAD

"Are you sad?"

"Why would I be sad?" Draig asked.

He stood on the shore of Raptor Bay island. The lighthouse, his home for more than a decade, rose at his back.

Draig stared out at the waves that were pounding with greater force against the beach. A storm was coming, and not just one that would roil the Atlantic Ocean.

"The ocean doesn't feel right."

That's what Seamus had told him recently. Then as a prelude to their engagement with Jinx, Typhon's daughter seeking to turn Draig and, failing that, killing him.

And he had been right.

If Seamus was standing next to him now, his friend would probably say the same as he did before.

The ocean didn't feel right to Draig. Not because of a specific threat like an Ancient seeking to conquer the Teg world. No, it was a general sense of unease that pervaded him. As if the world around him was shifting and in a way that he didn't yet understand. In a way that he wasn't certain he wanted it to.

"Your latest cause has left you." Riga stepped up next to Draig, slipping her arm through his.

Draig smiled. "She wasn't a cause. She was a catalyst."

"A catalyst for what other than chaos?" Riga asked.

"That's an excellent question," Draig murmured. He turned toward her. "Thank you for your help. I couldn't do what I needed to do without you."

Riga offered Draig a devilish grin. "How could I say no to tweaking your father's nose and then Morgase's. It was the most fun I've had in quite some time."

Draig chuckled softly. "Yes, I heard you put on quite a show in Williamsburg."

"You did?"

"Kassie filled me in. It seems that she had a great deal of fun as well."

Riga offered Draig a nod of pride. "Our daughter conducted herself well. More than well, in fact. I have no doubt that Mordred will have nightmares now not only about you but also her. The Dragon's daughter proved to be just as formidable an opponent as her father."

"I would expect nothing less."

"Is that why you're smiling so broadly? She's a chip off the old block?"

"No, not for that reason. Rather, I was pleased that she called to tell me all about it."

"Progress," Riga nodded slowly.

"It seems that way," Draig agreed, his voice containing a hint of relief.

"Don't muck it up. If you lose her trust this time, you may never get it back."

"Thanks for your faith in me," Draig replied with a heavy dose of sarcasm.

"Sorry," Riga replied, offering him a nod of apology. "That was uncalled for on my part."

"So what's on your mind other than the Witch who has moved on?" Draig asked.

"You mean other than to congratulate you on your victory?"

"I had a lot of help. Much of it from you."

"You always feel the need to share the credit. You're so unlike so many of the other warriors I know and have worked with over the centuries."

"That's because I'm just a baker," Draig replied in a deadpan voice.

Riga laughed deeply. "Of course you are." She reached out and squeezed his arm. This was one of the reasons she had become attracted to Draig in the first place. His sense of humor and the fact that he never felt the need to tout his achievements. His skill. The talents that resided solely within him.

Draig was the most dangerous Teg of the last few centuries.

More dangerous than Arthur. Morgase. Even Merlin.

Riga had known it when she first met him so long ago. Although she had kept that truth to herself, knowing that Draig would reveal himself when the time was right.

And he had repaid her belief in him by proving it to all the Teg, time and time again, banishing Typhon back to Tartarus only the latest and most powerful example.

Word of that achievement already was spreading among the Teg. Those ripples were gaining strength. And where they would lead ...

Riga had a sense. Just a sense.

Draig had a sense as well. She could feel it radiating out from him.

Because of that, she felt for him. Still, she couldn't help him with this new burden. He had decided to involve himself in a small matter that had become a larger one. And then larger still.

And now it was too late.

The Fallen Knight was no longer Fallen.

The Dragon had returned.

For better or for worse.

"You don't need to worry about me," Draig said quietly, his words barely heard above the roar of the crashing waves.

"Why do you think I'm worried about you?"

"I can see it in your eyes."

"You see more than you should."

"Sometimes I do," Draig admitted. "With you, never."

Turning to face him, Riga reached up and brushed her lips lightly against his. This was another reason she had been attracted to him. His way with words and his ability to read her like no one else could.

"You can sense it just like I can," Riga said.

Draig nodded. "It's not the end." He had seen something when Typhon was pulled back into Tartarus. Only a glimpse. Not enough to understand what it really was. But certainly enough to understand that Typhon wasn't the only threat facing the Teg. Perhaps not even the greatest threat.

"No," Riga agreed. "It's not."

"You don't need to hold back. There's something else you want to say."

"Just a suggestion," Riga replied. She caught his eyes, making sure he was paying attention. "There are a great many matters of import that seem to be converging upon you."

"That certainly seems to be the case," Draig sighed. "What's on your mind?"

"You don't like the game that's been set out for you."

Draig shook his head. "I don't."

"Then change the game," Riga said with a bright sparkle in her dark eyes. "Do the unexpected."

"Then see how all the pieces fall," Draig murmured.

"Exactly. Play the game that you want to play and see if your opponents can adapt to you."

"A fiendish approach," Draig murmured.

"And that's why you can't bear to be away from me for too long," Riga replied, lifting her lips up to his.

THE END

Keep reading for the first two chapters of *Stealing the Light*,
Book 1 of *Legend of the Dragon Lord*.

BONUS MATERIAL

If you really enjoyed this story, I need you to do me a HUGE favor – please follow me on Amazon and BookBub. And if you have a few minutes, consider writing a review.

Keep reading for the first two chapters from *Stealing the Light,* Book 1 of *Legend of the Dragon Lord.* Order Book 1 from my author website PeterWachtBooks.com. Also available on Amazon.

Stealing the Light
By Peter Wacht

Book 1 of Legend of the Dragon Lord

This book is a work of fiction. Names, characters, places, and incidents are the product of the author's imagination or are used fictitiously. Any resemblance to actual events, locales, or persons, living or dead, is coincidental.

Copyright 2025 © by Peter Wacht

Cover design by Ebooklaunch.com

All rights reserved. In accordance with the U.S. Copyright Act of 1976, the scanning, uploading, and electronic sharing of any part of this book without the permission of the publisher constitute unlawful piracy and theft of the author's intellectual property.

Published in the United States by Kestrel Media Group LLC.

ISBN: 978-1-950236-57-2

eBook ISBN: 978-1-950236-58-9

Library of Congress Control Number: 2025901347

 Formatted with Vellum

1. WORRISOME DISCOVERY

"This can't be right." Mikel frowned as he stared at the flakes of white that had hardened into ice and left several crusty shapes in their wake.

Lost in his own thoughts, he had almost missed them, never expecting to see footprints twice the size of a man's so far away from the jagged peaks that rose to the east.

The prints had the same number of toes as a human but the pointed indentations dug several inches down into the packed snow. They resembled claws more than feet. Those talons could rip open a man's gut with a single swipe.

"Not a good sign," he grumbled to himself. "Why would they come down from their caves?"

Mikel snorted, shaking his head, realizing that he was talking to himself again. It was a habit of his when he spent too much time by himself, which was a fairly regular occurrence these days thanks to his frequent trips into this frigidly cold often monochromatic landscape.

"No reason to ask," he murmured softly, answering his own question. "There's only one reason why a clan would come down from the mountains."

Adjusting the small pack that hung over his shoulder, he ignored the short sword scabbarded across his back, his hand instead drifting down to his hip. He took some comfort from the two-foot-long mace strapped there. Lightweight despite the hammer head on one end, a nasty curled spike on the other -- good for stabbing or slicing throats -- gave an experienced practitioner of the weapon a variety of options for defending himself ... or killing what required killing.

He knew that for a fact, having needed to do both more times than he cared to remember. Nightmares from several of those encounters ensured that he didn't sleep for very long or very well during the cold winter nights.

Those troublesome memories had no place in the here and now, however. Better to stay in the present. Better to live with his own nightmares rather than become a victim of one of the nightmares that had decided to hunt well beyond their mountain territory.

He stood atop a small bluff hidden by snow and ice, a barely visible trail snaking its way down the side to the Great Barrow. For the next few leagues, looking to the west and deeper into the Frozen Waste, he saw nothing else except for large, rectangular, snow-covered dunes that were a hundred yards wide and three times as long. Burial mounds Cadmus had explained, some containing the remains of creatures long dead and best forgotten.

There were broad paths between the mounds. Even so, when he entered the frosty ground set aside for the dead, he always stayed close to the side of a barrow and kept a wary eye.

Mikel was well aware of what to look for to avoid the death-traps hidden along those paths. Sinkholes dotted the space between the mounds, covered only by a thin crust of snow and ice.

If you didn't die from the fall, you'd die in the pit if you didn't have the proper equipment for climbing out.

He did. Nevertheless, he had no desire to risk becoming trapped in a sinkhole, even if only for a few minutes.

Not when he was more worried about what was haunting the Great Barrow.

The tracks he identified, although wiped away to a large extent by the blustery wind, led in the direction he needed to go.

He shook his head in aggravation. More at himself than anything else.

Teodor had been right. His friend had argued against making the trip on his own, believing that Mikel should wait until he could join him.

It would only have been a delay of a few days. And there was other business he could have conducted on the Crux during that time.

That didn't matter, however. Despite his friend's wise counsel, he couldn't wait. Not with what he needed to do.

Mikel had made a promise.

And he always kept his promises.

No matter what those promises might cost him.

The trust placed in him was too important.

It was hard earned ... and much too easily lost.

Mikel stayed where he was for a few minutes more. Wanting to get a better lay of the land. Seeking to identify anything out of the ordinary.

He didn't see anything from his perch that gave him any cause for concern. That meant very little, however. With the creature that made that imprint, he knew that he had virtually no chance of catching a glimpse of the monster before it buried a claw in him.

He needed to listen to have any chance of avoiding being caught by surprise, having little desire to be added to the cookpot.

He did that now.

Closing his eyes so that his vision didn't betray his hearing, he stood there for several minutes more. Not in a rush. Knowing exactly what he was listening for. And, thankfully, not hearing the rustle, sigh, or brief exhalation, that faint whisper or slight crunch, that meant his death approached.

Yet.

Because he had no doubt that it would only be a matter of time before he did.

Opening his eyes again, he studied the landscape of white that spread out before him. For as far as he could see, there was nothing but snow and ice. From where he stood, beyond the burial mounds that were closest to him, the environment appeared to be flat, the color and wind-swept nature of the ground hiding the rugged landscape, allowing it all to blend together.

A trick of the mind and the light.

A range of highlands extended toward the horizon to the west. In between, besides the barrows, there were a host of perils in addition to sinkholes and monsters with razor-sharp claws that viewed human flesh as a delicacy.

That thought stuck in his mind, Mikel reached down and rubbed his right leg. It was bothering him. That much-too-common ache that pulsed with greater intensity as he hiked down out of the mountains, his knee feeling as if it were filled with shards of broken glass.

An old injury. An aggravating injury. But not a debilitating one, and there was little else that he could do except deal with it.

Besides, there was a value to the pain.

It served as a reminder of what could happen if he lost focus in the Frozen Waste for just a heartbeat.

Maybe he would get lucky.

Maybe the monsters had moved on, not finding any worthwhile game here.

Yes, and maybe a street rat like himself could live just below the Royal Ring on the Crux. A ridiculous notion.

He hiked a few hundred yards farther down the trail. All the while he kept a sharp ear. Just as much keeping a sharp eye out for any movement, even though he believed that if he did see something it would probably be too late.

He stopped again when he reached the bottom of the trail, standing in shadow, the first of the burial mounds greeting him.

Studying the churned-up snow at his feet, he rubbed absently at his leg and knee, seeking to reduce the pain to a more manageable level.

He realized then that his hope that the monsters already had moved off was no more than that. Just as he believed it would be.

He identified the tracks of several different beasts, their claws punching deeply into the packed snow.

Intermixed was another distinctive print that he hadn't expected to see here. Almost lost in the crush. A boot. A good bit smaller than his own.

Those tracks wound their way along the edge of the barrows. The larger tracks followed.

Other than himself, what fool would take the risk of coming here on their own?

Everyone in the kingdoms to the south and east knew to stay clear of the Frozen Waste without the invitation of those who ruled this hard, unforgiving land.

And Mikel knew of only one human who currently had that invitation.

Even the bandits who roamed the mountains at his back stuck to the heights on the western side for the most part, having learned the hard way that the inhabitants of the Frozen Waste would be more than happy to make an example of them.

What to do about his unexpected discovery?

Mikel's own business called to him. His finding might serve

as an opportunity to avoid confronting these monstrous hunters himself.

Should he continue on his way and take a different path that led away from what would likely prove to be a bloody and gory mess?

Or should he follow the tracks and get a better sense of how many of these monsters had come down from the mountains?

Quite the dilemma.

He knew what he wanted to do.

But he rarely did what he wanted to do.

Usually he did what he thought he needed to do.

Even though that inevitably got him into trouble and made his life more difficult than he wanted it to be.

2. AN APPETIZER

Drin pushed herself up from where she crouched in the snow. Wary now. Scanning around her. Seeking any hint of movement. Any sound.

There was blood at her feet.

A lot of it with a few pieces of tufted fur and long slices of flesh dotted with red that were already frozen still clinging to what was left of the skeleton.

When she picked one strand up between her gloves, it was so thin, so delicate, the flesh snapped in two when she applied barely any pressure thanks to the frigid cold.

"What could have done this?"

The carcass was that of a reindeer. She was sure of it despite the missing head. The few hoofprints she spotted in the snow confirmed it for her.

"Not a polar bear," she mused. She swept her gaze once again around the sullied snow. There were no tracks suggesting one of the largest predators in the Frozen Waste was roaming close by. "So what then?"

Drin swiped her hair out of her eyes, realizing she was doing it again. Talking to herself. A habit her father said she needed to break before she assumed her rightful place in the Kingdom.

Thankfully, with her father in excellent health, she had little cause to worry about that happening anytime soon.

Still, he was right. Talking to herself wasn't a good look when she was in line for the throne of the Crux. The First Families were always looking for any hint of weakness. But she could work on that later.

Right now she needed to make a decision.

Should she head back the way she had come or continue on the route she had selected?

"It's a long way to go," she murmured to herself, Drin referring to the many hours and hard travel through the snow demanded of her to reach her current location.

The trail she sought that would take her back to the mountains and then home was less than an hour away from where she stood. It would save half the day. But it would lead her in the direction taken by whatever had killed the reindeer.

She decided on expediency in the place of caution. Drin took a few steps along the trail of blood that led away from the kill ground before she stopped abruptly.

She had been listening to nothing more than the whistle of the wind as it gusted through the spaces between the barrows.

Until just then.

A rustle that was different from any other noise she had heard since making her way down the trail to the maze of massive mounds teased her senses. It sounded like a snake sliding through the snow.

Without making a move, Drin searched around her, seeking any hint that might give away the cause of the noise that had set a bell of concern pounding in the back of her head. She saw nothing but white and heard ... nothing except for the wind playing across the icy tundra.

Her search was made all the more difficult because she lost

the sun when she left the trail, the shadows lengthening along the paths between the burial mounds. The wind grew louder in her ears.

She reconsidered her decision to come down here, ignoring her father's warnings and slipping away from her responsibilities for a few days. Slip away from the person who she believed was asking more from her than she was ready or willing to give.

Drin shook her head. "Think before you do," she murmured to herself. Advice her father offered her more times than she could recall. Irritating because of its frequency. Now, useful.

The blood led off between the barrows.

That was the fastest route out.

What to do?

She needed to decide. Quickly.

This was her first time in the Frozen Waste. Admittedly, she was barely across the eastern border of the great white expanse, which began at the mountains towering behind her. Still, it was an entirely different world compared to the one she was used to. And her few hours of exploration excited her in a way that nothing else had in quite some time.

It was beautiful.

Just as she had been led to believe.

Perilous as well.

Just as the blood at her feet demonstrated.

After listening to all the stories while she was growing up, the desire to visit this strange land became an irresistible urge. In large part because she felt the need to do something that wasn't what she was supposed to do.

For as long as she could remember, she always did what she was supposed to do.

She didn't view that as a weakness.

She believed it a good thing that she took her responsibilities seriously.

Nevertheless, with all that was pushing down on her shoulders, at least for once in her life, she needed to feel ... free.

Drin really couldn't explain it in any other way.

She wasn't running away from her responsibilities. She knew what was required of her, and she accepted the burden. Gladly, in fact, understanding that the power and privilege her family enjoyed came as well with an accountability that she couldn't ignore. That she wouldn't ignore.

When she returned.

She just needed to slip away from Innsbruck for a few days and gain a brief respite from the constant pressures of her position.

She shouldn't be here. She acknowledged that now.

The Frozen Waste was forbidden unless you were invited to cross the border by the Giants of the Rime. And from what her uncle had said, the keepers of this frigid wasteland had not issued an invitation for decades. Perhaps even a century. No one could really recall the last time the Frost Lord allowed a visitor into his domain.

Which made her all the more curious about how weapons, glass, and several other unique items were sold in Innsbruck. Items that were clearly of Giant making.

Though Drin had broken the bonds that formed the boundaries of her life if only for a few days, she hadn't broken the treaty between Innsbruck and the Giants of the Rime. She was just on the edge of the glacial, barren landscape. The border between the Frozen Waste and the Kingdom of the Crux was never really decided. Neither Realm put in the time and energy necessary to hammer out a resolution to the argument that had lasted since ... well, she really didn't know when.

Besides, her disobedience already had been rewarded. She would need to deal with the Giants eventually. Best that she got a sense of their world before she did so.

Much of what she had seen after trekking along the edge of

the Frozen Waste for only a few hours astounded her. Her lessons on what to expect not doing the captivating environment justice.

The massive barrows were only a part of it. Glaciers reached for the sky. Frozen rivers with ice thirty feet thick were so clear that she could still see the water rushing below even though she couldn't hear the surge. Crevices were hollowed out from the base of icy tors by the wind that polished the snow until it was blindingly bright when struck by the sun. Arches of strange and mesmerizing designs connected the tors to create what looked like natural aqueducts. Dozens of pingos, huge mounds of solid ice, dotted the barren landscape seemingly without rhyme or reason.

She had not anticipated half of what she had seen. She had anticipated the cold and believed she was ready for it. Learning much to her detriment that she wasn't. The frosty temperature and even more frigid wind chilled her to the bone despite being bundled up in a thick, fur-lined jacket and leggings along with a hat that failed to cut the bite of the wind.

Even so, she was glad that she had taken her uncle's advice, surprising though it had been. Particularly since he was even more wedded to his duty than she was.

Having made her decision, Drin took a step down the bloody path. But no more than a step.

She didn't see anything around her. Nevertheless, she sensed that she wasn't alone.

How close her stalkers were, she couldn't say. But she was certain there were more than one.

"Think before you do," Drin repeated to herself.

Another whisper of movement to her front. Then one more at her back.

Her hunters had set the snare, and she had walked right into it.

She took a few steps to the right. There was another path

there between the barrows that would lead her back toward the trail that she had taken down from the crag. The longer way home. Perhaps the only way home now.

Another dreaded whisper. This time from the west.

A shiver ran through her that wasn't caused by the cold.

Her hunters were herding her.

Either they wanted her to move in the only direction open to her or they hadn't closed the trap fast enough.

It was time to make another choice.

She heard the whisper again. Like a silk cloth being pulled across the ice.

Drin looked back over her shoulder. Her hunters were no more than twenty feet away based on the noise. Where could they be? She saw nothing more than the frosted side of a barrow.

No more time for thinking. There was only time for doing.

Hearing two more whispers of movement coming from both her front and back and only packed snow greeting her eyes, she selected the sole option open to her. She could only hope that there wasn't a fourth hunter waiting for her just up ahead.

She dashed off, pumping her legs as fast as she could, her boots crunching into the hardened snow as she ran between the short sides of two barrows.

The wind had returned. The blustery gale that she was running into slowed her down. Forcing her back toward her pursuers.

She pushed even harder, hearing the movement at her back. She didn't need to look over her shoulder to know that her hunters were right behind her and closing the gap between them, the terrifying whisper of their movements replaced by a heavy crunch.

The end of the path coming up on her quickly, a deep howl that sounded much like a wolf's ripped between the barrows.

It faded quickly.

Sinkhole.

It had to be.

She probably ran right over it without disturbing the trap. But her hunters were bigger than she was, and they were heavier. That realization and the fact that they could stay with her despite the punch of the wind narrowed down what could be chasing her, none of what came to mind what she wanted to think about.

Drin picked up her pace as best as she could. The wind slacking. Allowing her to move with greater speed down the path. Unfortunately permitting her hunters to do the same.

She was less concerned about how many hunters remained. Now more concerned with finding a better spot to defend herself.

Although she had no doubt that she stood little chance of escaping, what she saw to her front gave her a very brief moment of hope.

Racing out from between the barrows, she found herself on a small plain, her hope dying quickly. A large bluff on the far side ensured that she had nowhere else to go.

Still, right in the center of the plain a fantastical ice sculpture rose several hundred feet into the sky. Her uncle had told her about these marvelous creations.

They were crafted by the strange and powerful lightning strikes that often came with the blizzards that swept over this barren land. The energy blasted into the snow, throwing it into the air, the charge creating a design that froze in seconds because of the frigid temperature. What remained molded over time by the sun, cold, and wind.

Drin didn't stop to admire what waited before her. Instead, she sprinted right toward it, aiming for a spot where several of the razor-sharp branches carved of ice would offer her some protection.

She wasn't where she wanted to be, but it was the best that she could do.

She knew that she had to fight. There was no way to avoid it. At least here she could limit the number of hunters who could come at her at one time.

Skidding to a stop when she was between the razor-sharp branches, she spun back around, pulling the short sword strapped to her back in a smooth motion and ready to defend herself against whatever it was that hunted her.

Her heart froze when she identified the monsters that approached.

They peeled out of the white background as they drew closer.

Their confident steps confirmed that they didn't feel the need to rush. Certain that they could kill her whenever they desired.

Mikel couldn't understand why the woman was out here in the frigid wild on her own.

In a forbidden land.

Clearly having little real sense regarding the many dangers to be found in the Frozen Waste ... until some of those dangers found her.

Still, he was impressed.

The woman knew how to fight.

Short sword in hand, how she gripped the blade suggested that she had quite a bit of training.

That wasn't how she was defending herself, however.

Not yet.

Not until she had no other choice.

Instead she employed a unique skill rare in this part of the world.

Spikes of energy as well as other lethal creations made from the Talent shot from her palm. Keeping her attackers at bay for now, the position she selected ensured that she only had to worry about an assault from one direction.

A skilled fighter and a Magus.

Intelligent. Creative. Quick thinking. Headstrong as well to enter the Frozen Waste on her own without fully understanding the perils waiting for her, which suggested as well a worrisome obstinance.

A dangerous mix in his experience.

Mikel had to give the woman credit, though. She was doing well considering the challenge set before her.

She was facing off against Northern Trolls.

A fist all told, and there were more coming her way, drawn by the howls and barks of their brethren.

Mikel had fought Northern Trolls a few times before. He had never enjoyed the experience. And in each instance he had been grateful that he walked away.

Determined beasts. Cunning as well. And hungry. Always hungry.

The creatures were covered in a short but thick coat of white fur. It kept them warm in the below freezing temperatures of their homeland.

It also allowed them to blend in almost perfectly with their snow-covered environment. Quite an accomplishment since a Northern Troll was twice the size of a tall man in both height and breadth and exceedingly strong, muscles growing upon muscles.

Even their eyes were white. As were the tusks that curled up from their bottom jaw and the razor-sharp teeth that resembled fangs that were visible when they opened their short snouts to roar.

Each of the Trolls carried either a very large battle axe with a blade sharper than steel or a mace, both crafted from an ice that was harder than stone and found only in their mountain territory.

And, as the Trolls danced around her, seeking a way past her defenses, the Magus was learning that these gigantic creatures were terribly fast. Likely as well that they were strong enough to bear the brunt of her attack, knocking away with their oversized weapons the energy she sent their way.

Watching the engagement, Mikel also had to give the Northern Trolls some credit because they displayed a disconcerting cleverness. Rather than standing against the Magus' magical strikes, they used their speed to their advantage, evading her attacks more often than not. Ensuring that she did little more than tire herself out as they waited for more of their clan to arrive.

Based on how her expression had changed in just the last minute, it seemed that she had reached the same conclusion as he had.

Yet despite her difficulties and that blood-chilling realization, she demonstrated a tenacity that Mikel could only admire.

The Magus looked to be young. Maybe a few years younger than he was. And she clearly had not done her research before entering the Waste, because she had yet to figure out the best way to deal with Northern Trolls.

More than unfortunate for her. Likely a death sentence.

Once again, Mikel had a decision to make.

He could go about his business and leave the Magus to her fate. Some might even say a fate she deserved for so foolishly entering a forbidden land without the appropriate resources.

Or he could intervene.

Against a fist of Trolls.

With more of the beasts coming this way.

If this was strictly a business matter, weighing the advantages and disadvantages, the decision was quite easy. Besides, he needed to get moving. He had somewhere to be.

But this wasn't just a business decision now.

There was more at stake here than money to be made or a favor to be earned.

Mikel uttered several choice curses as all the relevant variables ran through his mind and he calculated the odds of the several paths open to him as he lay atop a barrow only a few feet from the crest.

With barely a thought, relying on his instinct, he flipped himself over.

Just in time.

The massive mace crafted from ice smashed down right in the spot where he had been lying only a moment before, punching deep into the crusted snow and leaving a large hole rather than crushing his chest. The Troll who had snuck up on him from behind hissed in anger as he pulled his weapon free.

When the Troll lifted the mace above his head to continue his attack, Mikel was nowhere to be seen, having scrambled back behind the creature.

"Come on, ugly. Time for you to go to the other side."

The Troll spun around upon hearing Mikel's words. However, instead of rushing at him, the Troll held his ground. Grunting and huffing. Brandishing his weapon.

Mikel frowned. Not the usual behavior from a ravenous …

He ducked and rolled, the huge axe crafted of ice sweeping through the space where his head had been just a second before, the blade taking a few locks of his hair rather than a large portion of his scalp.

He had just been thinking about the Northern Troll's cleverness, and his own attempt at cleverness had almost cost him his life.

And perhaps it still would, because now he stood against two of the giant monsters, the second approaching just as quietly as the first.

He turned sideways to his opponents. They seemed more

than willing to take a few seconds to study him. Not too concerned despite his discovering them before they could kill him.

He kept one eye on the Trolls while he searched the land-scape at his back with a quick glance over each shoulder. Mikel hoped that there weren't any more of the creatures lying buried in the snow, waiting to take him from behind when the combat began.

He didn't think there were. All he saw were the tracks made by the two who had crept up on him and the perfectly smooth snow atop the barrow courtesy of the always blowing wind. There were no lumps to suggest he needed to worry about a third Troll joining the party.

That was a good thing.

Not so good was the movement to his front.

Mikel took a step back and pivoted, allowing the Troll to pass by him.

The beast missed with his axe again, the power of his swing pulling the creature off balance.

Mikel was more than happy to make use of that mistake. Trailing a leg behind him, he caught the Troll's back foot, which sent the creature sprawling when that errant back foot hit his other foot.

All the Troll was going to eat that afternoon was a face full of snow, Mikel attacking before the Troll could push himself up.

Jumping onto the Troll's back with his knee and pushing the beast's tusks back into the icy crust, Mikel brought the sharp blade of his mace down, piercing the back of the Troll's neck. He could have used the hammer on the other end of his weapon, but Northern Trolls had notoriously hard heads. If he didn't crush the creature's skull in a single blow, then he likely was a dead man, a result that he wanted to avoid.

The Troll flopped a few times like a fish out of water, then lay still.

Mikel pushed himself up from the creature's broad back and turned to face the other Troll. The creature hadn't moved, surprised by what he had just witnessed. Never anticipating such a result.

Wanting to take advantage of the Troll's indecision, Mikel sprinted across the top of the barrow, mace held above his shoulder as if he was planning to swing down toward the creature's hip.

Mikel's movement jolted the Troll into action. The creature raised his mace, prepared to catch the blow.

But it never came.

Instead, Mikel ducked and rolled past. In the same motion he sliced with his weapon's blade across the back of the Troll's legs.

Cut across both hamstrings, one severed completely, the other partially, the Troll dropped to his knees, bellowing in anger and pain.

The Troll was fast.

Mikel was faster, and he did much as he had to the first Troll. Slamming into the creature's back with his knees, he forced the beast's maw into the snow while also punching his blade through the back of the Troll's neck.

Two kills in two minutes. Probably less.

A good fight.

Nevertheless, Mikel wasn't happy.

Grumbling to himself, he pushed off the rapidly cooling corpse and turned away from the dead Trolls, the heat from the bodies drifting up into the frigid air. At this temperature, in just a few minutes they would be no more than icicles.

It seemed like his decision had been made for him.

Taking a quick look from the top of the burial mound to

gauge what was happening below, he scrambled back from the lip. None of the Trolls were aware that he was above them.

Pulling free his snowshoes that were clipped to the back of his pack, he fitted them to his boots and locked them into place. He then pulled out two thin, fire-hardened boards that he fitted over the webbing on the underside of each snowshoe.

Knowing what would happen if he took a moment to think about what he was about to do, Mikel sprinted toward the lip of the barrow, mace in hand.

"You were a fool," Drin grumbled to herself as she carried on a constant commentary on her decision to enter the Frozen Waste. "Putting yourself at risk on a whim. Just because you …"

She didn't get a chance to finish berating herself, twisting to her right side and blasting a series of short, sharp bursts of magical spikes toward the beasts inching toward her from that direction.

Against other opponents, she already would have won this combat. Few had the strength and ability to stand against a Magus.

But she was battling against Northern Trolls. And much to her consternation, they knew how to fight a Magus.

A fact that she wished she had known before she began her ill-fated journey. Because if she had known, she probably would have stayed in Innsbruck.

She had gained very little in her many attacks against the beasts other than a few superficial wounds that failed to slow down the dangerously swift giants. Learning quickly that the best that she could hope for was to buy a few more minutes to search for some avenue of escape as she struggled to keep the Trolls away from her.

Drin shook her head to clear it. There was no point in castigating herself now or reminding herself of the many mistakes she had made, in particular with respect to this clash.

She needed to focus on staying alive, and that meant ensuring the Trolls kept to her front. If one got on her flank, she was done for.

That was becoming a more difficult task as the cunning creatures patiently brought a more intense pressure to bear upon her.

She had picked a good place from which to defend herself. Three sides protected.

But she had trapped herself as well.

With the jagged spikes that guarded her, she had nowhere to go other than through the beasts who, based on the drool dripping down their tusks, viewed her as that night's meal.

What really got her goat was that her use of the Talent didn't bother her hunters in the least. The creatures not only demonstrated an admirable skill in defending against her attacks, but also feinted toward her regularly. Keeping her on her toes. Inching toward her. Tightening the noose. Soon to be in a position to strike a fatal blow.

It wouldn't be long before one of the beasts came in close and forced her to use her short sword. When that happened, the other Trolls would rush her and the fight would be over.

Both Talent and steel of little use.

And she had no doubt that moment was approaching swiftly. Several more Trolls had joined the hunt, drawn by the sounds of the combat and the calls of their brethren.

Savvy creatures indeed. The Trolls were allowing her to tire herself out.

At the same time, they made sure she had little chance of getting away from them. They were more than happy to bide their time, looking for just the right opportunity, clearly unconcerned that they hunted a Magus as they sought to push her into that single mistake that would lead to her death.

Drin was angry.

At herself for taking this risk.

For not realizing what strategy these Trolls were employing before it was too late to break free.

Even more so for not really understanding the threat these creatures presented before she entered the Frozen Waste.

Big. Fast. Dangerous. Clever.

Clearly displaying attributes she had not learned about during her training.

A lethal mix as she feared she was about to discover.

An instant later what she dreaded most occurred.

She made a mistake.

One of the Trolls on her left side had climbed the mesmerizing ice sculpture, ignoring the sharpness of the frosty limb that cut into his claws, more concerned with coming at her from the flank.

She defended herself with the Talent, targeting the branch rather than the Troll.

The blast of energy shattered the ice, sending the beast flying backward, his body riddled with bloody shards.

She wasn't done. Sensing the movement on her other side, when she swept back around to manage the Trolls pushing in on her right who sought to take advantage of the distraction provided by their badly wounded brethren, her foot slipped in the snow, taking her down to one knee.

Recognizing her peril, she could do nothing more than rely on her instincts, raising her sword to defend against the battle axe already sweeping toward her head.

Drin knew without a doubt that her efforts wouldn't be enough.

The Troll was too fast and too strong.

The beast's axe would shatter her blade then split her in two.

Right before the icy blade bit into her flesh and bone, a blur slid by her, slamming into her attacker with a bone-crunching smack.

The collision left her rescuer just a few feet away from her while the Troll tumbled through the snow, coming to a stop when the beast slammed against the sculpture, a long shard of ice sticking out of his chest. The great weight of the Troll snapped off the branch, the creature sagging to the snow, only able to manage a soft gurgle as he died slowly, the icy lance having skewered his lungs.

Drin had less than a second to take in her unanticipated though much-appreciated champion.

He was big, almost hulking. Even so, he moved with a surprising nimbleness. Kicking off his snowshoes, he placed his back to hers.

"I'll take the right flank," he said.

She didn't have the chance to argue, the Trolls on her side pushing toward her once again. The shock of seeing their brethren impaled was wearing off quickly.

To hold them, Drin fired several bursts of energy at her attackers, forcing them back. A few even growled in pain, unable to avoid the searing heat she blasted in their direction.

Those few seconds she earned allowed her to observe the newcomer assisting her in this fight. Despite his size, he was deceptively fast. Efficient as well. Economical and graceful in his movements and his decisions. Almost as if he'd come up against Northern Trolls before.

Forgoing the short sword scabbarded across his back, he feinted toward a Troll to his right who was trying to sneak around them.

The Troll took a deft half-step back. A natural reaction, but also one that cost him as a slice of ice from the jagged branches behind him pierced his back.

Mikel left his adversary gasping out bubbly blood as the Troll dropped to his knee, struggling to breathe. Continuing his motion, Mikel spun around swiftly while bringing himself close to the snow-covered ground.

With all the strength that he could bring to bear, Mikel slammed his mace into the second Troll's knee, grinning devilishly when he heard the bone shatter followed just a breath later by a roar of agony.

Before the wounded Troll hit the ground, he was dead.

Mikel swiped with the other side of his weapon, his already bloodied blade slashing across the falling creature's throat.

One opponent eliminated, Mikel turned toward the beast with the bloody back.

The wounded Troll bellowed in rage. Ignoring the pain and the blood gushing down his back and between his fangs, the beast swung with his axe.

Mikel dodged out of the way. When the blade of ice swept past him, he kicked out with his boot, connecting with the beast's knee and bending it backward at a severe angle.

The Troll bellowed in anger again, though this time not only because of the pain of his second injury, but also because his wild swing threw him too far to the right, sending him stumbling into the icy branches on that side.

Mikel finished the Troll with a swift kick to his lower back, ensuring that the beast was fixed in place, caught on the frosty spikes that stuck out from his back in four different places, three of them fatal wounds all on their own.

Pivoting toward the Magus, Mikel ready for the next combat, the Trolls appeared to have lost interest in the fun of the hunt after losing so many of their brethren. They wanted only the kill now, and they were preparing to rush their quarry come what may.

"Target the ground in front of the Trolls!" he shouted.

Drin didn't hesitate even as she cursed herself for a fool. Sheathing her sword, she did as ordered, sending blazing bolts of energy blasting into the crust just twenty feet in front of her.

Right where the Trolls stood.

They were fast. They were strong. But they stood little chance against the power she exercised.

Particularly since the environment worked with her, the eruption of white blocking the sun.

When the gusts of wind buffeted away the snow and ice swirling in the air, several sinkholes were revealed that just needed a little nudge before giving way, taking three of the Trolls a hundred or more feet belowground.

She doubted that trio would be escaping their prison, assuming they survived the fall. Three more of the Trolls wouldn't be rising again either, their smoking and charred bodies confirming that fact.

That left only three of the beasts standing against her.

Feeling more confident after her first taste of success and with an ally covering her back, Drin decided on a different approach. Remembering what happened to the Troll who dared to climb the branches of ice, she made use of the sculpture that had offered her some much-desired protection. Using the Talent, she broke apart several of the branches above her then with a flick of her wrist sent the razor-sharp shards streaking toward the surviving Trolls.

Two died in seconds. They were able to defend against a few of the icy lances though not all. The third escaped harm except for a slice across his side only because his companions bore the brunt of the attack for him.

Realizing that he was alone, wounded, and stood little chance against the Magus and the human who wielded his mace as if it was a part of his hand, the last Northern Troll turned and fled as swiftly as he could.

With the wound he had sustained, it wasn't as fast as he wanted. His gait more a staggering stumble than a sprint.

Mikel reacted with barely a thought, refusing to allow the beast to lead more of his brethren after them. Pulling a slim dagger from his belt, tip of the blade between thumb and fore-finger, he flung the blade end over end through the air, the steel coming to rest in the back of the Troll's neck in much the same place where Mikel had dispatched several other Trolls at the beginning of the fight.

Nodding with satisfaction when the Troll crumpled in the snow, he kept his mace in hand as he walked across the battlefield. He checked each body to make sure they were dead. Then he examined the sinkholes with the same thoroughness to confirm that they had nothing to worry about from the beasts who fell through the ground. Heading toward the Troll farthest away from them, Mikel pulled free his dagger, wiped the blade clean on the dead beast's fur before sheathing it, and walked back completely at his ease, almost as if a clash against the most feared monsters of the mountains was just a normal day for him.

Stopping in front of Drin, Mikel gave the Magus an appreciative nod. For someone half his size, she certainly packed a punch. Sharp eyes matched her sharp features, and the lines around her mouth suggested that she liked to smile, although not now. Anger her primary emotion.

"This isn't a full clan," Mikel said, not put off by the Magus' close study of him. "I took down the last one so that he couldn't bring the rest this way. But I likely only bought you an hour. Best that you get moving now."

Drin heard what her unexpected ally said. She chose to ignore him. There was some aspect to the man that caught her eye, though she didn't know what exactly. And that bothered her. Usually she could read people with just a glance.

He was big. Not only tall, but also broad. Though it didn't look like he had an ounce of fat on him.

He wasn't particularly good looking. His nose had been broken several times and was permanently crooked. His short beard failed to hide the several scars that crisscrossed his cheeks and neck with a deeper one across his brow.

Yet his smile put her at ease despite his cold eyes. Colder than the gust of wind that blasted into her and turned the sweat covering her body to ice.

He wore clothes quite different from hers. A thin jacket unlike the bulky one that was doing very little to keep her warm. Thin pants as well, not lined with fur. Gloves. A knit cap.

All a mesh of grey, black, white, and blue that allowed him to blend into the environment almost as well as if not better than the Northern Trolls did.

Where did he get clothes like that?

And why was he there in the first place?

No one had permission from the Giants of the Rime to enter their homeland.

"Who are you?" she asked.

"You did hear what I said, right? You have an hour at most. You need to get moving."

"I did." Her voice took on a harder edge. "I ask again. Who are you?"

"No thank you?" He offered her a raised eyebrow. "I don't know that you would have made your way out of this mess without my assistance."

"I had everything well in hand," she replied, though her voice lacked the conviction to support her statement.

"Of course you did." His sarcasm dripped from his voice like molasses.

"Nevertheless, my thanks." She nodded as if she had completed a slightly unpleasant task and now it was time to move on to the next one. "Now answer me. Who are you?"

Mikel smiled in amusement. Just like every other Magus he had met. And he had met more than he cared to. They were single-minded to a fault and dangerously hard-headed. "No one of consequence."

"Are you always this difficult?" Drin demanded. He had aided her. Saved her life most likely, though she refused to admit that to him. Still, her natural curiosity was getting the better of her manners. That didn't bother her, however, because she was not used to being treated this way.

"Usually, yes," Mikel replied without a hint of embarrassment. "Now you need to get out of here. The snow is moving through the glass."

"The snow? Isn't it supposed to be ..."

"I was just taking literary license is all," Mikel explained, finding it harder to keep the smile on his face as the young woman poked and prodded. "You need to get moving, Magus. The Northern Trolls aren't done with you."

That last comment seemed to break her train of thought. "Why would they be down from the mountains?"

"Hunting," Mikel replied with a shrug, as if it was the most obvious of explanations.

"For what?"

"You."

"Me?" How could they know who she was? Why would they care?

Then it came to her. Who she was didn't matter to them.

"They're hungry. You crossed their path instead of the reindeer or polar bear they were seeking. Easy prey they probably thought. Though you'd be no more than an appetizer for them."

"I don't know how to take a comment like that," Drin replied, almost laughing because she wanted to avoid thinking about what would have happened if her rescuer had not arrived when he did.

"However you like. Nevertheless, I suggest you take my advice. Head out of the Waste. Quickly. If you get into the lower peaks and one of the forts along the trail before dark, you should be fine."

Mikel turned then. Picking up his snowshoes, he strapped them to his pack and strode toward the trail that would take him deeper into the Barrows.

"Pleasure to meet you, Magus," he called over his shoulder, giving her a wave without looking at her. "Now you know the Giants of the Rime are only one of the threats to be wary of in the Frozen Waste."

In just seconds, he was gone. Fading into the snow and ice. Moving just as quietly as a Northern Troll.

Drin took a breath, the moisture she released frosting. She had been holding it until he disappeared. More than just curious about him now.

Who was he?

Why was he there?

Perhaps most important, why did he risk his life for hers?

END OF CHAPTER TWO

To keep reading, buy your copy of *Stealing the Light* today.

WHAT TO READ NEXT

THE FALLEN KNIGHT SERIES

The Death of the Dragon (short story)*

The Dragon Awakens

Duel With a Dragon

Beware the Dragon

The Dragon Returns

THE REALMS OF THE TALENT AND THE CURSE

LEGEND OF THE DRAGON LORD

A Painful Truth (short story)*

Stealing the Light

Sacrificing the Queen

Roar of the Broken Bear

Rise of the Dragon Lord (Forthcoming 2026)

THE TALES OF CALEDONIA

(Complete 7-Book Series)

Blood on the White Sand (short story)*

The Diamond Thief (short story)*

The Protector

The Protector's Quest

The Protector's Vengeance

The Protector's Sacrifice

The Protector's Reckoning

The Protector's Resolve

The Protector's Victory

THE TALES OF THE TERRITORIES

Stalking the Blood Ruby (short story)*

A Fate Worse Than Death (short story)*

Death on the Burnt Ocean

Monsters in the Mist

The Dance of the Daggers

Bloody Hunt for Freedom

A Spark of Rebellion

Shadows Made Real

Shadow's Reach

Storm in the Darkness

THE SYLVAN CHRONICLES

(Complete 9-Book Series)

The Legend of the Kestrel

The Call of the Sylvana

The Raptor of the Highlands

The Makings of a Warrior

The Lord of the Highlands

The Lost Kestrel Found

The Claiming of the Highlands

The Fight Against the Dark

The Defender of the Light

THE RISE OF THE SYLVAN WARRIORS

Through the Knife's Edge (short story)*

www.ingramcontent.com/pod-product-compliance
Lightning Source LLC
Chambersburg PA
CBHW070240200726
48293CB00005B/1711